Murder in Lascaux

Terrace Books, a trade imprint of the University of Wisconsin Press, takes its name from the Memorial Union Terrace, located at the University of Wisconsin–Madison. Since its inception in 1907, the Wisconsin Union has provided a venue for students, faculty, staff, and alumni to debate art, music, politics, and the issues of the day. It is a place where theater, music, drama, literature, dance, outdoor activities, and major speakers are made available to the campus and the community. To learn more about the Union, visit www.union.wisc.edu.

Murder in Lascaux

Betsy Draine

and

Michael Hinden

Terrace Books

A trade imprint of the University of Wisconsin Press

Terrace Books
A trade imprint of the University of Wisconsin Press
1930 Monroe Street, 3rd Floor
Madison, Wisconsin 53711-2059
uwpress.wisc.edu

3 Henrietta Street
London WC2E 8LU, England
eurospanbookstore.com

Printed in the United States of America

Library of Congress Cataloging-in-Publication Data
Draine, Betsy, 1945–
Murder in Lascaux / Betsy Draine and Michael Hinden.
p.   cm.
ISBN 978-0-299-28420-6 (cloth: alk. paper)
ISBN 978-0-299-28423-7 (e-book)
1. Lascaux Cave (France)—Fiction.   2. Art teachers—Fiction.
3. Americans—France—Fiction.   4. Murder—France—Dordogne—Fiction.
5. Dordogne (France)—Fiction.   I. Hinden, Michael.   II. Title.
PS3604.R343M87   2011
813'.6—dc22
2011015989

This is a work of fiction. All names, characters, places, and incidents are either products of the
authors' imagination or are used fictitiously. No reference to any real person is intended or should
be inferred.

2574

For our brothers and sisters:

David

Bob

Patrick

Michael

Lucinda

Katy

Murder in Lascaux

1

Thousands of years before there was history, human hands created a masterpiece: the cave paintings of Lascaux. The brilliantly colored bulls and horses that decorate the cavern's walls are among the wonders of the world.

Lascaux is the reason I became an art historian, a career that might not have been in the cards for someone like me. Neither of my parents finished college. But as a child, I received a picture book called *Lascaux: The Story of Art*, and while I was growing up, those magical pictures held me spellbound. For years I leafed through that book just for the illustrations, dreaming that someday I would travel to France and visit the cave itself. Now I was going to get my wish—though before the day was over, I'd regret it.

It was a cool day in June. Toby and I had spent the night in Montignac, a bustling market town not far from Lascaux. After sleeping in and dawdling over breakfast, we still had hours to kill before our late-afternoon appointment at the cave. To fill the time, we decided to take a walking tour of the town. From our hotel, we headed down the main commercial street, passing old-fashioned shops with understated signage and attractive window displays. I dropped back at one point to admire the wares of a linen shop while Toby walked on ahead. I smiled at the thought that after six years of marriage, he still looked pretty good to me from behind.

Montignac spreads out along the banks of the Vézère, a tributary of the Dordogne River. It's the Dordogne that gives its name to the department, but the earliest human habitations were here, along the modest Vézère. I wanted to see the river, and soon we found our way to the balustrades of the quai. We stood there surveying the opposite bank, which was built up with tall, stone-and-stucco buildings. The bottom stories provided access to and from the river, and they were kept plain, with few windows, the better to withstand flood. The floors above were balconied and half-timbered, giving a medieval air to the whole ensemble. I tried to imagine what this bank might have looked like fifty thousand years ago, ranged with huts made of animal skins supported by wooden poles or maybe mastodon bones. I closed my eyes and pictured an ancient people—people like us—pursuing their domestic chores.

"Look," said Toby, pointing toward the lure of stone stairs leading down to the river level. Soon we were on a path that took us the length of the town, up a stairway to the bridge and over the river, along the bank we'd been watching from the balustrade, and back again. When we returned to our starting point, there was just enough time to buy bread and cheese, make a picnic at the quai, and get into our rental car for the drive to Lascaux.

By then, Montignac's main street was buzzing with tourists and bottled up with mid-afternoon traffic. We inched our way along, trying not to inhale diesel fumes from belching trucks. Worrying about the time, I didn't relax until we finally reached the tiny bridge that led out of town to the southwest, the cliffs, and the cave.

Those cliffs, I was thinking, provided shelter for the Cro-Magnon artists and may have been the reason why they settled here. They also provided building stone for the local houses, which blend in with the landscape and look so appealing to foreign eyes. As we left Montignac behind, we passed hamlets of limestone cottages whose harmonious colors changed with the light, from yellow to amber as the day grew overcast. How pretty, I thought; how serene it might be to live in one of those homes looking out toward the timeless cliffs.

But then as we drove on and it got darker, the houses began to seem gloomy and isolated, with individual cottages secluded in fields or set atop hillocks. The stone took on a grayish tinge, and the countryside turned flinty. After a few more miles, the landscape changed again. Cultivated fields gave way to overgrown patches by the roadside and copses of gnarled oak. Suddenly dark branches loomed over the narrow road. Before it was renamed the Department of the Dordogne, this province was called Périgord and this part of it "Black Périgord" because of its dark forests. I began to see why, as we drove deeper into the woods.

Our little Peugeot, no larger than a golf cart, by now was the only car in sight. The busy engine strained as the grade grew steeper. Had we veered off the main road? Were we lost? There were no markers along the way, no indication we were approaching a world-famous site. But after a long climb in second gear along a banged-up road where branches scraped the side mirrors, we came to a small sign with a wooden arrow, and following it, we arrived at a small parking area reserved for visitors to the cave. There were only two other cars in the lot. We looked at each other, got out, locked the doors and followed another arrow to a footpath, which led us into the forest.

It was unmistakably an oak grove—I know that leaf shape. But these were scruffy specimens, with thin trunks and low-arching branches. Whitish scales and gray moss made a mess of each tree's base. The atmosphere was creepy, and we felt our solitude uneasily. The modern world seemed far away.

In a few minutes, though, to my relief, we reached our destination, a clearing next to a small hut. Waiting there was another American couple, judging by their dress. An older man stood apart from them. Unsure of this other man's nationality, Toby greeted everyone in French; he speaks it better than I do. I struggled with French in college, but Toby picked it up during a summer in Quebec. Whether in Montreal or in Paris, he gets by pretty well on gumption, if not always on grammar.

The man who looked American replied in French.

"*Bonjour!* My name is David Press," he said, stepping forward. "This is my wife, Lily. We're from New York." Lily smiled and extended her hand. They were a bit younger than we were (early thirties, I guessed) and dressed for a suburban outing, in new jeans and cashmere sweaters. David was tall and broad, the massiveness of his frame countered by a boyish face. As we exchanged a few pleasantries, he seemed proud of both his competent French and his beautiful wife. She was ivory-skinned and jet-haired, with delicate features. She seemed shy, but perhaps it was just that, like me, she wasn't that confident in a foreign language.

We had nothing more than a curt "*Bonjour*" from the remaining member of our group. Everything about him looked world-weary, from his wrinkled suit to his deeply lined face. He made no attempt to join us and looked vaguely into the distance while dragging on a foul-smelling Gauloise. That told me he was French—nobody else can smoke those things. Out of deference to him, we continued to make small talk in his language, but after a few minutes, as he drifted away, I decided to relax into English.

"It's odd, isn't it, that four of us are Americans when only five people a day are allowed in. Are you here to do research?" (In recent years, the cave has been closed to prevent pollution, allowing only brief visits by scholars and VIPs. I couldn't easily ask David, are you a VIP?)

"Oh, no," David shot back. "I'm a lawyer—intellectual property. We had to pull strings to get in. One of my partners does legal consulting for the French government. He used his connections to get us permission, as a wedding gift. We were just married in March. In fact, we're on a belated honeymoon." He glanced toward his wife, as if seeking confirmation. One corner of her mouth tightened slightly, as her eyes lifted to his and then sought the ground.

Uh-oh, I thought to myself, trouble already on the honeymoon. Not a good sign. Of course it wouldn't do to notice. I offered my congratulations.

"What about you two?" David asked me.

I explained we were here under false colors as well. As an associate professor of art history at Sonoma College, I had the right letterhead for an application. It's just that I never mentioned my field. Now I felt guilty about it.

David laughed, acknowledging that our mutual grounds for admission were shaky. "So what's your research area if it's not prehistoric art?"

"Nineteenth-century painting."

David nodded and looked inquiringly at Toby, who said dryly, "I'm here in my capacity as the husband." His plan was to thoroughly enjoy our excursion. Toby, I should say, has about as much guilt as a radish. "At home," he added, "I sell antiques." In fact, he runs a very successful gallery. There's nothing he likes better than being on his own, driving from place to place on a scouting expedition and bringing home some special piece he's pried from a seller's hand.

There was a slightly awkward pause.

"And you, Lily?" I asked.

"I work in publishing at the moment," she said softly, "but I've been thinking of going back to school."

She gave us a weak smile, and David looked ill at ease. Why? I wondered. But any further conversation was forestalled by the entrance of our guide, who now appeared from inside the reception hut. It was precisely four o'clock, the hour for the tour. The dour Frenchman, who hadn't bothered to share his name with us, loped slowly up the path to rejoin our group. The guide gave him a disapproving glance and then stood grim-faced until he arrived within hearing distance.

The guide was thin, pale, and hunched-over. His gray hair was slicked straight back and looked wet. He announced his name as Pierre Gounot and set about checking our admission papers and spelling out the rules of the visit. No smoking (a glance at the French puffer, who crushed his cigarette underfoot). No photographs. No touching the walls or rock formations. No flashlights or other means of illumination apart from his own equipment. And we must stay together at all times. Understood? This recital of the regulations was punctuated by an alarming cough. Then, straightening up a bit, he announced: "*Bon. On y va.*" Let's go.

Toby and I donned the jackets we had been advised to bring, and we followed the guide up a trail leading from the reception area toward a grass-covered mound resembling a bunker. As we neared our destination, Toby took my elbow and hung back a little, so we lagged behind the others.

"Okay, who does he remind you of?" he asked in a conspiratorial whisper.

"The guide? I don't know."

"Come on. The long face, the batlike ears?"

"Who?"

"The children of the night," drawled Toby in his best rendition of Bela Lugosi. "They make such music!" Toby does two imitations, both out of date; the other is Groucho Marx.

Gounot did look a lot like Dracula, now that I thought about it. Besides the pointy ears, he had the pallor of someone who spent his days underground. Stifling a laugh, I shushed Toby, and we caught up with the rest of the group. We had walked about two hundred yards up the wooded trail. Now a stone staircase of about a dozen steps led down into the mound, where a huge iron door marked the entrance to the cave. The guide punched some numbers on a security pad next to the door, produced from his pocket a dungeon-sized key, and introduced it into the lock. The massive door swung open with a whisper, which surprised me: I had expected creaks and groans. On the other side of the door, the guide punched a few more buttons and then ushered us in. As he shut the door behind us, we had a moment to sense the chill. Not so cold, I thought. Those warnings about the need for a jacket were overdone. But in fact this was just the first of a series of temperature-controlled antechambers, each smaller and colder than the last.

In the third chamber, we had to step into a shallow tray filled with a chemical solution that would remove algae or pollen from our shoes. Ahead of me, Lily hesitated, and I sensed her reluctance to stain the leather of her expensive-looking flats. She winced as she waded through. I had come in rubber-soled running shoes and felt no compunction in complying. Toby splashed through after me, followed by the grim-faced Frenchman, who stepped lightly in and out of the tray as though he had gone through this strange ablution any number of times.

Then we were on the landing of a dimly lit stairway leading down into the dark. At once the air was different, with a cool smell of earth and rock. Gounot led the way. The steps were uneven, and I grasped the cold iron railing as tightly as I could. At the bottom, a smooth clay surface sloped gently down and away from us. I shivered, not so much from the cold as from the sense of entering a forbidden place.

"Come closer, please," Gounot wheezed. He detached a battery-powered lamp from his belt and announced he was going to turn off the lights strung along the stairwell. "For the paintings, the less light, the better."

Huddled together, we shuffled forward through a narrow passage, following the dancing beam of the guide's hand-held lamp. As the neck of the passageway opened onto a wider space, he turned off the lamp, encouraging us to inch forward in the dark. That's when I felt my first pang of fear. There was no reason for it, yet I reached out and grabbed Toby's hand. "It's okay," I heard David say to Lily. Our group stood for a full minute in the inky blackness, absorbing the alien silence. Then, with a theatrical flair, Gounot threw a switch, and a rack of floodlights lit the cavern.

"*Mesdames, Messieurs, regardez!* These paintings that surround you have existed for seventeen thousand years."

The effect was breathtaking. We were standing inside the entrance to the Hall of Bulls, a low rotunda perhaps a hundred feet long and thirty wide. A natural domed ceiling rose only a few feet above our heads, obscured by deep shadows. But all eyes were on the glistening walls. On either side of us, rows of magnificent animals galloped away toward the back of the chamber. There were bulls, horses, and stags, arrayed as if in a procession. Above my left shoulder was a strange-looking beast with a pair of long, straight horns. There was movement everywhere, and the colors were amazing: reds, yellows, browns, and blacks looking as fresh as if they had been painted yesterday.

Whereas the floors and ceiling of the rotunda were a rusty ochre streaked with yellow, the uneven walls were lightened by a whitish mineral that must have invited the imprint of images. And what images! All the animals were in profile. The herd was dominated by four enormous bulls, two on each side of the hall, the largest at least five yards across. On the left wall, one giant bull faced off against the other, while a line of red and brown horses fled toward and past him. That was the picture from my childhood art book, more spectacular in reality than in dreams.

Gounot had been consulting his watch as we stood in silence, taking in the spectacle. He now moved toward the back of the hall, where he flipped a switch. The lights went out. As he approached us again, in darkness illuminated only by his jiggling lamp, the images leaped to life. Now I could see how the artists had used the contours of the rock to create a sense of three dimensions. Where a boss on the wall protruded, the cave artist saw a haunch or a shoulder, and the rest of the animal followed. The images seemed even more alive emerging out of the dark, as the weak beams of Gounot's lamp created shadows, which defined the figures.

"*Mesdames, Messieurs*, this is how the Cro-Magnons saw Lascaux. They used torches for light, or they made sandstone lamps and burned animal fat, with moss for a wick. One of those lamps was found deep in this cave."

I strained to take in visual information, while listening as our guide recounted the story of the cave's discovery. Toby and I were able to follow along in French, but I could hear David whispering as he provided a running translation for his wife.

"In 1940, during the war, four local boys from Montignac were on an outing. You may have heard they followed the dog of one of the boys down a hole. That's a myth," explained Gounot. He hacked a few times and continued. "In reality, an old woman told them that a hole under an uprooted tree looked like it might start a tunnel leading underground. The boys took a flashlight, dropped stones down into the hole, and then one of them, a youth named Ravidat, fell into the hole. He landed here, in the Hall of Bulls. The boys alerted their teacher, and soon word spread. After the war, the cave was opened to visitors, and over a million tourists came to see it. But unfortunately, these visits contaminated the environment, making it necessary to close the site. You are among the privileged few who will ever see the original paintings."

"This is amazing," Toby whispered to me, squeezing my hand. The five of us were lined up single file on a concrete walkway with low curbs on each side to remind us not to stray too close to the paintings. But I leaned in as far as possible, to explore each image as the guide's light played over the wall.

As I peered at the figures on the walls, I noticed that almost all of them were drawn with miniature heads and shortened legs, with abstract ovals suggesting hooves. That meant the artists were following a set of conventions—and *that*, I always tell my students, is what defines a style. That also meant the artists had instruction of some kind. There must have been teachers—like me—who led apprentices into the caves to make sure they understood the fine points of the tradition.

While I was taking mental notes for a lecture I might give in the fall, I noticed Lily was acting strange. She had stepped back from the group, and she seemed unsteady. A touch of claustrophobia, I guessed. Her husband placed a protective arm around her shoulder and whispered to her in a tone of concern. She made a hand motion signaling that she didn't want to call attention to herself, then raised her chin and moved back into the group.

"Are you dizzy, Madame?" asked the guide. "That sometimes happens in the cave. Try to take a few deep breaths." She did so.

Toby whispered, "If he took a few deep breaths himself, he'd fall over."

I gave Toby an elbow.

"Do you wish to return?" pursued the guide.

"No, no, I'm fine," Lily said in English. She stood up straighter, brushed her long hair behind her, and gestured again to proceed.

"Very well," replied Gounot. "Our time is limited, and there are two other chambers to visit. But before we continue, does anyone have any questions? Monsieur?" This last remark was addressed to the silent Frenchman standing in the rear, probably because Guonot doubted whether any of the rest of us could speak his language well enough to pose a question. But the man shook his head in the negative, his face impassive.

"No? Anyone?"

Toby, who is never timid, piped up. "How do you know how old the paintings are?"

"*Bon*," replied the guide. "Everyone knows about carbon dating?" Nods all around. "Unfortunately, we cannot apply that method to the walls. The paintings are covered by a thin layer of calcite, which is how they have been so well protected. But calcite prevents the test. Nonetheless, other materials found on the floor of the cave have been tested—animal bones, charcoal sticks, and so on. We believe these objects were sealed inside when the original opening collapsed. And that gives us an approximate date of activity in the cave. Our estimate is about 15,000 BC."

Just then Gounot's lamp began flickering, and a few seconds later it conked out. There was not so much as a sliver of light. The darkness was absolute. I heard a tinny clank, as Gounot banged against the lamp with the palm of his hand. And at the same time I had an uncanny feeling there was someone else or something else moving about in the dark depths beyond us. A trick of the imagination, I said to calm myself, but the hairs rose on the back of my neck.

Gounot kept tapping his lamp until the light flickered back on. "Don't worry," he reassured us. "There's a spare battery if needed. Are you all right, Madame?"

David sought to comfort his wife, who looked shaken. Toby and I exchanged glances, and smiled. Since infancy, I've been fiercely independent. My long-suffering mother reports that my first phrase was "Me do! Me do!" as I rejected help in putting on a shirt. Toby knows how to leave me on my own until the right moment, which I appreciate. And though he looked at me inquiringly, he let me be.

"Well, then. Any other questions?"

Toby again raised his hand, its shadow enlarged on the wall behind him by the cast of the lantern. "It seems the artists painted only animals. What about human beings?"

"Ah!" declared the guide, standing a little straighter. "Yes, the paintings are always of animals. There are also symbols, though we don't know their meanings, but hardly any other subjects. Human images are extremely rare. Why? Perhaps there was a superstition against representing people in the paintings. Even today, in some cultures the making of human images is prohibited."

That made sense to me. The Bible condemns graven images. In some tribes it is feared that if one person possesses the image of another, he controls that person's spirit.

Gounot continued: "Nevertheless, here in Lascaux we have a famous example of human representation, but it is located in a part of the cave we can't visit. I'll tell you about it in a moment. First, please follow me. We are now going to enter the Axial Gallery." These observations were followed by another coughing fit.

Lined up again in single file, we shuffled toward the far end of the chamber, hurrying to keep up with our guide's bouncing light. Gounot led the way, followed by me, then Toby, then Lily, then David. The Frenchman brought up the rear. I found myself wanting to look behind me, but the path was uneven and difficult to follow. I had sensed something sinister, but what had prompted the feeling? Had it been fear of darkness lingering from a childhood scare, perhaps, or triggered by some obscure connection to our ancestors who once gathered here? I tried to shake off the feeling.

We squeezed into a narrow corridor with a profusion of images on both the walls and the ceiling. In places, the passage was so tight it was difficult to bend back far enough to see the paintings. The walls were uneven, with rock protruding from every angle, so it was necessary to watch your head. Once I turned to look over my shoulder, and as I twisted for a better view, I scraped my arm against a sharp formation.

"Attention!" barked Gounot. "Don't touch the walls! Every contact introduces noxious organisms." After a glare in my direction, he turned again to the depths of the cave.

We followed him toward the far end of the passageway, which came to an abrupt stop. There his lamp picked out the extraordinary image of an upside-down horse. "The falling horse," he called it. Indeed, the fawn-colored horse with a long, delicate head and thick black mane seemed to be flailing in the air, its belly pointed toward the ceiling.

"Monsieur asked a question about animals. You might well ask, 'Why were any of these paintings made?' The most common explanation has to do with hunting. We know from bones found at the bottoms of cliffs that the Cro-Magnons drove animals over the edge, where they fell to their death. Perhaps what we see here with the falling horse is a depiction of such a hunt or a magical ritual to ensure its success. But not everyone agrees. Please follow me."

The yellow lamp-beam jiggled on the walls as we began retracing our steps. By now I felt clammy, even though the cave was dry, not damp. Ahead of us, Gounot halted. "Look here, for example." His light picked out a charming frieze of miniature horses that seemed remote from any violence. The pretty horses might have graced a carousel.

"Others have suggested the artists painted purely for art's sake and no other reason. What do you think?" he asked rhetorically, gesturing toward the wall.

Above the little horses was a leaping cow painted in reddish brown. She reminded me of the cow in the nursery rhyme, the one that jumped over the moon. She had gracefully curved horns and a looping tail. Her forelegs were stretched out in front of her, while her hind legs were tucked up, as if she had just cleared an obstacle. Was she leaping over the horses, or had she been painted at a later time and posed so she didn't obscure the horses below? It was impossible to tell, but nothing in the scene suggested slaughter.

As we retraced our steps and entered another section called the Nave, we stopped at a striking painting of stags' heads in profile. Each followed the other, as if the artist had seen the stags paddling across a river, eyes wide, heads straining up, displaying their antlers, but with nothing visible below the neck. The scene hinted at the artist's pleasure in observing nature, but there was no sign of a hunt.

"This is as far as visitors are allowed to go." With his lamp, Gounot indicated a small domed chamber off to his right. "Beyond this corridor is a narrow shaft about twenty feet deep. It may have been the most sacred part of the cave. They call it the pit, and at the bottom is the painting I mentioned before. Its meaning is unknown."

We listened intently as Gounot recounted the drama depicted at the bottom of the shaft. Since then I've pored over photos of these drawings—and given what happened next, they are stamped on my memory.

At the bottom of the pit, drawn in black outline, are the figures of a man and a bison. The man appears to be hurt. He seems to be falling back on his heels, his arms flung out in alarm. Unlike the animals of the cave, which are lifelike in detail, the man is crudely sketched, like a child's stick-figure. Facing him stands the bison, its head turned sideways to examine its belly, where it has been wounded by a spear. The most baffling element of the scene is an object, also crudely drawn, that appears to be a bird on the end of a stick. Afterward, my mind would return again and again to this weird talisman, trying to connect it to the events that followed.

We were nearing the completion of our visit. Gounot had guided us back to the Hall of Bulls, where he paused to deliver the finale of his lecture. For the last few minutes of the tour, he had turned on the flood-lights again, bathing the rotunda in color. I was glad of this second chance to view the magical images from my youth. I looked up into the familiar face of the enormous bull, and suddenly the cavern was plunged into darkness.

And there it was, a sound—a scuffing sound along the dirt floor.

"*Merde!*" The guide's exasperation was audible. I could hear him muttering in the dark and trying to locate his hand-lamp, which he had placed behind him on the floor of the cave. I recalled there were two wall-switches for the ceiling floodlights, one near the entrance, close to where we were standing, and one behind us at the far end of the rotunda. Without the hand-lamp, which Gounot was fumbling blindly to locate, he couldn't find the switch nearest him, by the entrance.

"Who touched the lights?" he shouted angrily toward the far end of the hall. But there was no answer. Instead, I felt a movement of air and heard the wordless sounds of a scuffle: grunts, panting, the frightening thump of bodies against a cavern wall. "What's going on?"

The sounds of struggle continued. I reached blindly out to left and right, searching for Toby. I wanted to run, but in the dark I had no sense of direction. Instantly, Toby found me and threw his arms around me. His scent was comforting. From behind us came a gagging cry, followed by silence. Toby held me tightly.

"Don't move," Gounot commanded. We heard him wheezing and shifting about in the dark. "All right, I have it!" he shouted breathlessly. He had found the lamp somewhere on the floor, but it wouldn't go on. I heard him banging it against hard stone. "Wait. The battery." He muttered, working to change the battery by feel.

Somewhere close to us, David said, "I think we should join hands and stick together."

"Right," agreed Toby, and there was a sound of rustling jackets, as Toby uncurled himself from me and took Lily's hand, linking the two couples.

"Monsieur?" David called out to the stranger behind him, his voice echoing in the dark. There was no response. "Monsieur?" he called again.

"He's not there! I can't find him," David cried hoarsely, his voice rising in anxiety.

"Hold on to me," said Toby, grasping my hand more tightly.

It took Gounot forever to change batteries, or so it seemed. In reality, perhaps only two minutes went by. My hand, clasped in Toby's, felt sweaty. At last, the lamp came to life, and we looked at one another with relief. Lily was very pale, but Gounot's face was flushed with exertion.

"Stay where you are," said the guide, reasserting his authority. He moved to the wall-switch for the floodlights and turned them on. Around us, the great bulls and horses galloped across the walls.

Then we saw the missing Frenchman. He was sprawled on his back below the great white bull, with his arms flung out, his blank eyes staring at the charging beast. Blood oozed around his neck where a thin wire had been looped and tightened.

And lying next to him, its gray feathers also streaked with crimson, was a tableau out of the distant past: a dead bird impaled upon a stick.

2

INSPECTOR DAGLAN HAD what you might call a professional squint. It was designed to show just how shrewd he was. Short, square, balding, and nearing retirement age, he spoke in the chewy local accent and had the habit of ducking his chin into his chest to emphasize his points. He and his team—a gangly assistant, two tough-looking gendarmes, and a bearded medical examiner—had driven down from Périgueux as soon as they received the call. Waiting for their arrival, the four of us and Gounot marked time in the guide's hut in a state of shock. We had left the body in the cave without touching it.

Although Gounot seemed no more eager to return to the cave than we were, he was dispatched to point the police to the scene, while the tall assistant kept an eye on us. The gendarmes, with handguns drawn, led the team up the trail, with Gounot a step behind them issuing warnings and directions. In the hut, we sat in silence. Personally, I had no desire for conversation. It took all my energy just to quiet my unsettled mind. It must have been twenty minutes before the inspector returned alone.

"*Quelle horreur!*" was Daglan's first remark. He sunk down into the guide's chair, which his assistant had left empty. He expelled a sigh and looked from face to face, using his squint to good effect. "Do you all speak French?" Toby and I replied in the affirmative. David explained his wife understood a little French but did not speak it. She looked so shaken, she would have had a hard time expressing herself in English.

"Then permit me to begin with you, Monsieur. Your name, please."

"David Press."

"Your wife's name?"

"Lily."

"From?"

"New York."

"The *city* of New York?"

"That's right."

"American citizens?"

"Yes."

"Profession?"

"Lawyer," replied David. I noted Daglan did not inquire as to Lily's profession.

"How long have you been in France?"

David thought for a moment. "We arrived three days ago."

"The purpose of your visit?"

"Vacation."

"*En vacances.*" Daglan nodded to his assistant, who was making notes on a pad. "May I see your passports, please?"

David looked nonplussed. "I'm sorry. They're in our room. We'll be happy to produce them."

"Do you know that in France you are expected to carry your identification with you at all times? Where are you staying?"

"The Château de Cazelle. . . . That's near Beynac," David added, in response to Inspector Daglan's expression of curiosity.

"I know where it is. In fact, I know the family. We'll send for your passports. And you, Madame?" he inquired, squinting in my direction.

At that second I was too startled to respond. My international cell phone was vibrating in my pants pocket, and I didn't know what to do.

19

My brain ordered me to ignore the phone and answer the inspector's question. My body got there first, however. I had the phone out and was glancing at the caller ID. The number was my mother's, but this wasn't a good time for a family chat. I put the phone back in my pocket.

At the same time, Toby blurted in English, "Did you say you're staying at the Château de Cazelle?"

"That's right," replied David, with a puzzled look.

"We are, too!"

Lily's face brightened at the news. David's registered surprise.

"In French, please, Monsieur," said Daglan, looking from David to Toby.

"I said that we are also staying at the Château de Cazelle," Toby explained.

"Really?" said Daglan, raising an eyebrow. "So the four of you are traveling together?"

"No," said David.

"But you all know each other, yes?"

"No," replied Toby. "That is, we just met for the first time here at the cave."

"Quite a coincidence!" muttered Daglan. I thought so too, but I kept my mouth shut.

"When did you arrive at the château, then?" Daglan asked David.

"Yesterday," he replied.

"And you, Monsieur?" The question was addressed to Toby.

"They're expecting us this evening," he said.

"And where did you stay last night?"

"At the Hotel Vézère in Montignac."

Inspector Daglan's assistant was scribbling furiously on his pad. Daglan wagged his finger between Toby and David. "How long will you be staying at the château?"

"Ten days," answered David.

"The same for us," chimed Toby. At once I understood the coincidence.

"Then you must be here for the cooking class," I said to Lily in English.

"Yes, we're both enrolled," she replied, relieved to be following at least some of the conversation. Now things were becoming clear. The four of us had signed up for the same cooking class. It was scheduled to start this evening. I explained this state of affairs to Daglan.

"I see," he said, screwing up his lips. "And you claim that until meeting today you never knew each other?"

"That's right," I replied.

He scrutinized Toby and me. His look was doubting. "Your names and addresses, please."

"Toby Sandler, and this is my wife, Nora Barnes. We live in Bodega Bay in California. That's near San Francisco. We're American citizens."

"Passports?"

We had ours with us. We've both traveled enough to know that a passport can be demanded at any time. We had them in our jackets, along with our money and the car keys. I hate to have my passport checked, but I duly fished mine out and handed it over. Inspector Daglan did the usual double-take. "Ah, I see you have changed your coiffure, Madame."

The photo was taken in my last year of graduate school, when there was no problem with looking young and flirty. At my first job after finishing my degree, one week of teaching freshmen with raging hormones sent me to the hairdresser with a firm order: "The look we're going for is professorial." So much for the long mane. I do look different now from my passport photo. The bangs are still chestnut brown, but the overall length is to the chin, and I pull the hair back behind my ears when I'm working. Still presentable, I hope, but definitely less come-hither.

Toby, now, looks exactly like his passport photo. I'd say he was photogenic, but the truth is, he's always just as handsome in person as he is in his pictures: dark hair, high cheekbones, tanned skin, round brown eyes, strong jawline, and a twinkling smile. Average height but compact build. He stays in shape.

Daglan nodded as he continued shuffling through our passports.

"I see you arrived in France yesterday, is that correct?" It was. "And the purpose of your visit is to follow a *stage de cuisine* at the Château de Cazelle?"

"Yes," I replied for both of us, "but that's not all. I teach art history, and I'm here to do some research on an artist who was a member of the Cazelle family. I've been invited to use the family archives at the château."

"I see. And you, Monsieur?"

"I'm here for the cooking school, too, and to shop for antiques," replied Toby. "I'm a dealer. But the main reason for our trip is my wife's research."

In fact, attending the cooking school was a bonus added to our original plan, as was our visit to Lascaux. A year or so back I became interested in a minor artist named Jenny Marie Cazelle, and I traced her descendants to the current occupants of the château. I spent a full day working on a letter in carefully composed French inquiring whether the family could provide me with information about her life. In reply I received a friendly letter in breezy English from Marianne de Cazelle, along with a color brochure advertising her gourmet cooking school, which would start in mid-June. Should I be interested in attending classes, she wrote, she would be happy to grant me access to the family library containing the papers of her relative. I took the hint. The cooking-school tuition would serve as a permissions fee to examine the family archives. And once I knew we'd be in the vicinity of Lascaux, I applied to visit the cave.

I tried explaining all this as best I could in French.

Daglan listened attentively. "And how were you able to make an appointment to visit Lascaux on the very day your *stage de cuisine* begins?"

"That was luck," I replied. "When I wrote for an appointment, I mentioned I was planning to be in France at this time to do research, and we were given the date of June 18 to tour the cave. We planned our entire trip around the time the Cazelles would allow me to see their archives."

Daglan nodded and looked expectantly at David Press.

"We also started our plans with the cooking school," said David. "My senior law partner, who knows your minister of culture, arranged for us to visit Lascaux. He said it's easier to get on the list for a Monday, and he was right. When we learned the cooking school would start on that evening, we asked Madame de Cazelle if we could arrive at the château a night early, since it's so close to the cave."

"Make a note of that, Jackie," said Daglan, turning to his assistant.

"*Oui, Inspecteur,*" was the response. I spun my head to check who had spoken. Jackie, giraffe-like in height and thinness, had a voice like a teenage girl. And now that I was looking, I saw a mop of brown hair that could be a girl's as well as a guy's. Was "Jackie" short for Jacqueline or long for Jacques? I decided to watch the inspector's pronouns to find out. I didn't want to insult the young man—if that's what he was—by calling him *mademoiselle.* And a tall, flat-chested female would be just as miffed at being called *monsieur.*

"Please speak more slowly," said Daglan to David, whose face registered pride at this acknowledgment of his fluent French. Daglan nodded toward his assistant. "I want him to get all this down."

So Jackie was a "him." That settled that. But there was more to be worried about right now than gender politics.

Daglan next turned to Toby and me.

"I am going to ask you some important questions about the crime you have witnessed, and I would like you to think carefully before responding. First, where exactly was the guide positioned when the lights were shut off? Is it possible he extinguished them himself?"

"Impossible," I immediately replied. "I was standing right next to him, and he was never near the switch."

"That's right, Inspector," Toby added. "The guide was pointing to the paintings, and he was in the middle of his explanation."

"And just where was each of you standing when the lights failed? Madame, I think you said you were closest to the guide. Is that correct?"

I nodded yes.

"And who was directly behind you?"

"I was," Toby said.

"Then Lily, then me," said David.

"And where was the victim standing?" Daglan raised an eyebrow with his question.

"Behind me," David replied.

"So, if the victim was standing behind you, that means you were the person in the group closest to him, is that correct?"

"Well, I don't know about that. We were all close together. Now, look here. I wasn't very close to him. I don't know how far back he was. In fact, I was holding my wife's hand."

"No doubt she will confirm that."

David translated, and Lily nodded yes.

"Of course." Daglan's tone bore a trace of sarcasm.

David colored. "Are you saying I'm a suspect in this crime?"

"No, I haven't said that. But one thing is clear." His glance swept the four of us. "Unless someone else was present in the cave, either one of you or the guide is a murderer."

Lily, attuned to the raised voices, looked anxiously at her husband. David's face darkened. I found myself staring at him. Could he possibly be a killer? It hardly seemed likely. But the inspector was right: if not the guide or one of us, then who? Daglan moved on to the next logical question. Had any of us seen a shadow or heard a sound or noticed any indication of another person in the cave? I told him of the queasy feeling I had earlier in the visit that someone was lurking in the dark, but I had no evidence to support it.

After a moment, Daglan stood, turned his chair around, and sat down facing us with his arms folded across the top of the chair back. "So." He paused, with two fingers pinching the flesh under his lower lip. "Describe what you remember when the lights were restored."

David took the lead. "When the lights came back on, I was looking toward the back of the cavern, reaching for . . . the man who was killed.

24

I saw him slumped along the wall, choked and bleeding, with his arms spread out, as if in surprise. And he had that weird thing by his side. The sounds I heard occurred in the dark."

"What sounds, exactly?"

"Scuffling, punching, or maybe it was just bumping against the wall, and this terrible gurgling and gasping."

"Madame Barnes, does this accord with your experience?"

"Yes, that's right. But I was also staring at the bird next to the body. It was just like the one the guide described, pierced on a stick."

"And this bird, what did you make of it?"

I was surprised to hear Lily speak up, in English. "It was disgusting. A poor bird, speared, bloody, looking horrible." Daglan appeared to comprehend the emotion in Lily's voice and didn't request a translation.

"I was thinking," Toby said to the inspector, "that the killer must have meant to leave a message, referring to the scene drawn in the pit, which the guide described."

"What message?"

"*That* I don't know," answered Toby. "We never saw the scene ourselves. That area of the cave is off limits to visitors. But the image was so important that our guide wanted us to know about it."

"I see," said Daglan.

At that moment, Gounot himself charged through the door of the hut, looking harassed. "I've been sent back," he sputtered to Inspector Daglan. "I demand that you allow me to return to the cave to make sure your people don't harm the site, not to mention the paintings." He seemed out of breath. Daglan sat back patiently, waiting for him to resume. "I respect your position as a policeman. Please be so good as to respect my position as the guardian of the cave." He looked exhausted, but he also looked defiant.

"I do respect your position, but at this moment I am responsible for your safety. Has it occurred to you that a murderer may still be somewhere inside?" Gounot considered the possibility. "Now, if you will let the police do their job, I will ensure that they do it carefully. Did you provide my colleagues with a map of the cave's tunnels and chambers, as I asked you to?"

"Yes, and I showed them where the light switches are, and where the public paths are, as well as the forbidden paths."

"Is there any precaution you failed to mention to my colleagues, Monsieur Gounot?"

"No, but their job isn't to protect the cave. Who knows what they'll do if they think they see a clue? They might scrape at a painting or run their hands over a wall. Even one touch can start a process of destruction that will erase paintings that have been preserved for seventeen thousand years."

"Rest assured," Daglan said with authority, "my men will do less damage than any group of visitors you have led through the cave."

"That's not saying much," Gounot grumbled. He collapsed into a chair and doubled up, with his face in his hands.

"Calm yourself, Monsieur. I still have questions to ask you."

The guide looked up, as if in disbelief at Daglan's lack of appreciation for his distress.

"What else do you want to know?"

"First, tell me where you were standing when the cave went dark." Daglan had already extracted that information from us, so he was testing the guide for any inconsistency.

"At the head of the group, of course. I had led them back into the Hall of Bulls for the last lecture before the end of the tour. As we came near to the exit, I stopped the group and turned their attention to the wall on our right. That's when it happened."

"And at that moment, were all five members of your group within your sight?"

"Not at that very second, but I had just looked back to make sure they were all together. The fifth member, Monsieur Malbert, had the habit of falling behind. But I saw he was sufficiently caught up, just a few meters behind the rest of the group."

Daglan's face registered interest. "Ah, so the victim was close to the group. Close to which member of the group?"

"To this gentleman," Gounot replied, gesturing toward David.

"Do you recall this gentleman's name?"

"No. Actually, I must have read it when I checked each person's documents, but I don't remember it at this moment."

"Then how is it that you remember the name of the victim? You called him Monsieur Malbert. Why is that?"

"Because he was known to me. Admission to Lascaux is limited. In principle, no one visits more than once. Except for scholars who are working on a special project—and they come earlier in the day—or officials from the Bureau of Historical Monuments and Antiquities. I had seen this man among a group of visitors about a year ago. So I noted his name when I looked at his papers: Michel Malbert."

"Do you have any idea why Monsieur Malbert was visiting the cave on this particular day?"

"No, but from time to time the bureau arranges an unannounced visit of inspection to make sure the guide is enforcing the rules protecting the site. I assumed that Monsieur Malbert had visited for that purpose a year ago and that he was here for the same purpose today. The only other repeat visitors are scholars whose projects have been approved by the bureau, and they come earlier in the day."

"At what time?"

"From ten in the morning till noon. Even the scholars with special projects must be limited in the amount of time they spend in the cave. They pollute the atmosphere with their breath, just as public visitors do."

"And were there any special visitors here this morning?"

A little pink came into the parchment gray of the guide's skin. He looked embarrassed.

"There were supposed to have been. But I had to cancel the morning session. You see, I've been sick all weekend. Yesterday I called to put off the researchers for this morning. They're based in Périgueux, nearby, so they can come on another day. But the public appointments in the afternoon are sacred. People from all over the world wait months or years to get their appointed time. I had to come do this tour. . . . I should have stayed in bed." He again dropped his head into his hands, shielding his eyes, as if that would make the nightmare go away.

"Monsieur Gounot, I must still ask a few more questions. Where were you, then, before you arrived to lead the afternoon tour?"

"At home, trying to sleep off this flu, or whatever it is."

"Was someone else assigned to guard the cave in your absence?"

"No. When I go on vacation or have to be absent, there is a substitute I can call. But that wasn't necessary today, because the Périgueux scholars could be rescheduled. There's no guard on duty at night or for the hours of the day when no one is scheduled to visit the cave. But the security system is impeccable. The door to the cave is very secure. The manual lock is connected to an electronic alarm, wired to the gendarmerie in Montignac. If the key is turned without being preceded and followed by the secret code, the alarm is triggered. Also, there are motion detectors in the cave that are set off whenever there is movement inside except when the system has been disarmed, between ten and noon or between four and five in the afternoon."

"Then, if someone wanted to lie in wait for the afternoon tour group, he could simply enter between ten o'clock in the morning and noon."

"Yes, but he would need the key and the alarm code. And I have the key with me at all times. In any case, today there was no morning research session, so the alarm was not disarmed," Gounot added defensively.

"And this alternate who can be called, does he have a key and the code?"

"Yes, but he is as careful as I am. He's my nephew, and I have trained him to be vigilant in protecting the cave."

"His name?"

"Marc. Marc Gounot."

"Jackie, get the address of this nephew and arrange for us to visit him." Then, turning back to Gounot: "Who else had access to the cave besides you and your nephew?"

"No one. Not a single other person."

Daglan thought a moment and then asked, "Is it possible someone could have sneaked in behind the group today as you led them down into the cave?"

Toby shot out, "Impossible. We would have noticed it."

"What about after the murder?" Daglan asked. "If someone was hiding in the cave, is it possible he could have escaped afterward without your noticing it?

"I don't see how," Toby replied. "We've all been together here since then."

"Monsieur, from here I can't see the entrance, so you could not have either," Daglan asserted calmly.

Daglan was right. From here in the hut, we didn't have a view of the cave entrance.

Daglan turned again to Gounot. "When you led the group out of the cave, did you secure the door?"

"Of course I did. It's routine to lock the door immediately after exiting. I didn't lose my head. I locked the door, as always, the moment the last person in the group exited. That was Monsieur." He was nodding toward David. Having conveyed that information, Gounot fell into a coughing spell. "I don't feel well," he said.

"All right," said Daglan. There is one other thing I need from you. What can you tell me about the dead bird? Monsieur Sandler says you described a drawing of such a creature, which the group was not allowed to see."

"Yes, down in the pit a bird is represented below the hand of a man falling backward. What it symbolizes nobody knows. One theory is that the drawing represents an effigy of a bird that a shaman may have carried on a wand—in other words, not a living bird. But, then again, the fact that the drawing looks like a bird run through by a spear might mean the object is associated with the hunt. Another possibility is that it was the totem of a clan."

"Hmm," pondered Daglan, his chin supported by his fist. "How well known are these theories?"

"Everyone in the professional community knows them. Archaeologists. Anthropologists. Prehistorians. The image is famous, and there is no end of theories as to its meaning."

"I see. So, what do you suppose could be the message of a killer in leaving such an object at the scene?"

"I have no idea," Gounot replied. "None at all."

In the silence that ensued, I felt a sense of impasse, followed by curiosity, followed by worry that no answer would be found. Until someone could decipher the killer's motive, we were all under suspicion. At the very least, we were witnesses, which meant our return home could be delayed. That was a selfish reason for wanting to know who the killer was. Even stronger, though, was the primitive urge for justice. A man had been murdered. Someone must be held accountable.

All of us, Gounot included, instinctively turned our eyes to Inspector Daglan. We wanted reassurance that he would find the killer. But Daglan's features were closed. He checked his watch. "I must consult the medical examiner," he said evenly. "We'll continue this questioning tomorrow." He rose and, and turning his back to us, started for the door. At the threshold, he called back to Jackie: "For now the Americans are permitted to return to the château. Please see that they do. And collect the passports of Monsieur and Madame Press." Our own passports were tucked into a folder he was carrying as he strode briskly back toward the cave.

It's funny how the mind plays tricks when under stress. Right then what I couldn't get out of my head was the road sign we'd passed yesterday on the drive from Bordeaux to Montignac. The head of a Lascaux bull was on the panel. "You are now in the Dordogne," boasted the sign. "Welcome to the home of man." I remembered thinking "man the artist" as we drove by. "Man the killer," I was thinking now.

3

I N HIS HIGH-PITCHED VOICE, Jackie instructed us to go straight
to our lodgings. He would follow us. As we walked down to the
parking lot, David's composure cracked, and he grumbled audibly about
being ordered about like a suspect. Toby and I kept our own counsel.
We were rewarded by David's apologetic offer to lead us to the château,
since he knew the way.

We followed the silver BMW over the ancient bridges of Montignac,
then down a long woodsy highway, which led into the traffic-clogged
medieval town of Sarlat. After its vexing entanglements, we climbed up
and over a series of ridges opening onto the broad basin of the Dordogne
Valley. The river flowed between poplar-lined banks and curved around
cliffs topped with fairy-tale castles. Jackie brought up the rear in an old-
model black Renault with police markings.

As he negotiated the narrow road, Toby turned to me. "How are you
holding up?"

"All right, I suppose, considering."

"Well, I'm still shaking," admitted Toby.

"Me too."

"What the hell happened in there? And what do you make of those two?" he asked, nodding toward the windshield.

"David and Lily? I have trouble imagining either of them as a murderer. Lily is out of the question. She could never have fought with a man like that. Remember how long the thumping against the wall went on? But David is big enough. What do you think?"

"To me, it doesn't make sense. Why would a well-fed lawyer from New York strangle a Frenchman in a cave and leave a dead bird next to him? It's bonkers. Besides, David doesn't strike me as a killer. And he's too smart to have tried something so risky in such a tight space."

"It may have been risky, but if he had planned the murder that way, it worked."

"I don't think so," said Toby, shaking his head. "Whoever did this was desperate and probably a little nuts."

"That's what it looks like," I admitted. "But what if that was part of his plan, to make it look like the act of a madman? And how about his wife? She seemed nervous from the start. If they weren't plotting something, what was that all about?"

"I can't believe either one of them was involved in that struggle. Which means Daglan was right—there must have been someone else in the cave."

"You know, I had a feeling we weren't alone in there. It's creepy to think about it, but maybe we were being stalked the whole time we were inside."

"That's probably what happened. Otherwise, we're all suspects, which is what the inspector thinks," Toby replied.

A moment later he added, "I'd feel better if we had our passports back."

"Me too. What if we'd been scheduled to return home tomorrow?"

Toby nodded grimly. "We'd be stuck, that's what."

We fell silent, worrying. While Toby concentrated on his driving, I remembered my mother's call from home. Once we were on a stretch of road that looked like a straight shot for a while, I checked the phone and found there was no message. This would be my first attempt to place a call using the international cell phone I'd borrowed from my well-traveled friend Elizabeth, but after consulting the directions, which I'd stashed in my purse, I succeeded in getting through.

Mom started with a string of apologies—for interrupting our vacation, for calling so soon after our arrival, and for waking us up. Mom has trouble with time differences.

"No problem, Mom. It's just before dinner here. What's up?"

"It's your sister. She's doing it again. She's getting ready to spend all your grandfather's trust money on some crazy scheme of hers."

"Did Angie tell you this herself?"

"No, no. You know Angie. She never tells me anything. But she does talk to your father. Just out of the blue, she told him she's found out she can get money out of her education trust without using it for college, since she's over twenty-one. When Dad asked her what she wanted the money for, she wouldn't say. But I know it'll be like the last time, when she joined that yoga cult and pledged all her money to that guru guy. You know, your grandfather didn't work like a dog all his life to have his little legacy squandered by a bunch of ungrateful kids. . . ."

It went on like that for a while and would have gone on for longer, but I cut through to say this was not a great time to talk.

"Why, what's wrong?"

"Well, there's been an accident here. No, we're fine ourselves, but we were witnesses. I can't talk much longer because we're dealing with the police. I'll tell you all about it later, but don't worry, Toby and I are okay. No, not us. We were just bystanders. Yes, we're fine, but I have to go now. France is beautiful, yes. Okay, Mom, talk to you later. He sends his best. Bye. Maybe I'll do that. All right, I will. Promise. Okay, I will. Probably not today. Yes, Mom, bye."

She wouldn't hang up till she got me to promise to call Angie.

As I put the phone away, Toby glanced over. "Angie trouble?"

"Looks like it. I'll fill you in later. We're coming into Beynac, and the turnoff to the château comes right after that." In the car I'm the one who reads the signs. When Toby's driving, he just watches the road and daydreams. If I didn't say when to turn, we'd be in Toulouse before he noticed. But the system works—when he listens to me, he's a great driver.

Approaching Beynac, we had a full view of the castle stronghold, high on its cliff. I was glad we weren't headed there. Against the lowering sky, the castle looked threatening, and I had had enough threat for one day. We concentrated instead on the attractive drive through the riverside village. Just as we left its shops behind, David signaled a right turn. We rounded a curve of the cliff with the river on our left, and just as the curve straightened out, I spotted a small white wooden sign, waist high. On it were the hand-lettered words "Cazenac-Cazelle."

"That's it," I said. "Sharp right." The sleek BMW made a quick turn, then slowed to make sure we were behind it. When it confirmed we were following, it resumed its rapid pace, climbing a long and twisting road. We mounted for several kilometers, passing a hamlet and the side roads to some farms, and finally pausing at an ancient church at the top of the hill. From that perch, we could see across to the next hilltop, which was graced by a small but elegant château. It was built in the Renaissance style, with two conical towers capped by peaked roofs covered in slate. The château's cream-colored stone facade stood out against the gray sky, while dark, wooden shutters framed six large windows open to the air.

Ahead of us, the BMW climbed up a steep lane bordered by stately sycamores, pruned just the way the French like them, so as to produce a perfectly rounded crown. We followed up the hill, through a gate, and over to the pebbled parking area to the right of the château, with Jackie close behind. Two cars bearing rental tags were already garaged in the stalls of what once must have been the stables. They were built from the same light-toned stone as the house. Each stall door was topped with a straight stone lintel, decorated with an enigmatic symbol: a peculiar cross, seemingly with little balls on each of the four points. I couldn't tell exactly, since the soft stone had weathered over the years.

As we pulled into the last empty stall, Jackie parked in the lane, sprang from his car, and approached the welcoming party waiting on the wide, low steps of the château. As if posed for a family photograph, an old man and his middle-aged son and daughter stood with hands clasped in front of their waists. The daughter was the first to break formation, moving forward, extending her hand to the policeman, and nodding somewhat abstractedly to us, as she absorbed the news of the murder. After a long consultation with Jackie, she approached us with a tense smile, offering what welcome she could, given the circumstances.

Marianne de Cazelle was an attractive woman, in her fifties perhaps, with long, auburn hair and a trim figure. "We are desolated to learn what happened today," she began. "But in spite of everything, we will do our best to make you comfortable."

Marianne's English was excellent, though her word choice was distinctly French ("desolated" instead of "sorry"). Curiously, her accent had a touch of an American southern drawl overlaid on a Parisian glide. She introduced herself and said she was anxious to present us to the rest of the family. But first she noted the approach of her assistant, Fernando, who would take the luggage from our car to our room. With surprising agility, the wiry young man lifted our bags from the trunk and swung round to bring them into the château through a side door. Despite his dark good looks, he was not attractive. The air of acrobatic grace in his action was marred by a rude turning away of the head after he had given us one frowning glance. Bad-tempered, I thought to myself. Too bad. He'd be movie-star material without that scowl.

Taking me by the elbow, Marianne moved us toward the steps of the house, where she formally introduced us to her father, Baron Charles de Cazelle, and her brother, Guillaume. The brother welcomed us in less fluent English to "the domain of Cazelle." His father, warmer in the eyes than his son, bowed slightly and murmured, *"Vous êtes les bienvenus à Cazelle."* And with a nod, he signaled to a female servant, who scurried from her station just inside the doorway and proceeded into the hall. With a sweep of his hand, the old baron silently invited us to cross the threshold. Toby and I followed David and Lily into the mansion, while Marianne stayed behind a moment with Jackie.

The interior space was enormous—a huge square, lit from its back by evening light coming through a wall of glass-paned doors. To our left was a sideboard, from which the domestic was lifting a tray of delicate glasses. I couldn't help gaping at the ornate decor of the spacious salon. There was gold everywhere—gilt-framed mirrors, gold statuettes, and even gold etched into the intricate design of our fluted glasses. When all the glasses were full, the baron dramatically raised his. Looking each of us in the eye in turn, he saluted us: *"A votre santé."* Toasting our health was all the more apt, I thought, after we had been in the presence of death. With one voice, Toby, David, and I replied, *"A la vôtre."* Lily nodded, along with Marianne and Guillaume, and we all took our first sips of crisp champagne.

The baron, elegantly lean and straight-backed, led us across the parqueted hall and signaled us to settle ourselves on a set of three velvet sofas. They were arranged with their backs to the room, facing out to French doors, which opened onto a formal terrace. Beyond that, a lane of red roses led to a line of neoclassical statues set against a high wall of green topiary. Observing our admiration, the baron offered a proud smile. He took a sip of champagne, seated himself in one of the two armchairs in front of the windows, and looked to Marianne to continue the conversation.

At that moment, however, a new couple came clattering across the hall. Or, rather, *she* clattered, in high-heeled sandals that were never meant for parquet floors. He shuffled, in suede loafers. "I guess we are *en retard!*" chirped the clatterer, with a lilt in her voice that conveyed little remorse. "We just heard your cars arrive." She smiled toward Toby and introduced herself as Dotty Dexter and her companion as Patrick Greeley.

Obviously, Dotty and Patrick were our fellow students at the cooking school, but they made an unlikely couple. With her girlish demeanor and blonde bob, Dotty was trying to lop decades off her actual age—maybe late fifties, judging by her weathered neckline, which was amply exposed. Patrick's shaggy hair and casual manner said he was not very long out of school, and still finding himself.

Our hostess cut in, "I must tell you that our new guests have had an ordeal this afternoon." Once she explained the situation to Dotty and Patrick, they made murmurs of commiseration and adopted more somber expressions. "However," Marianne concluded, "we'll try our best not to let this event ruin everyone's stay." She informed us that since the police had asked her to reserve the next morning for interviews at the château, the original schedule for our cooking class would have to be changed. Tomorrow evening we would proceed as planned with a restaurant dinner, but there would be no cooking school during the day. As for tonight, we would all dine here.

"For now, please enjoy your champagne. In a bit, Madame Martin will show you to your room and you will have a chance to freshen up before dinner. Nora, we've put you and Toby on the second floor at the end of the hall. The door nearest your room leads up to the attic, but no one goes there, so you'll have your privacy. We'll serve dinner at nine thirty."

Dotty turned toward me and confided behind her hand in a stage whisper, "I can't get used to these late dinner hours. You know, it's murder on the waistline. They say that for every hour after six you eat dinner, you'd better add another two hundred calories to your day's total." I could see she wasn't about to let the news of our day cast a pall on her evening. She chuckled, jiggling her ample bosom, and twisted to her right to ensure that Patrick caught the view.

"Will your sister be joining us, Dot-ty?" asked Marianne, giving the name a hard accent on both syllables.

"You mean my sister-in-law." (There was a slight pause.) "Why, Marianne, Roz wouldn't miss your cooking. You know that. Here she comes now."

From the darkened hall emerged a commanding figure. Roz stood squat and strong, radiating motherhood gone to earth-motherhood.

Her thick black hair, streaked naturally with silver, was pulled back into a ropy bun. Her coloring was Rubenesque: creamy skin with rosy cheeks and rosier lips, free of makeup. A plain black dress fell becomingly over her rounded frame, and for jewelry she wore only a pair of silver hoops.

"Excuse me for being late," she apologized, turning first to Marianne, then to the father and brother, before turning to us, the newcomers. "I was taking a siesta. I hope I haven't held up dinner."

"Not at all," replied Marianne. "I'm sorry to tell you there has been a very bad incident today involving our guests. We'll need to give them a bit of a rest, so I'm delaying dinner by an hour. You've met David and Lily Press, but let me present to you our new arrivals, Nora Barnes and her husband, Toby Sandler." And turning to us: "This is Madame Roselyn Belnord, Dotty's sister-in-law." We shook hands, as Marianne proceeded to summarize the news of our tragedy.

As if sensing instinctively who was most shaken by our experience, Roz grasped Lily's hand, exclaiming with evident sincerity, "What a terrible thing to go through. Yes, of course, we should let you get some rest." She raised her eyes in concern to Marianne, who took this as a signal to send us off to our rooms and the good care of Madame Martin.

Marianne stopped David, however, to say she would need his passport and Lily's, since she had promised to deliver them to Jackie. David seemed about to protest, but a warning glance from Lily subdued him, and he promised to turn over the passports before dinner. Having stumbled past that snag, we repaired to our rooms on the second floor, to collapse, bathe, and ponder—in that order.

About an hour later, all of us except Dotty were assembled again by the south windows, which now gave out onto twilight in the garden. The sky had cleared, and the marble statues glowed a ghostly white against the dark background of topiary.

We stood, since Marianne and her men were standing. They seemed to be warding us off from seating ourselves on the sofas. Perhaps Marianne was eager to get us to the table, thinking that with a change of scene, the demons of the day could be dispelled.

While we were waiting, I struck up a conversation with Roselyn Belnord. "Is it Roselyn or Roz?" I asked.

"Oh, please call me Roz. Marianne was just being formal, showing her aristocratic side. Even ten years of living in America doesn't knock the finish off a well-bred chatelaine."

I was taken aback, momentarily. The word "chatelaine" has a suspect connotation in post-Revolutionary France—I remembered that from my undergrad course in French culture. Surprise must have shown on my face, since Roz continued: "Please don't misunderstand me. Marianne may be an aristocrat at heart, but she's the most loving friend in the world. She and I became close when she lived in Washington, D.C. Her husband and mine were college roommates, and they were both in the news business. Marianne's Ben was on the foreign desk at the *Washington Post*, and my husband is a political reporter with the *Baltimore Sun*."

"So you and Marianne have been friends a long time?"

"Yes, ages. She's the godmother to my older son, and both my boys call her "Tatie" because she's like an aunt to them. In the old days, she and her husband spent a lot of time with our family in Baltimore, and in summers at the Eastern Shore. But those days are over. Marianne was widowed early. You know, newspapers are a brutal business. I was always afraid my husband would die the traditional newspaperman's death— heart attack at sixty. But at sixty-four, Harry is as full of oats as ever, covering Congress like a hunting dog. It's Ben who's gone, and he was the one who jogged and didn't smoke and didn't drink. When Marianne lost him, she came back here to live with Guillaume and the baron."

"That must have been hard for her."

"It was, but she and her brother get on very well. Marianne has her cooking school, and he has his girlfriends. Though if he doesn't marry soon, there won't be an heir."

I raised my eyebrows, and Roz continued. "Marianne says she wants to see him settle down, but every time he starts getting serious about someone, Marianne finds fault with her. To tell you the truth, I think she's a little leery at the prospect of having to share him with a wife."

She suddenly sensed my distraction. "This probably isn't the time to talk about it. It's Nora, isn't it?"

"Yes, and Toby." As I looked in his direction, Toby turned and joined us. "And does your sister-in-law also live in Baltimore?" I asked, spotting Dotty flouncing back into the hall in her silky, clinging pants and low-cut top.

"For the moment," Roz replied, with a voice that noticeably cooled. "Now that my brother is gone, she's shopping for condos in Florida and New York. But it hasn't been that long. She may decide to stay based in Baltimore, and just spend a good part of the year traveling." She seemed to remember her better self and looked around the room with admiration. "I might do the same thing in her shoes. In fact, I was the one who talked Dotty into coming along with me on this trip. We both like to cook. We've had a little rivalry over who makes the better grits soufflé." She smiled, and then paused again, studying my face. "I'm sorry, you've had an awful experience, and here I am rattling on about food and family."

"Please, that's what I need," I replied. "It's a relief to talk about ordinary things."

As Marianne waved us in to dinner, I walked alongside Roz and confessed I was feeling a lack of confidence about the cooking school, because I was out of practice. "These days, it's usually Toby who makes our dinners."

"Well, why not? It must be very nice to come home to a man-cooked meal."

"It's not that I don't know my way around a kitchen," I explained. "I was a decent cook before graduate school, but I've been working nonstop at writing or teaching till recently, when I got tenure. The last few years, I've baked the week's bread every Saturday, but that's it."

In a lowered voice, Roz confided, "That's going to be a surprise for Marianne. She thought that, coming from the Bay Area, you'd be a disciple of Alice Waters and worship at the shrine Julia Child made for herself over there in Napa."

"Not *too* far off. I learned to cook young, from my Irish grandmother, working with her in our kitchen. No recipes. My mom was totally uninterested in cooking, so we didn't have a single cookbook. But when my little sister was born and I took over as supper-maker, I bought a paperback copy of Julia Child's TV-series and learned the basics from that. So I do sort of worship old Julia. She saved us from eating nothing but soda bread and lamb stew."

I didn't add that all through those years when the kids were growing up and I was in charge of supper, I looked forward to the daily food preparation as a way of bringing order to an unruly household. Mom worked late hours at a gift shop to bring in extra money, and Dad flopped into bed early, exhausted from his postal route. Most days, I was the de facto parent for my sibs. But cooking always set my mind to rest, and tonight I hoped thinking about cooking would help assuage the trauma of the day.

We were shown to assigned seats at the table, and Roz looked disappointed that the place cards forced us to separate. Marianne had put herself at the head of the table, with her father opposite. I was seated at Marianne's right, which I took as an honor. At the other end of the table Lily and David were seated flanking the baron. Guillaume, the brother, was on my right, and Roz was on his, while across the table Dotty turned on the wattage as she nodded to her swains, Patrick on one side of her, Toby on the other, and Guillaume directly across, with the best view of her cleavage.

Marianne silenced a buzz of polite chatter by tapping her knife on the side of her wine glass. "My father and brother join me in saying, 'Welcome to our table, and *bon appétit*!'" She moved graciously into her instructor's mode: "In spite of the unfortunate events of today, we hope you will enjoy our first meal together." Lily managed a smile, and I hoped mine was warmer. Marianne continued: "Even though it is Monday, we have decided to provide an abbreviated version of a Perigordian Sunday dinner. All the courses are typical, but we'll have only four, instead of the usual seven. We'll start with *soupe de fèves*, served as at home."

With that, Marianne lifted the top from a giant china tureen. This meal may have been intended to feel homelike, but the dish hardly looked like a peasant's pot. The china was bone white, decorated with the same elaborate cross that was incised on the lintels of the horse stalls outside. Here it was embossed in red over a band of gold around the tureen's rim. I was sure the china was Limoges; there's something unique about the color of Limoges ware, a balance of unmistakable depth and delicacy. With a long silver ladle, Marianne dipped into the soup, filled our bowls, and handed them to us to pass carefully down the table, family style.

True to the formal spirit of the china, we politely waited for Marianne to raise her spoon, and then we took up ours to sip a wonderfully creamy soup.

"It's delicious," said Patrick enthusiastically. During drinks he had hovered quietly in the background, but at table he suddenly came to life. To Dotty he said, "You know, there's nothing like tasting local food on the spot, especially this kind of cooking that's been passed down from mother to daughter."

Marianne looked hesitant and then seemed to overcome her misgivings. "But, you know, I did not learn to cook from my mother. It was Madame Martin's mother, Susanne, who was my teacher. Her greatest joys, she always said, were her 'two daughters,' as she called Agnes and me, and her work preparing meals for the baron's table."

Agnes, I thought. That history of closeness in childhood could make for an awkward employer-employee relationship. But it didn't seem to. I looked around to see if Madame Martin was in evidence as a server, and she wasn't. There hadn't been any servant present at the start of the meal, and that did give the air of a family dinner.

"I think I taste fennel or celery underneath the fava beans. Am I right?" Patrick asked seriously. He was more attractive frowning, with his soup spoon held speculatively in front of him, than he had been earlier, coming in like a trophy boyfriend on Dotty's arm.

"Both!" Marianne confirmed. "Very good, Patrick. You've got excellent taste buds, which every chef needs."

Trying to enter the conversation, since Guillaume, to my right, was occupied with Roz, I asked Patrick, "So you're a chef? Whereabouts?"

"Chicago, Evanston, though up until now," Patrick admitted, "I've never run a kitchen on my own. But next fall I'm planning to open a bistro in Madison, where I went to college."

"Will you feature Perigordian cooking?"

"That's the idea. Yes, with Marianne's help, I hope to learn enough to apply the traditional techniques to local Wisconsin ingredients. The two regions are closer than you'd think in what they produce—you know, cheeses and milk, walnuts and apples, and all the farm-raised meats."

"A new fusion cuisine," interjected Dotty, who had been following our conversation. I wondered again if she and Patrick were a couple.

At my end of the table, the talk continued about food and was all very agreeable, although it couldn't erase the shock we had suffered earlier. I tried hard to blot out images of death and to focus on Patrick's questions and Marianne's explanations, but I lost track until our server entered. It was the luggage-slinging Fernando. With the same angry expression he'd had outdoors, he abruptly removed the soup bowls. As he took Guillaume's, I thought I might as well try out my French on Marianne's brother.

"Monsieur de Cazelle," I ventured, "your château is very beautiful. When was it built?"

He dabbed at his mouth with his napkin and answered energetically, "That depends on which part you are interested in. There has been a château on this site since the thirteenth century, but it has been rebuilt on several occasions, so some sections are older than others. This section dates from the seventeenth century," he added, tossing a hand carelessly in the air. "Other changes were made in the nineteenth. Then there were the modern renovations."

"I see."

"You know, Madame, these great houses are very expensive to maintain. The roof alone—" Though poised to continue on this subject, he was interrupted by Fernando's reentry with a huge platter of what looked like overdone fried chicken.

As Fernando stood at her side, presenting the dish to the table, Marianne addressed us all: "Here we have the main course for a traditional Sunday dinner, *confit de canard*. This is duck that was preserved last fall in its own fat in a jar, then refried in the jarred fat this evening. Though the description sounds greasy, if the duck pieces are fried at a properly high temperature and removed at the right moment, they should be light and crispy." She waved Fernando to start serving me, and she got up herself to take a bowl from a sideboard. It contained a mass of tiny string beans glistening with a thin coating of oil.

When he'd taken his beans and passed the bowl on, Marianne's brother turned to me again and launched into a discourse on the tradition of preserving duck. Listening politely, I observed that Guillaume was rather well preserved himself. He appeared to be pushing sixty, but he affected the pose of a much younger man. He wore his dark hair slicked back and longish; the color at his temples suggested some recent touching up over gray. His cheeks had vertical wrinkles and pink blotches, possibly owing to too much wine. His voice was gravelly, his manner assured. While everyone else was casually dressed, Guillaume wore a dark, formal blazer and sported an ascot. All in all, he had the air of a practiced roué.

"Are you pleased with the *confit*?" he inquired, leaning over my plate.

"Excellent," I replied, sitting back a little in my chair.

"You won't find this kind of food in Paris," Guillaume sniffed. "Parisian cooking is not the real cooking of the people. For duck you must come to Périgord."

"Yes, it's delicious," I agreed. "Of course, I like all kinds of French cooking."

Guillaume's face clouded over. "French cooking?" he sneered. "There's no such thing! Here in the Languedoc we had our own cuisine and culture and language for centuries before France ever existed! And we still have them!" His insistent voice cut through the talk around us, but after a moment's hesitation, everyone returned to their conversation partners. Everyone but Marianne. She eyed her brother warily.

What made her nervous about Guillaume's little rant? I might be able to say if I knew what had set him off. I had done some reading about the history of the region and remembered "Languedoc" was an old term for the southern half of France. The northern and southern regions had strong differences of politics, religion, and even language. In the local dialect, the southerners pronounced the word "yes" as "*oc*," in contrast to the northerners' "*oïl*," which later became "*oui*." And that gave rise to the distinction between the tongue of *oc* in the South (the Languedoc) and the tongue of *oui* in the North (the Languedoïl). Obviously, Guillaume still respected the old division.

He must have observed my recoil from his bombast, because he continued in a less agitated manner. "I'm sorry if I have shocked you," he went on, "but I believe very strongly we must preserve our ancient traditions. My sister finds my attitude . . . old-fashioned, but that is how I am." Marianne indeed was looking worriedly at her brother.

"Guillaume, you'll make our guest uncomfortable with all your talk about the old ways. Nora has only just arrived, and you're already lecturing her."

"I thought our guests were here to learn about our cooking traditions. I was only making a comment about cuisine."

"Yes, but there's no need to be so insistent. You'll put our new friends off."

"Insistent, am I? Very well, we can change the subject; however, if you would like to learn more about our ancient culture and traditions, my dear lady, I would be honored to oblige."

"Yes, I would like that very much," I replied. "Perhaps at another time. Thank you."

"*À votre service.*" Guillaume nodded, smiled a small, cold smile, and concentrated on his dinner, spearing a morsel of duck with his fork and raising it to his mouth, all with his left hand.

"You'll have to excuse Guillaume," said Marianne. "He has rather firm beliefs."

"Not at all," I said. It was an awkward moment, but I had been waiting for a lull in the conversation to talk to Marianne about my research using the family archives. Perhaps now was the right time. "In fact, I'm interested in learning everything I can about Périgord for my work on Jenny Marie Cazelle. I was wondering when I might begin."

Marianne seemed to welcome the question. The horizontal lines on her forehead relaxed. "Tomorrow the inspector will be using the library for his interviews. When he's finished, I'll show you where the archives are located, and we can talk about your project. I'm curious about your opinion of Jenny Marie's work. Do you know you're the first foreigner who has ever expressed an interest in her career? How did you discover her?"

"Purely by chance," I explained. I had run across a beautiful little painting by her at an art fair in San Francisco. Toby was willing to buy it for his antiques shop, but in the end, we liked it so much we decided to keep it. A small oil panel, no more than eight by ten inches, it sketched an intimate scene of two women with their children sitting under a tree in a park. The style was impressionistic, with creamy, loose brush strokes. There was a signature, tiny, yet clear enough to read, but I'd never heard of the artist. And of course, that was the hook.

A quick check disclosed that during her lifetime (1870–1944), Jenny Marie Cazelle had exhibited in Paris at the Salon—a considerable achievement, for few women artists ever reached the level of Salon exhibition. But aside from a brief entry in *The Dictionary of Women Artists*, hardly anything was known about her life. The most interesting fact in the entry was that she was the daughter of a prominent aristocrat and had been raised in the family château near the town of Beynac in the Dordogne. That was enough to send me to the Internet. Castles don't disappear in France, I told myself, so it was possible the Cazelles still owned the château and that a descendant might be willing to provide additional information about the family artist—which proved to be the case.

I thanked Marianne again for allowing me to view the archives, and

I wondered aloud whether there were any paintings by Jenny Marie in the château. I had not seen any in the dining room or the salon.

"Yes, of course. A couple of Parisian scenes, as you'll see, in the library, and an interesting portrait, as well. You know, she made her living chiefly as a portrait painter, but nowadays no one seems interested in portraits of forgotten people. The little landscapes and park scenes are the popular ones, and every once in a while a new one turns up. We own several. You can see them tomorrow. As for the portrait, it is at the end of the corridor, outside your room."

We had passed a dark portrait hanging in the corridor as we came down to dinner, but the hallway had been dim. Now that I knew it had been done by "my" artist, I would want to look at it closely.

The dinner party broke up shortly after the coffee had been served, and we all headed back to our rooms. As we mounted the stairs, we heard urgent voices floating up from the dining room. The louder Guillaume thundered, the softer and more urgent Marianne's voice became. I couldn't make out the words, but the pitch of the argument mounted until it ended with the sound of a palm slapping the table and an exasperated "Oh!"

"What was that about?" I whispered to Roz, who was by my side.

"You know, I noticed when we arrived that Marianne seemed prickly. She went through a very bad patch when her husband died, and she's had her ups and downs. The smallest thing can set her off, like that little contretemps she just had with Guillaume. And then she'll be perfectly fine again and even sunny and charming like her old self. She just needs some time, I guess. This cooking school is just the thing for her. I'm glad she's taken it on." We had reached the landing. "Well, Nora, it's been a long day. I'm ready for bed."

"Me too."

The hallway on the second floor leading into the east wing, where the bedrooms lay, was dark. Toby, who had gone ahead, fumbled for a light switch and found a dial on a timer and gave it a good turn. A harsh ceiling light flashed on, hummed audibly, and after a minute shut off automatically to save electricity. Toby gallantly stood by the switch and turned it over several times as we all said our good-nights and sought our respective quarters. When everyone else was behind their doors, I asked Toby to stand at the switch a little longer, so I could get a good look at the portrait, which hung just opposite our door.

To my shock, I found it repellent. The style was realistic, bitingly so, with harsh shadows raking the face of the sitter. He was a severe-looking man in a tie and jacket in the style of the 1930s, seated at a desk and grasping a sheet of rolled paper in one fist, which rested on a blotter. His wavy blond hair was combed back to show off a high forehead and deep-set eyes. He was staring straight at the viewer. An unforgiving man, used to getting his own way. For all that self-assurance, he seemed young—maybe in his thirties. The background was black, the jacket brown, and the tie green, as was the desk blotter: a bilious color scheme. Who was the subject, I wondered, and why had Jenny Marie Cazelle rendered his portrait with venom? Was he a family member? If so, what had he done to incur her displeasure? At least it was clear why this portrait was hung in a dark corridor rather than in one of the public reception rooms.

"Mean-looking bastard," said Toby, making a sour face. I had to agree. The timer light clicked off again, and Toby fumbled with the key to our room. We were both exhausted.

As I undressed, the day's jangled images churned in my mind: a bloody bird, a strangled corpse, a police inspector who pegged one of us as a murderer. But it was the glowering portrait that lingered as I slipped into a troubled sleep.

4

I WAS TRYING TO WAKE, but I couldn't get out of the dream. I was running in the cave—running away, in the dark, from something awful. "Toby," I tried to cry, but no sound came out, and he didn't appear. Instead, a red bull leaped out from the wall and into my path. I had to spin round, to seek a route of escape. What I feared was there—the man who was chasing me, coming ever closer. I lowered my head and tried to charge him blindly, as if I were the bull and equipped with horns. But as I reached him, he pulled me up by my shoulders, and we stood face to face. It was the man in the portrait. His eyes were widened and staring, and he was bending forward to kiss me. "No!" I tried to cry, but the sound was muffled, as his whole face smashed into mine. I bucked back, with an effort of my arms—and found myself lifting my head from my pillow.

"Whoa, kitten, you're having a nightmare," Toby said gently, just coming out of his own deep sleep. "It's all right now."

I raised my head toward the thickly curtained windows, to see if there was light coming from the sides. There was—a little. It was past dawn, then. The outlines of our room slowly came into focus: the foot of a four-poster bed, a fireplace, an old armoire, a small table and two chairs, a standing lamp, the doorway to the bathroom. My glow-in-the-dark alarm clock read five after six. Too early for breakfast. Marianne had arranged that guests would be served in their rooms at eight thirty. But my heart was beating so fast that I would never get back to sleep. Toby seemed to surmise all this from behind closed lids. "Take your shower and wake me at eight," he grumbled.

By the time Madame Martin arrived with our tray, we were both dressed and ready to let her in. *"Bonjour, Monsieur-Dame,"* she chirped, in the singsong tone we'd learn was part of the local patois. Putting down the silver tray on a table by the window, she drew back the rose-colored curtains to reveal floor-to-ceiling windows looking out on the front lawn. "Soon the mornings will be warm enough for breakfast on the terrace, but not today."

As she chattered away, I realized Madame Martin was younger than I had first thought—perhaps in her sixties, which made sense if she had been Marianne's friend when they were girls in her mother's kitchen. She looked significantly older, though, because of an arthritic stoop and silver hair. But her face was round and youthful, with a playful smile.

"In Périgord we like to let the sun get up over the hills before we leave our sheets. Except, of course, for old folks like me. If you are ever up early and want your coffee, just come into the kitchen. I'll be there."

Toby thanked her. "You may see my wife, but not me. I'm a late sleeper."

"Understood, Monsieur," she grinned.

Late sleeper is right. How Toby gets anything done when we're at home is beyond me. He sleeps until nine or ten, reads two newspapers from front to back, and rarely leaves the house before noon; yet he runs a successful business.

As Madame Martin set out the breakfast, she added, "The walnut bread is my mother's recipe, and the croissants come from Monsieur Luco, the best *pâtissier* in the region. *Bon appétit.* Madame Marianne asked me to remind you to be ready for Monsieur Daglan at ten."

That threw a gloom over the coffee cups, as Madame Martin departed. Trying to distract myself from the prospect of another interrogation by the inspector, I asked Toby to tell me how his dinner conversations had gone. We had tumbled into bed without having had a chance to discuss the evening. The short version (and Toby's versions are always short before he's had his breakfast) was that Dotty had been flirty, Lily sulky, and David lawyerly.

"Lawyerly in what way?" I wondered. (I resolved to find out more about the flirty later.)

"He was bent on grilling the old baron about the family history. And the baron loved it. He talked about which baron begat which, and what battles each one fought in, from the Hundred Years War to the First World War."

"What about World War II?"

"They did get to that. Something about the baron serving for a year and then being sent back to manage affairs here. I wasn't quite following the French by then. I'd had one too many glasses of Cahors, and David speaks French pretty damn fast." Toby almost never gets annoyed by people. Either it was now too early in the morning for him to give a civil report on last night's dinner, or he was a little jealous of David's language skills. I'd be able to tell by the end of the day, but for now I'd better leave Toby alone. So per our usual morning routine, I went for a walk and left him to his second cup of coffee.

I wasn't going to get far in the hour before the inspector's arrival, so I decided to explore the back terrace we'd glimpsed the evening before. I headed into the main hall and found Marianne sitting on one of the sofas in front of the French doors, sipping at a bowl-sized cup of café au lait.

"Ah, *Bonjour*, Nora. You catch me at my morning duties. At this hour my guests are usually in their rooms, and I use the time to review the menus and the day's schedule. But in fact, I was just thinking about you."

"Really?"

"Yes, I realize my decision about where to put Monsieur Daglan will inconvenience you, and I regret it. Jackie asked me to arrange a room for the interviews, and because it had to have a phone, a table, and a closed door, the library seemed the best place. Now I realize you may lose all of today. Perhaps the inspector will finish his work by lunchtime, and then you could work in the library from after lunch till dinner."

"That would be fine, Marianne." The original plan was for us to cook in the morning and for me to do my research in the afternoon. "I wasn't planning on getting in much work today anyhow. I'll leave you to your planning if you'll permit me to walk out in the gardens."

"Of course, go right ahead. And if you walk back to the statues and turn right, you'll find a path that will take you along the cliff. There's a lovely view of the river."

"Will I be able to get back in time for the inspector?"

"Oh, yes. It's about a twenty-minute walk. The path ends at a little stone building, our modest Lady Chapel. If you head straight back, you'll be right on time for Monsieur Daglan. Jackie said the questioning will start with you."

Hurrying to keep to schedule, I moved quickly down a lane bordered by roses and passed the statues that shone white against the high boxwood hedges at the garden's limit, leading me to the cliff path. Its ample width signaled that this had once been a bridle path, though there was nothing underfoot to suggest the recent presence of horses. The well-trampled grass did suggest someone walked here often, but the path was informally tended. Woodsy plants crept in from the forest edge on the left—wild geraniums, tiny pale violets, and even red poppies where the sun struck a patch.

I took a big breath of cool, damp air and walked rapidly down the path, which grew darker as oak branches overhung ever more thickly. After perhaps ten minutes, I noticed that some of the boxwoods at cliff's edge to my right had been sculpted into topiary. The spaces between the topiary offered quick glimpses of the opposite cliff, now obscured, since it was backlit by the sun on its rise in the east. In the valley between one cliff and the other, the Dordogne River sparkled on its way toward Bordeaux. But I tried to keep my eye on the path forward, seeking the turn that would bring me to my destination, the chapel that Marianne had mentioned. It had been constructed at the outermost jutting of the promontory behind the chateau. The door had been propped open with a stone. Inside I found six wooden chairs, a kneeler, and an altar draped with a white linen cloth, which was a bit worse for weather-wear, though it looked as if it had been replaced since winter. A small statue of a Black Madonna stood on the altar, surrounded by half-spent candles and by vases stuffed with roses that were still fresh. Affixed to the walls were plaques thanking the Virgin for healing loved ones. A few were dated from the 1950s and '60s, but most were much older, and a badly eroded one seemed to have a date of 1818. The only plaque that didn't refer to an illness was dated 1944 and bore the inscription "Deliver us from evil." I felt like an intruder, stumbling upon these faded supplications from another era.

When I looked for a match to light a taper, I realized the statue had been blackened by smoke from countless candles lit for prayer. I was about to add my flame to the history but didn't see a match, so I turned round to head back. Stepping over the threshold, I nearly toppled into Guillaume, who was trying to enter as I was trying to leave.

"Excuse me!" he exclaimed, giving a deep bow. I had stumbled, and he reached out to right me as he rose from his position. When I looked up at his face, I thought I saw cunning, not apology, or even surprise. "Forgive me for interrupting your visit. But how did you know that our Lady Chapel was open at this early hour?"

"Marianne suggested I take the cliff walk; and the chapel door was open, so I stepped in. I wanted a walk before meeting with Inspector Daglan. I really have to rush back for that. He'll be waiting."

"That's a pity. There's another walk I could show you if you are interested, that is, if you are truly devoted to Our Lady. Am I mistaken? Are you one of her devotees?"

I didn't want to lie on a matter like this. But a true answer would have been more complicated than my rusty French could convey. So I stuck to the facts. "Well, as a girl, I went to Catholic school." A sweet memory came flooding back, and I let it out without thinking. "In fact, one year I even led my school's May Day procession. The nuns chose me to crown the Virgin with flowers that day."

"Did they? You must have struck them as a pious child."

"Not really. I was just a good student and also a little romantic about convent life. They may have thought I 'had a vocation,' as they used to say. But that wasn't so."

Guillaume's mood turned in a flash. "It's just as well you escaped from them." His eyes swept over my body approvingly.

I started to duck out the door.

"But if you still have an interest in such things," Guillaume continued, "perhaps you will allow me on another day to show you a famous local site, the Virgin's holy spring. It is deep in the chasm between Cazelle and Beynac, but that's only a few kilometers, by the footpath."

"I would like that very much," I replied, insincerely.

"The pleasure will be mine. I am delighted to find that you have an affinity for our traditions. I was just saying so to my sister last night, after dinner. She thought I might have offended you with my comments about the patrimony of Périgord."

"Not at all, Monsieur. I hope to learn more about your heritage." That much was true.

"Exactly! That's what I told Marianne. It's a question of heritage. My sister gets out of sorts when I talk about the old ways. She fears people will think it strange if I express my feeling for the past. But I find that—"

"I'm so sorry," I interrupted, "but I really do have to go. My appointment with Inspector Daglan. Perhaps we can continue this discussion at our next dinner. *A bientôt, Monsieur.*"

I hustled through the doorway and back along the cliff path, pondering the complexities of Guillaume's character. At dinner he had seemed a bored aristocrat and then suddenly a passionate traditionalist. And his religious ideas were a jumble—love of the Virgin Mary, but disdain for a nun's vocation. I wondered what turned his emotional switches on and off so abruptly. He'd be interesting to watch during our week's stay at his castle. But at a distance. I didn't want to find myself alone with him again.

I turned back and retraced my steps at a jogger's pace, hardly able to enjoy the views of the river and the ochre cliffs opposite. At last the château was in sight.

When I arrived at the rose garden and approached the terrace, I saw Inspector Daglan was seated outside in front of the French doors, waiting for me and sipping from a tiny cup of espresso. He stood up as I approached, extending a big, hammy hand for a formal handshake.

"*Bonjour*, Madame Barnes. Would you please follow me into the interview room?" I did as I was told, glancing down at my watch to confirm that I wasn't late. It was one minute before ten o'clock, but already I felt at a disadvantage.

After seating himself at the master's desk in the library, with me opposite in a straight-backed chair, Daglan gave me the full squint treatment—head cocked to the side, mouth pursed as if to muffle a scoff, and eyes like slits. He stared, and I waited him out. That seemed to earn his respect. He began with a series of perfunctory questions. How long had I been working at Sonoma College, where had I been born, had I ever been to France before, where else in Europe had I traveled? I replied calmly. Those were the easy questions. Then one took me by surprise.

"Now I'd like you to tell me about your work as an art historian. What exactly are your interests?"

This was a morning for complicated questions. First Guillaume, now Daglan. Why did he want to know about my work?

"Well, I have a number of interests," I began. "At the college level we make a distinction between what we can teach and what we do our research on, our area of specialization."

"Let's start with your research, then."

"All right. I wrote my dissertation on women painters in the nineteenth century who studied at the Académie Julian in Paris. The reason I'm here, as I told you yesterday, is that I'm doing research on Jenny Marie Cazelle. She attended the Académie, along with many others." I paused to see if he had a follow-up question.

"That is your primary subject? Women artists?"

"Yes, it is. I also teach a survey of European art, a general course in the nineteenth century, and—"

Daglan cut in. "This survey, what does it cover?"

"The basic history of Western art."

"And where do you begin?"

Now I saw where he was going. "With prehistoric art," I replied calmly. "*C'est logique*," I added—trying to appeal simultaneously to the French inspector's faith in logic and to his national pride.

"So then you have a professional interest in our cave paintings?" It seemed an accusation.

"I suppose so, but I'm not a scholar in the field. The fact that I can give an introductory lecture on the subject doesn't mean I'm an expert."

"Perhaps it is my ignorance of your profession, but I find your answer somewhat confusing."

"Then I haven't expressed myself well, Inspector. I regret my French isn't good enough to make these fine distinctions, so let me try again. What I meant to say is that as far as teachers of art history go, I am not an expert in prehistoric art."

"Then what was the purpose of your visit to Lascaux, when you applied to the authorities for permission?"

He had me there. I sidestepped the question. "Inspector, no one would pass up an opportunity to see the original paintings in Lascaux. They're world-famous. I'm not a Renaissance scholar either, but anyone interested in art would want to visit the Sistine Chapel if she were in Italy!"

"So you prevailed upon the authorities to make an exception to their rules and allow you to visit as a tourist."

That might have been the case, but it wasn't a capital crime. I didn't reply.

"And your companion, Monsieur Sandler, is he also here simply as a tourist?"

That was a strange way of putting things. I felt heat rising to my face. If the inspector was trying to get under my skin, he was succeeding. "First of all, Monsieur Sandler is my husband, not my 'companion,' and, yes, he is here as a tourist and also to shop for antiques."

"Indeed. Your husband surely knows this part of France has yielded antiquities of great value. Anyone in the trade would know what riches in statuettes and rock carvings have come out of our limestone caves."

What was he getting at? "Inspector, we simply wanted to see the paintings at Lascaux. Unfortunately, we became witnesses to a murder, about which we know nothing."

"That is precisely what I am trying to determine."

With this barb hanging in the air, Daglan's face underwent a transformation. His eyes widened, and he leaned forward confidingly.

"I'll tell you what I've been wondering. A young professor at a small American college in the provinces whose husband is an antiques dealer can hardly be making a fortune. It might be tempting for such a couple to use their knowledge of art and of antiques to profit illegally by a visit to Périgord."

"I don't follow you, Inspector."

"Then permit me to continue. We have a murder victim. In my experience, a victim usually has created a problem for someone, has become an obstacle to someone's plans."

"Whoever that poor man was, he certainly was no obstacle to us. We never saw him before."

"So you say. In fact, the man who was killed in Lascaux was Monsieur Michel Malbert, and Monsieur Malbert worked for the Bureau of Historical Monuments and Antiquities, the agency that authorized your admission to the cave on the day of the murder. In addition, the focus of his recent work was the recovery of goods stolen from archaeological sites in Périgord."

"I hope you don't think my husband and I have stolen any artifacts!"

"We don't know that you have. And we are trying to determine whether Monsieur Malbert was working on a particular case. For now I am only speculating, but could it be he had information about your activities that made him suspicious? I wonder if that is why he arranged to join you at Lascaux when he saw your names on the visitors' list. Why else was he there that day? Was he following you?"

His questions bore down like a drill, each one with a larger size bit.

"That's ridiculous. I know nothing about any plans to steal valuable artifacts. And my husband sells antiques in the American sense—objects that go back only to the eighteenth and nineteenth centuries."

"That may be. But there are wealthy collectors in your country who will buy antiquities of questionable provenance at very high prices, isn't that so?"

"I tell you, we don't know anything about such things," I answered with a catch in my voice. This interchange had unnerved me. I had not been prepared for it. We had witnessed a crime, but it was absurd to consider us suspects. Daglan gauged my reaction and drew back a little. He had been pushing hard.

"I am not making any accusations at this point. As I said before, I am simply speculating."

I suddenly felt alone. But there was Toby, thank God.

"Monsieur Daglan," I said, trying to keep my voice firm. "I'm wondering if we need a lawyer. Would you advise me to contact the American consulate in Bordeaux?"

"You are free to do so, but to be frank, I would advise against it. You don't need a lawyer just because I have asked you a few questions. You are not under arrest, and once the diplomatic bureaucrats become involved, everything gets more complicated. Try to have a little patience, Madame. Justice will prevail in due course."

We exchanged volleys for a few more minutes, but Daglan's expression had relaxed, and his questions became less pointed, until at last he sat back and folded his hands in his lap. I took this signal as an end to the interview and rose to my feet. Since Daglan didn't object, but merely tilted back in his chair, I turned and left the room. When I checked my watch and saw it was only twenty after ten, I was astonished. It felt as if I had been in that room for hours.

The library gave out onto the salon, where we had sipped our champagne and where I had talked with Marianne that morning. Jackie now sat in the baron's chair, ramrod straight, waiting, apparently, for me to emerge. He leaped to his feet and came over to meet me.

"Madame Barnes, I must ask you to sit here for a moment while we call the next witness. We would like each person to approach the interview without having talked to someone whom the inspector has interrogated."

This was beginning to feel more and more like a police station. It helped a little to see that Toby was the next one called, since that meant my wait would be over soon and we would be free to talk.

As Toby entered the library, Jackie asked, "Do you have something to read, Madame? This could take some time."

"Well, then, I think I'll go to my room and read there."

"No, I'm sorry but that won't be possible. I am to stay with you, and the inspector asked that we stay here, outside the library, in case he wants to call you in to his interview with your companion."

"Why do you keep saying 'companion'? He's my husband. Where are you getting these ideas?"

"Gurgle, Madame." At least that's what it sounded like.

"Do you mean Google?" I asked.

"That's what I said."

"And Google says Toby is my 'companion?'"

"It does not say you are married."

"Well, it's nice to know there's still some privacy on the Internet. Could we go get my book, then, and I'll read here under your surveillance?" That was acceptable.

On the way back from my room to the salon, I had a glimpse into the dining room, where Guillaume and Marianne were seated closely together engaged in a tête-à-tête. Literally. Their foreheads were almost touching as they talked intensely in low voices. The baron stood at a window with his back toward them. From my angle, I could see his face in profile. He seemed to be staring into the past, where the very old spend much of their time.

Nearly an hour later, the library door opened. Watching the time slowly tick by, I had assumed Toby was getting the third degree, but he seemed relaxed as he emerged from the room.

"How'd it go?" I asked anxiously.

"I'll tell you about it. Let's go outside, and we'll compare notes." With Jackie's permission, we walked out into the back garden and shared our stories. Daglan had put Toby through the same round of questions he had used on me, including the innuendos and sarcastic asides. He had wanted to know all about Toby's business, his supposed dealings in prehistoric artifacts, the reasons for our current trip to France, our prior connections in the region (none), and what we knew about the other guests at the château, particularly David Press. But Toby was convinced Daglan was going through the motions rather than seriously pegging either one of us as suspects.

"What makes you think that?" I asked.

"Just a hunch. The way he was asking the questions, I guess, sort of mechanically. Then toward the end he changed the subject and started asking me some random questions about our life."

"What sort of questions?"

"Well, that's just it. They didn't seem connected with the case. He wanted to know whether we have any relatives in France, whether my father fought in the war, and how Americans feel about Germany now. He asked about California, and what kind of house we live in, and what my favorite television show is. I asked him why in the world he would want to know that. He said he was watching re-runs of *Santa Barbara* on French TV and he just wondered if it gave an accurate picture of life in the United States."

"Sounds like he was trying to put you off guard," I ventured.

"Maybe he was, and he seemed to be enjoying himself. But he can't really think we had anything to do with the murder. It doesn't add up."

"So what did you tell him?"

"About what?"

"*Santa Barbara.*"

"Oh. I said it was just fantasy and that only a few rich Americans live in monster mansions by the ocean and drive fancy luxury cars, while the rest of us live normal lives like the average Frenchman."

"Hmph. Well, he took a much more intimidating tone with me."

"He's not as gruff as he wants us to think he is. He's clever, though."

I shot Toby an irritated look. "What? You're not taking this seriously enough."

"I am. It's just that I doubt we're going to end up in jail. And since we're not headed for the clinker, I have a suggestion."

"Wait a minute. We very well could wind up in jail. This isn't a joke, Toby. We could be in trouble here."

"All right, take it easy."

"Don't tell me to take it easy. You mean keep quiet and leave everything to you because I'm getting all worked up over nothing."

"Nora, you know I didn't mean that."

"No? You cut me off every time I try to get you to see the seriousness of this situation. Someone has been murdered, Toby. We were there. Daglan thinks we had a motive."

"Oh, come on!"

Now I was getting mad. "Look, just because you've led a charmed life doesn't mean that you're invulnerable. I've seen the inside of a jail. I don't want that to happen again."

"That was a very different thing, Nora. Spending one night in jail for having occupied the chancellor's office during a student protest at Berkeley doesn't make you into a case for Amnesty International. And what do you mean, I've led a charmed life?"

"You know what I mean. Private school, help with setting up your business, everything you've ever needed."

"I'm not ashamed of that, if you're suggesting I should be. I know you're upset, but don't take it out on me."

"Upset? Well, it makes sense to be upset when you've just witnessed a murder, you're suspected of committing it, your mother's on your case from thousands of miles away, and your little sister is about to blow her trust fund on God knows what. And by the way, do I get any sympathy for the family stress? No. As usual, you act like my family is best ignored."

"Hey, one thing at a time. I do care about your family. I just think you're a little too involved with them."

"You wouldn't say that if you'd had a little sister to bring up. You never had anyone to look after but yourself."

"That's a low blow," Toby sighed. (True, it wasn't his fault that he was an only child.) "All right. Truce? Look, I hate it when we quarrel. Maybe you're right and I'm not taking this as seriously as I should. But it won't help to get all upset. I was going to say, let's put all this aside for a few hours and go out to lunch. How about it?"

Typical. But perhaps a good idea. I hate it when we quarrel, too, and I was sorry that I had jumped down his throat.

"Lunch," I deadpanned sarcastically.

"Lunch," repeated Toby, casting a doleful look requesting absolution. "In Castelnaud."

"I *am* upset, and frightened too."

"I know," he said. "That's why we need a break. What do you say?"

I sighed, and the air began to go out of our argument. Toby went for the car while I whisked back to our room to pick up my purse and a sweater. As I came down the stairs, I could hear Toby bringing the car up to the front entrance, tires crunching on the pebbled driveway. Just as I ducked out the door, I saw David Press being ushered into the library. His attempt to look casual seemed forced.

Once we were in the car, the rest of my anger dissipated. "Sorry I chewed you out," I said. "I think I lost it back there. Daglan really got to me."

"We're good," said Toby. "Look." He nodded toward the passing scenery.

I willed myself to look out the window and enjoy it. The road followed the river through verdant fields planted with corn and tobacco and framed by honey-colored cliffs, four of them topped by imposing castles. The mightiest was Castelnaud. With its great round artillery tower baking in the sun, it dominated the valley. We passed a field of swaying sunflowers, crossed a bridge, and climbed a steep road up the side of a cliff with precipitous switchbacks, which brought us to the village.

Besides the castle, there wasn't much else to see in town: a tiny square boasting an old stone cross, a *mairie* (town hall), a few shuttered shops, and a sleepy outdoor café shaded by a sprawling linden tree. We parked in the small lot nearby—since it was lunchtime, the tourists had deserted—and we seated ourselves at a dented metal table at the café. We were the only customers. A cluster of yellow stone houses built against the steep hill blocked our view of the fortress, but we could still feel it looming over the village as we enjoyed our lunch: a bowl of soup, a slice of pâté, and a piece of homemade walnut cake. The cake was drier than Madame Martin's, but because it was feather-light and yet full of walnut flavor, it tasted heavenly. For the first time since the murder, I was starting to unwind.

Or at least I was, until Toby started talking about the forbidden subject. "You know, I've been thinking about that bird that was left at the scene. It was put there for a purpose, but whether the purpose was rational or crazy is the question."

"Do we have to talk about the murder? Now that you got me away from that hothouse, I like being out here and I don't want to spoil it."

"Not if you don't want to, but just listen to one point. The motive for the killing has to be connected to the cave art, because the bird is a specific reference to it. So who would have a grievance against Lascaux?"

"There are lots of nutty people who get worked up about art and do crazy things to desecrate it. Remember the madman who attacked Michelangelo's statue of the Pietà with a hammer? But chalking the crime up to a madman doesn't get us very far, and besides, I'd rather think about other things right now. Can we change the subject?"

"Right," said Toby. He could see I was tensing up. "Let's go see the castle, then, and make the most of the afternoon." He pushed back from the table.

"Thanks." We rose to go.

The *mairie*, just across from the café, was connected to a small stone house to its left by its second story, making a sort of overpass, leaving a passageway beneath for pedestrians. A little sign saying "château" pointed through the passageway. We followed, to discover a steep path lined by cozy rectangular houses, all hewn from the same limestone. The colors of the stone changed as sun or shadows played over its surfaces. Sometimes the blocks appeared yellow, sometimes ochre, sometimes orange or even white in the bright daylight. The village, especially now during its quiet hour, seemed little changed from the Middle Ages.

Up close, the castle was enormous. Although it had been heavily restored, there were sections left in partial ruin as a reminder of its age. The interior now housed a Museum of Medieval Warfare, with exhibits of arms and armor, computer projections of the castle's stages of construction, and dioramas of sieges. But nothing prepared me for the panoramic view of the valley as we exited the castle onto the terrace. Toby took a perch on the low wall of the terrace, his legs dangling in space, as we gazed out across an immense vista. To the west, the Château of Beynac, also perched high on its cliff, glared at Castelnaud as an equal—and indeed, the two fortresses had been bitter rivals, in war and in peace. Straight ahead, the Château of Marquesac soaked up the afternoon sun. To the east, the lovely village of La Roque-Gageac could just be made out in the distance.

I sat down next to Toby, smooched his cheek to cement our truce, and began to read aloud from the visitor's brochure as he gazed across the valley. And as I was reading, something in the narrative caught my attention. The Château of Castelnaud first entered the historical record in 1214, when the ill-named Pope Innocent III launched a bloody crusade against a heretical sect called the Cathars, who were plentiful here. The master of Castelnaud, one Bernard de Casnac, was a follower of the count of Toulouse, a leader of the heretics, when the pope unleashed a brutal warrior named Simon de Montfort to wipe out the group. Which Simon did.

What piqued my interest was a sentence in the brochure that described the pope's "crusade against the Cathars of Languedoc." "Languedoc" was the term Guillaume de Cazelle had used the night before at dinner to describe his pride in the region. For him, the old name still meant something. But who were the Cathars, exactly? I made a mental note to myself to find out more.

"All very interesting," said Toby, swinging his legs back onto the ground and getting to his feet. We made our way down the path to the village, admiring the views of the valley as we descended. Back in the tiny main square, we checked out a couple of shops that had been closed during the lunch hour. One sold local products for the tourist trade (canned pâté, walnut liqueur, souvenirs bearing the image of the castle), another sold hats and scarves, and one featured miniature châteaus.

The *mairie* had two doors dividing the ground floor of the building between the mayor's office (closed) and a provincial one-room library, which doubled as a bookshop. Inside, a petite young woman with freckles and short red hair greeted us and asked if she could be of assistance. *"Merci,"* we said, but we added that today we were only looking. The room was orderly and attractive, with stone walls and wooden shelves piled high with books. The subjects were fiction mainly, with a hit-or-miss selection of other items and an entire wall of books of regional interest: volumes on local history, cooking, archaeology, prehistoric art, medieval warfare, architecture, and agriculture; as well as books and pamphlets on the Resistance in Périgord. A table displayed glossy photograph books; these had price stickers on them. We thumbed through a couple and moved to the door.

"Be sure to visit the exposition of fossils before you leave," the librarian advised us in a pleasant voice. "It's free." Indeed, a sign posted on the outside of the building indicated that a display of fossils was open to the public on the second floor. We climbed the outside staircase and took the open door as an invitation to enter without knocking.

Inside, rows of trays and glass boxes displayed minerals and stones containing traces of small sea creatures, or imprints of their shells, or insects trapped in amber. There were some odd lots of arrowheads and other Neolithic tools. The old wooden floor squeaked as we moved from case to case. The proprietor, seated behind a desk, was a slightly heavy, nervous-looking man in his middle years wearing jeans and a checkered shirt. He had thick brown hair and a walrus mustache. Although we were the only customers at the moment, he tried not to hover, but he gave us a welcoming smile and followed us with his eyes as we wandered around.

"Would you like to see the earrings, Madame?" he asked optimistically, as I paused over a case of jewelry featuring items made of purple quartz.

"No thank you," I replied. "I was just looking."

"Perhaps you are interested in fossils, Monsieur?" he shifted to Toby, raising his bushy eyebrows and getting up from his desk. "Everything you see here is authentic, I can assure you. And some of these are quite rare, like this (here he mentioned the name of a creature we had never heard of), which dates from the Pleistocene." He lifted a rock fragment from one of the trays and explicated the squiggles on its surface. "Or this trilobite, which is a very fine specimen and over 4 million years old!"

"Thank you," said Toby, declining the offer as affably as he could. "In fact, I'm interested in antiques, but nothing that old."

"Monsieur is an *antiquaire?*" asked the proprietor. Toby nodded yes.

"American?" he asked again. The French are very good at figuring out your accent.

"That's right. We're from California."

His face folded into a frown. "You are the Americans who are staying at the Château de Cazelle?"

"How did you know that?" Toby asked, surprised.

"And you were in Lascaux when that man was killed yesterday!"

"That's true," admitted Toby, who was now off balance. "But how—?"

"It's in the newspaper, Monsieur. Here, look." He went to the desk where he had been sitting when we entered and came back with a copy of the *Sud-Ouest*. A stark headline announced the death of a visitor to the famous cave of Lascaux. The accompanying photo showed Inspector Daglan speaking to a reporter. Our names were not mentioned, but the story identified as witnesses several American tourists who were currently lodged at the Château de Cazelle. They were described as an American lawyer and an American antiques dealer who were visiting the region accompanied by their wives.

"Besides, I heard about it last night from my uncle. I am going to be questioned myself later today."

"Your uncle?" I asked.

"Monsieur Gounot, the guardian of Lascaux. He was extremely upset."

I remembered Gounot mentioning a nephew to Inspector Daglan, a nephew who had access to the key and alarm code of the cave. I now looked at the fossil vendor with interest. He seemed to catch my glance. "Of course, I had absolutely nothing to do with it. I was here in my shop all day yesterday, as the librarian in the *mairie* will attest. But you were there yesterday. Can you tell me what really happened?"

"We've already spoken to the police," I said. "I'm not sure if we're allowed to talk to anyone else about what we saw." (Especially to a potential suspect in the case, I thought to myself.)

"Perhaps I can be helpful," he persisted. "After all, I know every corner of that cave."

"Look," Toby interjected.

"Marc," said the proprietor. "Please call me Marc."

"Marc," Toby complied. "I'm Toby, and this is my wife, Nora." Marc nodded. "I don't think Inspector Daglan will be happy if we talk to you before he has a chance to question you himself. And I don't want to make him angry. When are you supposed to speak to him?"

"This afternoon. Here."

"In that case, it may be best for us to leave."

"I don't expect him before six. I'm anxious to hear what happened. Can't you tell me anything at all?"

"I'm sorry," I stammered, "but . . ."

Marc raised his palms. "I understand. We're being questioned, so we're in the same boat. Look, I'm about to close up shop for the day. Will you let me buy you a drink?"

"I don't think . . ."

"Please. There is a café right next door. It would be my pleasure."

Toby looked at me. I could tell his curiosity was aroused. So was mine.

"All right," he said to Marc, "but we won't talk about the murder."

"*D'accord,*" Marc agreed. He closed up shop, and we moved next door, taking the same table where we had eaten lunch a little earlier. Now several of the other tables were occupied too. Marc ordered a pastis, a cloudy, licorice-flavored liquor mixed with water. Toby and I each ordered a glass of white wine. Marc avoided the topic of the murder and asked us the usual questions posed by locals to visitors: how we had learned French, what our impressions were of Périgord, what we thought of the view from the château. We responded, nursing our drinks.

After a pause, Toby sat back, searching for another neutral topic. "So, how did you become interested in fossils and minerals?"

"That's a long story," replied Marc, giving his long mustache a nervous twist. "But the short version is that I was always interested in ancient things, ever since I was a boy. My father was a prehistorian, and I thought of becoming a scholar myself. But I wasn't able to go to university. I had a friend who was in the business of dealing in fossils, and he taught me something about it. Showed me I could make a living at it and keep my interest in prehistory at the same time." He shrugged.

"I get by. Business is quiet right now, but when the full tourist season starts in July, I'll make enough money to get through the winter."

"And what do you do in the winter?" I asked.

"This and that. I help out my uncle when he needs me, and I sometimes get work as a substitute guide in the other caves. But I also have time for my own interests. You might say I'm an amateur prehistorian. I do a lot of reading and my own research. I've even published an article in one of the professional journals."

"Then you're an independent scholar," I said. "I know several art historians in the United States who are doing important work but who never were lucky enough to get university appointments. I admire them very much."

"Independent scholar? Yes, I suppose that's what I am. I like the sound of that. And what about your work?" He looked intently at me from behind bushy eyebrows.

Feeling a little too well attended to, I talked about my teaching and research. Then Toby talked about his shop. Marc wanted to know where exactly it was and what kinds of pieces Toby specialized in. Toby described the Russian River valley north of San Francisco where his gallery is located, in Duncans Mills. Marc responded by telling Toby about an upcoming antiques fair in a neighboring town and how to drive there.

At the end, we were getting on rather well, I thought—until a police car bearing Jackie and a glowering Inspector Daglan turned into the square and screeched to a stop in front of the *mairie*. Daglan got out and closed the car door with exaggerated care.

"Old friends, I see," he said with a smile, approaching us with a leisurely stride. He inclined his head toward Toby, rubbing his hands. "You will excuse me if I interrupt your aperitif to talk to your *copain* about a matter of homicide."

"Shit," muttered Toby under his breath.

5

WELL, THAT'S JUST GREAT. First Daglan suspects us of lying about knowing David and Lily Press. Now he thinks we're in league with the guide's nephew." Toby's clenched grip on the steering wheel had turned his knuckles white.

"It's not going to be easy to convince him otherwise."

"And since Marc had access to the cave, he's a serious suspect."

"I know. Still feeling all chummy toward the inspector?"

"Not so much," Toby retorted, taking a curve in the road a tad too fast.

When we reached Cazelle, Madame Martin was waiting in the hall with a message. We would be leaving for the restaurant in La Roque-Gageac earlier than planned because Marianne had arranged for our group to be given a tour of the kitchen before dinner. Madame Martin explained that the hotel-restaurant Le Beau Soleil was run by an old family of the region and kept hours that suited the locals. Only in the high season of July 15 to August 15 did it permit fashionable diners who arrived as late as nine. At all other times of the year, the desk accepted reservations at seven—period. Marianne wanted us to see the kitchen before the staff was in full frenzy, preparing hors d'oeuvres for as many as twenty tables. If we arrived by six thirty, we could get a good look at the kitchen and talk to the chef before he and his staff were under stress.

The plan put *me* under stress, though, since I needed to call my sister before we went out, and we both needed to get cleaned up. Being cooperative guests, we went into overdrive for our hostess. I tried to put the inspector out of my mind and called Angie while Toby showered. Then while I bathed and dressed, we discussed the call.

Now, you have to understand about Angie. She's my little sister and she's absolutely adorable. At least to me. Toby sees her from another angle. According to Toby, she's a bombshell, and as he reminds me, bombshells tend to explode. I'll admit Angie is lovely, and there has been a little trouble associated with that. At fifteen, she almost flew off to London with a photographer who claimed he could get her signed up with an international modeling agency. (I came back from grad school to help Mom and Dad talk her out of that.) At her junior college she became the object of her math teacher's obsession, and though she claims nothing ever came of it, the professor's pregnant wife smelled lust in the air and denounced the non-couple to the dean. The randy teacher kept his job, but Angie was so embarrassed that she left school. And then there was the yoga master who wanted both her fortune and her flesh.

Angie emerged from all these entanglements with her optimism intact, and that is just the trouble. She never sees the caution light when it comes to men.

So it was no surprise when I learned that Angie's plan for Grandpa's trust fund involved her latest boyfriend, who roasted coffee at the café down the street from the beauty shop where she works. Hank made her coffee, and she cut Hank's hair. But he had higher sights for them both. His idea was to start a business that would truck your motorcycle from your home in icy Boston to your warm-weather destination—Miami, say, or San Diego. All he needed to make it happen was $30,000. With that sum, he'd buy a used Winnebago, and he and Angie would fix it up to serve both as their home-on-the-road and as a motorcycle-transport truck. Of course he'd pay her back when the business was up and running. It sounded fishy to me.

Toby snorted. "I'll say. Something's wrong with his business plan. Guys with motorcycles like to ride them. They don't hire a service to get the bike from one place to the next. How long has she known this Hank?"

"Only a couple of months. Do you think it's just a coincidence that he needs exactly the amount of money that's in Angie's education account? It makes you wonder whether there's any plan at all, other than to get Angie's money and run."

"So how did you leave it with her?"

"Well, I told her what I was worried about. She was pretty ticked with me for interfering, but she said she'd think it over."

"In this case, I think you're right to interfere. Your sister doesn't have another penny in the world. You need to talk her out of this."

"I said as much as I could without alienating her. I'll let her think about what I said for another day or two and then call again."

"Fine." Toby put his hands on my shoulders, told me I was a good sister, and that Angie would listen to reason in the end. I felt better.

Together we hustled into the hall just before six, the last to arrive. Marianne informed the group that at the restaurant kitchen we had to stay close together and be out in twenty minutes. We weren't to touch anything. And we were to address all our questions to the chef, so his staff could stay focused on their work. "Monsieur Mazière is being extremely generous to us with his time," Marianne impressed upon us. "You must help me keep my good credit with the family for future visits."

I felt like a schoolgirl being lectured into submission before the class outing to the chocolate factory, but I chalked up Marianne's severity to the strictness of the French school system. I would be happy to keep quiet and observe the cooking equipment and the way the staff was organized for an evening's work. I hoped the kitchen tour and meal would banish my family worries and my mental image of Inspector Daglan's suspicious squint.

We climbed into a white Volkswagen van, which had enough seats for all, and found the grim-looking Fernando at the wheel. It was only a short drive to the restaurant. We passed Castelnaud perched high on our right, then drove alongside thick green cornfields until a bend in the road brought our destination into view. La Roque-Gageac has been called one of the most beautiful villages in France, and it is. While some of the towns in the Dordogne are built atop cliffs, La Roque-Gageac is built into one, with its back to the limestone sheaf out of which its houses are hewn. The cliff and the town face the Dordogne River, which holds the golden townscape in reflection.

The van drove through the village and parked in the lot at the end of town. Walking back toward the restaurant, Toby and I let the others get ahead of us and ambled behind them to savor the setting. We passed a small grocery and a café but then had to change to single file, pressing against the buildings to avoid a truck that came barreling along the narrow road between the houses and the river bank. In a minute or two we caught up to the others, who had entered the restaurant. From the street, Le Beau Soleil was easy to overlook, its yellow stone facade indistinguishable from the neighboring buildings except for a faded "Hotel-Restaurant" sign that hung above an alcove leading to an inner courtyard. Inside the alcove, the group stood in a circle perusing a menu on a wrought-iron stand.

Seeing we'd arrived, the group crossed the flowered courtyard and climbed the stone staircase to the second level, where we were all greeted by the chef and his wife, Christine, who stood waiting for us at the hotel reception desk. Madame Mazière was thin, with limp, brown hair and a pasty complexion; she extended her pale hand to each of us in turn. Her husband, Michel, looked ten years younger, his cheeks ruddy from kitchen heat and his eyes dancing with a mirth that seemed to say he was supremely happy. He waved us into the kitchen and proceeded to walk us clockwise around the work stations: nearest the door (and farthest from the stoves) a counter that doubled for preparing hors d'oeuvres and desserts; in the middle of the room a table for putting together the first and second entrée plates; on the far wall one stovetop for broths and soups and another for sautés, two ovens, and a grill for meats; and, as we rounded the room, a huge stainless-steel refrigerator-freezer. Salads, we were told, would be put together after the main courses were served, using a bar to the right of the refrigerator. Besides the chef, there were just two under-chefs, one hard at work at the hors d'oeuvre counter and the other tending the soup pots.

The pots held my interest. While the chef lectured in French and Marianne translated, I tuned out, thinking of our kitchen back home and that our pots and pans were ready for the Goodwill bin. I noticed that, with the exception of a nest of sauté pans, Monsieur Mazière's pots weren't copper. I had been intimidated from buying a new set of cookware by friends who said a serious cook had to have either copper or copper-lined equipment, and I couldn't afford either. I was working up my courage to ask the chef about the material and weight of his pans when I noticed he was already engaged in an interchange with one of our party.

Dotty was asking in colloquial French how the chef and his two handsome assistants managed to keep so trim when they were surrounded by such tempting food. Monsieur Mazière answered the question with a laugh and an assertion that cooking was very hard work. "One doesn't need a gym when one has to lift these," he declared, suddenly using both hands to raise a heavy roasting pan filled with a dozen or more duck breasts. Dotty gave his shoulder a little flick of her hand, and winked.

Marianne intervened. "We've overstayed our agreed time, Michel. We look forward so much to the meal. Thank you for enduring this intrusion."

"Not at all. It's been our pleasure," he replied with a little bow of the head. And then Marianne shooed us out of the kitchen and into the competent hands of her friend Christine, who showed us to our tables—the two best ones, at the ledge of the second-floor terrace, over-looking the Dordogne. The open-air dining room was inviting. A tangle of overhead grapevines provided shade, while the lowering sun filtered through and danced on the cutlery and immaculate white tablecloths. Across the road, the river flowed gently by. Aside from the buzzing of a wasp, all was quiet; there was little traffic at this hour. In France, when it's dinner time, it's dinner time.

Patrick, Roz, and Lily were my companions. Toby was seated at the table next to us, with David, Dotty, and Marianne. I liked that arrangement, since we were a small enough group to talk, and yet at each table there was someone knowledgeable about the cuisine. Patrick might not be local, but he'd studied enough Perigordian dishes to be our guide. Sure enough, he explained that Marianne had deputized him to give us a running commentary on the meal. Our dinner had a main course from time eternal—a pot of braised boar meat. But the accompanying cornmeal cakes were an up-to-the-minute variation on shortbread recipes from medieval times. The lightness and sweetness of these corncakes was just what the boar needed, Patrick explained. Boar was a heavy meat and needed tenderizing with long cooking and a good dose of vinegar in the pot. Cornmeal was just the thing to stand up to the boar without adding more heaviness. Patrick guessed it was because of the strength of the boar course that the other plates were so light—first a thin slice of vegetable pâté (striped orange, white, and green: carrots, parsnips, and spinach), then a small square of filo pastry with crayfish and leeks inside. After the boar course that followed, we were offered a ball of melon sorbet to clear our palates.

Between all this instruction about the food and the pleasure of eating it in these lovely surroundings, there was not much social chatter at our table. As we rested over the sherbet, I asked Roz about her life in Baltimore. She told me she still lived in Guilford, the neighborhood she'd grown up in, just a block from the old family home, which her brother had inherited at their parents' death. That was now Dotty's house. Roz's mother, as a proper southern debutante and then southern matron, had not had a career, but she'd always done charity work and had established a neighborhood center in Hampden, a working-class area not far from the family home. After graduating summa cum laude from Sweet Briar, Roz had earned her master's in social work at Princeton, where she met her husband, Harry. When they settled in Baltimore, Roz took up her mother's work, but on a professional level, seeking grants for the neighborhood center, getting her mother and her friends to raise money to fund programs that there weren't grants for, and making the center the local hub for social work, day care, and after-school education.

"That sounds like worthwhile work," I said. "Baltimore has had its challenges, with drugs and gangs, I hear. How has that affected your work at the center?"

"We've had the same type of problems since my mother's day," she replied calmly. "But now the percentage of the population involved is higher, and the children are affected at a younger age. That's why I've worked so hard to ensure the future of the neighborhood center." She suddenly looked worried.

"Are you afraid it won't survive?"

"I'm not sure. We were in the middle of a capital campaign to buy the building we're in when my brother Tom died, and his gift was the anchor of the whole campaign. There's a dispute with my sister-in-law over whether his pledge will be honored by the estate. Dotty keeps saying it's not worth fussing over, but the lawyers are at work on that even as we speak."

Dessert arrived to distract us from this touchy topic. Madame Mazière herself came to assist the young waitress (her daughter, it appeared) in serving *oeufs à la neige*, Périgord style. Eight rounds of soft meringue were nestled, as usual, in a silver tureen filled with crème anglaise. The local difference was that each meringue was drizzled with caramel syrup and powdered with minced walnuts. Even with all that to savor, I mused a bit privately, thinking about what Roz had told me. She and Dotty had a good deal at stake between them, now that Roz's brother had passed away. What would happen to the pledge for the neighborhood center? Perhaps it was a good instinct that had sent the sisters-in-law off on a pleasure trip together before a battle could break out at home.

The silence over dessert gave me an opening to connect again with Lily. Earlier I had asked how she was feeling, but she had remained quiet, concentrating on her meal. Now I thought it was only polite to bring her into the conversation.

"Lily, I'm wondering why you and David decided to take a cooking class for your honeymoon. It's not the typical choice for a June bride."

"Well, I'm not a June bride," she bristled. "We were married in March. But David's work at the firm wouldn't allow for a honeymoon then. We thought at first we'd be able to go to Venice in April, but then a case David was working on blew up, and our trip wasn't possible. In the end, David's boss set up this vacation as a gift to us. He arranged the visit to Lascaux and gave us tickets to Paris for a two-week trip."

"I've heard that the law is an exacting mistress," Roz interjected, "but I didn't know it also set the terms for a honeymoon!"

Rather than bristling again, Lily smiled shyly at Roz, as if grateful for an ally who would speak up against The Firm and its tyrannies.

"And did your husband's boss also arrange your stay at Cazelle?" I asked, with a bit more curiosity than was politic.

"No, that, at least, was our decision. David's recently been warned to reform his diet, since his father and brother have heart problems. David's a Francophile, and he's read people in Périgord have the lowest incidence of heart attack in Europe. The theory is that it's the diet, maybe something to do with wine or walnut oil. So he went on the Internet and looked for a cooking school in the region that would teach us how to cook the traditional food."

"You chose the right place," promised Roz. "Marianne is a master of Perigordian cuisine. And even better for your purposes, she's lived in the States and can tell you how to cook these dishes using ingredients you can get at home."

"I hope so," Lily almost whispered. There was a plaintive tone in her remark, as if she lacked confidence that this honeymoon would go well. I felt sorry for her. She seemed to have a sensitive temperament, prone to sadness. In an attempt to raise her spirits, I lifted my still half-filled glass of Baumes de Venise, which had been brought with dessert, and offered a toast to the hoped-for success of our week together. Patrick and Roz raised their glasses. I noticed then that Lily hadn't accepted any of the sweet wine. "Dessert wine not to your taste?" I asked.

"It's not that," she denied, turning her eyes down in seeming embarrassment. "I don't drink." It seemed to cost her something to say so.

"Then how about coffee? I'll bet they have decaf." They did, and after finishing dessert we all four ordered some. As we sipped from the tiny cups and nibbled at a small tray of chocolates and candied walnuts, we stuck to safer topics—what we'd read about local restaurants and what we so far liked best about the food of the Dordogne. Meanwhile, I felt a little envious of Toby's place at the other table. There had been much laughter over there, not only from Toby and Dotty, whom I could see, since they were facing me, but also from David and Marianne, whose backs were to me. David gave another of his loud, warm laughs, as Dotty giggled, grabbing Toby's arm and sort of nestling her head into his shoulder in a show of being convulsed by mirth. Toby was getting the full merry widow treatment. Well, it was certainly more appealing than Lily's mode of lady in distress, which had brought the spirits at our table low.

By now the sun was setting, lending a rosy glow to the river and the fields beyond. I excused myself from the table and went over to extricate Toby, who looked up at me with mischief in his eyes.

"You'll never guess what we've been talking about. Dotty has discovered that there's a nudist colony at a nearby campground—well, not a colony, exactly, but a beach on the river."

"Clothing optional," reported Dotty. "It's called l'Espace Cro-Magnon Club Naturiste. 'The Cro-Magnon Nudist Club.' Can you believe it? I'm trying to talk Patrick into going with me. If you two come along, I bet he'll do it. We could go as a foursome."

"You know what? I don't think that would work for me," I replied lightly, preempting any comment from Toby. I may like to see my husband having a good time, but I'm not crazy.

"At least think about it," said Dotty, with a grin. "It could be an adventure."

"It would be different, that's for sure. What do you say, Nora?" asked Toby in an innocent voice, rising from the table.

I hooked his arm and led him toward the stairs. "The only foursome you'll ever be part of is on the Northridge Golf Course."

He laughed. "I thought as much." He turned to Dotty and said over his shoulder: "Enjoyed talking to you. We'll see you later."

"Right," she waved, airily, going back to her glass of wine.

"Tell me something," I said as we made our way out of the dining room. "Do you think Dotty's attractive?"

"Please." Toby wore his put-upon look.

"What?"

"That question is the third rail of marital politics. Touch it and the man is dead."

"No, seriously. I'm curious. Is Dotty the type of woman you'd be attracted to if you were single?"

"Nora, *you* are the type of woman I'd be attracted to if I were single. The proof is I married you."

"And I'm glad you did. But say I wasn't available. Would she be your type?"

"Not really. She's a little too obvious. Of course, some men like that."

"But not you."

"No, because I'm happily married."

"But if you weren't?"

"I'd be unhappy."

"You won't answer my question, will you?"

"I'm trying not to."

"Why?"

"Because if I said yes, you'd be mad, and if I said no, would you believe me?"

"Probably not."

"The defense rests."

At the threshold to the kitchen, the chef, his brow now glistening with perspiration, was shaking hands and acknowledging compliments as his dinner guests filed out. Until now it had been a pleasant evening. But at the bottom of the stairs, in the entryway of the hotel, stood Marc.

"I have to speak with you," he said urgently. "Can we go somewhere to talk?"

"How did you know we were here?" asked Toby, after recovering from his surprise.

"Everyone knows where you are staying. I telephoned the château to ask where you were dining. I've been waiting for over an hour. Please, it's important."

Toby looked worried, but after a pause, he said, "All right. But we have to meet our van soon, so we can't go far."

Marc led us down the street to the town's sole café, which was busy with a boisterous after-dinner crowd. Inside, we found a table in the corner and ordered drinks, whiskey for Marc and for us small glasses of sweet walnut liqueur. Marc leaned forward and spoke earnestly. "The inspector questioned me for hours. He's convinced we know each other—I mean, we do know each other now, but he thinks we've known each other for a long time and that we're all involved in some conspiracy. You've got to convince him otherwise."

"I'd like to," said Toby, "but he may be hard to convince. What did he say about us?"

"He asked me all sorts of questions about you, but of course, I told him I had just met you and didn't really know anything about you. He didn't believe me."

"What kinds of questions?"

"Whether we had ever done business together, whether you deal in ancient artifacts, whether you knew Monsieur Malbert, the man who was murdered, those kinds of questions."

"We never saw Malbert before in our lives. And I hope you told him you and I had never met before this afternoon."

"Of course, that's exactly what I told him. But he doesn't believe what I say. And I'm not in a good position."

"Why not, just because you're the nephew of Monsieur Gounot?"

"That and other reasons."

"Yes? Can you tell us what they are?"

"It's complicated. It has to do with my father."

"I don't think we can help you unless we know what's going on," said Toby.

We waited.

He decided to continue. "Do you remember that I told you earlier today my father was a well-known prehistorian?" We nodded. "Well, there was a controversy about him after the war. He was accused of collaborating with the Germans." He could tell we were shocked. "It wasn't true, not what they said he did, but it was true he was friendly with a German archaeologist who was working here in the Dordogne when the war began. That was the only collaboration my father took part in, a scholarly collaboration. They had similar research interests. But after the war, the authorities twisted the facts and accused him of working for the occupiers, helping them with propaganda. It ruined his career. He lost his appointment. And in a way it ruined my chances at a career."

"How?" I interrupted. "Whatever your father might have done, you weren't to blame."

"I didn't have enough money to attend the university. My father couldn't help me, and, in fact, his disgrace in the profession hurt whatever chance I might have had for a scholarship. And now look what's happened: I'm a suspect in a murder." I saw he was twisting his mustache again. Was that a sign that he was lying, or just that he was nervous?

"I'm not sure I follow you," I said.

"The man who was killed—Malbert—was my father's accuser. He was a young man at the time, just starting out to make his name in the Bureau of Antiquities. He built his reputation at my father's expense."

"Whew!" whistled Toby. "Now I get it. And I see what Daglan is thinking. In my country we would say that not only did you have a motive for the murder, but also the means and the opportunity to commit it. Isn't it true you have access to the key and security code to Lascaux?"

"Maybe I do. But I assure you, I had nothing to do with this man's death, and I have a witness who can verify I was in my shop all day."

"You mean the young woman who works in the library?" Toby asked.

"Yes, she works directly below my shop, and she will swear I never left it on the day of the murder. And that's the truth."

"Then Inspector Daglan will be speaking to her, no doubt," Toby said sharply. "Based on what you just told us, I can see why Daglan suspects you. But why would he think you are connected to us, other than that he saw us together today by chance?"

"No reason I can think of," answered Marc. "But the police are always looking for connections. And you were there in the cave when it happened, weren't you?"

"That's true," I admitted. Daglan was putting two and two together. In this case, though, his arithmetic was wrong.

"Marc, who else may have had a reason to kill this Monsieur Malbert?" asked Toby.

"That's just it, you see. Lots of people. Over the years Malbert made enemies in the profession. Some he denied permits to excavate. Some he charged for pilfering artifacts, some for forgery. Others, like my father, he discredited. There are more than a few who will not mourn his death."

"Including you?" I asked.

Marc sighed and swigged down his whisky. "Yes, including me. But that doesn't mean I killed him. I didn't."

"And your uncle?" Toby asked.

Of course! Our guide at Lascaux must have known Malbert was the man who had denounced his brother. But he didn't mention that connection to Inspector Daglan during questioning. Instead, he mumbled something about seeing the name on a visitors' list and assuming Malbert worked for the Bureau of Antiquities. That was misleading. I wondered whether Daglan knew anything yet about this history.

Marc's expression was unreadable. "Yes, of course, my uncle recognized Malbert at the cave," he admitted. "He knew the name beforehand, but he didn't kill him, either. I'm sure of it."

I was sure of it too, but only because Gounot had been standing in front of us when the lights went out and couldn't have attacked Malbert, who was at the rear of the line. But now that I knew he had a motive—the same motive as his nephew—it left me wondering. Could Marc and his uncle have been working together? It certainly would have been possible for Marc to slip into the cave before the tour began and then to coordinate the moment of attack with the guide.

We sat in silence. The din of the café seemed suddenly louder. "Maybe you can help us understand something else," said Toby after a while. "The object left beside the corpse, that bird. What do you think it was supposed to mean?"

"It means whoever killed Malbert knew something about prehistory. The image of the bird is famous. But what the message was, I can't say." He paused. "Unless it was left there as a sign of revenge."

"Does the scene in the pit have anything to do with revenge?" I asked.

"Perhaps not, but obviously it has to do with death. The man in the scene is dying, or at least he is falling; the bison is dying, or at least he is wounded with a spear in his side; and then there is a bird on a stick that is lying next to the falling man. No one knows exactly what to make of this picture, but maybe the death of the man avenges the death of the bison, or vice versa."

That didn't seem to me a likely interpretation, but it did seem plausible, the more I thought about it, that the murder was committed for revenge. If so, why leave a clue next to the body? Was it a message or a warning?

"What else can you tell us about the bird in the pit?" Toby asked.

"I know all the major theories about it," Marc answered. "And unlike some of the scholars who write about it, I've seen the original with my own eyes."

"Really? What's it like down there?"

"Mysterious. You have to descend into the pit by iron rungs that have been built into the side of the wall. It's like going down a ladder into a well. The space is narrow and difficult to illuminate. You can hardly turn around. As to the theories, some say the scene tells of a hunting accident. The bird is a simple decoy on a stick. Then there are those who argue the scene is symbolic. One professor thinks this, another thinks that. But I can tell you this much: whatever the scene means, the artist reserved it for the most remote part of the cave with the most difficult access. So it must have been important."

That struck me as true. This strange scene hidden deep in the cave must have carried special significance for the artist who created it. And special significance for the killer, as well.

Toby caught my eye. I could tell he too was mulling over Marc's story about his father's exposure. He sipped his drink with deliberation.

"I'm sorry to learn about the difficulties your father had," I said. Is he still living?"

"He died a long time ago. He committed suicide."

"I'm very sorry to hear that. Very sorry."

Marc was tight-lipped. He kept worrying that mustache.

"We certainly don't mean to pry into your affairs," said Toby. "Remember, we're under suspicion, as well."

"I know that," said Marc, taking a breath and exhaling slowly. "And that's why you have to talk to Inspector Daglan. Tell him we have nothing to do with each other. Tell him you never saw me before this afternoon."

Toby said, "I certainly will, since it's the truth."

"*Bon*." Marc nodded. He looked at the table. The silence was awkward.

To smooth things over, Toby asked, "How about another drink?" Marc nodded again. Toby went to the bar and ordered whiskey for Marc and Perrier for us. We'd both had enough alcohol.

Just as the drinks arrived, so did the rest of our group, entering the room in a loud gaggle of English-speaking voices. Dotty hailed us and came over to our table, while the others clustered near the bar. "So here you are!" she exclaimed. "We wondered what had happened to you. *Bon soir*," she added in Marc's direction, waiting for an introduction.

Toby, relieved at the interruption, smiled and rose. "Dotty, this is Marc Gounot. Marc, may I present Dotty Dexter." Toby had launched the introduction in French, having observed earlier how well Dotty spoke the language. I noticed he had avoided the predicament of addressing Dotty by "Madame" or "Mademoiselle," as he wasn't quite clear which title was appropriate for a widow. I would have thought "Madame" befitted her status, but then again, Dotty's persona was decidedly "Mademoiselle."

"Very happy to make your acquaintance," replied Marc automatically, as he pushed back his chair and rose to take her hand. "Will you join us?" He pulled an empty chair over from the next table, and Toby went to the bar to fetch Dotty a glass of wine.

"We walked the length of the town and back," said Dotty. "It's so beautiful at night, with the reflections of the lamplight in the river. Are you from La Roque-Gageac, Monsieur Gounot?"

"Marc," he said. "No, I live nearby."

"And how do you all know each other?" Dotty's question was addressed to me with frank curiosity.

"We met Marc yesterday when we were in Castelnaud. He was telling us about the region."

Dotty's face lit up. "It's magical. I think it's the prettiest part of France. The castles, the stone houses, the cliffs! Have you lived here long?"

"*Oui*, Madame, all my life. Is this your first visit?"

"Please call me Dotty. Yes, but it won't be the last."

"You are from the United States, too?"

"Baltimore. On the East Coast. I'm here with my sister-in-law at the Cazelle cooking school, with Toby and . . ."

"Nora," I prompted.

"Nora, of course. And what do you do, Marc?"

"Excuse me?"

"What kind of work do you do for a living?"

"I have a little shop in Castelnaud, where I sell fossils and minerals."

"Oh," said Dotty, flagging momentarily. "Fossils and minerals! I'll have to visit your shop while we are here."

"It would be my pleasure," said Marc.

Dotty stole a glace at his left hand. No ring. "Maybe tomorrow? In the afternoon?"

"If you like."

Tourist chatter filled up the next few minutes. Toby lingered at the bar, talking with Patrick. Meanwhile, at our table Dotty enthused over Périgord and Marc played the role of helpful local. When Dotty began asking him questions about fossils, he grew animated. With slightly flushed cheeks, he leaned over the table in Dotty's direction and expounded on the life cycle of ammonites. It occurred to me that he had been drinking while waiting for us to finish our dinner, and now, with two more whiskeys under his belt, he was beginning to unravel. Dotty was a practiced listener. In fact, by the time Toby returned from the bar with her glass of wine, we were all getting quite friendly. Unluckily for Dotty, Toby interrupted her siege on Marc by asking him about the other restaurants in town.

I turned to Dotty and, reverting to English, complimented her on her French. "How did you get so good at it?" I asked enviously.

"Not in charm school, like some I know," replied Dotty, with an unguarded candor. "My father was out of work for a long time, and so I was sent to my aunt in New Orleans. I worked at the Café du Monde. A girl can pick up a lot of French waiting tables in that town."

"You must have a good ear," I complimented her, and I meant it. I never "picked up" any language, no matter how long I was exposed to it. Visiting my mother's relatives in Portugal for a month as a teenager, I came home with no more than *"muito obrigada,"* and that's because Grandma Silva drilled "thank you" into me before letting me get on the plane.

Perhaps my impression of Dotty required a second take. Blinded by her girly manner, I'd underestimated her. When Marianne called time, I paired up with Dotty for the walk back to the van. "How'd you like New Orleans?" I asked.

"Loved it! How could I not? It's a long way from the coal mines to The Big Easy. And I sure do know which I prefer." I didn't reply, walking along the street toward the car park. She continued, "Don't get me wrong. I love my family, but life was pretty tough in West Virginia. I lost my daddy and one of my brothers to the mine, and that killed mama pretty young. So I'm grateful today for every nice thing life has to offer." I couldn't argue with that. We settled ourselves in the van, with Toby back at my side.

On the return drive, we passed Castelnaud and Beynac floating high above the valley, both dramatically illuminated by floodlights from below, standing out against the star-filled sky. I was sleepy by the time we pulled up in front of the château. We said our good nights and climbed the stairs to our room. Toby entered, flicked on the light, and headed for the bathroom. I hung back, pausing again before the strange portrait hanging outside our room. It was eerily lit by the light from our doorway.

I saw now that the painting had strength of a kind, but it wasn't in the least attractive. Again I wondered what had prompted the artist to paint such a portrait with bitter brush strokes. He looked down at me with the hint of a snarl, this arrogant young man. The rolled sheet of paper in his grasp seemed brandished as a threat. Tomorrow I would start work in the archives. Maybe then I would find out who he was.

6

SLEEP DIDN'T COME EASILY. As I tossed in bed, I blamed my edginess on the after-dinner drink. But it wasn't the walnut liqueur that had unnerved me, nor was it the portrait this time. It was our conversation with Marc. I had identified with his panic at being a suspect—being one myself. And his story about the injustice done to his father sparked my sympathy. With immigrant grandparents on both sides of my family (Portuguese and Irish), I tend to empathize with outsiders who can be pushed aside by the establishment. And now, between my sympathy for the underdog and Toby's sociability, we had allowed ourselves to be drawn into a public alliance with Marc. How were we going to convince the police we weren't involved with him?

When dawn filtered through the curtains, I dressed quietly and went to seek that cup of early-morning coffee Madame Martin had said would be waiting in the kitchen. She looked startled to see a guest that early, but she cheerfully left off cleaning raspberries to pour me a cup, served with a pitcher of steaming milk. We chatted about what types of raspberries were ripe and when, and by the time I had finished my coffee, we were both ready to leave the kitchen. She was off to the patisserie in Beynac to pick up brioches for the breakfast trays. Sensing that I was out of sorts, she offered to take me along. I hated to say no to her, but I had another idea in mind. I thought a walk to the little chapel on the cliff might repair my spirits. (It was early enough that I probably wouldn't risk meeting Guillaume.)

Following Madame Martin's instructions, I turned the key in the French doors at the back of the salon and took the path into the gardens and around the cliff. Already near seven, the sun was warming the earth and the dew was burning off into mist. I made an effort to take deep breaths, savoring the moist air and the calm of the wooded path. My stride grew long and free, and I felt calmer by the time I reached the shrine at the end of the path. Its door was open.

I took two resolute steps and stood before the Black Virgin on her white altar. Once again I noted the offering plaque on the wall inscribed "Deliver us from evil." Murder, suspicion, and uncertainty had thrown me off balance, and the message seemed to speak for me. This time, I would light a candle. The roses were still in their vases, and there was the same mix of spent and half-used candles piled next to the four-pronged candle-holder. And again, there was no match. Even in the growing morning light, the grotto was dim. There must be a match-holder somewhere on the altar. I fumbled around with my hands, first behind the rose vases, and then to each side of the statue. Feeling nothing but altar-cloth, I leaned forward and reached back to explore the area behind the Virgin.

"*Ah, non, Madame!*" I heard, as I felt my right arm seized at the elbow. I swerved, to see Fernando looming over me, about to grasp my other arm and pull me back.

"Stop!" I protested.

"No, you stop, Madame!" he replied harshly.

I mustered just enough French to ask him what he was doing. He rudely shot the question back to me: What was *I* doing?

"Nothing but looking for a match to light a candle with," I replied.

"Ah!" He looked surprised, then suspicious. "You are a believer?" He still had me by one elbow.

"Do I have to be a believer to light a candle?" I asked testily, shaking my arm free of his grasp.

Confusion played across his features. He grunted and took a step backward. "*Excusez-moi, Madame.* I'm responsible for this shrine, and no one is allowed to go beyond the candle stand in front of the statue."

"Very well," I conceded. "Next time I come, I'll bring my own matches. And of course I'll respect the boundary line in front of the statue, as you wish."

He nodded curtly. The rudeness with which he stood his ground irritated me. Not to stoop to his level, I uttered a polite, "*Au revoir, Monsieur*," as I turned to regain the footpath and return to the chateau.

Describing this encounter to Toby over brioche and coffee only roused my ire. Toby was incensed. "Let me know if he ever tries to lay a hand on you again. He'll end up looking like pâté."

"Don't worry, I will." While Toby showered, I lay back on the bed, reliving my misadventure with Fernando. I must have fallen asleep, for it was almost ten when Toby waked me gently, saying it was time to get ready for the cooking class. The nap had done me good. I felt much better.

When we arrived in the dining room, all but Dotty were assembled. Roz and Patrick were chatting about whether brioche was properly French or, rather, Italian. David and Lily were peering, with some repugnance, at the stuffed heads of deer and boar mounted on the long wall of the dining room.

As we approached our fellow students, we heard Dotty calling from the salon behind us, "Don't start without me—I'm coming!" And sure enough, she made a grand entrance, swishing great volumes of flowered skirt. Her waist was cinched tight, and the lace on her white blouse dipped recklessly at the strategic point. I tried not to notice. And not to disapprove. The woman needs a man, I told myself, and she's using what she's got to get one.

At this moment, the kitchen doors opened, and Marianne appeared, to lead us into the great *cuisine*. She looked different today. Her hair was pulled back in a bun, and she was dressed in chef whites. Very clean, very efficient. "This will be your classroom," Marianne said with a smile, looking more attractive as she did so. "We hope you'll enjoy learning here as much as I did, many years ago." She led us deeper into the kitchen. "We have kept the grand fireplace, as you see — now it's a display space for the big old pots and the copperware. Today we have ovens and stovetops to do the work the fireplaces used to do. And here at this oaken table, which has been in this room, we believe, since the beginning, we are going to cook — and eat, and talk — just as our ancestors did, in centuries past."

A length of about four feet in the middle of the long oak table was covered by red oilcloth, which was stabilized at one end by a wooden cutting board, flanked with knives and pounders. The other end was weighed down by four white bowls, each filled with ruby-red raspberries. Marianne motioned us to seat ourselves on the cane-backed chairs flanking the two bare ends of the table.

"I think you already know my helpers," she continued. "Madame Martin will be my sous chef, which is ironic, since I learned to cook at her mother's knee." Madame Martin, standing just behind Marianne, smiled proudly.

Gesturing toward the big sink in the corner of the room, she pointed out a male figure in a white outfit, with a bright blue scarf holding back black curls. He had been hidden from view as we entered. "Our assistant will be Fernando, who, you will find, is a jack-of-all-trades."

I flinched as he turned his unsmiling face and gave us a quick, severe glance. I was sorry to be seated so I had a full view of his station, but I was glad my back wasn't to him — that would have made me even more nervous. Toby shot a warning look in his direction, but by then Fernando had already turned away. I patted Toby's arm to reduce the tension. He nodded reassuringly; we didn't need a scene.

"This will be your menu for the day," Marianne said, producing for each of us a single sheet headed with an announcement of the three courses for our lunch:

Salade de chèvre et d'huile de noix
Green salad with goat cheese and walnut oil

Escalopes de dinde sautées aux morilles et noix
Turkey scallops pan-fried with morel mushrooms and walnuts

Coupes de framboises marinées
Cups of marinated raspberries

Underneath the menu, the salad title was repeated and there was a list of ingredients followed by a blank space. I looked on the other side of the paper and found that the turkey and dessert dishes were treated the same way. The name of the dish and a list of its ingredients were there, but there was an empty space where recipe directions ought to be.

"Our sessions will be collaborations," Marianne explained. "For each class, I have selected two courses for which the technique is easy. I will prepare those quickly in front of you. Then there will be one course where you need to practice a technique, and I will call on you to do that. Meanwhile, for all the dishes, you will write the directions down as you observe me. Don't worry, at the end of the course you will receive a booklet of the recipes with my directions—but what you write down yourself is what you'll remember best. So, have faith in your eyes and ears, and don't forget to keep taking notes."

The raspberries got tackled first. Marianne cautioned simplicity in treating fresh fruit and yet encouraged creativity in choosing an accent flavor. She proceeded to toss one bowl of berries with a few tablespoons of sugar and shreds of freshly cut mint. There was no mixing spoon, just Marianne's clean hands, taking care not to bruise the tender berries. With each bowl, she upped the ante—adding lemon juice and a larger quantity of sugar to the second bowl, dousing the third bowl with two tablespoons of raspberry eau-de-vie and a dash of sugar, and lacing the last batch with cognac and honey.

Toby, I noticed, had lost his focus because he was periodically casting about for Fernando, who was in and out of the room. Whenever their eyes met, Toby sent him a piercing glance, which Fernando shrugged off nonchalantly. I began to worry that Toby was getting too worked up.

Within a short time, Madame Martin was carrying the berry bowls to a closed cupboard, and we were on to the next course, or rather, to the first. Marianne explained we had started with a dish that benefits from advance preparation—those berries could marinate for half a day, if necessary. We would proceed to a dish that should be prepared just before serving, a simple salad dressed with walnut oil. And we would serve it (to ourselves) immediately, as a first course, even though in France the traditional place for salad is after the meat. The salad proved delicious, a concoction of lettuce leaves coated with walnut-oil vinaigrette and topped with a slice of warmed goat cheese and a fresh leaf of basil.

I was totally absorbed in the lesson and for the time being forgot about Fernando—until his sudden presence at my right side put me back on edge. He was only taking away my salad plate, but I reflexively pulled in my elbows and avoided his touch. As Fernando reached to remove Toby's plate, Toby stayed his hand by grasping his wrist. "I'm not finished yet," Toby said slowly, looking down at his plate, which still held a few leaves of lettuce. Then he relaxed his grip, a second later than was friendly. Fernando shrugged and moved away. "Just a little pissing contest," Toby whispered cheerfully, "to give him something to think about."

"Men!" I muttered, shaking my head. But I wasn't entirely sorry he had done it.

As Fernando continued with his removals, Marianne began preparing the meat course. She stood at the cutting-board end of the demonstration area and accepted from Madame Martin a plump but small turkey breast, about the size of an open hand. With a thin carbon-steel knife, Marianne cut quarter-inch slices and gave each a light pounding, to halve its thickness. As she worked, she explained this turkey breast came from the aviary kept by Fernando's wife, Elena. The household relied on Elena's bird pens for quail, partridge, and pheasant, and on her fowl runs for free-range chicken, duck, geese, and turkeys. Marianne added that we should make a point of walking over to their cottage to see the birds. I looked up at Fernando, who was about to wash the salad dishes, but he seemed not to have heard. He stood stiffly, with dishes in either hand.

For the next hour, we worked at the stovetops, frying bacon and onions, tossing morel mushrooms in the bacon fat, and creating a vegetable sauce by adding chopped green peppers, shallots, celery, and white wine. While all this simmered, we sautéed the turkey scallops and sprinkled them with chopped walnuts. It was almost time to eat. I turned from the stoves to get another glimpse of Fernando, and there he was, rapidly resetting the table for the main course—that is, working well in tandem with his boss, Marianne. I turned my attention back to our teacher and took notes on her instructions about presentation. Then, like the rest of the students, I returned to my place at table, with a filled plate in hand. Marianne and Madame Martin sat in the middle, where the oilcloth had been, and ate with us, while Fernando attended, pouring wine and water, and waiting for the time to clear.

In true French fashion, coffee came after dessert, and we chatted about our plans for the rest of the day. David and Lily were going to visit the archaeology museum at Les Eyzies, but David suggested we four should take a walk over to the bird coops beforehand. I was for it. That would revive my energy, before my long sit in the library. And I was secretly grateful I'd have company with me when I ventured onto Fernando's turf. I was curious to see the birds, but I wouldn't want to go alone.

A path led us behind the old stables and across a mown field to a group of outbuildings. Between a wooden shed on one side and a two-story house on the other, the ground had been cleared and covered by a neat structure of poles and chicken wire, creating an open-air aviary that was almost as large as the house itself. All manner of fowl were caged in there, kept from flight by a mesh roof. They huddled into the half that was shaded by a linden tree. I recognized the quail and pheasants

Marianne had mentioned, but there were many smaller birds too. The pen was clean, and the birds looked alert. They gave only a healthy pungent scent, which was lucky, since the house was feet away, and outside the kitchen door there was a pebbled patio with table and chairs, where Fernando and his wife doubtless took their summer meals.

Lily and I lingered in front of the aviary, trying to name the birds and wondering whether the medium-sized ones were crows or some French species with a more appetizing name. Our men had moved quickly toward the vegetable garden, which lay beyond the house. We noticed the garden was as large as a tennis court, and its rows were meticulously hoed. The midsummer crops were closest to the house—lettuce, peas, beans, peppers, tomatoes, and summer squash—with ranks of corn and leeks and onions behind, followed by plants that would ripen later: carrots, potatoes, and winter squash. Behind the aviary a grassy field was cordoned off for a pen containing ducks and small turkeys. Next to that was a chicken yard with a thickly canopied tree and a roofed hut for egg-laying and chick-tending. Beyond the pens was an orchard of walnut trees, fenced round to keep in a huge flock of geese. Wherever there was shade, fowl were waddling and pecking at the ground.

David returned, tapping his watch, and announced he and Lily had to hurry off. I didn't see where Toby was but assumed he was exploring, so I decided to do the same. I said goodbye to the Presses and started walking toward the goose yard, when I noticed the squat tower at the left of the house's roof-line. That was a *pigeonnier*—or dovecote. The tiny windows were for the entrance and exit of mourning doves. I raised my eyes, hoping to see one emerge. But I didn't have to wait for that. A pair of slim gray doves was perched on the roof. I hesitated and then tried my version of a coo. That did it. One of the two birds flapped down and landed within two yards of me, on the doorstep of the dovecote. Suddenly I felt my pulse racing. The pierced bird in Lascaux could have been the twin of the one at my feet.

I bent forward, to try to catch the bird, but it flew away. I was leaning on the dovecote door when I felt myself grabbed from behind by both shoulders. Brute force twisted me round, and there was Fernando, preparing to march me off his property.

"*Qu'est ce que vous fàites?*" he growled—What are you doing?—omitting the obligatory "Madame."

But Toby, who had observed Fernando coming toward me, was on his heels. He gave Fernando the same treatment Fernando had given me—grabbing him by the shoulders and spinning him round. I was flung back and landed on my backside.

"Take your hands off my wife!" said Toby in a steely voice, giving Fernando a hard shove, propelling him backward. Fernando's legs went out from under him, and he went sprawling in the dust. It was over in a matter of seconds. Fernando scrambled to his feet and looked for a moment as if he were ready to give battle, but he thought better of it and retreated.

"Those are my birds," he said sullenly. "You have no right."

"And you have no right to touch my wife," said Toby, helping me up.

The two men glared at each other for a tense moment. Then, abruptly, Fernando turned and strode off toward his house. "You have no right," he muttered again over his shoulder.

Oh God, I thought, we've really done it now! What will Marianne think of us? "Toby, you shouldn't have done that."

"What did you expect me to do?"

"Look, we're guests here, and he's staff. He had a right to object to my snooping around his yard."

"But he doesn't have the right to manhandle the guests. He's lucky all I did was push him. What's so awful about looking around his yard?"

I told Toby of my discovery. "Look." He followed my pointing finger. The two doves were perched again on the roof.

"So that's what made him so hostile. Maybe you're on to something."

"Maybe. It's just possible the dead bird in the cave came from that dovecote."

"It's possible. But I'll bet there are hundreds of dovecotes in the Dordogne. It could have come from any one of them."

"Even so, we'd better mention it to Inspector Daglan, don't you think? I wonder if there's any way of telling whether a bird came from a particular dovecote?"

"I doubt it, but yes, we should mention it to Daglan. And look, if you're worried about Marianne, you can say I apologize for pushing Fernando and I'll be a good boy from now on. Say I'm overly protective or whatever."

"You think maybe you are?"

"Not really. But the way you're standing with your hands on your hips tells me you think so. Am I right?"

"I could have handled the situation myself, Toby. Now you've created a problem for me."

"Do you want me to apologize to Fernando?"

"It might help."

He paused and took a breath. "All right, I can do that. And meanwhile, I'm going to act as if nothing happened. I'm going off to scout antiques and leave you to your research for the afternoon. Are you still up to that?"

"Yes. Just promise me there won't be any more fighting."

"I promise not to start anything, how's that?"

"Toby . . ."

"All right, I promise."

"That's good. Now off you go."

"Are you sure you're all right?"

"Yes, I'm all right. Go on. I'll see you later."

Marianne was waiting at the entrance to the library at two o'clock, as we had arranged, but she was not looking friendly. "Nora! What's this I hear about your husband brawling with Fernando?" she demanded. "He told me you were trampling all over his bird pens and that when he asked you to leave, your husband threw him to the ground. I can't have that sort of behavior from my guests. I'm surprised at you."

"I'm sorry it happened, Marianne. But Toby sometimes goes all chivalrous on me. He gets rather protective if he thinks someone is threatening me."

"What do you mean, threatening you? Fernando told me he found you trying to enter his dovecote, where you had no reason to be."

"I just wanted a closer look at a bird. I didn't realize he would consider that breaking into his property."

"In fact the property belongs to me, but that doesn't make any difference. My workers are entitled to their privacy." Her eyes narrowed. "And what was so interesting about our dovecote?"

Was it just my imagination, or was her anger turning into suspicion?

"I'd never seen one before. And I thought you said we could take a look at the bird pens."

"A look is one thing. Going into them is another. Our doves aren't for show; they're valuable. Fernando has every right to keep people from disturbing them."

"Of course. But he had no right to grab me. That was wrong."

"What?"

I explained what had happened and added an account of how menacing Fernando had been at the chapel.

Marianne took a small step back. "Well, I'm surprised to hear that. He shouldn't have touched you, on either occasion. I'll talk to him. But in the future, please mind where you walk. We want our guests to enjoy their stay at the château, but you can't just go anywhere you please. This is our home."

"I know, Marianne. I'm sorry. I thought when you said we should visit Fernando's aviary, it would be okay if I looked around. I guess I got too close. And the men got too macho. It shouldn't have happened. I'll be more careful from now on."

I was doing my best to mollify her, and my efforts had some effect. "And what about your husband?"

"Don't worry. There won't be any more trouble with Fernando."

"I hope not. She held my gaze steadily for a moment, then sighed, leaving me with the impression Fernando had caused her difficulties in the past. "All right, let's say no more about it. We'll go into the library and I'll show you to your work." She opened the heavy oak door and led the way in. "And where will your husband be while you are working?"

"Toby is out looking for antiques this afternoon. He'll be busy, too."

"Good, I'm glad to hear it." She gestured for me to follow her into the room.

"I can't tell you how grateful I am for your help with my research," I said, trying to lighten the atmosphere. "I want to learn as much as I can about your great-grandmother—that is, if I'm right about her relationship to you."

"No, Jenny Marie Cazelle was what I think you would call my great-great-aunt. But you'll see for yourself when you look at the family records. I've already pulled things together for you."

The library was comfortable rather than imposing, with floor-to-ceiling bookshelves on three walls crammed with all types of volumes: old leather-bound tomes, more recent hardcovers, even paperbacks and some cardboard document files. Three brown leather armchairs ringed the room, each accompanied by a standing lamp. A well-worn oriental rug covered the stone floor. On the fourth wall, a tall window with leaded panes was cranked open to admit the afternoon air. Hanging on either side of the window were two beguiling paintings in a style I immediately recognized.

"Are those by—"

"Yes, of course," interrupted Marianne. "I thought they would interest you."

"They certainly do." I walked over to study one, then the other. The one on the left showed several figures strolling in a park. The other featured children playing in a city street. "They're lovely," I said. Marianne waited a few moments while I took them in. Near the window were an oak table and a matching desk chair. On the table several books and boxes were carefully laid out. In spite of a pleasant breeze from the window, a whiff of old tobacco smoke hung in the air.

Marianne bent slightly at the waist and placed both palms on the table as I sat myself in the chair. "Here, first of all, is the family Bible, with records of births, baptisms, marriages, deaths. I've put bookmarks on the pages that refer to Jenny Marie." The Bible was oversized, old, and covered in black cloth. "In the boxes on the left you will find some old letters and documents that might be useful." She paused briefly. "But I think the sketchbooks and journals will interest you most." She pointed to a small stack on the right side of the table. Sketchbooks and journals? This was more than I expected.

"We have some, not all of them," Marianne continued, "which means the record is incomplete, but even so, you are welcome to look through these and to use whatever may be important for your research. I've gone through them all several times, but you are the first person outside the family to look at them."

"It's a privilege. Thank you so much." My day, which had started so badly, now held real promise.

"If you like, you may borrow any of the books in here, but I would ask you not to remove Jenny Marie's records from this room. For safety's sake, you understand."

"Of course, Marianne. I'll handle everything with care."

"I am sure you will," she said, without warmth.

"Thank you again," I said, meaning it. She walked away, closing the door behind her.

I took a breath, held it, and exhaled slowly. I needed to stay in Marianne's good graces if I wanted to accomplish my research. But now that I was here, I wasn't sure where to begin. I had been hoping to find sufficient material for a journal article. There was more than enough here for that. My challenge was to sort through the documents and decide what to use, given the limited time I'd be here. I was so excited to find a cache no one else had ever examined that my anxieties melted away, and I reverted to type: Nora Barnes, sleuth of archives.

Like most academics, I have my tics about getting down to work. I shuffle papers, rearrange my desk, stack items in their order to be read, and so forth. I even have a ritual for opening a new book. I start with the cover blurbs and descriptions on the book jacket. I look at the flyleaf and prefatory material—all of it. Then I flip to the back to see if there's a biographical squib on the author. Finally, I zip through the table of contents, and only then do I turn to the first page. I guess this procedure gives me context for what I'm about to read. It's also a warm-up, like a pianist stretching her fingers before playing.

True to form, I started with a quick inventory. The records in the family Bible were the obvious place to begin, but first I couldn't resist a quick thumb-through of the sketchbooks. Pictures before words: the art historian's mantra. Many of the drawings were in pencil or charcoal, and some were in ink that had started to brown. There were studies for portraits—though nothing resembling the one outside our bedroom that had disturbed me so much—as well as figure studies, anatomy drawings (dozens of hands were painstakingly rendered), sketches of animals, trees, and plants. Some drawings were partial or unfinished, others quite polished. One of the pads held a number of spatial compositions that might have been studies for large paintings. Each of the sketchbooks was dated on the upper left-hand corner of its inside cover, which would make them useful for tracking the artist's development. For now, I stacked them in chronological order (the oldest was dated 1888, the latest 1924) and moved the long pads to a corner of the table.

Next I gathered the four thick, blue-covered notebooks Marianne had left for me and looked to see whether these too had been dated on the inside cover. Yes, in a careful hand, the artist had noted the beginning and ending dates covered in each volume, and the individual entries were dated as well. I stacked the four journals in front of me too, with the oldest on top. It would be easy enough to correlate the journal entries and sketches by dates. The earliest journal was dated 1886–1892, the next volume 1892–1905, the next 1905–1917, and the last 1917–1938. But Jenny Marie had died in 1944, so the series didn't cover the last six years of her life. That was a pity. I wondered if there had been a fifth volume, now lost, perhaps, or located elsewhere. I'd ask Marianne.

Next I checked the family Bible. A page at the back separated by a leather bookmark opened to a neatly drawn genealogical chart. Additional pages recorded dates of baptism, marriage, and death for each member of the family going back to the eighteenth century. I was right about Jenny Marie's dates. She was born in 1870, the eldest of two children born to the Baron Émile de Cazelle, and she died in 1944, without children of her own. In fact, she had never married. (That didn't surprise me. It wasn't easy in the nineteenth century for a woman to combine a full-time career with a family. I wondered, though, about possible suitors and hoped I would find out more about her private life in the journals.) Jenny Marie's younger brother, Antoine (1875–1944), inherited the title and passed it on to his son, Pierre de Cazelle (1900–1965). Pierre's son Charles, the current baron, was born in 1924, and his two children were Guillaume (born 1949) and Marianne (born 1952). And so, I calculated, that made Jenny Marie the aunt of the current baron's father, and therefore the great-great aunt of Marianne, as she had correctly stated. Complicated, yes, but reasonably easy to follow with the genealogical diagram in front of me.

Now that the family lineage was clear, I realized the old baron was the one remaining member of the family to have known Jenny Marie during her lifetime. He would have been twenty years old at the time of his great-aunt's death, during the war. Come to think of it, didn't Jenny Marie's brother, Antoine, die in the same year? Yes, according to the records. So were their deaths related, and were they connected to the war? What had been the experience of the family during the German occupation? I wondered if the old baron would be willing to talk about that period. I knew many French families were reticent when it came to talking about the war years, since France had capitulated so easily (or at least that's how it looked to the Brits and the Yanks). Still, he had mentioned the war to Toby and David the first night, so it would be worth asking.

I was taking notes on my laptop as fast as I could. Even though I knew there would be no Internet connection for guests at the château, I had brought my computer along for this purpose.

I hadn't yet peeked into the boxes of letters and documents Marianne had provided. I did now and was relieved to discover that someone, Marianne no doubt, had already sorted the letters by date. Most of the correspondence was business-related, with letters to the artist from clients or galleries, art juries or professional societies. However, a few handwritten letters appeared to be personal, and those might be interesting. I scanned through the letters to the back of the pack, curious to see whether the correspondence continued through the war years, but again the last item was dated 1938. It was a letter from a collector acknowledging receipt of a portrait of his wife.

By now I had finished my inventory and arranged my materials. The next step was to start reading methodically, and this was the point at which I always get up from my desk. As the French say, "*Reculer pour mieux sauter*": "take a step back, the better to jump." (It's plain old fidgeting, really, but that's how I work.) I edged my chair back, careful of the carpet, and took a turn around the room. I paused again in front of the two paintings, delighting in their details. Then I let my eyes sweep the bookshelves, checking whether Marianne could have missed the final volume of Jenny Marie's journals. Unfortunately, I found no prize. My tour ended in front of a bookcase crammed with volumes about Périgord and local history, including several old volumes on the Cathars. I'd been hoping to learn more about the sect but didn't want to get side-tracked, so I glanced through the tables of contents quickly and chose *The Heretics of Southwest France* for later reading. I tucked it into my purse.

My goal for the remainder of the afternoon was to speed through the first volume, which covered the period of Jenny Marie's life from ages sixteen to twenty-two. Her handwriting was large and flowing and not very difficult to read. However, she was not regular in her entries. Sometimes she jotted thoughts on sequential days, but sometimes weeks and months went by without a note, and when she was eighteen, there was a halt for more than a year. But for my purposes, even this early notebook was useful. From the start it was clear she treated her journal as a work diary—there were few entries about bruised emotions, crushes, or the other usual teenage subjects. Instead, she wrote about her ambitions as a young artist and her struggles to master various techniques. By sixteen she was already serious about her drawing, and at seventeen she was locked in debate with Monsieur Chaliflour, her art teacher. Even at that age, she showed an independent spirit, complaining that her school exercises were too rigid.

3 May 1887

He tells us art is made by the hand and eye, but I think art is also made by the heart. I find it hard to like M. Chaliflour, he is so cold. Plan for today: I will draw the trees and pathways leading to the chapel. There is an old man who visits there every day at noon. I will ask to draw him, and what I want to capture is the sorrow in his face. For that is what is important about him, not the length of his fingers. What does M. Chaliflour know about sorrow? Or life? He has no wife or children. He lives by himself. I should feel sorry for him, yet there is no sorrow in his face, nor joy, either, come to think of it, nothing but sternness. Maybe that is because he is an art teacher and not a true artist. That's what I want to be—a true artist or nothing. And I will work as hard as needs be to become one.

The more I read of Jenny Marie, the more I liked her. On an earlier page there was an affectionate description of her younger brother, Antoine, who must have been about ten at the time.

14 September 1886

What a rascal he is. Today he made Papa cross and received a spanking (but not too hard). It all had to do with a broken vase in the courtyard. Yet ten minutes later he was laughing and running about as if nothing had happened, and even Papa was smiling again. I tried making him sit still so I could draw him, but he refuses to hold a pose. What can you expect? He gets bored so easily. And besides, how hard it is to draw a smiling face! I did a quick sketch of him today, but I couldn't seize his likeness. How could anyone? It's always changing. Now off he goes with his friends. And they follow him into the woods carrying those big sticks to knock walnuts from the trees. A knight with sword raised high, leading his soldiers onto the battlefield. And they seem happy to follow. Antoine, oh he's a good fellow, they tell me. I know he is, I say. And what I don't say but think is that my brother is the kindest boy of any his age. What lies in store for him? What kind of man will be become? A good one, that's for sure. Yes, of that I am certain.

I turned to the sketchbooks to see if I could find the drawing of her brother, and sure enough, there he was, captured in charcoal: a bright-eyed, towheaded boy of ten or eleven, face half turned toward the artist, mouth wide with laughter, his neck and trunk barely suggested by quick black strokes. A skillful drawing for a young artist, I thought, and a sweet face.

But soon I felt the time slipping away and began skimming more quickly. By nineteen, Jenny Marie had exhibited at local fairs and competitions; by twenty, she was earning money from her portraits; and at twenty-two she was off to Paris to study at the Académie Julian.

18 October 1892

Arrived this morning in Paris, the city of my dreams, and I can hardly believe I'm here. At the academy we were introduced to our teachers and toured the studios where we will be working. The studios are so grand. I met several girls my age who are also enrolled and have even found a flatmate. Her name is Aimée Laurance, from Lille, and she is already a very good artist—she showed me her sketchbook. She has taken a small apartment in Montmartre and needs someone to share expenses. Well, that's me. Or Papa, to be more exact. He has agreed to support me in my studies at least for a year. So tomorrow I say goodbye to my hotel and take up my new life—as a student in Paris, where young artists come to study from all over Europe. Paris, the capital of the art world!

And there, I thought, I will leave you until tomorrow, for I had reached a logical stopping point after a good afternoon's work. I glanced at my watch; it was already half past five.

I was relaxing with my feet up on one of the patio chairs, reading about the Cathars and wondering whether I should call my sister again, when I heard someone crunching over the pebbles of the terrace. It was Madame Martin carrying a tray of drinks.

"Would Madame care for an aperitif? I can offer you a kir, white wine, or sparkling water."

"*Merci*! A kir would be lovely," I replied. I watched as she carefully poured white wine into a glass already lined with a half-inch of cassis liqueur. I thought of asking her to call me Nora, since "Madame" felt so formal, but then I realized this would raise the question of whether I would call Madame Martin by *her* first name. Instinct told me she would feel more respected if I addressed her as Madame, so I stifled my American impulse toward familiarity.

"Thank you, Madame," I said. "I've just spent hours in the library, and it's time to clear my mind."

"That is our habit," the older woman replied. "Generations of Cazelles have come here at the end of day to find repose."

"It's the perfect spot," I agreed. "How long have you worked for the family, Madame Martin? Which barons have you served, out here on the terrace?"

"Before Baron Charles, I served his father, Baron Pierre. And my mother served his father, Baron Antoine."

"Really? Then your mother must have known Jenny Marie, his sister."

"*Mais oui, Madame.* My mother esteemed Mademoiselle Cazelle very highly."

"Then I have a question, Madame Martin. I don't know much about the naming tradition in France, so I'm probably all wrong, but the name Jenny doesn't sound French to me at all."

Madame Martin looked pleased, as if her pet pupil had just come up with a smart question. "You're right."

"Since the Cazelle family is so traditional in other ways, what led them to pick a name like that?"

"That was her mother's decision. Isabelle. Of course, she wasn't a Cazelle by birth. Baron Émile met her when he was studying at the Sorbonne. It's true she was from an aristocratic line, which made her acceptable to the family, but she was one of those radical women devoted to all sorts of new ideas. That's where we get to Jenny Marie's name."

"Then it was a choice for the name to be nontraditional?"

"Yes, you could say that. In fact, Jenny Marie was named after Jenny Lind, the famous opera star from Sweden."

I'd heard of Jenny Lind, the Swedish Nightingale. She'd been an international star in the nineteenth century and later had done many good works for charity, but I'd never thought about her as a role model for women. Of course, she would have been.

Evidently, Jenny's mother thought so. She named her daughter after Jenny Lind, in tribute and perhaps in hope. True to her mother's wishes, Jenny Marie had lived life her own way, as an artist and an independent woman.

"What else can you tell me about Jenny Marie Cazelle?"

Madame Martin paused. After a moment's silence, she replied. "She was always serious, that one, even as a girl. And strong-willed. That was true throughout her life."

"In what way?"

Madame Martin looked thoughtful. "It must have taken courage to leave the château and to go live alone in Paris to pursue her career, don't you think? In those days, women didn't fly off by themselves so easily. But you see, *Maman* knew Mademoiselle Cazelle both in her youth and after she came home, after the First World War. She used to say Mademoiselle Cazelle was a brave one, a woman who was true to her beliefs, first to last."

"Did she mean by that her dedication to her career?"

"I suppose so."

"Or perhaps she meant something else. What were her other beliefs? Was Jenny Marie religious, for example?"

A laugh lightened the mood. *"Au contraire! Maman* always said that however aristocratic her blood, Mademoiselle Cazelle was a daughter of the Revolution. She believed in liberty, equality, and fraternity. That's why she stopped calling herself 'de Cazelle.' As soon as she started signing paintings, as a girl, she dropped the 'de' from her name because she thought it stank of aristocratic pretension." As if realizing suddenly that her employers used the "de" and that she might seem to be criticizing them, she stopped short. I waited for her to continue.

"Yes, *Maman* always said Mademoiselle treated her as one of the family. *Maman* was just the cook, and Mademoiselle was the sister of the baron, but when Mademoiselle died, it was as if my mother had lost her own sister. I never saw her weep like that again."

"Do you remember when she died?"

"I was only five years old, but I'll never forget my mother weeping that time. It was near the end of the war, but we didn't know that. My father was away, and we feared he would never return. Then suddenly the two elders of the Cazelle family died within months of each other. It was a catastrophe."

"That would be Jenny Marie and her brother, Antoine. How did they die, if I may ask?"

Madame Martin stiffened and replied, "It is not easy to talk about those days. It was a terrible time. And these matters are private to the family. It's not for me to discuss." She bent to pick up her tray and depart.

The distant sound of shifting pebbles made us both look to the side, to see Fernando entering one of the garage stalls with a rake and hoe in his grasp.

"Could I ask you one more indiscreet question?" A change of subject might get Madame Martin to stay. "It's about Fernando. Am I the only one who has found him difficult?"

"How do you mean, Madame?"

"Well, a bit rude and not very friendly. *Pas sympathique.*"

Madame Martin nodded her head knowingly. "I can tell you about him. You see, Madame Marianne has a forgiving heart. Fernando's father was a mason who came from Portugal to work on the Château of Beynac, years ago. He was well respected in the village. And he was training Fernando to work beside him. But when Fernando was young, only about sixteen, he was arrested for stealing objects from an excavation at the castle."

"Did he go to jail?"

"Yes, he did. The objects were of archaeological value, very precious, very old. He spent two years in prison."

"Then how did he get a job here, after such a disgrace?"

"The mayor heard Marianne was starting her cooking school, and he asked her to take Fernando on. Fernando's father is so well regarded that the mayor wanted to help the son get back on his feet. And many believe the accusation was false. There's some prejudice against the Portuguese around here. Madame Marianne says we should remember that, when Fernando acts resentful. If he spent time in prison for a crime he didn't commit, he would naturally feel angry from time to time. And the authorities never leave him alone, like that poor inspector from the Bureau of Antiquities who was killed the other day. He was here pestering Fernando the very day before he died, so I don't wonder that Fernando is upset." She hesitated, and began to blush. "I have said too much. I am turning into an old gossip. But I didn't want you to have the wrong impression of Fernando. He is a good worker."

She straightened up and turned to leave, smiling apologetically as she said, "I must return to the kitchen. Enjoy your kir, Madame."

For a good while I sat sipping my drink, thinking about what I'd just heard.

7

I FOUND TOBY IN OUR ROOM, leaning over the bed, examining a large sheet of parchment. He turned his head my way and grinned, without rising from his bent position.

"You look like an ostrich. What have you got there for prey?" I asked.

"A map! And we're on it. Come take a look." Toby always wears a sheepish smile when he's made an impulsive purchase.

"Did you get a chance to apologize to Fernando?"

"I did. Briefly."

"And what did he say?"

"Nothing. He grunted. I think that means a ceasefire." Well, at least Toby had made an effort. "Now let me show you something."

I knew that whatever this map was, I'd better like it. There was no need for me to feign enthusiasm. I was so struck by the total effect of the artistry that the writing didn't register until Toby said, "See, it's the diocese of Sarlat, with all the churches drawn in black like little steepled huts and inked over in red. Look, just along the river here, there's Beynac, and right above it is Cazenac—that's the church on the hill opposite Cazelle."

"But the style doesn't look local. It doesn't even look French."

Toby put a finger on a small bit of script at the lower right corner: "Amsterdami. Apud Guiljelmum Blaeu."

"Dutch, mid-eighteenth century," he informed me. "The midline crease has been mostly ironed out, but you can see the map was stored folded in a boxed set of prints. It comes from a collection of maps of the ecclesiastical domains of Périgord."

"It's beautiful, and one thing you can be sure of. There was a wealthy patron behind the project. Someone who loved the Church bought the talents of an exquisite printmaker, this William Blau."

"I'm going to ask the baron about it. I got the print from a Dutch antique dealer in St. Cyprien. But she told me her father purchased the set from a family in Beynac in the late 1930s. She doesn't have a record. There was so much chaos during the war, she said. Important papers were lost."

"You know, this lull before the dinner hour would be a good time to find the baron. Why don't you see if you can consult him while I take my shower, and then we'll go out to eat?"

It was nearly an hour before Toby returned, looking bemused. He raised his eyebrows high and announced, "I've had quite a time with Baron Charles. Let's get going, and I'll tell you on the way." Our destination was a café Toby had spotted on the main street of St. Cyprien. He wanted to return for the fricassee of rabbit that he'd seen on the chalkboard.

"Want me to drive, so you can talk?" I asked, moving to the driver's seat.

He gave me a sideways smile and settled in as my passenger.

"This family is full of surprises," he announced. "Did you know we are living in a hotbed of heresy?"

That word again. "You mean, as in the Cathar heresy?"

"That's my guess. When I showed him the map, the baron nearly pushed it off the table. He said he had nothing but contempt for the wars of the Church and their genocide in Périgord."

"What did he mean by that?"

"I asked him, but I didn't entirely follow. I think it goes back to what you were reading aloud to me when we went to Castelnaud. Charles kept pointing at the Cazenac church symbol and saying 'this holy site' didn't rightfully belong to the Church. It belonged to 'the pure'— whoever they were—and their champion, Bernard de Casnac. He also kept mentioning Toulouse."

"Did you ask him if his family might have commissioned the set of maps?"

"That's what got him agitated. He said his family would never give tribute to the wolves of Rome. Leave that to the lords of Beynac, he said."

"So it looks like there's a family feud between this little castle and the big one on the opposite cliff? And it has to do with Rome and the Cathars?"

"That's what I understood, but, I tell you, this is one touchy topic. I'm not going to ask again."

All this heat about churchly things made me think of Madame Martin's declaration that Jenny Marie had turned away from religion on Revolutionary grounds. However, being anticlerical in honor of Bastille Day seemed quite a different thing from being anti-Rome in deference to a medieval sect. I also wondered how the chapel of the Black Virgin fit in with what we'd heard. I had assumed that the activity at the chapel—clean altar cloths, fresh flowers—meant that the Cazelles were pious Roman Catholics. Apparently not.

These musings were put to rest by our arrival in the little cathedral town of St. Cyprien. The café occupied the corner of a busy street, but there was a sheltered terrace in the back. We took a table outside and enjoyed the late light of midsummer. The waiter suggested a bottle of chilled Beaujolais; we accepted. It paired nicely with the savory rabbit. We ate with relish, recounting our separate afternoons. I told Toby what I had learned in the library about Jenny Marie and what I had learned about Fernando from Madam Martin. Over coffee, we made our plans for the next day.

Toby wanted to visit Lascaux II in the afternoon. This elaborate copy of Lascaux, famous in its own right, is located just a few miles from the original. It was built in the 1980s for the general public, who were no longer permitted inside the authentic cave. Toby thought that by visiting the facsimile we might learn something that could have a bearing on the investigation.

"Look," he said. "We now know of two people who might have wanted to kill Monsieur Malbert—Marc and Fernando. Three, if you count the guide, who would have had the same motive as Marc. Both Marc and his uncle had access to Lascaux. As for Fernando, we don't know how he could have entered the cave, unless one of those two was helping him. We need more information, and one way to get it is to take the tour and refresh our recollections of what happened."

"Isn't this kind of thing the inspector's job?" I asked. "I'm here to find out about Jenny Marie's paintings. I need tomorrow afternoon to work on her journals."

"Then I have an idea. In the morning, I'll go to the cooking class, and you go to the library. You can work straight through lunchtime. Then in the afternoon we'll go to Lascaux II and get a bite on the way. They give tours till six. I'll ask Marianne to call and reserve tickets for us."

Except for having to skip cooking class, I liked the plan. I now had so many questions about Jenny Marie that I could hardly wait to get back to her papers. I've also always liked mornings. Getting to work in the library before others were up and reading through the lunch hour would suit me very well.

"Okay," I conceded. "But let's find Marianne when we get back and explain what we're doing. I don't want her being surprised if I miss the class. If we tell her tonight, it will be all right."

The next morning, the dawn of Midsummer's Eve, I tiptoed down the dark hallway toward the main salon, which was dimly lit by the faint light coming through the windowed doors at the back of the room. I hugged the left wall, found the library door, and fit Marianne's key into its lock. Entering, I was pleased to see nothing had been disturbed, and eagerly I resumed my reading of the journals.

Soon I was absorbed again in Jenny Marie's life. Volume 2 of the journals found her at the Académie Julian in Paris. I'd done previous research on the Académie and was delighted to come across a firsthand account of student life there. At that time, women were excluded from the other studios, but Rodolphe Julian's art school was open to both sexes, giving talented women a unique opportunity to pursue a career in art. The journal entries described Jenny Marie's newfound friends at the academy, her teachers, and her daily exercises—and brought to life what for me had been a historical footnote.

20 November 1892

At last. After weeks of drawing only plaster casts, we have a live model in the studio, and a good-looking fellow he is, too, as naked as the David (though a bit of his modesty is preserved by drapery). No one is embarrassed, either, though there might have been some squeamish ladies if the men had been painting alongside us. Monsieur Lefebvre trains us separately. So here we are, thirty women sitting in a circle, each behind her easel and dressed as formally as if she were being presented to nobility. Instead we concentrate on our drawing while M. Lefebvre walks from one to the other, making comments here and there. For me today there was a word of praise, though poor Aimée was less fortunate. I confess I felt a touch of pride. Monsieur Lefebvre is a good teacher and a fine artist himself. He showed us an exquisite portrait he did of a Japanese lady with a fan. The delicate shading of blue is marvelous. The woman, of course, is a French model and doesn't look the least bit Japanese, but her costume is authentic and she grasps the fan lightly and gracefully. I think I am learning a great deal.

The strong suit of the academy was figure drawing, and Jenny's sketchbooks from this period were filled with studies of models, both male and female, drawn from every conceivable angle and pose. But the young artists were exposed to newer trends in painting as well, including impressionism, now a generation old. In the most exciting entry in her journal, Jenny recorded a meeting with Berthe Morisot, the most prominent female painter in the movement. Morisot, who had married Manet's brother, had her first solo exhibition in Paris in 1892, and Jenny Marie went to see it with her friend Aimée.

3 December 1892

The first thing we saw as we went up the stairs was a magnificent work in the style they call impressionism. The idea is not to get lost in details but to reproduce the sensation of seeing, and the approach creates startling effects. Here you see two young women sitting in a boat on a lake against a background of shimmering water. Nothing in the painting is sharp or clear. Next to the boat are several ducks, but you can barely make them out. Still, somehow you feel the pleasure of a lazy summer's afternoon. You can see the sunlight in the choppy colors, and the brushstrokes are irresistible, free and thick, with no attempt to smooth them out. I found it very beautiful. The room was filled with such canvases. Everywhere you looked, the colors were so bright that you were taken aback. The artist paints mainly women and children in outdoor settings. It seems as if the colors are reflected from mirrors, with dancing beams of light.

Imagine how excited we were to see Madame Manet herself standing in a corner, receiving visitors. We stood in line waiting our turn. When we introduced ourselves as students of the academy, she took an immediate interest in our work and asked us many questions. No longer young, she is still a handsome woman, slim and dark-haired, with a youthful bearing. Her manner is unaffected. She received our compliments with grace. We asked which other artists of the day she favored. She now thinks Daubigny's works much too dark but remains devoted to Corot. Renoir is a favorite, and of course she idolizes Manet, who was her brother-in-law. He died some years ago. After speaking of these other artists, she grew serious, and looking very directly at the two of us, urged us never to waver in our devotion to painting. I know how difficult art is for women, she said. Consider my sister, Edma. She was as talented a painter as ever I was, but when she married, she renounced her career. Young ladies, do not let that happen to you. Continue on your course. So do you advise us never to marry? asked Aimée. Not at all, she replied. I married and now have a grown daughter whom I love dearly. But you must choose a husband who will value your talent and give you the freedom to use it. Never forget that.

These words I have taken to heart. Afterward, Aimée and I had a long talk about marriage. Would you marry if to do so you had to give up your career, I asked. Aimée replied with a grave expression, yes, I think I would, if I deeply loved my husband and if he asked me to stop painting. Would you? No, Aimée, I said. You may do so, but I never shall.

I pondered these words. Jenny Marie had never married. So far, her journal revealed nothing about a romance, and I wondered if there had ever been a man in her life. In any event, this entry documented Jenny Marie's interest in impressionism and was of interest for that reason. I pushed back from the table and rose to take a closer look at the two paintings in the library, both done in the impressionist style. The ornately framed oil painting to the left of the window was identified by its nameplate as *Parc Monceau au printemps*. It depicted a bright scene of well-dressed women walking haughtily by an old couple trying to sell flowers from a park bench. The small painting hanging on the other side of the window was called *Gamins au jeu*. It showed two thin but lively youngsters playing a game with sticks and stones in a dirty cobblestone street. She had dated this one next to her signature, and it was the date given in the journal, 1894. Yes, I thought, the influence of Berthe Morisot was apparent.

A rap on the library door interrupted my reading. "May I come in?" It was Marianne. "I'm sorry to disturb you, but Inspector Daglan is here and wants to speak to you and your husband. They are waiting in the salon. I'm afraid I have to get back to the class, so could you lock up here and meet the inspector as soon as possible? "

"Of course. I'll be there in a minute." Frustrated, I marked my place, closed the journal, turned off my laptop, and picked up my purse. I was careful to lock the door behind me.

When I entered the salon, Daglan was seated in an armchair with his legs crossed, talking to Toby. I sat down beside Toby on the couch and exchanged greetings with Daglan.

"Will you take coffee?" he asked. I saw that he was nursing a small cup himself and that there was a pot and an empty cup beside it.

"Yes, thank you." I had missed my coffee this morning. "How may we help you, Inspector?"

Before he could reply, Toby said he had just been telling the inspector about our meeting with Marc Gounot and how little we knew about him, despite appearances.

"Yes, that is my question to you," rejoined Daglan, handing me the cup he had just poured for me. "Would you mind telling me how long you and your husband have known Marc Gounot and how you met?"

Just the right amount of anxiety coursed through me—not enough to make me glance up at Toby, but just enough to caution me not to. I didn't want it to appear that we were coordinating a story. I kept my eyes on the inspector as I recounted how we had met Marc by chance at his mineral shop, consented to a drink with him at the nearby café, and then were sought out by him after our restaurant dinner with the cooking-school group.

Toby jumped in. "I know it seems suspicious we would meet the nephew of Monsieur Gounot on the day after the murder, but that's what happened. And we might not have met him if we hadn't visited the library in Castelnaud. The librarian there told us not to miss the rock exhibit, which was in Marc's shop."

"The young woman who has provided Marc Gounot with an alibi?"

"Yes, I suppose so."

"Very convenient. So Marc Gounot can claim you never would have met him without her suggestion."

Toby countered with the facts, but the inspector seemed determined to believe, or to pretend to believe, that we had met Marc by prearrangement. He just wasn't sure for what purpose. After fruitlessly grilling Toby again on his antique business and his knowledge of paleontology, he took another tack.

"Madame, did you think it advisable to socialize with one of the possible suspects in this murder investigation?"

"No, I didn't, Inspector. In fact, it made me uneasy. But Marc was insistent. We agreed to have a drink with him, that's all, and we said we wouldn't discuss the murder. But then when Marc started talking about himself, he seemed so vulnerable. I felt sorry for him." At the quizzical rise of the inspector's eyebrows, I retold the story Marc had related of his father's disgrace.

"So, you know something about that, eh?" Inspector Daglan looked down at his shoes. "I wonder if you really know the whole truth about the father, Henri Gounot. He behaved very badly during the war."

"What exactly did he do?" Toby asked.

"Evidence wasn't collected formally, because he committed suicide as soon as the charges against him were brought to the head of the Bureau of Monuments and Antiquities. But the evidence is right there in the personnel files of the bureau."

"Evidence of what?" I pressed.

Daglan considered a moment. "First, Henri Gounot systematically purged from the bureau all employees of Jewish extraction. For this we have ample proof. His letters of denunciation were found in the bureau's personnel files. There were only three cases of dismissal, but this was not a small matter. All three—two men and a woman—were later deported and died in concentration camps."

Toby looked as stunned as I felt.

"But that's not all. Henri Gounot also served his German masters by

118

spreading their racial propaganda, and he ended by compromising his profession."

"How do you mean?" I asked.

Daglan sat back and sighed. "How much do you know about the ideology of the Nazi SS?"

"A little," said Toby.

"Do you know what attracted their interest in the Dordogne?"

"No, I don't."

"Well, then, let me tell you. No doubt you know Herr Hitler believed in a race of superior 'Aryans' that supposedly went back to prehistoric times. Well, he gave his friend Himmler the assignment of finding archaeologists sympathetic to that view. Their mission was to prove that the cave art discovered at the turn of the century in France and Spain was Aryan—that the cave men had come from Northern Europe, not from Southern Europe, or worse, Africa."

"You're not saying," I asked in shock, "that the French Bureau of Antiquities collaborated with Himmler's project?"

"Unfortunately, Madame, for some in Périgueux that was the case, both before the war and later during the Vichy regime. And Henri Gounot was the principal liaison between Himmler and the bureau. He personally escorted Himmler's emissary to Les Eyzies at the end of the thirties. His correspondence with his Nazi counterparts documents their arrangements to tour the caves of the Dordogne and to meet with French archaeologists. He even arranged for them to meet with the venerable Abbé Breuil. But this brush with evil could not stain that good man's long career."

"But it did stain Henri Gounot's," I stated, as flatly as possible.

"Exactly, because with him it was not a brief contact. His association with Himmler's entourage lasted from 1938 to 1945. And his nemesis in the bureau, Michel Malbert, had the documents to prove that."

"When did Malbert make his accusations?" I asked.

"Not until 1969. That is what gives the son a bit of ground on which to stand. He claims Malbert was motivated by his ambition to replace

Henri Gounot as head of the archaeological section. That could be true. But the documents show the accusations were accurate. I tell you this to warn you about Marc Gounot. He is in his own way a fanatic, blinded by loyalty to his father."

"Do you really think Marc would murder Monsieur Malbert in revenge for his father's death? If that was the motive, why did he wait nearly forty years to do it?"

"The answer may be as simple as opportunity. Consider this: All his adult life, Marc Gounot resents Michel Malbert. Then let's say he becomes involved with foreigners in a project to traffic in prehistoric artifacts. Once again Malbert appears on the scene threatening the plan. His uncle, the guide, reveals that Malbert's name appears on his visitors' list for Lascaux on a certain day. Marc finds his opportunity to eliminate Malbert, and *voilà*."

It was maddening the way Daglan shifted from lulling conversation to potshots of insinuation. With the word "foreigners" he raised his eyebrows and darkened his tone. Again we protested the implication that we were involved in any plot to sell artifacts. For a while Daglan stubbornly gnawed on this subject like a dog with an old bone in his mouth, but then, just as abruptly, he let it go and the conversation took a new direction.

"Tell me. How long have you known the other members of your *stage de cuisine*, Madame Dexter in particular?"

"Dotty? We met for the first time here at the cooking school," I replied, "and that's when we met the others as well. Why do you ask?"

"Because Madame Dexter visited Marc Gounot at his mineral shop yesterday, and I would like to know why she did."

I tried explaining that Dotty probably went just to flirt with Marc, but Daglan continued to look skeptical. Exasperated, I encouraged him to ask our fellow students at the school about Dotty. He would soon learn how plausible my explanation was.

"Inspector, Dotty doesn't have anything to do with this," Toby declared. "But there's someone else you should be looking at. The handyman here, Fernando, had as much reason to murder Malbert as Marc had. We've been told Fernando once served prison time for stealing findings from an archaeological site, and Monsieur Malbert came to Cazelle on Monday morning to see Fernando—perhaps to accuse him of other thefts."

The canny inspector smiled wearily. "He was not here expressly to see Fernando. And yes, we know all about Fernando's past. We also know from the authorities at the Bureau of Monuments and Antiquities that this was Monsieur Malbert's third meeting with the baron and his children. They were engaged in discussions about opening their private cave to archaeologists and scholars."

"What cave?" Surprise showed in my voice.

"There is a long and complex history about a cave located on the property. Inside there may be markings that would be of interest to the authorities, or so Monsieur Malbert thought, on the basis of a rumor. But the family denies it. At any rate, they oppose any examination of the cave."

Now *that* was interesting. There was a cave located somewhere on the grounds of the château, and the family was jealously guarding it. Were they merely trying to protect their privacy, or something else?

Daglan seemed to read the expression on my face. "You can be sure we are questioning members of the family about the visit, but that doesn't concern you. Right now I'm more interested in what you can tell me."

Toby bristled. "There's something else you should know about Fernando. He keeps a dovecote, and his doves look exactly like that bird that was speared and left at Monsieur Malbert's feet on Monday. Would it be possible to determine whether the bird came from Fernando's flock?"

"I doubt it. There are few large properties in the Dordogne that lack a dovecote, and the doves all look very much alike. There was nothing unusual about that particular dove except the manner of its death."

"Do you know anything more about it that you could tell us?" I asked.

He shrugged. "I am told the symbol is quite well known by the experts."

"Yes, we know that much. So perhaps Monsieur Malbert had other enemies in the profession," I pointed out.

"Oh, he certainly did. But only Gounot and his nephew Marc had access to Lascaux," snapped Daglan. His eyes narrowed. "And what if this bird is merely a distraction, something that was left to throw us off the track?"

"Are you saying that the dove may have had nothing to do with the killer's motive?" asked Toby.

"I have to consider that a possibility," replied Daglan. He was about to say something else when he was interrupted by a knock on the door. Marianne entered, looking more than a little flustered.

"Inspector, we have finished the lesson, and the students are almost through with their meal. Do you want me to ask Monsieur and Madame Press to wait, to talk with you after you are finished talking with Toby and Nora?"

"Yes. Would you be so good as to ask all the members of the class to go to their rooms? I will talk to each one shortly." Marianne looked disturbed but walked quickly back toward the kitchen to execute her orders. "We are finished here for now," Daglan said to us. "I must ask you to say nothing to the others about any part of our conversation."

"Of course," said Toby. "Actually, we have plans for this afternoon. Do you mind if we leave now?"

"You may go. I know where to find you."

We managed a cursory goodbye as we hurried away to our rooms to get a few belongings before going out to the car.

In Montignac we stopped at a busy café for a late lunch (ham sandwiches on baguettes) and claimed our reservations for Lascaux II at the ticket office in the center of town. The lines were intimidating. Luckily, since we had reserved in advance, we went through the pick-up line in a reasonably short time. Lascaux II has become a popular attraction. Visits are staggered at half-hour intervals, and the daily operation of shuttling hundreds of tourists to and from the artificial cave is planned with military precision.

With tickets in hand, we killed some time by window-shopping on the main street of Montignac before driving to the well-marked site on a wooded hill on the outskirts of the town. Arriving at the parking lot, we claimed one of the few open spots and joined the line waiting at the entrance. There were picnic tables scattered about and kiosks selling soft drinks, ice cream, souvenirs, and booklets.

From a professional standpoint, I had my doubts about Lascaux II. A copy can never replace an original. I scold my students who rely on reproductions instead of looking at original art when they can. But that's just it: because of conservation worries, the real Lascaux is no longer accessible to the public. So wasn't it reasonable for the government to construct a facsimile to satisfy their curiosity? Tour books tout it as an amazing technical achievement, faithful in every respect to the contours of the original cave and to the size, placement, and colors of the paintings. That may be, said a competing voice in my head, but after all, it is still just a copy. It's a pity the fake cave has been seen by far more people than will ever see the original.

Those were my first thoughts as we waited in line, but it wasn't long before my mind reverted to the murder. Then I began to worry that this visit might trigger memories of the violent scene we had witnessed only days ago. Toby seemed to sense my disquiet, and he placed an arm around my shoulder.

"They move these groups through pretty quickly. We won't be in there long, and we need to make the most of our time inside. I want to check out the size of the space and see if we can re-create where we were standing when Malbert was attacked. Try to look around and get a feel for any hiding places someone might use to conceal himself. Are you up for it?"

Yes, I thought so. The line was moving. We were approaching a sheltered overhang with a cement staircase leading down into the ground. The crowd pressed in, and in another moment we were milling around inside a dark antechamber with illuminated wall displays and diagrams. The guide, a young woman, began her introduction. She described the construction process for Lascaux II and went over the history of the real Lascaux's discovery and the reasons for its closing. She pointed out that only the Hall of Bulls and a section of the Axial Gallery had been reproduced in Lascaux II. We were invited to consult the wall diagram if we wanted to get a sense of the entirety of the cave, which was of course much larger than the replica. I tuned out the rest of her spiel as I studied the map, trying to trace the sections we had visited three days ago and to situate them in relation to the Hall of Bulls.

It was obvious at a glance that there were significant sections of the real Lascaux we hadn't visited during our tour—in other words, any number of hiding places where a killer might have been concealed. There were in fact two passageways leading into the Hall of Bulls. One led from the Axial Gallery, but we had gone most of the way through that one, and I remembered it as too narrow to have shielded a person from view. The other passageway, though, led to the Nave, a much larger area, which we had entered briefly but never explored. Beyond the Nave was still another gallery, and off to the side was the mysterious pit containing the falling man and the bison. What better hiding place for a killer who was planning to leave a duplicate of the pierced bird as a calling card?

Soon we were herded into the faux Hall of Bulls, forty or fifty of us pressed together as if in a crowded elevator. Familiar outlines of bulls and horses surrounded us, but the magic I felt at seeing the authentic art was gone. Besides the crowding, what made the experience so different from the original was the impact on the senses. Lascaux is a natural cave, smelling of earth and stone. Its limestone walls are glossy, whereas the walls of Lascaux II are made of polyester resin and have a dull matte finish. The floor is concrete, the air paper-dry from the anodyne air-conditioning. Yes, the murals are replicated in their proper spatial relationships. The lines and colors are right; even the bulges in the walls are reproduced down to the last centimeter. It's very well done but—like all copies—lifeless.

Lifeless: the thought drew me back to the murder. Toby, I could see, had barely glanced at the paintings. He was trying to find his approximate position in the real Hall of Bulls before it had gone dark. I jostled my way toward him until we were pretty close to our original locations in the cave. We imagined Gounot in front of us near the entrance and then the others behind us. Yes, there was room enough for Gounot to have circled around us, but how much time would he have needed to get behind us, strangle Malbert, and return to his place before being discovered? I remembered Gounot fumbling in the dark for a replacement battery for his lamp. Might that have been a cover for his movements? How much time had actually passed before the lamp had been made to work again? Several minutes, at least. And yet I felt sure Gounot had not doubled back on us. No, I concluded, whoever killed Malbert had stalked him from behind, had emerged stealthily from some hiding place deep in the cave.

"What about David?" asked Toby. We were back outside again, comparing notes. Toby agreed Gounot could not have outflanked us without attracting attention, but he reminded me David had been closest to the victim and need not have emerged from some lair.

"I just can't accept that," I said.

"I'm only pointing out that, in terms of logistics, eliminating Gounot leaves only David as a suspect, along with anyone else who may have been hiding in the cave before we went in."

"Do you mean Marc?" I asked.

"Yes, Marc. He could have acted on his own or as Gounot's accomplice, but 'could have' isn't the same as evidence. The same goes for Fernando."

I sighed. "So that leaves us pretty much where we started."

"Pretty much. Do you feel like checking out the shop?"

"Sure, why not?"

The shop on the grounds of Lascaux II was well stocked with prehistoric paraphernalia, everything from T-shirts with images of bulls, to Lascaux ashtrays, models of dinosaurs, and children's picture books on cave art. While Toby slowly spun a rack of postcards, I was drawn to the back of the shop, where a large color poster of "the scene in the pit" caught my eye. There it was hanging on the wall, larger than life-size, its details much sharper than in smaller photographs. What was its meaning? The wounded bison with its entrails dragging; the spindly man in profile falling backward, arms flung out; the bird or effigy of a bird on a stick, either planted in the ground or dropped from the dying man's hand? I peered more closely and now noticed with surprise that the man in profile was shown with an erection. That was puzzling enough, but so was the fact that his nose looked more like a beak, suggested by two horizontal dashes. Stylistically, his nose was the mirror image of the beak of the bird on the stick, which faced in the opposite direction. Was the man wearing a mask? Were his hands really bird's feet? The Birdman— the word popped into my mind. Who or what was he? And why did the artist who otherwise was so sparing of anatomical detail depict him as sexually aroused?

"I'll tell you one thing," said Toby, who had quietly crept up behind me and was nuzzling my neck. "You wonder what the old boy was doing before the bison interrupted him."

"Okay, wise guy, maybe the artist simply wanted to indicate the person's sex."

"Well, he certainly did that," said Toby, with a Groucho Marx wag of the eyebrows. "Speaking of which, there's something I've been meaning to bring up since we got here."

"Cut it out," I laughed in spite of myself. "There's a time and a place for everything."

"True. But we do have a room," said Toby, nibbling my ear. "And plenty of time. It's Midsummer's Eve, the longest day of the year."

8

T HAT'S WEIRD."

"What?"

It was later—close to ten and still not yet dark. We were reading in bed. Toby had a paperback mystery, and I was browsing through the book about the Cathars that I had borrowed from the baron's library.

"What's weird?" repeated Toby.

"I've been looking through this book, trying to find out whether the Cathars had any special iconography, you know, symbols or images that would be used as motifs in their art."

"And?"

"And as far as anyone knows, they had almost no art of their own. There are only a handful of artifacts that anyone's ever associated with the movement. One was the Cross of Toulouse, which has what looks like the tips of little crowns on each of the four points. I know I've seen that image before. I think it's carved on the lintel of the stable doors where we park our cars. And it also looks like the motif on the family china."

"So the family is interested in historical symbols. What's so strange about that?"

"Well, here's the thing. The other image was a bird, a dove in flight with outstretched wings. An archaeologist studying the Cathars found a small stone sculpture of a flying dove in the ruins of Montségur, which was where the believers made their last stand in 1244. The pope's army laid siege to the citadel, and when it was over they burned two hundred heretics at the stake."

"Awful," said Toby. "What were they fighting about?"

"What religious fights are always about, power and ideas."

He nodded, pursing his lips.

"But listen. What I'm trying to tell you is that it's strange that the Lascaux artists and the Cathars and whoever murdered Monsieur Malbert all used the bird as a symbol of something. I'm trying to figure out if there's a connection."

"How can there be a connection between Lascaux and the Cathars? We're talking about a difference of thousands of years."

"I know that. It's just curious, that's all."

"Or weird, as you said."

"Yes, weird."

Toby rolled over and propped his head on his hand. He walked the fingers of his other hand across my shoulder. "Okay, what else have you found out?"

"Well, the origins of the sect are obscure, but their stronghold was here in this part of France, extending south to Marseille. The Church did such a good job of wiping them out that there aren't many traces left of their culture. But at the time they were considered a real threat to Rome."

"How?"

"Basically, they thought everything connected to the material world was corrupt, including the Church, and they wanted to become spiritually 'pure' or 'perfect.' By the way, that's where their name comes from, the root of the Greek word 'catharsis,' meaning 'purification.'"

"Wait a minute, that's what the old baron was going on about, something about 'the pures' and the Catholic Church."

"Exactly. The Cathars were also known as the Albigenses because the sect was numerous in Albi, near Toulouse. The Count of Toulouse was one of the leaders of the movement."

"That ties in with the baron's animosity about my map!" exclaimed Toby. "He mentioned Toulouse."

"It does, but we're talking about a heresy that died out hundreds of years ago. The question is why the baron is still worked up about it. Here's the only tie-in I can see," I added. "As a result of the Albigensian Crusade, the South, which before then had been independent, was annexed to the kingdom of France. Political resentment can go back a long time. Remember the remark Guillaume made at dinner the other night about the Languedoc and the Parisians?"

"Yeah. But you don't think they're still practicing the old religion here?"

"It's the politics I'm wondering about. I'm thinking about the hostility Guillaume has toward the northerners." I reached behind me and plumped up the pillows.

Toby shot me a sly glance. "You know, you're awfully cute when you talk about politics."

"And you're awfully cute when you lie there helplessly asking questions."

"I'm lying here helplessly only because I've had a long and fulfilling day, and I've earned my rest."

"You have." I patted him on the knee.

Toby sat up and punched his own pillows behind him. "So, what else did the Cathars believe, I mean besides that the world was corrupt? Hell, I believe that myself."

"Well. What really got them in trouble was they preached that the Devil, not God, made the world, and so the goal of life was to renounce the world, that is, to become pure—though only a few would be able to do it. Those are the 'perfects.' The rest of us will be reincarnated back into the world until we are able to attain perfection."

"Sounds more like Hinduism than Christianity."

"There's definitely a tinge of Eastern philosophy to it," I agreed. "But the Cathars did believe in Jesus. They saw him as a messenger from the world of pure spirit. Then they claimed the Devil created a false church to distort Christ's message, and that was the Church of Rome."

"And oddly enough, the pope took umbrage on that point."

"He did. According to the sect, there would be other messengers in the world, and those would be the 'pures,' or the 'perfects.' To become one you went through a ceremony called the Consolation, and then you had to live like a saint, fasting, praying, avoiding violence, never swearing, never lying, never eating meat, and of course, no having sex."

"So much for us," said Toby with a grin.

"Not really. You'll like this part. In practice, the Cathars were pretty casual about sex. There was no point rushing into the Consolation; you had to be strong enough to follow its demands, which is why it often took place as a deathbed conversion. Before that you were simply a follower and you could do pretty much what you liked, as long as you were kind."

"Hey, that doesn't sound so bad."

"It did to the Catholic Church," I said. "The Cathars reasoned that if all worldly practices were evil, then everything worldly was on the same plane. Like sex. All sex was sinful, so why was unmarried sex any worse than married sex? It wasn't. Members of the sect married late, and their enemies accused them of licentiousness. In a way, since everything was forbidden, everything was allowed. That is, until you accepted the Consolation."

"You've got to hand it to them. So what happened at the Consolation?"

"Nobody knows the details. The ceremony was kept a secret. The believers went to their deaths rather than reveal it, and if there were any written Cathar texts, the Church destroyed them. Most of what is known about the heresy was handed down by word of mouth and through trial records made during the Inquisition."

"And that was the end of the Cathars?" Toby slid his legs over the side of the bed and inserted his feet into his slippers.

"As far as I know. But here's something else. During the persecution of the heretics, there were two methods of execution. One was burning at the stake. The other was the garrote, and that's how Malbert was killed."

"What do you make of that?" he asked, heading toward the bathroom.

"I don't know. But there could be a connection."

"Between Lascaux and the Cathars? I don't see it."

"Neither do I. Yet."

Next morning, Toby was up early for him, and we walked to the twelfth-century church at Cazenac, admiring its gargoyles and wondering whether it had ever served as a Cathar sanctuary. Back in our room, we devoured the spice bread that Madame Martin brought with our coffee, and still we were hungry, having skipped dinner the night before. But we had been eating all too well on this trip, and today would feature a cooking-class lunch that was sure to make up any deficit in the calorie department.

Even as I entered the dining room and said good morning to Roz, my stomach grumbled. She looked at me quizzically, but it seemed she had other things on her mind.

"We missed you at the class yesterday," she started. "And then in the afternoon, we looked for you before we set out for Cahors."

"I'm sorry. We should have mentioned that we decided to visit Lascaux II. Did you have a good day?"

"It turned out that we did, even though we got a late start. Your Inspector Daglan gave Dotty the scare of her life, I must say."

From behind me, I could hear Dotty complaining energetically to Toby about "that inspector" and his "ridiculous notions."

With an effort, I remained attentive to Roz. I asked her what Inspector Daglan had said that upset Dotty, and then I remembered the inspector had asked us not to discuss our conversation with the other guests. Surely he simply meant not to talk to them before he had talked with them, but he might want us to keep mum about all we had discussed, even now. My dilemma was resolved by Patrick's entrance. He walked over and joined us, and he and Roz began to recount the adventures they had with Dotty, exploring the old quarters of Cahors on foot and then driving to the train station to dine at the fashionable Restaurant Terminus. Patrick was thrilled to have tasted a great chef's take on southwest cuisine. Eagerly, he began comparing the dishes to those we had sampled at Le Beau Soleil.

From then on, the focus stayed on food. Marianne entered the dining hall, passed out our menus for the class, and led us to the teaching table in the kitchen. I thought she avoided looking at either me or Toby. In her typically intense way, she launched right into a discussion of *magret de canard*, sliced duck breast, explaining that this signature dish of contemporary Dordogne cooking was still considered an abomination by traditionalists. Her own brother turned up his nose at the plate. Traditionally, she told us, duck was cooked on the bone, whether roasted, stewed, or fricasseed. That brought out the depth of flavor that distinguishes duck from chicken. In addition, the frugal way to cook a duck is to use every piece of it in the same meal. This business of selecting only the breast, for its tenderness, strikes the older generation as wasteful and pretentious. Nonetheless, deboned breasts of duck have become a staple of Perigordian cuisine both at home and in restaurants—and we were about to learn how to cook them perfectly.

I looked around to see if Fernando had turned up today, but Marianne was doing this lesson solo. Her first step was to set up a cook-off, with each team assigned a different method for preparing the duck. Toby and I were instructed to grill our breasts, while Lily and David would roast theirs in the oven, and finally, Patrick, Roz, and Dotty would sauté theirs. Each method had its appropriate sauce: mashed cherries and vinegar for us, a tapenade of chopped olives and shallots for the Presses, and a berry sauce spiked with Grand Marnier for Patrick's team. Marianne helped each group, but she also pointedly publicized our gaffes. This produced laughs, except in the case of Lily and David, who seemed clueless. Their duck breasts stuck to the roasting pan, which charred and ripped the skin, and their sauce looked like chunky tar. Marianne was unsparing. She called the Presses on every fault, and when David burned himself removing the pan from the oven, she rushed over, pushed him aside, and grabbed the pan from him.

"*This* is the proper way to grasp a roasting pan," she hissed. "Arms extended, and elbows bent, with the forearms held close to the chest." Her tone was strident. It seemed unfair to criticize David for failing to execute a maneuver she hadn't taught us. Marianne seemed to realize that quickly, but she had trouble lightening her tone. Her face stayed grim and her voice rasping as she apologized, "I'm sorry to make an example of you, David. But, class, this is most important. You must always address the stove respectfully, straight on, with your arms in position to perform any necessary action with strength. Shoulder blades flat on your back, spine straight, abdominal muscles taut." She gave a disapproving glance at David's girth. And then she made each of us practice lifting a pan in and out of the oven.

The room became tense. I, for one, dreaded Marianne's scrutiny of our final products. We were all nervous for ourselves, I think, and even more so for David and Lily. I hoped that in spite of their misadventures, their dish would be edible. The communal tasting doused that fantasy. Their *magret* was tough, dry, and bitter. Ours was crusty on the outside and pink on the inside, just as it should be, but the sauce could have used more sugar. Patrick, assisted by Roz and Dotty, produced tender slices of rosy duck steak, with a blackberry sauce that was just tangy enough to give the dish complexity. There was no question who won the cook-off. But a mystery remained for me. What were David and Lily doing at a cooking class aimed at people who knew the basics and were looking to learn a niche cuisine? What they needed was Betty Crocker 101.

I'm no expert myself. In fact, I had expected to be the dunce in the class, and it was fine with me to have someone else fill that slot. Given my own inadequacies, I wasn't worried these kitchen virgins would lower the level of instruction, but I was curious. David had told Inspector Daglan that he and Lily were thrilled to find out they could combine the cooking school with a trip to Lascaux. Yet if they were so keen to study cookery, wouldn't you think one of them would have honed just a little skill in the kitchen already? And how likely was it that two people with no cooking experience (as it appeared) would be overjoyed to spend their honeymoon learning sauté techniques?

Maybe I was being overly suspicious. With all his questions, Inspector Daglan had made me wary of everyone. Still, this unease about David and Lily and their supposed honeymoon had bothered me from the outset. Even though I found them endearing, I was puzzled. I decided to watch them more closely.

For a while, the buzz at the table was all about the food. Each person had taken a slice from each of the three platters of *magret*, and Marianne asked us to analyze how the different cooking methods affected the meat. As the expert chef, Patrick held the floor, being wonderfully tactful in glossing over the failings of David and Lily's sample. I extolled the purée of parsnips and apples Marianne offered as an accompaniment. And soon we drifted into separate conversations.

I tried to calm Marianne down by continuing to talk about vegetable purées, but I was also keeping an eye on Lily and David, who did not speak at all. Perhaps that was because Dotty, who sat next to David, was on a rant, complaining to her side of the table about how insulting the inspector had been. Toby, seated opposite her, took on the challenge of teasing her back into good humor. I heard Marc's name mentioned and the sound of girlish laughter. Out of the corner of my eye, I glimpsed Dotty admonishing Toby with a brush of her hand on his forearm. At the same time, she glanced over to Patrick, to pull him into the foolery. David and Lily were poker-faced.

Roz had overheard a bit of Dotty's drama and sensed I had too. She frowned and leaned toward me, across the table. "I'm good and sorry we took that trip to Castelnaud," she said in a low tone. "Dotty insisted it would be rude to ignore Marc's invitation, and I didn't want her visiting him alone, so I drove her there, knowing full well she would flirt with him. She doesn't mean anything by it. It's just her southern-belle pose. But look at the complications. Now Inspector Daglan thinks Dotty is involved in some monkey business with Marc that may be connected to the murder."

"And you weren't even at the cave when it happened," I replied in commiseration. Just then I noticed Lily was following our hushed conversation.

I turned to her. "So, Lily, was the inspector as hard on you as he was on the rest of us?"

She looked startled, and then determined. "Actually, Nora," she said in a firm voice that caught the attention of Dotty's group as well as ours, "the inspector requested that we not discuss the content of the interrogation. I don't think I should say anything more. What do you think, David? Am I taking the inspector's request too literally?"

"No. He was quite clear," David asserted. He sat up straighter in his chair, looking pompous, with his chin tucked down into his neck.

Well, well. Was this just a lawyerly display of rectitude, or were David and Lily hiding something? From then on, the atmosphere was awkward. Marianne tried to lighten the tone, as she served us an ice-cream bombe straight out of its grocery-store box, claiming that, for the French, who adore ice cream, a frozen confection makes a welcome end to a company meal. But even as we enjoyed the treat, we all remained unsmiling, with David and Lily silent again in the middle. When coffee came, I was glad to make my excuses. The group was going to spend the afternoon at a local distillery, but I was going back to the library and my research on Jenny Marie.

I was glad to find everything as I'd left it yesterday. The second volume of Jenny Marie's journal sat closed in the middle of the table. It took me a while to settle down to work. So many other thoughts were swirling through my head: the scene in the pit from Lascaux, the dead body in the cave, the strange cult of the Cathars, my suspicions about David and Lily, my doubts about Marc. Eventually, though, I found myself drifting back into the past, immersed again in my research.

I picked up where I had left off in volume 2. After several years at the Académie Julian, Jenny moved on to open a small studio, which she shared with Aimée Laurance and two other friends. She set up as a portraitist and began to earn a living, though not much of one, it would appear. The pages from this period were preoccupied with financial matters. But then, when one of her canvases was accepted for exhibition at the Salon of 1898, her fortunes took a change for the better.

5 May 1898

They have hung my portrait of Mme. Roissy so high up on the wall, never mind in a corner, that it is barely recognizable, or in "the sky," as the artists say, with dozens of other paintings underneath it, reaching from the floor to ceiling. But even so, I heard a few favorable comments about it from the judges as we circulated around the hall. That may be because there aren't many portraits in this year's competition. So many landscapes with peasants and military subjects and even mythological scenes, which everyone thought had gone out of fashion. Well, so much the better for me! In Paris there are scarcely a dozen collectors willing to buy a painting without the imprimatur of the Salon. Not to mention clients who will order portraits. M. Julian always said to us, if you can make a splash at the Salon, the buyers will come knocking. Well, finally I have been accepted. Will it make a difference? We shall see.

With her debut at the Salon behind her, Jenny began to prosper. She started receiving regular commissions, and she was able to rent an atelier of her own. I now read through pages detailing sales and exhibitions. Her friend Aimée seemed to drop out of her circle, for she no longer was mentioned. In fact, there was little of a personal nature in the remaining pages.

The third volume of Jenny's journals dated from 1905, when she was thirty-five years old, to 1917, when she was forty-seven. Almost at once I noticed a livelier tone. These were the years of her flowering and success. They were also the years when love entered her life.

4 August 1906

I have met the most wonderful man, a fellow artist. I shall call him P———.

This was the first time in her journals Jenny had mentioned a romantic interest. I didn't learn her lover's name, for she continued to refer to him only by an initial.

19 October 1907

We have found the perfect studio for us both. It is a walk-up flat in Montmartre with four large rooms and good light where we can live together and do our work. P——— worries that working where we live may harm our relationship, but I tell him that is foolish since we aren't in competition. Our styles are completely different, and so are our buyers, especially now that I am doing only portraits. My clientele wants realism, his, impressionism. In fact, we get on so well that you might take us for a baker and his rosy-cheeked wife, except our smocks are daubed with paint instead of flour.

A warm, sunny afternoon today. We were both at our easels until the last bit of good light was gone. I am finishing a portrait of an old dowager whose son has paid me well.

These were the best of times for Jenny Marie Cazelle. Paris was in its heyday: after all, it was the belle epoque. Realism, impressionism, and post-impressionism jockeyed for favor, bohemian life was in full bloom, the cafés glittered, and Jenny Marie was in love.

23 May 1908

This afternoon we went to see the new landscapes by Monet and Renoir at the Galerie Durand-Ruel. Glorious paintings, filled with light and joy. I prefer Renoir's landscapes to his women, but Monet outshines him, no matter what he does. Unfortunately, we quarreled on the way home. As usual, P——— indulged his habit of ranking artists. We agreed about Monet, but what set me going is that he had unpleasant things to say about Berthe Morisot. Well, she was every bit as good as the men, I said, and then we quarreled.

I know I am right, but when we argue, I sometimes lose confidence in our love and start to worry that one day he may leave me for a younger woman. He says he never will and that the difference in our ages is unimportant, but still. Then we make up as we did tonight, and I feel calm again. I think he does love me deeply. Tonight we talked again of marriage, and I told him I am happier with him than with any man I've ever known. But marriage? This way we each have our work and independence, and perhaps it is better not to spoil things. Now look who is holding back, he said. I have given you my heart, I told him. There is nothing I am holding back. Besides, you're the one who says that marriage is a convention. That's right, it is, he says, but I want you for myself. Well, then? We laugh and go to bed. And afterward I remind him Morisot was just as good as any of them, certainly Renoir.

So Jenny Marie was capable of wit as well as feeling—good for her! During the next few years her life was both happy and productive. She was living with P——— and working well. She sold paintings and exhibited regularly at the Salon (though whether P——— did is unclear). Her corresponding sketchbooks from the period showed her at the height of her powers. But it all came to an end with the Great War.

5 June 1914

More talk about war. You know, if the war comes, I may have to go, P——— says. Why, I ask. To fight for the industrialists? The nationalists? It has nothing to do with them, he says. Then with what? With me. With my father and brother. But you hardly see them, I say. I'm French, after all, says P———. We can't let the Germans take what they will. You don't understand.

No, I don't. I don't.

22 August 1914

P——— has enlisted, despite my protests. All his friends are going, and he says he can't stay behind.

Don't worry, P——— tells me, they say the war will all be over in a few months, you'll see, and then everything will be fine again. Paris will be different after the war. We'll live in a fine house with a garden and I'll build us a great studio in back with good light. And who knows? Maybe you will marry me.

Maybe. And if he doesn't return? My heart trembles with fear.

P——— didn't return. He was sent to the trenches and died at the second battle of Ypres. Jenny was disconsolate. In her notebook she recorded a single line on what must have been the day she received the news.

26 April 1915

Gassed. Humanity is mad.

The next day she continued railing against the war.

27 April 1915

So many dead for no purpose. It will go on until everyone is exhausted, and then it will stop, but only then. Afterward life will be no better. What will happen to art? How can we paint with so much horror and ugliness in the world? What will happen to me?

Her work went badly. She broke off recording her thoughts. And two years later, she gave up her life in Paris and returned to the family château in the Dordogne.

I was ruminating on these events when the door to the library swung open without a knock and in walked the old baron. He was wearing a rumpled vested suit and tie, though shuffling in his bedroom slippers. It was obvious my presence was a surprise.

"*Ah, Madame! Excusez-moi!*"

"Not at all, Baron. Please come in."

"I had no idea you were working here today, or I would have come some other time."

"Please, Baron. I was just getting ready to leave. I've been doing research on your relative, Jenny Marie Cazelle."

"Yes, I know. Marianne informed me. But do continue." He turned to go. I decided to seize what might be an opportunity.

"Baron, would you be willing to spare me a few moments to tell me a little about your father's aunt?"

"*Ah, oui?*" He seemed surprised by the request, thought for a moment, shrugged, and walked slowly across the room to a brown leather armchair. He now seemed amused, his eyes twinkling—but not kindly, I thought—his pink, tight skin crinkling his bald pate. "If I can be of service to you, I shall be happy to, although my memory is not altogether clear about those days." He crossed his legs, fished in his vest pocket for a pouch of tobacco, withdrew a pipe from his jacket pocket and filled it. He lit the pipe, sucked a few times, blew some smoke toward the ceiling, and raised his head. "What do you wish to ask?"

"Do you have any personal memories of your great-aunt that you could share?"

"Memories? Of course. She was living here when I was born. That is to say, there was a great difference in our ages. But she was a member of the family. Naturally I knew her."

His response left me feeling foolish. "Yes, of course, Monsieur. What I meant was do you remember anything of particular interest about her life that might be useful to me in my research?"

"I'm not sure. For example?"

"For example, I was just reading in her journal that the reason she decided to come home in 1917 was that her fiancé had been killed in the Great War. Do you know anything more about him?"

"He was never her fiancé, but they were living together in Paris. The family did not approve. All I know is that my father thought very little of that man."

"Did you know his name?"

"Philippe something or other. She never spoke of him, not to me, at any rate. But my father often said that perhaps it was best he died in the war. He was something of a radical, it seems, without money or morals. The family welcomed her back, I can tell you, when she needed us."

"I see. Was there anyone else in her life after she returned to the Dordogne? A man, I mean."

"If there was, she kept it a secret. No, no, there was no one else. She lived quietly here, always working in her room or in the garden." While his answers seemed casual, the old man was scrutinizing me with his eyes, clearly trying to size me up.

"Painting, you mean."

"Painting, drawing, yes."

"And what became of all those paintings, besides the ones here in the château I have seen?"

"Who knows? Many she gave away, to friends, relatives, comrades from her student days. She sold a few, as well, but really, I do not know much about that side of things. She had talent, but she was lost down here, far away from Paris and the art world. Everyone forgot about her. Except the family."

"I think she was a very fine artist. Did she ever talk about her work to you?"

"I was just a boy at the time. She lived as a recluse as far as I remember. She took her meals with us but spent most of her time alone and had few visitors. No, now that I think about it, I knew very little about her habits or her thoughts." He paused, tamping down his pipe. "There was one time I remember she tried to give me a drawing lesson, but I was very bad at it and bored, too, to tell the truth. I think I disappointed her. After that, she never spent much time with me. And later I was away at school. In those years I saw little of the family."

"I understand." Shifting gears, I pretended to consult my notebook, as if I were checking a list of questions I had jotted down during my reading. Looking up, I asked, "I wonder if you know whether she was religious?" I was thinking of Madame Martin's description of Jenny Marie as a daughter of the French Revolution.

The Baron's face darkened a shade with suspicion. "Why do you ask that question?"

"Only because I am curious about her views."

"Her views? She was absent, as I recall, at family religious services, but I never discussed the subject with her. It was of no concern to me." Here I sensed the old man was concealing his feelings, but I hesitated to force the question, as I had been slowly moving toward the subject I really wanted to ask about—the war years.

"There is one other thing, Baron, if I may. I don't seem to have any information about Jenny Marie's death. She died, I believe, in 1944, during the Second World War. Can you tell me anything about the circumstances?"

"That, Madame, is a painful subject I do not wish to discuss in detail. She was ill, she died, along with many others who suffered and died. My father, my comrades, many patriotic Frenchmen. It was a terrible time."

"Yes, of course. I certainly don't wish to bring back painful memories, Baron. But I have been wondering what life was like here during the war. Was the family able to remain in the château?"

"It was our home. Where else would we live? Of course, there was hardship, but still it was better here than in the North, thanks to Marshal Pétain, who made a necessary arrangement with the Germans."

He meant the Vichy government, which was accused after the war of collaboration. "We had to make accommodations, and we did." The baron said this as if he expected to be challenged, but I let it pass.

"Was there fighting here?"

"Some," he nodded, with a grunt. "The partisans only made things worse for the population. They weren't always the heroes you hear about, I can tell you that."

"I don't understand."

"They would provoke the Germans, and then there would be reprisals against the local population. And many had their own reasons for fighting, which were not the reasons of France. Communists—I don't say all of them, but some nevertheless."

"Were you involved in any of the fighting?" He had been in his late teens, old enough to have fought.

"I served briefly, but for most of the war I remained here, helping the local people." That was a vague, disquieting answer.

"As a member of the government?"

"No, as a private citizen but one who, along with my father, had responsibilities as a result of our family's position. We provided aid and assistance to those who were in need." Here the old baron knocked the ashes from his pipe, uncrossed his legs, and rose with slight difficulty from his armchair. "Madame, you will excuse me if I interrupt this interesting conversation, but I must go now. I only came into the library for a moment to search for a book." He strode to one of the shelves, pulled a book out by its spine, checked the title, and tucked it under his arm. "I wish you success with your research. Until later . . ." His words drifted off inconclusively, as he nodded and rounded the door at a sprightly clip for an old man in slippers.

Like me, Toby had skipped the group's excursion. While I worked in the library, he'd spent a few hours antiquing around Beynac, but he returned to the chateau empty-handed. Not to call the afternoon a loss, he proposed that we go off on a little jaunt before dinner. Without even

143

asking "Where to?" I agreed, on the condition that he'd put up with listening to my end of a call home as he drove.

Our destination was a picturesque hamlet tucked away on a side road between St. Cyprien and Les Eyzies. Tiny as it is, Meyrals has a reputation as an artists' colony, and we were ready for a distraction. As we headed that way with the windows rolled down to savor the breeze, I dialed my sister's cell phone. I reached her during her work break, which was good, but she was having her cup of coffee at Hank's shop, which was bad. Nonetheless, after determining Hank was not at the table, I plunged in.

"Got a minute to talk about men?"

"Not really. Unless you're having trouble with Toby."

"No, but I'm a little concerned about you and Hank."

"What is it with you and Mom? Every time I let slip I've got a boyfriend, you two are on my case, badmouthing the guy. Even when you haven't met him. Do you want me to be single forever?"

"I'd just like to see you take it a little slower, Angie. Till this week, you'd never mentioned Hank, and all of a sudden you're giving him $30,000. You're going to be penniless once you write that check. And you'll be without a job if you walk away from the beauty shop and go on the road with Hank. It's not such a great idea for a woman to be that dependent on a man, even if she's married to him, and I haven't heard you mention that."

"Oh, brother. Is that what this is about? You and Mom want me to marry Hank before I invest in his business? You two are living in the Dark Ages."

"That isn't what I meant, Angie. This is coming out all wrong. I'm just worried for you."

"Well, stop worrying. I'm not fifteen anymore, you know."

"Are you telling me I'm being too much the big sister?"

"You could say that." I heard a grudging smile in Angie's voice.

"Okay, I'll back off. I'll just be plain old sister, sending love from overseas."

"Good. Forget about me for a while. Have a great vacation. You're in France!"

That made me realize I'd said nothing about our ordeal at Lascaux. For a second, I wondered whether the murder at the cave had hit the press in the United States. Angie wasn't much of a newspaper reader, so she wouldn't have seen any coverage. But someone else in the family might hear about it soon. I let the moment pass, and we said sisterly goodbyes.

I turned toward Toby. "Was that awkward, or what?"

"Not so bad. You've said your piece. Are you really going to cease and desist with Angie?"

"I promised to, didn't I? But I have this terrible impulse to call my brother in Boston and ask him to help. Angie's always respected Eddie's opinion."

"Would that be in the spirit of—"

I interrupted him. "No. I know that. It would violate Angie's privacy. It would undermine her independence. And she told me to lay off. So it's not happening. I'm just telling you, I have the impulse."

For the remainder of the drive, we enjoyed the scenery in silence. We drove past slender stands of poplars swaying in the wind, yellowing pastures where the hay was rolled up like carpets, remote farmhouses, beehive huts, crumbling manors, and roadside chapels, all made of the same attractive tawny stone. For the moment, thoughts of family and murder were banished from my mind.

The sleepy village of Meyrals has a sixteenth-century château and an old church but is otherwise unremarkable, except for half a dozen signs planted here and there directing visitors to this artist's home or that artist's gallery. We turned off at the third sign and followed the arrows to a rambling old stone house set back from a side road about a mile from the village entrance. The house was well hidden by a tall hedge, but a sign out front read: "Nigel Simmons, *Peintre. Bienvenue.* Welcome. English Spoken." A Brit, most probably—there were a quite a few of them living in the Dordogne. Alerted by the slamming of the car doors as we got out, the artist himself appeared in the doorway and invited us in.

Nigel Simmons was in his fifties, had a ruddy face that complemented the red cravat around his neck, and was sloshing a gin and tonic in one hand, with which he motioned us inside. He had longish hair combed wet and wore a long-sleeved white shirt and white pants. Delighted to see us, he was, and more than happy to show us around. "Americans! We don't see too many of your lot around here, do we? But please come in. Have a drink? You've come at the right hour. Just having one myself, as you can see."

He showed us into a large, open room with walls of exposed stone and old worm-eaten beams that supported the upper floors. After brief introductions, he left us to wander around while he fetched the drinks. The ancient manse had been smartly renovated with an eye toward maximizing exhibition space but at the same time preserving as much of the original architecture as possible. The walls were hung with plentiful examples of the artist's work, mainly watercolors of popular subjects: flowers, birds, fruit tumbling from baskets, vegetables portrayed from interesting angles. They were attractive.

"Please don't leave without buying one," he implored with disarming frankness. "I could use the money!" This was said with a self-deprecating smile as he handed us our drinks. After taking our time looking around, we did select a small, unframed painting of a watermelon, sliced into triangular pieces, which was nicely done and inexpensively priced. It would make a sweet gift and would be easy to pack. That broke the ice.

Highly pleased, Nigel invited us to make ourselves comfortable. He pulled a wicker chair across the room and gestured for us to take seats on an old sofa set against the wall. As cash-paying clients, we were entitled to freshened drinks and conversation. In ten minutes we had his full life story—divorced, living in the Dordogne for the past twenty years, bibulous, garrulous, lonely, and, except for the house, which must have been valuable, a bit down at the heels. He was delighted to learn I was an art historian and flattered that I appreciated his work. He also seemed genuinely interested as I described my research project on Jenny Marie Cazelle.

Did he know of her? Was he familiar with the family and their château?

Yes, he was aware of her work, but he'd seen only one painting of hers. As for the family, he didn't know them well but certainly knew *of* them, especially the baron's son, Guillaume, who had something of a reputation among the arty set.

"Really? In what sense?" I asked.

"Well, it's all just rumor," Nigel replied, "but he's been selling old paintings for years at the Bordeaux auction houses, and people have been wondering where they came from."

"Why is that? They live in a château," I pointed out, "so there's obviously wealth in the family, and it wouldn't be unusual for them to have acquired a number of works of art over the generations."

"That's not what I'm talking about," Nigel said. "It goes back to the war, at least that's what people around here say."

Pushed for an explanation, Nigel spun a tale about Nazi-looted art during the occupation and the suspicion—it was common knowledge, he said—that the Château de Cazelle was used to store some of the stolen works during the waning days of the Third Reich. "Too friendly by half" was the phrase he used to describe the family's relations with the occupiers. By war's end, the works had been moved elsewhere or dispersed, but local gossip had it that the family retained a portion of the secret cache from those days and that from this cache Guillaume pieced out works to auction.

"What kinds of paintings?" I wanted to know. "Were the works museum-quality?"

No, Nigel said, they were paintings for the most part by less well-known artists, but still paintings that can bring a good price, the kinds of paintings the Nazis expropriated from people's homes when they were rounding them up.

I listened with a queasy feeling, recalling Inspector Daglan's observation that before Malbert was killed, he had visited the château to discuss the status of a private cave located somewhere on the Cazelle grounds. What if this hidden cave had nothing at all to do with prehistoric art but instead concealed paintings that had been stolen during the Holocaust? If so, had Malbert been killed to prevent him from uncovering that secret?

Of course, I knew that the Nazis had looted art from both public and private collections during the war. One famous episode came to mind. Before the war, the Bernheim-Jeune family had operated one of the most prominent galleries in Paris, featuring a stunning array of impressionist art. With the fall of France, the owners, who were Jews, faced the prospect of German confiscation, and worse. And the worst happened: the Nazis seized the gallery, and while some family members escaped, others were sent to concentration camps where they met their deaths. However, before the Nazis arrived, the family managed to send the best part of their collection to friends who owned the Château Rastignac in the Dordogne. At the beginning of the war, the Dordogne was part of the so-called free zone, run by the Vichy government rather than governed directly by the occupiers, and the family had reason to believe the paintings might be safely hidden there. But toward the end of the war, as the German army suffered reversals and the French Resistance stepped up its activities, German troops began exacting reprisals in the Dordogne. In 1944 the Nazis ransacked the château and burned it to the ground. Just before they set the place ablaze, several German army trucks loaded with loot were seen leaving the site. To this day, no one knows whether those trucks contained the hidden paintings or whether they perished in the ashes. The paintings have never been found, including a famous Renoir and a van Gogh.

It was plausible that the Château de Cazelle had played a similar role during the war as a hiding place for art, especially if there were rumors to that effect. But how could we find out? The old baron didn't want to talk about those years, and I wondered if Marianne would be willing to shed more light on the past.

Meanwhile Nigel was becoming agitated. "And I'll tell you something else about that lot. Mean misers, they are. Guillaume and his sister have both been to my studio and never bought a thing. You'd think they'd be willing to support a local artist, but no. Just cheap, I tell you." By now, he was slurring his words as multiple gin and tonics took their effect.

"Nigel," Toby interrupted, "where did you hear these stories about paintings that were hidden in the château during the war?"

"Hmm? Common knowledge," he mumbled. "Just ask around. Would you like a refill?"

"Thanks, but no," I said, glancing at Toby. I was beginning to think we ought to leave.

Toby looked at me, mumbled something about the time, and thanked our host for the drinks. We paid for our purchase and edged toward the door. Before we got there, Nigel clapped Toby on the shoulder and began offering advice about antique shops in the region where a dealer might find a few good pieces. Toby feigned interest, and the men shook hands.

Outside, the air was still hot and dry. As we drove off, Nigel Simmons stood in the doorway and waved goodbye with a tipsy up and down motion of his fingertips.

For dinner that evening we were on our own. We drove into Sarlat and joined the throngs of tourists who roamed its medieval lanes lit by lanterns that cast pools of yellow light on the cobblestones. We found space at an outdoor table at the Café du Centre, which anchored a courtyard surrounded by half-timbered buildings with wooden balconies. In the soft lamplight, it seemed a stage setting for a play by Molière. We asked for a kir, lingered over its bittersweet taste, and put off ordering for a while. We eventually settled on the classic bistro dinner of steak frites. The thin steak came with a baguette, a bowl of French fries, a salad dressed in walnut oil, a pitcher of local red wine, and no surprises.

"What do you make of Nigel's story?" I asked Toby, trying to slice into my rather tough steak.

"It depends on how much credit you can give to rumors."

"I wouldn't put it past that family to come to some sort of arrangement with the Germans."

"They wouldn't have been the only ones."

"Right." I was thinking of the Château Rastignac. "If Guillaume is selling paintings from a hidden cache, they have to be stored somewhere, either in the château or on the family grounds. What about that cave we've heard about? Is that why the family is keeping it off limits? It would be worth finding out."

"It would if we knew where it was, which we don't," said Toby. "But you've given me another idea. What about the attic? We know where that is, and we can get up there from our room without anyone knowing."

"If the door's unlocked."

"True, but either it is or it isn't. There's one way to find out."

"I'm game, but what if they catch us?"

"Look, I'll go by myself. I'm already in hot water with Marianne, so what's the worst that can happen? I'll apologize."

"I don't know, Toby."

"Nora, there might be something to Nigel's story. I'm going up there."

"All right, but not without me," I said, "and not without dessert." Our waiter had arrived bearing cups of crème brûlée prepared with a hint of walnut liqueur in the caramel sauce.

"Deal," said Toby, tucking into his custard. "Scrumptious." He made a show of licking his spoon upside down.

It was half-past ten by the time we got back to the château. All was silent and dark, except for a few lights in the family wing. We let our voices carry as we climbed the stairs to our room and went through the usual preparations for bed: we closed the shutters, ran the water, flushed the toilet, stretched out on top of the bed with our clothes on, and doused the light. We lay there quietly for thirty minutes, before rising stealthily. Toby went to the dresser and dug out the pocket flashlight he carries around for examining antiques. Though smaller than a pack of cigarettes, the light has a high intensity bulb that casts a brilliant white beam. "Knew this would come in handy on the trip," he said in a pleased-with-himself tone of voice. "Let's go."

We eased into the hallway, lightly closing the door behind us, and made our way shoeless to the door at the end of the corridor. Toby tried the handle. It was unlocked. "That means there's nothing to hide up there," I whispered. "I think we should go back."

"You're probably right, but I'm going up for a peek. You can stay here if you like."

"No way. I'm not going to stand here in the hallway looking guilty. After you."

The door creaked open on old hinges to reveal a spiral staircase made of iron leading up into darkness. Toby beamed his light up, sweeping the stairs. "Come on." I eased the door closed behind us, and we mounted slowly and as quietly as we could. The iron treads were solid, but the armature supporting the suspended stairwell swayed slightly under our weight. We stopped and listened. Nothing. We continued. After four complete turns around the central pole that held the stairway up, Toby reached the top. "Trapdoor," he whispered down to me. He gave it a push. "It's unlocked. Here, take the flashlight."

I held the beam vertically as Toby pushed with both hands at the trapdoor, raising it open. He climbed a few more steps until his head and shoulders disappeared from view. "I'm in. Hand me the light." He reached down to take it from me. The open trapdoor rested against a post at an angle, but it was stationary. Toby disappeared into the dark space above. "Okay, come on up." He shined the light on the steps between us and extended a hand. In another moment I was beside him.

We were standing under a peaked roof supported by enormous beams of bowed oak that gave the appearance of the framework of some upside-down ship. Motes of dust danced in the flashlight's glare, while moonbeams filtered through tiny triangular windows built for ventilation just a few inches above the floor. The combined smell of old wood and animal musk was powerful. Toby's light swept the attic floor, penetrating into obscure corners and illuminating odd pieces of furniture here and there: old night tables, hanging clothing under plastic wraps, and not much else. Even from where I was standing, I could see that our quest for art stashed under the eaves was fruitless.

Suddenly I froze. There was a door creaking below, followed by tentative footsteps on the spiral staircase. Someone was coming up. Toby instantly killed his light and stepped back into a dark corner, gesturing that I should do the same. An old steamer trunk was near me, standing on its end. I ducked behind it, waiting for inevitable discovery. Soon a yellow beam of light played across the side of the open trapdoor, and in a moment a head appeared in the opening on the floor. Another step, and the intruder stood half in and half out of the attic. I glanced in Toby's direction. For now he was invisible, and I hoped I was, too. The figure moved up another step, and his features became recognizable in the moonlight—it was David Press. Had he followed us? If not, what was he doing here?

Almost at once, there came another sound from below, and David started. Quickly he doused his light. He hesitated, listening, and retreated backward down the stairs. I heard the door below open and close, followed by absolute silence. I was certain he hadn't seen us. Some minutes passed, then Toby was at my side. "That was close," he whispered. "What do you think he was up to?"

"Who knows? What do we do now?"

"Wait. Something spooked him, and that might mean someone else heard us come up here." So we waited in the dark, with pounding hearts, as the minutes dragged by.

"Let's chance it," Toby finally said. "I don't think anyone's down there now." Gingerly, he stepped through the open trapdoor, placing his hand on the iron railing of the stairwell. "Come on," he whispered. "We're going." He flicked on his light, and I followed him down, pulling the trapdoor shut behind us.

The dark corridor was empty. "Quick," Toby whispered. We tiptoed to our room like villains in a pantomime. Once back inside, we locked our door.

It was three o'clock in the morning. After a restless start, I'd been sleeping soundly. Suddenly I was alert. The light in the corridor was on, and someone was at the door of our room. I could hear the floorboards creaking and could see the shadow of a pair of feet in the crack of light at the bottom of the door.

"Toby!" I whispered. "Wake up. Someone's trying to break in." I shook him lightly on the shoulder.

"What?"

"There's someone out there. Listen." The creaking stopped. And at the same moment the timer light in the corridor went out.

"I don't hear anything. What time is it?"

"It's after three. There's someone out there. I know it."

"David Press?" Now Toby was alert as well. He sat up, rolled out of bed, and tiptoed toward the door. Dim moonlight fell across his naked back. Outside in the hallway I heard footsteps shuffling away. That's not David, I thought; the sound brought to mind the old baron hurrying out of the library in his slippers. Toby reached for the door with one hand and balled his other fist.

"Wait!" I called out in a hushed voice. "What if whoever's out there has a weapon?" I could see Toby scouring the room for something to protect himself with. "And put something on." He strode to the bathroom and wrapped a towel around his middle. Then he walked quickly to the fireplace and grabbed an iron poker, stepped back to the door, pulled it open, and leaned out. The hall was dark, and whoever had been at the door was gone. Toby slipped into his pants and stumbled out into the corridor. He was back in a minute.

"No one's there now except the ugly customer in that portrait. You sure you weren't imagining things?"

I was sure.

"Then someone was trying to scare us."

"He succeeded. But why was the light on in the hall, unless he was checking on the portrait?"

"At this hour of the night? What for?"

I couldn't imagine a reason.

"Anyhow," said Toby, "there's no one there now. I need to sleep." Toby made sure the latch was securely closed, shucked his pants, and crawled back under the covers. Soon he was breathing deeply and evenly. I tossed and turned for a long time, and it was much later when I finally dropped off again.

9

W E WOKE TO BRIGHT SUN and the prospect of a blistering day. I did my best to banish the memory of last night in order to enjoy the morning's class, but the baron was standing at the foot of the stairs.

"Good morning, Baron."

"Good morning, Madame. I trust you slept well last night."

Was he being polite, or sly?

"Yes, I did, thank you," I lied. "And you?"

"Pah! At my age one never sleeps well. Old men are up at all hours from necessity."

I must have looked blank.

"The WC. And then I find myself wandering the halls."

"Ah."

"Besides, there are curious sounds in these old houses late at night, you know. Sometimes they prevent one from sleeping."

"That's a pity. We didn't hear anything. We got back late from Sarlat and went straight to bed."

"Yes, I heard you come in."

"We didn't disturb you, I hope."

"Not at all. I was awake."

"Even so, I'm sorry if we were noisy."

"No, no. *C'est normale.* Your room is comfortable?"

"Oh, yes, quite comfortable. And quiet too."

"*Bon.*"

There was an awkward pause. I felt like a mouse at the mercy of a cat. I decided to press my luck. "Baron, may I ask you another question related to my research?"

"*Oui, Madame.*"

"It's about the transport of paintings during the war. I read somewhere that several important collections were sent from Paris to the Dordogne to keep them safe. Did anything like that happen here?"

He raised his eyebrows. "Not to my knowledge. We heard such rumors after the war, but whether they are true or not, I cannot say. Why do you ask?"

"I was only wondering whether Jenny Marie might have been involved in any project to protect important art during those years. Her notebooks seem to end before that period."

"Nothing of that nature happened here, so far as I am aware. I thought your research concerned the paintings of my aunt. Yet you keep asking about the war. I think I told you I cannot help you very much on that account."

Madame Martin appeared in the doorway of the salon. "Ah." As if he had been expecting her, the baron dipped his head and made off in her direction. "*Excusez-moi, Madame. Bonjour.*"

By ten we were assembled in the kitchen for our next lesson, and I tried to clear my head. Our assignment today was a dessert extravaganza. Last evening while we were in Sarlat, Marianne had prepared a batch of ice cream and left it overnight in the refrigerator for finishing this morning. As we gathered around the table for instructions, my eyes sought out

David's, testing for any flicker of complicity that might confirm his movements of the night before. But if he had been following us, or if he'd spotted us in the attic, he gave no sign. Instead he listened intently as Marianne outlined the procedures to be followed. Toby, who had been staring just as hard at him, caught my eye and shrugged.

Our first task was to process the ice cream and get it in the freezer. The flavors were local: walnuts and honey and caramel. That would be a perfect accompaniment to the strange cake we were baking. Its base was pumpkin mash and corn flour, its oil was goose fat, and it was flavored with rum and chopped prunes: a winter cake, but we would make it summery by accompanying it with ice cream and by eating only a big salad of greens, goat cheese, and pear slices beforehand.

I was distracted by my plan to catch Marianne alone to probe for more information about the family, but I didn't know how to approach her. I considered my options as she assigned teams for preparing the cake. Marianne put Dotty with us and paired Roz with Patrick. I kept an eye on Dotty as she sidled up to Toby and asked for hands-on assistance in tackling our pumpkin. Meanwhile I observed David and Lily. Admittedly, a pumpkin is not an easy vegetable to handle, but they both seemed unusually inept with a knife. This time, Marianne used their awkwardness to good advantage, demonstrating on their pumpkin how to take a slice off the top and another across the bottom, so that the pumpkin had a firm base when she used a small but sturdy knife to pare the skin from top to bottom. All would have been well then with the Presses, except that when we cooked the pumpkin chunks in milk, their pot boiled over, getting milk scum stuck to the pot and the burner. Marianne's patience was tried as she explained that milk has to be watched carefully or it will develop a skin (the first warning sign of things gone wrong) and then boil over. Once again, I was confirmed in my assessment that the Presses were newcomers to cooking.

At one point, each half of the team had a separate task. Toby and Dotty were doing one job (folding the egg yolks into the boiled pumpkin mash), while I did the other (whisking the egg whites). I was standing next to David, who was also on the white-whisking duty, so I took the opportunity to chat him up.

"At home, are you the baker, or do you leave that to Lily?" (The way he was frantically stirring, not whipping, the egg whites was a clue.)

David hesitated before saying he kept more to the main course. We then both looked over at Lily, who was having trouble executing a simple turn of the mixing spoon in the heavy batter.

"Um, we usually don't make desserts. There's an Italian bakery right on our corner."

Marianne swept in at that moment to correct David's arm action. I stepped back to my team just in time to extricate Toby from an embrace Dotty had artfully engineered under the guise of getting some help in batter-folding. From then on, I stuck with my team, and we produced an aromatic cake, without further entanglement.

Both the salads and the desserts were served on the utilitarian white dishes we always used in class. At the end of the meal, looking down at my empty dessert plate, I remembered the pattern I'd seen on the family china the first night, and it gave me the opening with Marianne that I was looking for.

"Marianne, I'm wondering if you could show me some of that beautiful china you used the first night we were here. I'm interested in Limoges patterns, but I've never seen one like yours."

"I'd be happy to show you after class. There's a reason you have never seen the pattern. Perhaps your husband would be interested also, since he knows antiques." The glance she gave Toby communicated that he was still on probation.

A half hour later, the class dispersed, and Toby and I were standing with Marianne in front of the dining-room's china cupboard. Marianne carefully carried over to the table a dinner plate, a soup bowl, and a cup. She turned the plate over to show the Limoges stamp in the center. Where the pattern name would normally be, the notation was "Château de Cazelle."

"This is a private pattern," she explained. "My grandfather commissioned it in 1922 as a wedding gift to his bride." She turned the plate over again and placed it in my hands.

"It's lovely," I said. "The colors on the rim ribbon are so rich, especially the ruby red of the crosses against the gold. It's an odd shape for a cross, though, isn't it—I mean, the way the stem and arm-piece are equal and thick, so that the cross is round, like a flower." I brought the edge of the plate up to my eyes for close examination. "Is that a fleur-de-lis on each of the tips of the cross?"

"Those are crowns on the tips. It's the Cross of Toulouse, you see."

"Oh? Is the family related to the house of Toulouse?"

"Yes, rather far back, there's a connection to the count of Toulouse. One of us was one of his lords, once upon a time. I don't know all the details."

"The Cathars—this cross is their symbol, isn't it?" Toby, who can be blunt, pointed to the design repeated around the rim of the plate.

Marianne gave a start and took a step back. "I don't know that it is. It's the Cross of Toulouse, and it's on our coat of arms because a branch of the family derives from the line of Toulouse." She sounded defensive.

Toby and I exchanged glances, and then we set about being polite, admiring the dishes, getting out the bigger serving pieces to see how the design was placed on their various shapes, and then helping Marianne put everything safely back. As she turned the key on the cupboard, she said to Toby, "If you're interested in heraldic symbols, you may enjoy Sunday's outing. Do you know about the Félibrée at Domme?"

"Yes, I'm looking forward to it. Does the celebration take place every year?"

"Every year since 1903. The festival rotates from town to town, to all four corners of Périgord. It's usually the first weekend in July, but it's a week earlier this year, to coincide with a special celebration at Domme. Four hundred years ago this week, the people of Domme began rebuilding their church, which had been demolished during the Wars of Religion."

"Religion is a delicate subject around here, isn't it?" Toby ventured.

"It is everywhere," she answered.

"At least, in France, your government stays out of religious matters," I said, trying to be agreeable.

"You think so? You know, today the government finds other places to stick its nose. They've been harassing us at Cazelle—those people from the Bureau of Antiquities." She caught herself. "Of course I'm sorry about what happened to their representative, but really, it has been very unpleasant for us."

Now I saw my way. "Inspector Daglan mentioned something about that," I said. "Something about a cave on the property?"

Suspicion tightened her features, and her voice developed a jagged edge. "Daglan said that? Yes, well, there are caves all over the countryside. In fact, there's one on practically every estate, so there's nothing special about ours. But somehow they've got it into their heads that there must be prehistoric art down there. There isn't. I used to go there myself, as a girl. There's nothing but a long, narrow tunnel and a small rotunda at the end with pretty stalactites. It's no concern of anyone's, including the inspector. But you must understand my father's position. He finds it insulting that the bureau will not take his word, and, as Guillaume says, the cave is on private property."

"Monsieur Malbert's visit here must have been uncomfortable for you," I commiserated.

"Visits. It wasn't just once. This last time, I didn't have the patience for it. I left it to my father and brother. I was busy getting ready for your arrival, anyhow, and then you know what happened. I didn't like that man, but how awful."

"And yet," I said, "in spite of everything, you've been an excellent host. You've had to change so many things because of the investigation, but you've managed to accommodate everyone's needs. We appreciate it."

"It's good of you to say that," Marianne replied curtly, moving back at the same time, as if to send us on our way. I pretended not to pick up on her signal.

"May I ask one other thing?" I interjected. "I hope you won't think I'm prying too much into family matters, but we heard another story yesterday about the château, and I'm wondering if there's anything to it."

"Oh, yes? Who else is telling you stories about us?"

"It was an artist we met in Meyrals. He was talking about art that was hidden from the Nazis during the last world war. It seems some people think there may have been paintings hidden here in the château. Could that be?"

"*Mon Dieu!* That's another ridiculous rumor. People will believe all sorts of things, but nothing like that ever happened here. You say an artist in Meyrals told you the story. Which one?"

"His name is Nigel Simmons," replied Toby.

"The drunken Englishman. I thought as much. Half the time he doesn't know what he's talking about, and the other half he makes things up. For some reason he doesn't like us, and he's a terrible gossip. But, no, nothing like that ever happened at Cazelle. I assure you, if it had, I would know about it." She turned to go, then turned back again. "You know, I asked you once before to respect the boundaries between our private domain and the parts of our property that we have made available to our guests. Perhaps I didn't make myself clear."

Did Marianne know about our visit to the attic last night? Her eyes were cold. "This is our home, it is not a museum. I've asked you not to wander about wherever you fancy. And that goes for letting your imagination wander about, as well. I don't wish to be impolite, but is that understood?" She was trembling now with anger. We'd obviously crossed a line. "And now, please excuse me. I have work I must do in the kitchen."

"Of course," I said, "and, Marianne, I'm sorry if you think we've taken advantage of your hospitality by asking so many questions."

She paused to take a deep breath. "I'm sure you meant no harm. Americans don't think anything of asking personal questions. Our customs are different."

"I'm sorry if we offended you," offered Toby.

"*Bien*," said Marianne, but she wasn't smiling as she left.

When she was gone, I asked Toby, "Do you think she knows we were in the attic?"

"Can't tell, but she's definitely hiding something. Did you see her expression when you asked her about the cave? I wonder what it would take for us to get a look at it. If there are paintings hidden anywhere, that would be the logical place."

"I know. But we can't ask her anything more about the cave after that. In the meantime, maybe we can try to find out more about what went on here during the war. I'd like to go back to that little bookstore in Castelnaud this afternoon. They had a whole section on the Resistance in Périgord. We might be able to find out a few things."

Toby agreed. In late afternoon, we would drive up to the village. First, though, I was headed for the family library, and Toby was taking Dotty antiquing. I squinted like Daglan and suggested that it would be only polite to ask Roz to join them. "Already did," he replied with a wink. "She's coming. She knows her job."

The library had been shut up since yesterday, and the air felt stale. I could still smell traces of the baron's pipe smoke, so I opened the window wide before returning to my place at the table.

I felt useful, getting back to work. By now I had gone through all but one of the notebooks. The fourth in the series dated from the artist's return to the Dordogne in 1917, up through the summer of 1938. The early entries in this notebook recorded news of the First World War and were sparse and somewhat impersonal. An exception came on November 1, 1918, the day of the armistice.

> Thank God it is over. My love, you and how many others paid with your lives for this debacle. Why did I let you go? As if I could have stopped you. So many young men rushing to their deaths, what did you know about war? At least now Pierre will be spared—may this news bring Antoine joy. For me this must be a day for bitter regrets.

I rechecked the family chronology. Pierre was the son of Jenny's brother, Antoine (and would become the father of the current baron). Just a month before Jenny's entry in the notebook, the boy had turned eighteen and had been conscripted. Now he would return safely. By this time, Antoine was the head of the family. He was the one who had urged Jenny Marie to return to Cazelle.

As the months went by, the entries, like the weather, became sunnier.

3 July 1918

We are in the heart of summer, and the days begin to pass more agreeably. Antoine sees to it that I want for nothing. He manages the château as well as Papa ever did. Of course, everyone speaks well of him. He has been encouraging me to get back to my art, and now that I have a little atelier in the south tower, I have begun painting again. The family leaves me to my work until dinner time and then sends for me to come to table. It suits me well, this routine. This morning I was sketching the big linden tree in the garden and finished before noon. Antoine tells me the notary wishes to have a portrait done. Why not? This afternoon perhaps a walk to the chapel when the sun is not so strong, and then repose.

By now Jenny Marie was in her forties, and in those days she would have been considered well past her prime. Even so, she seemed to find renewed energy for work. She wrote of rekindling old acquaintances and busying herself with new projects. Judging from sales notations, her career took an active turn in the mid-1920s. There were details about exhibitions and commissions—and something else that caught my attention. She began selling works at auction. Not often and never her own works, which seemed exclusively to be handled through private transactions, but the works of other artists about her own age. Few of the names were well known, but all struck me as familiar. It took a while for my memory to work, but when it did, the explanation was obvious: I had come across them in an earlier notebook. Jenny Marie was selling paintings she had acquired in her student days from her friends at the

Académie Julian. I went back to the notebook from that period, and sure enough, I found references to most of the names that surfaced in the auction accounts. At the Académie, the students often traded works or bestowed them as gifts of friendship; Jenny gave away many of her own works, as well. Now, to promote the careers of her friends, she was helping build a market for their works by placing some at provincial auctions. I cross-checked the box of letters from the period and confirmed that Jenny Marie had shared the proceeds from successful sales with her former comrades. Aimée Laurance was not among them.

This information also provided a potential explanation for the source of paintings Guillaume de Cazelle was said to be flogging in Bordeaux these days. What if, instead of selling paintings from a secret stash of Holocaust art that was supposedly at the château, he was innocently selling works left over from Jenny Marie's private collection? There was no law to prevent him from doing that. If the family members needed money, they were certainly entitled to sell works that had come down to them through inheritance. That possibility undermined Nigel Simmons's rumor-mongering. Then again, said a voice inside me, possibilities aren't the same as facts. In this case, what were they?

I was losing time with these speculations and needed to get back to the notebook. In the remaining pages covering the 1930s, Jenny Marie's entries were sporadic. There were fewer sales and a section of confusing pages of accounts and balances. Of course, those were the Depression years. Months went by without an entry; there was nothing at all from the years 1933 through 1936. Toward the end, though, there were several pages decrying the rise of Fascism in Germany and expressing fears of another world war.

18 July 1938

That lunatic Hitler is wringing the German heart. Blood will stain French soil again. Can it really be possible that another war is coming so soon after all the slaughter we have seen? Have we learned nothing from it? How the French can quarrel about politics with no sense of the future and no understanding of the past! It will end in ruin, Antoine says, and he is right, but the others are too stubborn to see the danger. They are like schoolboys wrestling in the yard while a hungry wolf watches from the forest.

There were also allusions to dissension within the family, a quarrel involving Jenny Marie's brother and nephew, but no details were given.

16 August 1938

It pains me to say so, but Pierre and his father are no longer talking. Antoine is distraught but refuses to say a bad word about Pierre. I suspect it's about politics, and sooner or later I will penetrate the shroud that has fallen between them. Antoine is the kindest of men and a doting father. I can't believe he is at fault.

Nothing further explained the misunderstanding. The final entry was dated two days later, but the handwriting was unreadable, blacked over with a heavy felt-tipped pen. Had that been Jenny Marie's doing? Did they even have black felt-tipped pens in 1938? Or had some other member of the family censored the passage? I flipped to the end of the notebook. There were twelve blank pages left between the last entry and the back cover. The three previous notebooks were each filled to the very end. Something seemed wrong.

Maybe she had a breakdown. Maybe it was depression. There could be lots of explanations." Toby was responding to my unsettled thoughts about the notebook as we maneuvered along the narrow, twisting road through Beynac on the right bank of the Dordogne. Our line of traffic came to a standstill while a tourist bus squeezed by, inching between the oncoming cars and the cliff face alongside the road.

"Or maybe she switched to a more private diary, where she could confide her thoughts," I speculated. "She had another six years to live, and she had been keeping some sort of journal ever since she was a teenager. How likely is it she would have just stopped cold like that?"

"But you said Marianne told you there were no notebooks other than the ones in the library."

"That she knows about. Yes, so she said. But I have friends who keep diaries and colleagues who keep journals, and once you start, it's a lifetime habit."

"Well, if there is another notebook and the family knows about it, it's obvious they don't want you to see it. Anyhow, you've got enough material for the article you want to write, don't you?"

"More than enough. But I want to know what happened to Jenny Marie during the war, and so far I've drawn a blank. It's frustrating, is what I'm saying."

"Who else can you ask about it?"

"Marianne's the only one. But I don't want to push her too far. I think we kind of hit the wall with her this morning."

Toby nodded.

The truck ahead of us had at last cleared the bottleneck and was receding, trailing black fumes of exhaust. Toby shifted into first, and we started moving again. In the distance we could already see the Château of Castelnaud mounted on a wooded cliff above the valley.

At five in the afternoon, the sun was still high and the day hot. As we continued, the massive fortifications of Castelnaud grew larger, commanding the valley from their strategic height. In another ten minutes we crossed the river on a narrow stone bridge and arrived at a bustling intersection. Behind a row of shops, we heard the delighted shrieks of children at a beach along the river bank. A quick left turn, then an immediate right, put us onto the steep road winding up to the village. Around every bend, the castle loomed, its limestone façade glowing orange in the afternoon sun. The tiny parking area for locals was full, so we followed the signs directing us to a large field for parking on the outskirts of the village and then made our way on foot to the little town square.

The door to the combination library and book shop stood open. The door to Marc Gounot's mineral shop on the floor above it was open as well, but we didn't want to run into him on this visit. Warily, with an eye to his entrance atop the building's outside staircase, we entered the library below. The freckled librarian recognized us and greeted us as if we were old friends.

"Ah, the Americans," she said, with a smile. "How may I help you?"

"We thought we would take another look at your books on Périgord," said Toby.

"Go right ahead. And let me know if you have any questions." She gestured to the section of books for sale on local topics.

We browsed casually, pulling volumes off the shelves here and there and flipping the pages. Toby picked up a book on traditional furniture, and I found a paperback on the Cathars that looked interesting. But my focus today was on events in the region during the Second World War. There were a dozen or so books on the subject, and one of them, *Tales of the Resistance in Périgord*, illustrated with photographs, looked most serviceable (meaning not too dense or difficult to read). We brought our finds to the counter and roamed around the room while the librarian tallied the cost.

I could hear the old boards creaking on the floor above, as well as voices engaged in conversation, which reminded me that Marc's alibi for the day of the murder had been provided by the young woman who was now ringing up our purchases. It would be forward of me to mention it, but I had nothing to lose.

"Excuse me," I said. "I wonder if you would mind answering a question for me. You know, we're staying at the Château de Cazelle, and everyone there has been questioned as part of the investigation of the murder that took place in Lascaux."

The smile on the librarian's face froze as if she had been botoxed. I thought I detected a tic of the eyelid. "Is that so?" she asked in a neutral tone.

"Yes. And now that we know Monsieur Gounot, who owns the shop upstairs," I continued, pointing toward the ceiling, "we were concerned to hear that he was questioned at length by Inspector Daglan." I went on breezily, without pausing: "But we understand it was you who told the inspector that Marc was in his shop during the time the murder took place."

"That's right," she replied, coloring. "Listen for yourself. You can hear everything that happens up there. I know Marc was in his shop all afternoon on that day. It's impossible to think anything else. And besides, it's absurd to believe he would ever be involved in such a thing."

"Without a doubt," Toby asserted. "We think very highly of him ourselves."

Her features relaxed just a little. "That's nice to know. He is a good and honest man," she added, wrapping our books. She stood stiffly now, unhappy with the conversation.

"Thank you for suggesting that we visit his shop," said Toby. "It sounds like there's someone with him at the moment, so we won't go up today, but please tell Marc we said hello."

"*D'accord.*"

Her body language told us we had worn out our welcome. We smiled, acknowledging the awkward moment, but said no more, paid for our purchases, and left.

We were halfway across the square when I heard a familiar, guttural voice speaking French with a thick accent. Fernando. He was poised on the upper landing of the iron staircase leading to the mineral shop, saying something back to the person inside. He hadn't seen us. I pulled Toby behind a column supporting the roof of an open shed, so that we were both out of sight. What was Fernando doing in Marc's shop? He was standing in the doorway, gesticulating.

"Don't let him see us," I whispered.

There was a little souvenir shop next to the shed. We ducked inside and watched while Fernando continued his dialogue with his invisible partner. He appeared to be annoyed. Then he stood still and listened, finally nodding gruffly. In another moment Marc stepped out onto the landing, shook Fernando's hand with a curt nod, and dismissed him with a pat on the shoulder. Marc turned back inside as Fernando skipped down the stairs. We watched unobserved as he swaggered to a motorbike leaning against a wall, kicked up the stand, gunned the engine, and roared off.

Just then the owner of the souvenir shop approached and asked what she could do for us.

"Thank you, Madame, just looking," said Toby, placing a hand at the small of my back and steering me outside.

We crossed as quickly as possible to the road back to the parking area, where we found our car so hot that we opened the doors and stood there talking while it aired out.

"I don't want to believe Marc is involved in this," I said.

"Remember, he has an alibi."

"It's a good thing he does. I keep thinking about the war. At home it's history, but here it's still alive, part of the present. There's that business about Marc's father as a collaborator, which is nagging at me. Then there's the rumor we heard yesterday about Nazis and hidden art at the château, not to mention the blank I've drawn about Jenny Marie during the war years. And now we discover there's some connection between Marc and Fernando. I don't have a good feeling about any of this."

"Let's slow down a minute. So what if Marc and Fernando know each other? Everyone knows everyone around here. And as for the rumors about art and Nazis, how trustworthy is Nigel Simmons? Not that I'm dismissing the idea. I'm just saying we don't know very much. And I still don't see the link between any of this and the murder. Maybe we should stick to our sheep, which in my case is antiques and in your case is art."

"Stick to our sheep?"

"It's a French saying meaning let's get back to the subject. Don't you know it? *Revenons à nos moutons.* 'Let's return to our sheep.' I think it's from a play by Molière."

"What have sheep got to do with anything?"

"You need to know the story."

"So?"

"Something about stolen sheep. Or maybe they were lost. I don't remember."

"Sometimes you can be infuriating."

"I admit it. But get into the car."

Toby's suggestion was to go to the beach. It was still egg-frying hot at a quarter to six in the evening, and the Castelnaud beach at the foot of the cliff was inviting. We drove down the looping road from the hilltop village and parked in the dirt lot with its cluster of shops fronting the river. There was a café bustling with vacationers who had come from the beach to enjoy an aperitif before dinner. By contrast, the beach itself, a sandy strand shaded by trees, was pleasantly uncrowded. The Dordogne River, clear and wide at this spot, burbled gently and sparkled in the late sun. We found a comfortable patch of grass beneath a tree on a rise set back a little way from the beach, and we plunked ourselves down to relax.

Couples and groups were scattered along the river's edge, spread out on blankets or lolling in plastic beach chairs. Some had picnic baskets at the edge of their little patches of territory. Most of the families with young children had pulled up stakes by this hour, but teenagers and older folks were enjoying the scene. Three teenage boys were wading out to a bit of exposed land in the middle of the river—it was too small to call it an island—where two girls were stretched out sunbathing. A man in charge of the canoe concession was pulling his boats up onto the beach and aligning their prows; this was the landing point for canoes that had been launched upstream and were now being returned at day's end. A light breeze rustled the leaves. I folded my arms around my knees and breathed in slowly. The air felt good.

This being France, many of the women were topless, and not just the twenty-somethings. Women of all shapes and ages were following the fashion. It seemed quite natural. Maybe that was because no one was staring (aside from Toby). On some blankets women bare from the waist up were sitting next to others who were covered up, and nobody seemed to find anything amiss. I couldn't help thinking of Manet's *Déjeuner sur l'herbe*, which had caused a scandal by depicting a naked woman sitting on the grass beside two fully clothed men. But that had been a century ago and might as well have taken place in a different country.

Off to the right about fifty yards in front of us sat a slim man in trunks and a blonde whose back was bare. They were gazing at the river. There was something familiar about the pair. Almost at the same time, Toby and I recognized Dotty and Patrick.

"Should we say hello?"

"I suppose we have to," I said.

"But she's . . ."

"Yes, I can see that."

"Maybe we should go."

"Too late."

Patrick had stood up and spotted us. He said something to Dotty, who turned and waved. And jiggled.

"Toby, you can put your eyes back in your head."

"Huh?"

"And for your information, those are implants."

"How can you tell from here?"

"Because they look like megaphones."

"Yeah, they do, sort of. It's embarrassing."

"True enough."

Dotty was shimmying into her halter. Once ensconced, she waved again and started to troop over, followed by Patrick, who gathered up their towels and slung them over an arm.

"I didn't know you were coming to the beach today," said Dotty brightly, directing her remark more to Toby than to me.

"We didn't either," replied Toby. "It was a spur-of-the-moment decision."

Patrick spread out their towels, and they sat down. He gave a wan smile. It occurred to me, and not for the first time, that he might not be attracted to women. That must have dawned on Dotty too, for she fixed her attention on Toby.

"Still thinking about that armoire?" she asked, with a tilt of the head.

While I had been working in the library, Dotty, Roz, and Toby had spent the early part of the afternoon at an antique fair in Le Castang. Toby told me he had thought of buying a small cherry wardrobe but had decided against it.

"It was a nice piece, but awfully expensive," he answered. Toby dutifully made eye contact with Dotty rather than letting his gaze drop lower. I gave him points for that.

"What about you, Patrick?" I asked. "What did you do today?"

"I've been reading up on local restaurants, comparing reviews from various guides, you know, Michelin, Gault and Millau, and a couple of others."

"Got any tips?"

"Well, tomorrow in Domme we're scheduled to have lunch at l'Esplanade. They say it's very good. It had a Michelin star until a few years ago when the original chef retired, but it's still supposed to be right up there. And the site, they say, is spectacular, with a dining room overlooking the whole valley."

"I'm up for that," said Dotty. "You know, I never really was into haute cuisine until Roz took me in hand. Until I married Tom, I never had the money for it. But I will from now on, and I won't mind spending it. Making up for lost time, you might say."

"Why not?" said Patrick, "though from what you said the other night, I gather you and Roz don't always see eye to eye."

"Not always. There are a few issues about Tom's will that need ironing out, and we're talking about them." She shifted her attention to the river. "Isn't it gorgeous here?"

"It is," I replied. Shading my eyes, I looked up at the castle, behind and high above us, looming atop its jagged cliff. The sun had now dipped behind one of its towers. People around us were slowly getting up to leave, shaking out blankets and gathering their belongings. No one spoke for a few minutes. Then Dotty pointed to a couple just arriving at the beach.

"Say, isn't that our friend Marc with that redheaded woman?"

The woman carried a towel in one hand; the man had an arm wrapped around her shoulder. Sure enough, it was Marc Gounot, and the woman he had his arm around was the librarian.

"Look who's an item," Toby said quietly.

Yes, I thought to myself, and so much for Marc's alibi.

10

SUNDAY MORNING FOUND ME groggy and regretful. "Everything hurts," I whined to Toby. "I can't even face the coffee. Can you get me a couple of aspirins to go with my croissant?" Soundless bells were clanging in my head.

The meeting on the beach had led to an epic drinking bout. It was Dotty's idea that we splash in the river and then go for tapas at the Spanish restaurant by the bridge. She jumped at the chance to charm three men at once. I figured she couldn't get too far with Toby right under my nose, and over drinks we'd learn more about Marc. So I said yes for both of us. It didn't work. The tapas were tasty, but the six of us drowned our social discomfort in sangria, and no one but Dotty found anything much to say. The hours were wasted, if we'd expected to find out anything about Marc's relationship with the little librarian, never mind why he was arguing with Fernando. The talk was about spiked wines—the merits of Spanish, Basque, and Perigordian versions of the same.

Having drunk less than the rest of us, Toby was in reasonably good shape, in spite of what was for him an early wake-up call. This was lucky, as I needed a helper or I'd never make it to the van in time for our departure. Marianne wanted us to start early, because thousands of visitors would be converging on Domme for the Félibrée. The police had restricted entry to one narrow road, which winds up a high hill to the town gate. "Grand as it is," she warned, "the gate can accommodate only one car at a time." We needed a two-hour start to make the journey. Our first scheduled event was ten o'clock Mass, so we had to depart by eight.

Thanks to Toby's ministrations, I was ready in time to mark the entrance of Marianne and Guillaume, who appeared on the front steps of the château in full holiday regalia. Marianne wore a white lace bonnet that framed her face becomingly. Her ankle-length dress was topped by a snowy lace collar so wide it formed a shoulder shawl. The fabric of the dress was royal blue, with gold bees as a repeated pattern. The beehive, she explained, is the emblem of the Félibrée; the bees symbolize the *félibres*, the celebrants, and their industrious preparations. She looked attractive as she smoothed her skirt down with one hand and motioned the gathered group into the van with the other. As usual, Fernando was the driver. We gave him a wide berth as we waited near the van, and he in turn avoided eye contact with us.

Guillaume, in contrast to his sister, looked austere. He was dressed in stark black and white: round-brimmed black hat, black vest, and black pants, tighter than they should be, possibly because they had been in use just once a year since his slimmer days. A black string tie at the collar of his white shirt gave him the air of a stern Amish patriarch, a contrast to his usual persona of dapper aristocrat. I saw him glance up at Marianne as if unsure of his appearance, searching for approval.

After giving his sister an arm's assist to mount into the van, he seated himself next to Fernando in front, and turned to the rest of us to announce proudly that Marianne was wearing the same dress their mother had worn when she was queen of the Félibrée.

"It was the summer after the war," Marianne added. "They say it was the happiest of all the Félibrées. We have photographs of it—but of course we weren't there. It was the year before our mother was married, in her hometown of Montignac. But now let me tell you about Domme."

As our van made its way slowly down the wooded road that descends from the château to the river, and then through the morning-lit streets of Beynac, Marianne gave us a lesson about *bastides*. These rectangular walled towns were built in the thirteenth century as military strongholds when England and France contested dominion over Aquitaine. Domme, built by the French at the edge of a towering cliff, is irregular in plan, but its spectacular site makes up for what it lacks in symmetry. Marianne predicted that Domme would be a glorious setting for today's celebrations.

Every Félibrée starts outside the city walls. The queen of the festival throws open the city gate to admit the waiting crowd, who then parade up the town's cobblestone streets, under arches of brightly colored paper flowers made by women from nearby villages. All through the cold evenings of winter and early spring, the women meet to make flowers that will transform a summer street into a floral arcade.

Marianne guessed that we'd miss the opening ceremony, but we'd be there in time for the next event, which was the Mass to bless the Félibrée. This year the Mass would be sung by the Bishop of Sarlat, and since the *langue d'oc* is the language of the Félibrée, he would sing in Occitan. At this point Guillaume spoke up sharply in rapid-fire French, seeming to forget that half the group wouldn't understand him.

"At least this bishop speaks Occitan," he declared in an offended tone. "Last year the festival was held in another diocese, and their bishop didn't speak the language at all. He was from the generation after the war. They were too bent on being modern to learn the patois of their parents. Besides, they were forbidden to speak it in school." He sounded angry now. "In fact, people in that generation didn't realize their dialect was a form of Occitan. They were told it was peasant language and they had to speak proper French to be civilized. Now, I'm happy to say, children are taught Occitan in school."

Marianne took over in unruffled English, observing calmly, "Our bishop is young enough to have learned to speak and sing in the old language. You will hear the old words and the old music from morning Mass to the end of the day."

It took the full two hours to get to Domme. Not to miss Mass, we piled out of the van before it reached the Porte del Bos and left Fernando to park while we climbed the steep, flower-bedecked streets. Walking with us were groups led by men who carried poles sailing the flags of their towns and cities. As we approached the church, I spotted someone carrying the flag of Castelnaud, with its yellow rampant lion, and I wondered whether we would run into Marc.

When we reached the church, we found a long line ahead of us in front of the entry. Once inside, we sought the back of the church and found seats together in one of the last pews. There was quite a din, so Marianne felt free to continue her tour-guide functions as we waited for Mass to begin. She fell silent at the first notes from the choir, and the congregation hushed too, as an all-male chorus began singing in plaintive tones. They were up at the front of the church, at the bottom steps to the right of the altar: twelve men, all dressed like Guillaume, in black and white. Their round-brimmed hats hung at their backs. Two strummed guitars as they sang, and one played a small keyboard instrument like a miniature harpsichord. The music was mournful, with a sad and longing tenor part, set against a bass part that sounded low and strong like a drum. To this strange chorus, the bishop, attendant priests, and altar boys marched in step from the church door, up the aisle to the altar.

I remembered enough from my upbringing to follow along, since what the bishop and congregation sang was an Occitan version of the Latin Mass with all the familiar phrases and gestures. The most memorable parts were the choir's haunting choruses, which punctuated the ritual. I wasn't prepared, however, for the finale, when the bishop, having said the Occitan equivalent of *"Ita missa est"* ("The Mass is ended"), raised both hands, gestured for all to rise, and then led the assembled hundreds in a full-throated rendition of an Occitan song, which all the locals, including Marianne and Guillaume, knew by heart.

As the bishop and his entourage "recessed" from the altar, down the aisle, and out the door, the choir continued with verses the congregation didn't know. Once the church was half empty, Marianne huddled us into a side chapel. There she explained the parting song was the hymn of the Félibrée, "La coupa santa," taught to every Perigordian child at least once, maybe twice: first, in school in the curriculum of Occitan studies and, then, if you were the child of Catholic parents, in catechism class in preparation for First Communion.

"What are those black boxes all over the wall?" asked Dotty, as if she had not been listening at all to what Marianne was saying.

Marianne turned to look where Dotty was pointing, the left and right sides of the chapel, which in the middle had an altar topped with a very old bust of the Virgin and Child. "Those are—I don't know the word in English—sort of offerings. On the face is a plaque with writing that thanks God, or Mary, for an answer to the person's prayers. In this church there's a little box behind each plaque where the grateful person can put money or jewelry as an offering. In some chapels, there's one locked box for the offerings. The priest collects the offerings periodically and gives the proceeds to the poor of the parish."

"That's done in some way all over the world, isn't it?" I asked, accessing dim memories of my grandmother's church in Gloucester—and the more recent memory of plaques in the little chapel on the château grounds.

"I think so," said Marianne. I've seen this sort of thing in Spain and Italy, I'm sure."

"That is so sweet," said Dotty, taking note of a quaint foreign custom.

Guillaume looked at her reprovingly. "Gratitude is a universal duty," he intoned. His posturing broke the mood, and Marianne told us we were free to go.

"Enjoy the festival, and let's meet at twelve thirty sharp in front of the Hotel Esplanade just across the way from here. Don't eat too much at the stands. You'll want to have an appetite for our lunch!"

In the jostle of exiting the church, Toby and I fell in with David and Lily, and we drifted into touring the town together. Following the crowd, we veered to the left, which brought us to the square with its old covered market. The stone pillars were swagged with pink paper roses, and more strings of artificial flowers were strung up to the rafters. We entered into this giant bower, stopping at tables where women sold walnut candies, or slices of walnut cake, or the wafer-thin crisps they called *gaufres*. Lily and I were debating whether we could split a treat, when Toby said he'd catch me at the same place in a few minutes.

By the time David had devoured his walnut candies and Lily and I had powdered our lips with confectioners' sugar from the crispy *gaufre* we shared, Toby was back. He held a brochure in his hand. "Sorry, I wanted to get a map of the town, and I saw that the tourist bureau was open. They recommend a walk along the ramparts. Anyone game for that? We'd have just enough time before lunch."

"I'm in," said David, looking over to check with Lily.

"I'm not feeling too athletic this morning. But you go ahead. I just feel more like strolling the town. I'll meet you for lunch at the hotel."

I surprised Toby by opting to stay with Lily. Toby knows I generally crave a daily walk, but I wanted to get to know her better, and besides, I hadn't quite recovered from last night's overindulgence. A leisurely stroll round the town would be better for me than a hike.

Lily and I made easy companions as we walked slowly down the steep main street without talking much, motioning to each other when we wanted to go into a shop or pointing out particularly nice decorations. We remarked on the costumes of the local women. Many wore white lace blouses with dark skirts and colorful aprons. Others wore full dresses like Marianne's. Those in costume looked as if they were going to have to peel off layers, because it was already hot and it was still before noon. The tourists, in their shorts and T-shirts, looked out of place but comfortable.

Walking gently down the shopping street, we stopped to peer into windows, which featured the old instruments of each shopkeeper's trade—ancient scales and weights at the greengrocer's, old mortars and pestles at the pharmacist's. At the window of the pastry shop, decorated with nineteenth-century cake molds, we looked at each other and simultaneously asked, "Coffee?"

Inside the pastry shop, we sat back to watch the mix of locals, *félibres* from out of town, and tourists like us, ordering and receiving their goodies with relish. Over coffee, Lily asked me to tell her about our life in California, and I did, asking her in turn to tell me about her life in New York with David.

"We haven't been married long, actually. So we haven't really got a rhythm to our life together, not like yours, with you teaching all day and coming home to a nice dinner cooked by Toby. Right now, I'm alone a lot. I do my copyediting job nine to five, but then there's not much to do unless I go to visit my mother or sister. David's job is very demanding. He's often at work till ten or eleven at night. And he's at the office all weekend."

"I've heard the hours are grueling for lawyers who are trying to make partner."

"Of course. . . . But with David, it's not just that. There's no doubt he'll make partner, but I don't think that will change how much he works."

"Is it that he loves his work so much?" I replied cautiously.

She looked up at me soberly. "I don't call it love." Then she fell quiet.

When the silence threatened to become awkward, I asked, "Is this a sore topic?"

"Sort of. David is dedicated to his job. It's a passion with him. And I know it's very important work. But it's going to be difficult now."

I gave a puzzled look.

"We'll be having a baby. We just found out, before we left on the trip." I might have guessed. That explained Lily's fatigue, her demurral from drinking, and her lightheadedness in the cave. Not to mention David's solicitude toward her.

"Congratulations! You must be so happy," I said excitedly, and the inappropriateness of the comment was clear before it had completely come out of my mouth. Lily plainly was not happy. "You'll work this out," I predicted, more on faith than on evidence. "David is obviously crazy about you. When he sees you need him, I'm sure he'll get his life in balance. If it comes to the office or the wife and baby, he'll make the right choice."

"Sometimes it's not a matter of choice."

I was flummoxed. And kept my mouth shut for once. After a moment, Lily spoke, with a mixture of conviction and despair.

"Sometimes the work chooses you, and you can't say no."

"I suppose," I replied, a little anxious to break the gloomy mood. "I never realized intellectual property law could be so compelling."

Lily looked as if she didn't understand my remark. Then she seemed to remember something, pushed her coffee forward, and said, "Well, in this case, I'm afraid it is." She stood up and turned away, ending the conversation abruptly.

We made our way silently back to the square and then moved toward our restaurant. We arrived just as the church belfry sounded two clangs to mark half past the hour. Lily excused herself to use the ladies' room.

Toby looked as if he had worked up an appetite. "How was your walk with David?" I asked.

"Good. There are some great views from the ramparts." David and Patrick were examining the day's menu, posted on a wrought-iron stand at the edge of the hotel patio.

"Ready to order, gentlemen?" I asked.

"Nothing to order," Patrick informed us. "In honor of the festival, there's a set menu of traditional dishes."

"Fine with me," David declared enthusiastically.

When Lily rejoined us, she gave me a hesitant smile. I realized she'd probably been fighting morning sickness at every meal.

Marianne waved to Dotty and Guillaume, who were clinking glasses at one of the patio tables, and soon she had us all assembled for an announcement: "We have a table for six and a table for three, so I'm asking if there are three of you who would be content with a little table by the window. You'll have the best view."

Roz spoke up. "I'd be happy to join a couple at the little table. Nora and Toby?"

"Great," declared Toby.

We did have a great location, right in front of an open window, looking out over the valley. I could see all the way to the bluffs at La Roque-Gageac. Toby, opposite me, looked over the esplanade down to fields along the river. And Roz, facing the window, looked straight across a meander of the Dordogne in the direction of the little village of Vitrac. Our companions had a more ample table, but it was in the interior of the restaurant, away from this stunning view.

We started with medallions of foie gras, paired with a Sauterne from nearby Monbazillac. After a sherbet of red Cahors wine "to cleanse the palate," we moved to grilled *magret de canard.* That gave us plenty to talk about, as we compared the chef's masterpiece to what we had done with our duck breasts in cooking class. There was no comparison. We drowned our chagrin in a good round glass of the local Pécharmant.

"I swear, I've let my cooking go," Roz confessed. "I'm been so busy with the neighborhood center. But I do love good food, and I think that now I'll have more time for it."

"You mean, you'll make more time, now that Marianne has renewed your interest?" Toby asked.

"Well, yes, but what I was thinking is that I'll actually have more free time now. I'm expecting the center to close."

"But," I replied, "isn't there a possibility of saving it, if your brother's bequest comes through?"

"We did talk about that, didn't we?" Roz seemed surprised to remember she had been so self-disclosing. "Well, yes, if we get the bequest Tom planned before he died, we'll be able to buy the building. If not, there's no way for us to keep up with the rent increases. The problem is that Tom never put the bequest into his will, and Dotty can't make up her mind whether to honor his promise. I've asked Tom's lawyers to explore options with Dotty's lawyer while we're away, but when we return my sister-in-law will have to make a decision. For now, everything's in limbo."

"Maybe it will all work out," I offered, optimistically.

"I hope so. But Dotty and I have been talking about it, and she doesn't really see the value of a neighborhood center. It's hard to get her to think of anything but herself," Roz added, with a note of bitterness.

"Maybe she needs to see the programs at work. Have you given her a tour?" I asked.

"No, and that's just what I've been thinking. When we get home, I'm going to take her there and show her the classes for single mothers and the day care operation." She caught herself. "Not that Dotty is exactly maternal. It might do more harm than good."

As the conversation continued, Marianne pulled up a chair and joined us for dessert. It was clear she and Roz had been talking about Dotty earlier, for she already knew the details and was clearly incensed. "It's a scandal what your sister-in-law is trying to do, ignoring your brother's will. Why don't you let me speak to her about it?"

"Marianne, you're my oldest friend, but please don't interfere. I'd like to handle this my own way."

"I know you. You won't say anything. I wouldn't keep quiet if someone were trying to tarnish my brother's legacy. I'd fight."

"I know you would, but please do as I asked. I'll fight in my own way."

"You're too nice; that's the trouble," sputtered Marianne. "To think of it! What did your brother want? Only to help the charity you've worked so hard for all these years, not to leave all his money to you instead of his wife. There still will be plenty left for Dotty, am I right?"

"I do have lawyers working on this, Marianne, believe me."

"Lawyers. Once you start with them, it never ends. In France, we would settle this matter within the family."

"Marianne, please don't make things more difficult than they already are. I'm asking you as a friend." The finality of her tone put an end to the conversation.

"Very well," said Marianne, rising from the table. "But you know how I feel." She strode brusquely off to find the others, who had moved on to the next event.

Roz let out an exasperated sigh. "She's been at me about Dotty ever since we arrived. I know she means well—I couldn't imagine a friend more loyal than Marianne. But her idea of forcing a confrontation would only make things worse. I know Dotty, and she doesn't like to be pushed."

I nodded. "Do you suppose Marianne feels so strongly about your sister-in-law because of the way she feels about Guillaume? I mean, she dotes on him, anyone can see that. And the idea of Dotty coming between you and your brother Tom, even after his death, must strike her as intolerable."

"You may be right. And it *has* felt pretty well intolerable. But I haven't given up on convincing Dotty to honor Tom's bequest, and I don't want to stiffen her resistance by fighting with her while we're over here. That's what I've told Marianne, and she'll just have to trust me on this." Roz pushed her chair back from the table. "Come on, let's see what's next on the schedule."

We strolled down to the town gardens, where an outdoor lunch was just breaking up. Marianne had reassembled our little group there. She gave a slightly disapproving nod to Roz but then resumed her tour-guide patter. Gesturing toward the tables, she explained that the core celebrants—such as people staffing booths or doing craft demonstrations, dancers, and musicians, as well as everyone in traditional costume—had been invited to a communal meal. We may have enjoyed the finer cuisine at our lunch, but they seemed to have had a more boisterous time, for all were merry and ready to start the next activity, the Court of Love.

We couldn't understand the words in Occitan, but Marianne explained that by tradition the nobles of the area—today, the queen and her consort—would settle romantic disputes according to the rules of courtly love. The other main activities of the afternoon were musical. At the back of the garden, there was a low stage, where three women played ancient instruments in their laps, and a man strummed a guitar. At the side of the garden, a costumed mother and son played accordions under a tree, with spectators surrounding them. A group of young girls, from eight to eighteen, danced together in facing lines. Couples were also dancing, with the women holding up their skirts with the left hand.

It was hard to pull ourselves away when Marianne said it was time to find Fernando's van. "If you want to return later, you can do that," she announced. "With this heat, I'd advise coming back after dinner for the outdoor ball. That will start at nine."

By the time we found the van, it was mid-afternoon, and we had wilted. We were suddenly a quiet group, glad to cool off in the air-conditioned car.

Back at the château, we freshened up by splashing cold water on our heated skin. Toweling himself dry, Toby said he needed a real soak in the pool, but I wanted a nap, so we parted ways. I must have fallen deeply asleep, because when I woke to the ringing of my phone, I was befuddled. At first I didn't recognize my brother's voice.

"Is that you, Nora?"

"Eddie—I'm surprised to hear from you. Is anything wrong?"

"No, everybody's okay. I just need your help. It's about Angie's new boyfriend. I'm looking into his background."

My stomach knotted. "Eddie, I'm not sure it's such a good thing for us to be all over Angie's love life. There's such a thing as being over-protective. Did Mom put you up to this?"

"No. If she had asked me to, I wouldn't have. Angie asked me."

"You're kidding. Just yesterday she told me to mind my own business about Hank."

"Maybe she decided she didn't want opinions, just facts. And since I work in I.T., she knew I could get facts fast."

"So what did you find out?"

"Before I tell you, I want to say I don't really go for this business of family members knowing every detail of each other's lives. I wouldn't be doing this search if Angie hadn't asked me. And I wouldn't be telling you the results if Angie didn't want me to."

"I'm with you on the principle. But what do you need to tell me?"

"I have a question. Do you remember Jack Havens from high school? He was in your class."

"Sure do. I had a few dates with him in my junior year. He was a football player and a real charmer, but too slick for me. He wound up with the prom queen."

"Did he ever get into trouble?"

"There was something in senior year about running a gambling pool or throwing a game and getting paid off by a gambling pool, or something like that, but it all got hushed up."

"That's consistent with what I found out. Jack has all kinds of liens against him for unperformed contracts and defective work when he was a builder, and he served time for conducting an Internet con on elderly people."

"What's this got to do with Angie and Hank?"

"Jack Havens is Hank's older brother, and Jack is living in Hank's apartment right now. That's where he took refuge when he got out of jail last spring."

"So, what's the conclusion here? That Hank has a slimy brother, or that in high school I had bad taste in dates?"

"More to the point, Angie's boyfriend has a con man living with him. The older brother may be teaching Hank how to run a scam with this motorcycle-moving service. Or he may be using his influence over his younger brother to run a scam without the kid knowing it's a scam."

"Have you told Angie?"

"Yes. She's met Jack, and she knows he's been in jail, but she believes Hank's story that Jack was framed. She thought you would remember Jack as a football star, an all-around great guy. You were supposed to be the glowing character reference."

"If Angie already knows that I knew Hank's brother, why didn't she mention that when we talked on the phone?"

"She was feeling cornered by you and Mom. So she kept her business to herself. But she began to have doubts, so she asked me to do a background check on Hank and Jack."

"What about Hank, then. Did he come up clean?"

"Nothing criminal. But for a young guy he's had a lot of failures. Angie tells me he dropped out of two job-training programs. I found out he went bankrupt trying to run his own coffee-roasting business. Then he was unemployed a year, until he got this job at the coffee shop. If the motorcycle scheme flops, it'll be par for the course."

"And what if his older brother is involved in the motorcycle scheme? His plan could be to steal motorbikes in one state and drive them in a Winnebago to another state for 'resale' on the black market."

"All I can do now is to tell Angie what you remember, and we'll see what she concludes from that."

"Okay, thanks, Eddie."

Sometimes it isn't easy being a sib. Marianne always seemed to be soothing her agitated brother, and Eddie and I had our hands full with Angie. I was glad Eddie was helping out, told him so, and we were off the phone in short order.

Now wide awake, I needed a walk to work off the adrenaline from the phone call. To be ready for the heat, I changed into shorts and a T-shirt and set off along the cliff path, which was shaded and not too strenuous. I vowed to set aside Angie's troubles. To take my mind off my sister, I steered my thoughts back to my research.

Loping down the path, I wondered whether Jenny Marie had ever painted here. The woodsy path would have been a perfect subject for her style of realism heightened by effects of light. To the left, the stunted scrub oaks of Périgord clung to the cliff and arched over the path, providing puddles of deep shade. To the right, the view to the river played in and out between those tall topiary figures I'd noticed the first morning. On the initial stretch of topiary, the figures were taken from a deck of cards: a man-sized heart, a chubby club, a fat spade, and a sharply chiseled diamond, all about seven feet high. For a moment I thought my over-stimulated brain had projected me into *Alice in Wonderland*. And sure enough, the topiary figures at the bend ahead were a fat queen and a tall king. Around the corner must be a jack and an ace. Not forgetting to peek out between these fabricated wonders to the views of the river that they framed, I walked along slowly, feeling delighted by the effects of human artifice on nature.

As I rounded the last bend, I stopped short. Ahead of me, men in black Félibrée costume, broad-brimmed hats and all, were standing in front of the chapel, looking somber and speaking quietly. Guillaume was one. I stepped back and hid behind the topiary just at the bend. Thankfully, it was the fat queen—wide enough to hide me. Immediately I felt ridiculous. When I did have to reveal myself to the men, how would I explain why I had hidden behind the bush? Calming myself with slow and measured breaths, I peered through the needled branches, trying to find an angle that would provide a peek. Yes, that was Guillaume. And the cadaverous man he was speaking to was Marc's uncle, Monsieur Gounot. The other four I didn't recognize. There was something furtive about their movements. They whispered among themselves and then, led by Guillaume, they filed through the opening arch of the chapel and into its interior.

I wasn't going to be able to see a thing from my present position. With curiosity overcoming caution, I crossed the path and positioned myself behind a scrub oak near the barred window on the left side of the chapel. The angle allowed me to see most of the interior. Although the men obscured my view of the altar, it looked a little different from my previous visit. The white linen cloth was the same, but, as Guillaume moved his hands up and down in a theatrical gesture, I saw there was an outsized book—maybe a Bible—and several napkins. A brass basin filled with water rested on a side table that had not been there before. Long white candles burned on the altar, spotlighting the book and giving a glow to the Black Madonna behind it.

I watched as the men removed their hats and began to chant in unison. Though I couldn't make out the words, I sensed the similarity to the Occitan hymns sung in church at Domme. As the chant ended, one of the group, who appeared to be younger than the rest, was brought around to the side table. Two others, who moved with an air of authority, motioned him to draw closer and kneel. One of the men directing the youth was Gounot. He and his companion spoke some words and ceremoniously washed their hands in the basin, drying them with the linen napkins. Then, from his place in front of the Virgin's altar, Guillaume spoke in low tones to the kneeling man, who appeared to repeat the words, as the ritual proceeded. After a few minutes, the man prostrated himself twice, then rose, assisted by Gounot.

Now the young man spoke solemnly to each of the older men in turn, and they nodded in approval. Guillaume lifted the Bible, carried it a step over toward the young man and twice touched his head with the book. As Guillaume turned back to replace the book on the altar, Gounot laid hands on the young man's shoulders. A low chant went up from the group, and I still could not make out any words. The neophyte walked slowly around the little table and was kissed once on the cheek by each of the men standing. When the youth returned to his starting point, Gounot raised both hands in benediction and then washed his hands a second time in the little basin. With that, the ceremony neared its end. I was afraid the men would start back toward the château and their path would lead them directly toward me. But no, each of them now approached the altar and bent forward to touch his forehead to the skirt of the Black Madonna.

I quickly crossed the path and ducked back behind the topiary, where the men would not see me as they passed by. But that was a terror, because the topiary was perched on the edge of the cliff.

I reached into the greenery, searched for the thick trunk of the bush, and holding onto that, scooted myself to the cliff edge, confident the queen-shaped bush would hide me as long as I could hang on and keep my balance. I kept my gaze on the trunk, to which I was clinging. Minutes went by without the men leaving. I wasn't going to be secure holding on there much longer. So I looked up again and tried to get a peek at the opening of the chapel, through the branches. The room looked empty. And the air was silent.

I shifted my weight and swung back toward the path. Leaning my head left of the bush, I verified that I was alone. I stayed still for a moment, waiting to hear or see something. But sensing I was safe, I finally stepped back onto the path and moved forward far enough to peek through the window again. No one was there. The side table and its basin were gone. The Bible was gone from the altar too. But the candles still burned. That was my proof this whole event had not been a mirage.

Instinct turned me on my heels and sent me swiftly back toward the château. I was relieved that the bend in the cliff put me quickly out of view of anyone who might still be at the chapel. Yet no one was ahead of me on the path back. How could they have vanished so completely?

11

PEOPLE DON'T JUST DISAPPEAR, and they couldn't have come out the door. I was watching."

"Then there has to be another way out of the chapel," reasoned Toby. "A hidden exit of some sort. Let's take a look."

"But what if they return and find us poking around?"

"So? We're two Americans out for a walk before dinner. We stopped in to see the chapel. Nothing unusual about that, is there?"

"Maybe not. But I'd hate to have Guillaume think I was spying on him."

"Don't worry, we have the perfect cover. We're tourists. We look at old buildings."

Despite my hesitations, I wanted to revisit the chapel, with Toby along for protection. "Are you thinking what I'm thinking?" I said. "That there might be an entrance leading from the chapel to that cave that's supposed to be hidden somewhere on the grounds?"

"That's exactly what I'm thinking," replied Toby.

There was no sign of activity as we approached the chapel, strolling as nonchalantly as we could. Inside, nothing had been touched, though the candles had burned down and were guttering. We scanned the enclosure carefully, from the left of the altar all the way around the room to its right. We ran our palms over the walls at shoulder level, searching for a gap or irregularity on the surfaces. Next we examined the stone floor, but it too was smooth and solid. We crouched down and passed our hands over the walls again, this time at knee level, with the same result. But what about the wall plaques and the offering boxes behind them? Maybe one of them concealed a spring or lever to operate a secret exit.

I shared my conjecture with Toby and voiced a fear. "It's one thing if they find us admiring the chapel architecture, but what if they return and catch us fooling around with the offering plaques?"

"All right," Toby offered, "I'll stand watch at the entrance while you look around."

"But what if they suddenly pop up from wherever it is they disappeared to?"

"We'll hear them coming, won't we? Look, you go ahead. I'll keep an eye out for them. Go on, we don't want to hang around here too long."

So I began, with Toby standing guard. Most of the plaques, as I remembered, bore messages of thanks or else pleas to cure illnesses. Some could be flipped open using thumb and forefinger. That revealed a space cut into the wall, into which notes or coins or small devotional objects could be placed. Gingerly, I began testing them. Behind one plaque was a sealed envelope addressed to the Holy Virgin; behind another, a small religious medal on a silver chain. Several of these little coffers sheltered withered flowers. But after opening a few, I grew uneasy with prying into the devotions of living people, as well as those long gone. These offerings were not meant for strangers' eyes.

I paused before the simple plaque that had caught my eye during my first visit to the chapel. It was different from the others in that it bore a general prayer rather than a request for a specific cure. "Deliver us from evil," it read, beside the inscribed date of 1944. I grasped the edges of the plaque and lifted up, but it budged only a fraction; it seemed stuck. I repeated the motion using both hands and the firmest grip I could muster, but still no success.

"Toby, could you help me, please?"

He walked over and quickly sized up the job. "Hold on," he said, reaching into his pants pocket for his Swiss Army knife, which he's never without. (He claims it was his best friend as a child and is now his best tool as an antiques man.) He tried using a dull-looking blade to pry at the sides of the plaque, loosening grit, and then he switched to a shorter one and applied the leverage of his body's weight. It worked. Toby reached in.

"There's something in here, all right," he grunted, groping around. "Feels like a book. Okay, I've got it."

With that, Toby withdrew a sooty hand holding a familiar-looking blue notebook covered in dust.

"It's Jenny Marie's!" I exclaimed. "The notebook I've been looking for—I knew it had to exist."

"Here, take it," said Toby, quickly restoring the plaque to its original position. "And let's get out of here before someone finds us."

Back in our room, I began scanning the notebook's pages and was immediately arrested by one passage with a drawing opposite it.

17 November 1938

Dinner last night for the professor, who talked again about his racial ideas. I know my brother will keep his head. But as for Pierre? Can't he see another war with Germany is coming? Does he think Hitler will stop with Austria? Or does he think making friends with these Nazis will protect us when they arrive on our doorstep? Next time it won't be archaeologists with polite manners but soldiers with guns and tanks.

Jenny Marie was sixty-eight when she wrote this. Her brother, Antoine, was sixty-three. Her nephew, Pierre, was in his late thirties.

Our professor seems to believe the Cro-Magnons were the fathers of the Nordic race and therefore the Germans, who are their descendants, invented painting and civilization. That's ridiculous! Nothing but Nazi propaganda. Maybe he knows about bones, this one, but about art he is as ignorant as a badger. Then like a badger, let him go dig in Germany. Our painted caves are the glory of France, and if the Cro-Magnons are the progenitors, they are the ancestors of all Europe, not just some imaginary race of Nordic geniuses. The professor flatters us and pretends to be gracious, but really he is arrogant and could be cruel, I think, like the others.

On the facing page was a sketch of a supercilious young man with wavy hair and steely eyes. It was a disturbingly familiar face. I had found a study for the repugnant portrait hanging in the dim corridor outside our room.

A summons to dinner prevented me from reading further. We changed clothes quickly, and I stuffed the notebook into a dresser drawer. Toby locked our room, and we headed downstairs, past the chilling portrait in the hall. What was a Nazi archaeologist (if that's what he was) doing at the château the year before the war broke out? I was impatient to get back to Jenny Marie's notebook to find out what had happened between her brother, Antoine, and his son, whether they had quarreled about the Nazis, and if so, what had been the outcome. I was also thinking of the old baron's reluctance to talk about the family's experiences during the war years. But people were waiting for us.

Everyone looked refreshed and happy. While I had been out in the heat walking and stalking, they had been napping, dipping in the pool, or enjoying a cool drink on the veranda. They stood around in the front hall, exchanging reports of their post-Félibrée relaxation and making plans for after supper. Marianne said the van would be at the front door at eight-fifteen. I didn't want to make a big show of not joining the group, so I remarked casually that Toby and I had decided to stay at the château for the evening.

Guillaume didn't like the sound of that. "You know," he said reprovingly, "the evening ball is the culmination of the Félibrée. You and your husband should go." He raised his chin in Toby's direction. His glance was frosty, and for a moment I wondered if we had been observed entering the chapel. I didn't think so but couldn't be sure.

"And I hear," added Dotty cheerily, "that many a romance has started on Félibrée night!"

Marianne was opening the dining-room doors when that comment was made. She looked up at Guillaume, who announced rather stiffly, "Yes, our parents met at a Félibrée dance. It is one of the most honorable ways for a couple to meet."

Marianne reinforced her brother's remark. "My father, as one of the barons of Périgord, claimed a dance with the queen of the Félibrée, and within a year, they were married, in Montignac." She took in a breath, and then welcomed us to the table.

The seating was informal this time (no place cards), but the Limoges china was there, just not so much of it. Marianne's father was accompanied in from the hallway by Madame Martin, who kept a hand near his elbow, watching to see that he made his way safely to his end of the table. He kept his upright posture and never swayed. In spite of the absence of place cards, we mostly found the same seats we'd had on the first night, except Roz put herself in Dotty's old place between Patrick and Toby, which left Dotty to take Roz's former chair. Dotty must have been pleased. From her new position, she was in chatting distance of Guillaume on her left, Toby opposite, and David on her right. She had given up on Patrick, and the baron was too old to draw her interest.

Of all the meals we had eaten at Cazelle, this was the simplest, as well it should have been, after our lunch at l'Esplanade. We started with small Perigordian salads at each place: tender greens, crisp chunks of duck bacon, and toasted walnuts. As we were finishing our salads, Madame Martin and Fernando entered, each bearing a round metal casserole. Madame Martin at the baron's end of the table and Fernando at

Marianne's held their casseroles out at waist level and raised the lids simultaneously, to reveal two perfect, puffy omelets.

"*Omelettes aux truffes et aux champignons,*" Marianne announced. "The truffles are from our own woods. The Paris mushrooms are the ordinary grocery-store type, but they make a nice bland backdrop for the truffles."

As Marianne rose to assist Madame Martin and Fernando in serving each guest a portion of omelet, I stole a glance at Guillaume. But Dotty had already engaged him. He looked a different man under the influence of Dotty's blandishments. His face was crinkled by an amused smile, as he leaned in to listen to her softer-than-usual voice. I couldn't distinguish her words, but I could hear the melodies of southern-fried flattery. Across from me, Patrick, Roz, and Toby had their heads down, giving the omelets a discreet sniff, while discussing whether truffles lived up to their hype. Patrick defended the truffle's reputation for unparalleled delicacy of taste and texture, while Roz and Toby looked skeptical. I waited for Marianne to be seated and to take the first bite. Then we all pitched in, hoping not to be disappointed. And we weren't.

When the talk of truffles had worn down, Patrick gave Marianne a high toast with his glass and congratulated her on another beautiful meal. The talk at the table turned to the Félibrée.

"I was wondering," began Roz. "At the covered market this morning, I saw the flags of the four baronies of Périgord, but Cazelle wasn't one of them. How is it that Cazelle has a baron if it is not one of the baronies?"

"There's a reason for that," Marianne replied, giving the last truffle on her plate a quick stab. With her eyes still cast down on her plate, she began what seemed a carefully worded statement.

"Things change over time, don't they?" She looked up and continued, with a bit of steel in her jaw. "At one time there were only four baronies in Périgord, and Beynac was ours. However, there was a falling-out among brothers, and our ancestor set up a rival barony to his older brother's. They quarreled about politics and religious matters," she added.

"Of course, ours was the rightful claim," asserted Guilluame.

"So we believe," said Marianne in a conciliatory tone. "Our ancestor set his château, more modest but more elegant, on this hill opposite the cliff of Beynac. The two châteaus face each other, but being on the same side of the river, the English could never tell whether we were rivals or fellows in arms, opposites or comrades, each with opposing claims."

"Claims to what, Marianne?" asked David.

"To the land, to our heritage," Guillaume responded.

"I don't follow you," said David, with unfeigned puzzlement.

"Are you talking about the religious divisions between the Church and the Cathars?" I asked. Guillaume ignored the question.

"Who are the Cathars?" asked Dotty.

"They were a sect in the Middle Ages who quarreled with the Catholic Church," I explained.

For the first time that evening, the old baron looked my way. "Our quarrel was nothing of the kind," he said, responding to my question. "It had to do with the title."

Now everyone looked puzzled. Marianne intervened. "The barony," she said, by way of clarification.

Guillaume harrumphed assent. "These are things perhaps too complicated to explain to those who weren't born here." He chewed for a moment, nodding in agreement with his own opinion. That put an end to further discussion, and a lull followed, punctuated by sounds of silverware scraping plates.

"Nora," said Marianne, in a gambit to change the subject, "why don't you tell us how your research is going."

"Very well," I replied, welcoming this opening. "You had the papers in such wonderful order. That's been very helpful. But I've been wondering about Jenny Marie's paintings. For example, just now coming from our room, I looked again at that interesting portrait hanging in the corridor. Can you tell me who the subject was?"

"I've been told he was a friend of my grandfather," she replied coolly.

Guillaume sat up straighter in his chair.

"I don't know his name," she added. "A family friend."

"I see. Do you know about when it was painted?"

"Before the war, I think. You can tell by the style of clothes."

"Yes, that's what I thought, too. Somehow, though, he doesn't look French. Was he from Périgord?"

"I don't think so."

"With that blond hair, he looks like he might even be German," I ventured, growing brazen. Toby raised an eyebrow, telegraphing me to ease off. Marianne shrugged, seemingly unconcerned. Not Guillaume, though. He riveted me with hostile eyes.

"In the period between the wars we had many visitors, not only from France but from all over Europe," explained Marianne. "It's possible he's German, but, as I said, I don't know who he was."

"That's too bad, because it's an interesting portrait. Not typical of her style, but very powerful in its own way."

"Do you think so? To be frank, I never liked it. He looks disagreeable to me."

"Do *you* happen to know anything about him?" This time, I directed my question to Guillaume.

"No," he replied firmly. Then he turned to his father. "When we had to identify it for the insurance records, we called it *Portrait of a Young Man*, didn't we, Papa?"

"I don't recall," replied the baron softly, turning back to his conversation with David.

My inner radar warned me I had gone far enough for the moment. Since dessert was about to be served, I simply smiled, in anticipation of the fruit platter that was making the rounds. I let the others pick up the conversation while I enjoyed my pear, laboring to eat it with knife and fork, French style. After coffee was served, I turned again to Marianne. Dotty was now bantering with Toby, and Guillaume was following their interchange with a bemused expression.

"Marianne," I said, lowering my voice so as not to override the others, "there's another matter I'm curious about, and that is the cause of Jenny Marie's death. According to the family Bible, it was in 1944, so I know the war was still on, but no one seems comfortable talking about it. Did she die as a result of the war, or was she ill, or what exactly happened to her?"

"She was ill. Cancer is what I've been told. But it's true nobody likes to talk about the war. Those years were painful. My father has stories. . . . But I don't like to ask him too many questions. It upsets him. As for Jenny Marie, yes, she was ill, and amid all the other unfortunate events of that time, the family lost her too."

"I see," I said. "I didn't mean to pry. Really, I'm extremely grateful for all your help. I'm sure I can write an informative article about Jenny Marie and her work, based on all I've learned here."

"I'm glad to hear that, Nora. It will be good to see her work appreciated."

Guillaume was looking my way again, with an expression of displeasure. He was no longer paying the slightest attention to Dotty, who was telling Toby an animated story.

You were pushing them with those remarks about the war," said Toby.

"Wasn't I, though? It's a subject that makes them uncomfortable. Maybe Jenny Marie can tell us why."

We were back in our room, leafing through the discovered notebook. It was different from the others in that it contained both diary entries and sketches, whereas earlier Jenny Marie had relegated her thoughts to the notebooks and had kept her drawings in separate sketchbooks. Here pages were given over to faces and figure drawings, as if she were trying to capture the people around her in rapid pen strokes while there was still time. In addition to the sketch of "the professor," there were portraits of family members, though none was identified by name. That is, I assumed they were family members, for they were drawn affectionately and with a sense of intimacy. I was pretty certain that one was of her brother, Antoine, since it occupied a full page opposite a diarylike entry devoted to him.

12 December 1938

In the coming troubles, Antoine can be counted on. I know he will remain faithful to his principles, even if so many others are weak and hypocritical, concerned only with their self-interest. Antoine was never like that. I can depend on him. As for the others, we shall see.

If indeed he was the subject of this drawing, Antoine was a handsome man with a lined face, a large rueful mouth, and a shock of white hair. I thought I could trace a resemblance to the current baron, Antoine's grandson, who was now more than a decade older than Antoine had been when Jenny Marie sketched him.

Antoine's son, Pierre, looked very little like his father, judging from another sketch accompanying an entry about their growing estrangement. Pierre would have been about forty at the time. The man in this drawing looked that age but had a rounder face than Antoine's, a less aquiline nose, suspicious eyes, and a pursed mouth with bow lips. His features may have resembled his mother's. I rechecked the family chronology and was correct in my recollection that Antoine's wife had died in childbirth in 1900.

Pierre, wrote Jenny Marie, was becoming a constant worry to his father—and to her.

15 December 1938

How intolerant Pierre has become. He talks only of order, order, order, and says scandalous things about the Jews. Bitter arguments divide us. Antoine accuses Pierre of abandoning "Liberty, Equality, and Fraternity" for Fascism, Racism, and the Fatherland. Pierre retorts that the Revolution has taken France down the path of anarchy and degeneration. To his father he says, you are blind to the true enemies of France, namely the Jews, the Communists, and the Freemasons. My God, what has become of my nephew?

"Freemasons?" asked Toby, with a quizzical expression. "What were they doing on the list?"

"Beats me," I replied, "I thought they were some quaint eighteenth-century club with secret handshakes, but obviously they were an issue in the thirties."

"And not the Germans?"

Not for Pierre.

8 February 1939

And now my nephew has struck up a friendship with this German professor who comes to the Dordogne and into our home to spread his fantasies about the cave art of the Cro-Magnons. Why is he here almost every day? What does he expect from us? He takes an interest in our patrimony, so he says. I know he makes drawings and sends them back to Germany, but he has no talent for depiction. Neither does his friend Gounot. I won't help them, though. I want nothing to do with them.

Gounot. Would that have been Marc's father, the one who was denounced after the war as a collaborator?

"Has to be," said Toby. "Remember that according to Daglan, he got involved with an archaeologist Himmler sent to visit the caves around here to prove Hitler's theory about racial superiority. It couldn't be anyone else."

Then it was true Marc's father had been working with a German on some archaeological project in the Dordogne that was of interest to the Nazis. But why were they working here at the château? Unless there was prehistoric art on the grounds or, rather, under the ground, there was no reason for them to be focused on Cazelle.

"This provides a link between Marc and the Cazelle family," observed Toby.

"But that doesn't give him a motive for murdering the man from the Bureau of Antiquities."

"It might. We need to learn what's in the Cazelles' cave."

"Marianne swears the cave is of no importance. Do you still think she's lying?"

"Why wouldn't she lie, if there really is a hidden trove of art? That's something the family would want to protect and keep secret from the government. And Malbert was trying to inspect the cave."

"Yes, but how does Marc come into the picture?"

"We know Malbert exposed his father's wartime past. But what if there's another part of the story that still hasn't come out, some secret involving an archaeological discovery at Cazelle? Maybe Marc feared Malbert would uncover that secret. That would explain why Marc might try to silence Malbert now rather than at any other time in the past when he could have found an opportunity."

Yes, that made sense. And there was something else in this journal entry that leaped out at me. Drawings, wrote Jenny Marie. The young professor was making drawings to send back to Germany. Of what? Prehistoric frescoes? If none existed, what else was he after? There was that rumor about paintings that had been stored at the château during the war to keep them out of Nazi hands. Could the professor have been making an inventory? But surely Jenny Marie would have known about that secret had she been asked to participate or to copy paintings, and no reference to anything of the kind appeared in the notebook.

Instead, what the notebook recorded was a moving, ground-level account of life in southwest France during the war years. I read with foreboding that as hostilities with Germany neared, Jenny Marie grew increasingly estranged from her nephew.

3 May 1939

Pierre spouts slogans from the Parti populaire français, with their fascist salutes and disgusting talk of welcoming the Germans if they invade. To purify the nation, he tells Antoine. Such rot. What's galling him is the flood of refugees from the Spanish Civil War who have settled in the Dordogne in the past few months. It's easy enough to talk of expelling immigrants, but where will the French go when the Nazis invite themselves in, unless we make them at home and lick their boots?

And when war finally broke out and France capitulated in the summer of 1940, it was no surprise to Jenny Marie that Pierre embraced the collaborationist government set up in Vichy under Marshal Pétain. Antoine was despondent after the armistice was signed. Jenny Marie made plain her views about Pétain.

2 February 1941

They have pasted propaganda posters glorifying Pétain on every available wall. This is the so-called Art Maréchal. It is a disgrace both to art and to France.

Nor was she solaced by living in the phony free zone, unoccupied by German troops but managed by Vichy on behalf of their Nazi masters. "What we do ourselves is more humiliating than what is done to us by our conquerors, because it is we who do it," she wrote in August 1942. The occasion was the roundup and deportation of Jews in the Southwest, abetted by French officials.

They say the children were screaming as they were taken from their parents. Where is France? Where is the Church? At least there is the Archbishop of Toulouse. He condemns the arrests, but otherwise the Church is silent. Soon it will be as bad in the Dordogne as in the North.

Jenny Marie was prescient. By 1943, Hitler saw no reason to prolong the sham of a free zone in the South and ordered the total occupation of France.

15 January 1943

The Gestapo has arrived in the Dordogne. Now the enemy wears German uniforms, and they are no longer disguised as our neighbors. Not that our complete capitulation has done anything to heal the rifts between us. The Resistance is growing stronger, but the right has organized the Milice, who are no better than the Nazi SS and help them do their dirty work. Neighbors go on killing one another. The ones who join the Milice are the worst of the worst. Even Pierre has his doubts about them. He thinks Pétain does not approve and that his monster of a deputy, Laval, is responsible for this group of thugs, but who knows for sure? There is just one piece of good news. Pierre has prevented Charles from signing up with them. Can you believe it, Antoine told me, Charles wanted to join the Milice but Pierre said no. It's the first prudent step he's taken since the war began.

So Pierre's son, Charles—the current baron—had toyed with the idea of joining the Milice! Charles was then nineteen. He had entered the French army in 1939 but had been released and sent home after the 1940 armistice. I had no trouble picturing the baron as a young man recently demobilized, panting for membership in a right-wing terrorist organization. That his father had doubts about the Milice was provident, for as the war ground to an end, the Resistance exacted heavy reprisals on its members. Charles had survived the war, but he might not have survived the peace. No wonder he was hesitant to talk about those years, except in the vaguest terms.

As we came to the end of the journal, what surprised and moved me the most was Jenny Marie's account of the circumstances of her brother's death. Cross-checking her final journal entries with the volume on the Resistance that Toby had picked up, we were able to piece together the following events.

During the first two years of the occupation there had been very few efforts on the part of the local population to try to help French Jews. But after the roundups of August 1942, cracks began to appear in the wall of public indifference. There were some who tried to hide Jewish families and, if possible, to spirit them out of the country. In the Southwest, the most effective of these networks was the OSE, Œuvre de secours aux enfants, or Children's Relief Organization. Routes were established to smuggle Jewish children over the Pyrenees into neutral Spain, and from there to safe harbors elsewhere. Word spread throughout France that a path of escape led through the Dordogne, and news of it brought a plea to Jenny Marie from her old friend Aimée Laurance.

She hadn't heard from Aimée for many years. Unlike Jenny, Aimée had given up her career for marriage and had raised a family. She was a widow now. Her daughter had married a Jewish pharmacist, and there was a grandson. Now she wrote to her former comrade, desperate for help.

17 April 1944

Today received a heartbreaking letter from my dear old friend, Aimée, reminding me of our days at the academy. So long ago, such happy days. And such a pitiful letter from one who has nowhere else to turn. Her grandson, Arnaud, a boy of seven, is classified as a Jew according to the Vichy racial laws. Deportations in the North are speeding up. It is no longer safe in Rouen. Aimée begs me to shelter the boy at the château until arrangements can be made with the OSE for his rescue. Her son-in-law has already been deported, and she fears the boy will be taken next. Will I do it? Will I? Yes, Aimée, send Arnaud to me, not just for the sake of our friendship, but for the sake of humanity. France has lost its reason, not only the war. Send him to me, Aimée, and God help all of us.

The boy came in May. He arrived at twilight in the back of a truck, hidden in one of several sacks of potatoes. Antoine, old as he was, carried the sack inside himself.

3 May 1944

He is safe now in our attic, and Antoine has gone to find our contact in the underground to make arrangements for the transfer. A beautiful boy, with big, wide eyes and soft brown hair. I can see a bit of Aimée in his features. Trembling like a rabbit, but considering the situation, very brave for his age. Quiet, intense. He seems to understand exactly what we must do, so we needn't speak very much. I have written to Aimée using the phrases we agreed on to let her know he's arrived. No one besides Antoine knows he is here. Just now I brought him milk and bread with cheese, which he gobbled up, and then I covered him with a light blanket. He is sleeping now. It may be days or even weeks before he can be moved, but meanwhile he is snug above my head.

But events forced a move more precipitously than Jenny Marie and Antoine anticipated.

5 May 1944

For two days all has been well, until this morning, when Charles, growing suspicious of my trips to the attic, discovered Arnaud in his hiding place. He said not a word to me but informed his father, and Pierre ran up the stairs and flew into a rage. He went on and on. We must turn this boy over to the authorities. If not, we'll be ruined. We'll lose the château. We'll be arrested. I'm sorry for the boy, but we have no choice. Antoine refused. There were words exchanged that should never pass between family members. I was beside myself with emotion. I said, if you denounce this child, I will never speak to you again. Never.

Jenny Marie was shaking with anger when she wrote this line. I could tell, because her pen wavered. She must have been trembling with outrage when she spoke it, too.

In the end we arrived at a bargain. Pierre will keep silent but only if we send Arnaud back to his mother immediately. To make peace, I agreed, and we began packing the little boy's things. But after Pierre left, Antoine took me aside to confide his fears. He is worried about Charles. We must move tonight, he thinks, without waiting another day. And so Antoine has sent word to our contact in St. Cyprien to arrange the rendezvous this very night. After curfew, he will bundle the boy in the trunk of the car and set out for the meeting. Yes, it is dangerous, very dangerous, but what else is there to be done?

6 May 1944

The worst has happened, a catastrophe. At dawn the police found Antoine's car by the side of a ravine and summoned Pierre to identify it. They had traced the license plates. Doors riddled with bullets, tires spattered with mud, bloodstains on the front seat. It looks very bad, said Pierre, but the family knows nothing about it. Yes, it's our car, but it went missing a few days ago. We know nothing about this at all. That's our story, he said to me later, better stick to it. Oh, Antoine, my dear brother, what happened last night? Was it the Gestapo? The Milice? Did you make the rendezvous before they caught you? Is the boy safely away?

There was no further news of either Antoine or Arnaud. There never was.

"Do you think our friend the baron betrayed Antoine to the Milice?" asked Toby.

"Betrayed his own grandfather? I hope not. Jenny Marie didn't think so, or she would have written about it."

But whatever she may have thought after that night, Jenny Marie said no more. Following the narration of these events, there was a melancholy sketch of the face of a young boy, but no other entry in the notebook for a full three months. Then, in September, she wrote: "*Je vais mourir.*" A doctor had come and delivered grave news about her lungs. The outcome was inevitable, the doctor said. "I am going to die, and perhaps that is just as well."

I wondered whether Jenny Marie, ill and with no end of the war in sight, had placed this last notebook behind the offering plaque in the chapel—she who had never been religious. The last page of the notebook was undated and filled with sketches of tiny crosses, quite distinctive ones, with the stem and crosspiece of similar thickness so the form looks almost round. I recognized the pattern from the family's Limoges china. Scrawled across the drawings, as if to cancel them out, in capital letters from the lower left hand corner of the page to the upper right, was the prayer repeated on the offering plaque: "Deliver us from Evil." *DÉLIVRE-NOUS DU MAL.*

12

IN THE HOURS BEFORE DAWN, I brooded over Jenny Marie's sufferings, the fate of her friend's grandson, and the unselfish death of Antoine. I wondered if the family had ever acknowledged his sacrifice. I wondered how he was remembered by his grandson, Charles, who was now the old baron. I wondered what other secrets about this family had yet to be revealed.

I also worried about the coming day. In the afternoon, our group was scheduled to visit the cave of Rouffignac, but I was reluctant to go. Although not as famous as Lascaux, Rouffignac is known for its prehistoric paintings, and the trip into its interior by electric train makes it a popular attraction. Back in California, when we first read Marianne's program brochure, I'd checked that box on the itinerary as a plus. I thought it would be fun to compare Rouffignac to Lascaux and exciting to ride the train. But that was then. By now I had no further need of underground excitement. Finally, I gave up on further sleep, got dressed in the dark, and sat for what seemed a long time, until my glow-in-the-dark alarm clock said six o'clock. Then I thought it was decent to go to the kitchen and cadge one of those emergency coffees from Madame Martin.

This time she wasn't surprised to see me and in fact gave a welcome. "Ah, Madame Nora! You and I are the only ones in the house who enjoy being up before light. I'll be glad to have your company. Will you join me in a café au lait?"

That was just what I wanted. "Yes, with pleasure. But then you'll have to let me repay the favor by helping you prepare breakfast."

"No, no, no!" she protested. "There's hardly any preparation this morning. We're serving on the terrace, just a bare continental breakfast. If I'd been cooking something interesting, I'd be happy to let you help me. In fact, why don't we do that tomorrow morning? Get up early, and I'll show you how I make baked eggs. I do it my mother's way, without a water bath. We call that *oeufs sur le plat.*"

"I'd like that very much, thank you." I let her serve me a wonderful bowl full of milk-laced coffee, and we chatted about her life in the kitchen when her mother was its queen. I couldn't resist an opening to ask her something I'd been wondering about.

"Madame Martin, do you remember Jenny Marie's brother, Antoine, at all?"

"Only vaguely; I was so little then. But *Maman* thought very highly of him. He was brave, she said."

"I've been reading Jenny Marie's notebooks in the library, and she mentioned it was Antoine who invited her back to the château after the man she loved was killed in the Great War."

"Yes, that's right. Antoine had been a widower for a long time, and he was lonely. By then, his father, who disapproved of Jenny Marie's life in Paris, had also died. With the baron gone, Antoine had the right to invite Jenny Marie back, and they had always been close. I'm sure it was a comfort to him to have her with him again at Cazelle."

"She speaks lovingly of her brother in the notebooks."

"They were a devoted pair. The time between the wars was a good time for this house."

"But then war came again."

Madame Martin winced. "Those were terrible years."

"I'm sure they were. I have another question, though. It's about the year Jenny Marie died. Out at the chapel, there's a little plaque that was put up in 1944, and it reads 'Deliver us from evil.' I've been wondering whether it was Jenny Marie herself who put up that plaque."

"Oh, no." Madame Martin shook her head. "It was my mother who installed that offering plaque, in Jenny Marie's memory."

"Do you know why she chose those particular words?"

"Well, yes, because, according to *Maman*, those were Jenny Marie's last words." She paused, as if thinking of something for the first time. "I suppose *Maman* must have been surprised that Jenny Marie would repeat the Lord's Prayer at the end. Jenny Marie was never religious, you know."

"Your mother never wrote any of this down, did she? I'm asking because I'd like to use some of this information in my article."

"My mother was a simple cook. She never wrote anything but recipes, grocery lists, and letters when our men went to war."

"Then I'd need to attribute the information you just gave me to my conversation with you."

This suggestion changed Madame Martin entirely. She stood, looked uncomfortable, and turned away, saying indistinctly, "I can't say. The family might not like it. You don't really need to write all this down, do you? I just thought we were talking entre nous. I should have remembered you are here to uncover stories about the family."

"That's not my purpose, Madame Martin. I only want to understand Jenny Marie."

"You have your work to do, and I have mine. Excuse me while I get the breakfast ready. I need to work alone now, if you don't mind."

She had spoken to me so freely up until this point that I regretted her change of tone and felt a twinge of guilt that I had been its cause. But now I knew who had discovered Jenny Marie's notebook after her death and who had placed it behind the offering plaque in the chapel.

When Toby and I arrived on the terrace an hour and a half later, the ambiance was elegant, with white linen cloths on little round tables placed just in front of the rose garden. The breakfast tables were set for three, a clever way to mix up the group. David and Lily were already seated with Patrick. Roz and Dotty arrived with us. We hesitated a moment, and Marianne, acting as hostess at the French doors to the terrace, directed us where to sit. I was sent to start a table with Roz. Toby and Dotty were told to join Guillaume, who was seated at the farthest table, poring over a copy of *Le Figaro*.

I was still disturbed about the tense end to my conversation with Madame Martin and so was grateful to be seated with Roz. I'd always found her good company. It would be soothing to have a quiet breakfast with her on the terrace.

Each place was set with an empty coffee cup, a small glass of apple juice, and a lunch plate filled with four square toasts, a pat of butter, and three strawberries. Shallow bowls were brimming with jams in three colors: red, orange, and brown. Marianne came to our table and clinked her glass for silence.

"The breakfast is a bit Spartan today, because our class is going to follow immediately, and we're preparing brunch. But it might interest you to know those dry toasts on your plate are the commonest breakfast food in France. We call them *biscottes*. The British call them rusks. And you Americans call them melba toast. Your coffee is coming round. After breakfast, please join me in the dining room. We need to start promptly, so we can have a good class and you can get to your afternoon outing on time. Your appointment at Rouffignac is at two o'clock."

"Won't you be coming, too?" asked Dotty.

"I have marketing to do for tomorrow," Marianne explained. She reached into her apron pocket. "We already have your tickets." She handed them around. "I'll meet you there when the tour is over to take you to the old walnut mill in St. Nathalène, where they'll show us how the walnut oil is pressed. Now, please, don't wait for me: enjoy your breakfast." She signaled us to dig in.

Roz and I sampled all three jam bowls, discovering that the brown stuff was sweetened walnut paste, the red glob was currant jelly (too sour for me), and what looked like orange marmalade was apricot jam with lemon zest. The toasts were pretty tasteless, but the jams filled the lack.

When Marianne finished helping Fernando supply us all with coffee and hot milk, she sat down at our table. We hadn't said a word to Fernando since Toby had apologized for the incident at the dovecote, and that seemed all right with him.

I felt uneasy facing Marianne, since I knew I had an issue about whether to use family secrets in my article. The chat with Madame Martin had just turned the knife in a wound that was already there. Over the last few days, I'd learned a number of things about the Cazelle family that Marianne and Guillaume might not want publicized. I was going to have to decide whether to regard that information as fair game. If I thought I needed permissions beyond those Marianne had implicitly given, we would need to have a serious talk, and that prospect made me nervous. Now, though, to my relief, Marianne smiled in greeting, looking happier than I'd left her yesterday. She was her best self, and most content, when she was talking about food.

We complimented her on the jams, found out her source for the walnut spread (better than she was able to make at home, she said), and agreed that yesterday's outing to the Félibrée was a success. "I hope," said Roz to Marianne, in a lowered voice, "that the little tiff Dotty and I had didn't spoil the outing for the rest of you. I didn't expect Dotty to get so miffed." Apparently Toby and I had missed a family drama.

"Not in the least," said Marianne. "Don't you think my brother and I have a quarrel every now and then? Tensions are a part of family life— that's all there is to it."

"Yes, well. It's not my habit to air tensions in public. I always told our boys they could quarrel all they wanted within the walls of our house, but outside there were to be no fights. I'm not a very good illustration of my own rule."

"You were only trying to get Dotty to rejoin the group. I was grateful, in fact. Fernando had been waiting a long time for us, and I knew he had to be up early to take his wife to work. Speaking of which, I should go help him now."

"You're very gracious, Marianne. I'll take it my apology is accepted."

Marianne took her leave, and that left me wondering whether to ask

Roz about the tiff or let it go. Lately my questions had been ruffling feathers. So I kept silent.

Roz turned to me with a rueful grin. "I'm not the best sister-in-law," she confessed.

"I'm sure that's not true. Anybody'd be lucky to have you as family."

"I don't know about that. I've been thinking about what it means to be a good in-law. For one thing, it involves accepting that when a newcomer to the family has different habits, or different opinions, or different values, they aren't necessarily wrong. They're just different. I know that's easy enough to say, but it's hard to live by. It's not natural for family members to see an outsider who really *is* different as truly acceptable, never mind lovable." She sighed, as if tired of her struggle with the problem.

"That's always the case, Roz," I offered, trying to be comforting. "Anyone can see how different you and Dotty are. It's just that you're a—well, a Renoir earth mother—and she's a Toulouse-Lautrec Follies girl."

Roz laughed, sputtering her coffee. "Well, I guess you can be smart-mouthed when you want to be! As a matter of fact, the tiff we had *was* about Dotty's dancing."

"Oh?"

"Yes, she danced the night away at Domme, which was of course what we were there for. But the problem was Dotty took it to heart that a girl might find her future husband at a Félibrée ball."

"Yes, she mentioned that yesterday."

"Nora, I can't tell you how mortified I was. She found Marc Gounot early in the evening, and after dancing a few with him, she got him to be her personal dating service. She had him going up to perfect strangers and asking if they were married and would they like to dance with a lovely American widow. It was just shameless. But Dotty wasn't the least bit shy about it, and Marc seemed to find it a big joke. I think they'd both had more than their share of wine punch."

"Did you know he's seeing someone? A woman from Castelnaud who works in the library."

"Really?"

"That's right. We saw the two of them together at the Castelnaud beach. Did you happen to notice if he was with her at the dance?"

"I wouldn't know who she was, but now that you mention it, there was a young woman there who seemed to have a claim on him. She wasn't best pleased about the time he spent with Dotty. And that just added to my embarrassment."

"Maybe nobody noticed but you, Roz."

"I only wish. I did keep telling myself it was none of my business how she carried on, and I kept my mouth shut. But when she wouldn't listen to Marianne's call for us to leave, I just couldn't help myself, and I made a few sharp comments as she was dancing by. At first she pretended not to hear. But then, when she and her dance partner came back to where I was standing, she said some nasty things to me. Marianne heard, I'm sure."

"That's too bad. I wouldn't expect Dotty to get mean."

"Oh, yes, Dotty is lots of fun, till she gets crossed. And I suppose that disagreement I told you about, over the center and my brother's will, has her feeling crossed—by me."

"I can imagine. She must realize it makes her look selfish not to honor her husband's wishes, and she resents you for wanting the money. But she resents you even more for making her look bad for withholding it. So she's touchy if you try to tell her what to do."

"That's about right. I try to avoid bossing her around, but she just keeps doing the most childish things."

"Roz, you know what I think you need? A little time away from your sister-in-law. Why don't you stick with me today, and we'll let others deal with Dotty." We shook on it, and Roz's face relaxed. With that, we were off to cooking class.

Marianne had decided to pair us again, so Roz and I went into our own little corner, playing with flour and eggs and powdered sugar. The subject of the class was *gaufres*, the wafer-light confections that Lily and I had loved at Domme. But we learned the *gaufres* in our area were an exception to the rule. Everywhere else in France, they are made thick, like waffles. In Périgord they are made thin and crisp, like cookies, and draped over a rolling pin, to curl them.

Marianne made a batch of the classic batter, with just vanilla for flavoring, and told us her secret, which was to use yeast granules, not baking powder, as leavening. Then she gave each pair of us a way to distinguish our batch. Roz and I were shown how to make the version from Domme. The others, making flat, square waffles, made theirs unique by adding tasty ingredients: coconut shavings in David and Lily's, cinnamon and cloves in Patrick and Dotty's. Marianne joined Toby to lace a batch with lemon zest and vodka (they call it "eau de vie" in France). When dozens of *gaufres* were piled on platters, we sat at the long kitchen table, served ourselves liberally, and treated our *gaufres* to the finishing touches. As Marianne explained, it's customary to serve them with a choice of confectioners' sugar, jam, or raspberry sauce. All options were on the table (literally). With all this sweetness, everyone's mood soared. There was laughter and silliness, including some combative blowing of confectioners' sugar between Dotty and Toby.

As we left the room, I was happy to see Dotty giving Roz a mischievous smile. She'd just had a very good time, so she could feel benevolent toward her stick-in-the-mud sister-in-law.

With this family spat momentarily at rest, my mind drifted back to the more serious family drama recounted in Jenny Marie's hidden notebook. On the way to our room, Toby and I stopped again in the corridor in front of the portrait of the Nazi archaeologist. (That's how I now thought of him, and with that identity tag, he looked even more menacing than before. Had Jenny Marie captured a gleam of fanaticism in his eyes, or was that just my imagination?) I was considering how to treat the information Toby and I had discovered. While I had an obligation to my hosts, I also had an obligation to the truth. Would I be able to tell Jenny Marie's story without offending her family?

Back in our room, we had time for a short rest before the afternoon's excursion to Rouffignac. Almost as soon as I stretched out on the crisply made bed, I dropped off to sleep, with Toby by my side. A half-hour later, he ear-nibbled me awake.

"Time to get ready to leave."

It felt as if I had slept for hours. "I don't want to go."

"You'll regret it if you stay behind," Toby assured me. "Who knows if we'll be back this way again?"

"But to go into another cave after what we've just gone through?" I frowned petulantly and rolled over to go back to sleep.

"They're waiting for us," said Toby, with another ear-nibble.

"I'm sleeping," I whined.

"It's one of the few painted caves left that are still open to the public," said Toby, poking me on the clavicle. "It's art."

I guess that did it (the art, not the poke), and after more half-hearted foot dragging, I agreed to go.

Lily, on the other hand, stayed home. As we waited for Fernando's van, David made her apologies to the group, which weren't necessary for Toby and me. We understood all too well why she would blanch at the idea of entering another cave. At one-fifteen, Fernando pulled up with unnecessary speed, scattering pebbles and punishing the brakes. Today he had one of his sullen looks. No one greeted him as we climbed in and took our seats.

"This should be fun," Dotty said to Patrick. "And look here." She turned to Roz and me. "I picked up these cute berets at the dance last night. There's one for each of us girls for the cave. They say it gets chilly in there. I have one for Lily too, but I'll save it for her. Go ahead, try them on." We did. I guessed this was Dotty's way of trying to smooth things over with Roz, so I played along. Toby said I looked chic. After posing a bit for fun, I took mine off and put it in my tote for later.

Traffic at this hour was light. We drove through St. Cyprien to the tiny village of Campagne, followed the bend in the Vézère River to Les Eyzies, passed below the town's dramatic cliffs, and headed to Rouffignac along a rural road.

David was reading from his guidebook. "Did you know," he

announced, "that Rouffignac was the site of one of the worst Nazi massacres during the war? The Germans burned the village to the ground in reprisal for a raid launched by the Resistance. March 1944. The only building left standing was the church. The whole town was rebuilt after the war, so there's not much to see in the town itself." We were solemn for a few moments as the van skirted the town.

"What does your book say about the cave?" Patrick asked David.

"Well, it says it's enormous. 'The galleries and chambers extend for more than eight kilometers,'" David read. "That would be, like, five miles. That's why they built a narrow-gauge track for an electric train to take visitors through it. It's too far to walk in the dark. Plus the train cuts down on dust and pollution."

"How far does the train go in?" asked Dotty.

"About four kilometers, it says here," replied David. "You see paintings and engravings of a variety of animals, mostly mammoths. They call it the Cave of a Hundred Mammoths."

"Neat," said Dotty, sounding like a little kid.

We came to an isolated farm, followed a sign directing us to the cave, and pulled up at the side of the road in front of a gaping entrance. Metal chairs were arranged so visitors could wait outside until the train was ready. A few steps inside led to a huge antechamber that had been developed to hold tour groups. A ticket booth, a souvenir stand, and a variety of educational displays were spaced throughout the chamber.

We wandered around, looking at the exhibits. Roz stayed outside, sitting on one of the metal chairs, sunning herself while waiting for our tour to depart. Fernando strolled around inside, looking at the displays. Normally he remained with the van while we were making our visits. It was odd seeing him mingle with us.

After about fifteen minutes, our tour group was called, and we filed through a metal security door leading into the cave. Immediately there was a temperature drop, but the air felt dry rather than damp. Dotty, Roz, and I donned our berets anyhow, more in the spirit of playfulness than for warmth. The mini electric train was waiting for us. It looked like a row of toy wagons, the sort that might take tourists around a fairground. The cars were open, with banquettes for seats and iron handrails in front of each row. When full to capacity, each car could seat perhaps a dozen people if everyone squeezed tight. However, as this was the first tour after lunch, the cave wasn't crowded. Toby and I had a bench to ourselves, and there were even a few empty rows here and there. Besides our cooking companions, the other passengers were French, and among them were excited children, abuzz with chatter.

The little train had four connected wagons with small platforms at each end for an engineer, who doubled as the tour leader. Our guide looked college-aged; he was probably a student earning summer money. "I should warn you that much of today's journey will be in the dark, to protect the paintings," he announced, swinging into his seat and putting the train into gear.

The wagons started rolling with a mild jolt, like a subway train pulling out of a station. That impression was reinforced by the low tunnellike ceiling of the passage we now entered and by the screeching of the wheels. The train's headlamp threw a cone of light ahead of us, but otherwise all was dark. As the little train picked up speed, the screeching grew louder, and the walls flickered in front of us in the headlight's gleam.

Our first stop must have been several hundred meters from the entrance. The guide switched on a low-intensity wall light to reveal four mammoths and two bison, but the drawings were indistinct. We continued on our way again, rattling in the dark, until we paused to examine a bear burrow, illuminated this time by the guide's flashlight. There were a number of these round hollows throughout the cave, he told us. The giant bears, which were three times larger than their modern equivalents, had dug their nests out of the cave's soft walls so they could hibernate.

After swerving gently to the right, we passed a cul-de-sac containing the drawings of two more mammoths and a rhinoceros. A short distance beyond was another mammoth, engraved on the wall by a Cro-Magnon artist who had used a pointed rock. The beast's eye was a natural bump on the wall that must have inspired the artist to draw the rest of the body, and it could be seen only by oblique light. The guide used his flashlight to make the point, and then we set out again. The train rocked and clattered deeper into the cavern.

Afterward, I was able to retrace the stages of our journey with the aid of a diagram of the cave. The train tracks in Rouffignac are laid out in the shape of a Y, with the bottom stem of the Y at the entrance. We were now about a half-mile from the entrance, where the tracks fork to the right and to the left, along the two upper branches of the Y. At the end of each branch is a gallery. When we reached the junction, we took the fork to the right, leading to a small gallery. But to visit the main gallery, which is at the end of the other branch of the Y, our train would have to reverse, back out again to clear the junction, and then take the branch to the left.

In the gallery at the end of the right branch we saw a frieze of seven mammoths. The images were all painted in outline, using manganese. (The animals of Rouffignac come only in black.) Now we were ready to reverse our tracks—quite literally. The guide hopped off his seat at the front end of the train and walked to the other end, got on again and set the train in reverse, using the rear engine.

As we backed up toward the junction, the bright beam from the headlight of an oncoming train suddenly lit up the tunnel, blinding us when we turned our heads to look. "Don't worry," said our guide, "we do this all the time. Just wait." By signal, the train coming toward us stopped to give us room to back up beyond the junction. We did so, and for a moment the two stopped trains stood facing each other on the same track, casting dueling headlight beams at their passengers. Our guide hopped down again from his perch, walked to the forward end of our train, retook his former seat, and steered us onto the left-hand fork, while opening the way for the oncoming train to fork to the right, along the track where we had just backed up.

As the two trains branched off in separate directions, I caught a glimpse of the second train's driver—it was Marc Gounot. With one hand on the throttle and the other waving at us, he was smiling broadly, as if he fully expected our trains to meet. Dotty saw him too, and waved excitedly. In the half-light, her smile looked conspiratorial. She must have told Marc about our group's visit to Rouffignac while they were dancing at Domme and learned he'd be working here today, since neither of them seemed surprised by the encounter.

"How about that?" said Toby in my ear. "What's he doing here?"

Our train screeched and jostled along in the dark again until it reached the terminus of the left branch of the track, where we found ourselves in a domed chamber, softly lit and wide enough for the track to loop around for the return ride. This was Rouffignac's most famous gallery, the hall of the Great Ceiling, covered with dozens of images of animals. The guide invited us to dismount and examine the ceiling more closely.

I strained to make out some of the outlines. Children were pointing out animals to their parents; it seemed easier for them to spot forms than it was for the adults. As I stared up intently, the images gradually resolved from a mass of lines into individual creatures. But the figures overlapped each other in a confusing way. Horned mountain goats were drawn right over mammoths, with no attempt to keep the animals distinct.

Dotty latched onto us when people in the group began moving around to get a better look.

"How old did he say these paintings were?" she asked.

"Oh, between sixteen and twenty thousand years old, I think," answered Toby. "They're not exactly sure."

"Really! How could they last that long?"

"Well," I volunteered, "there's no weather down here to erode the walls, and the cave was sealed off from the outside for most of that time."

Ignoring me, she kept talking to Toby. "Which is your favorite? I like that mammoth with the big curved tusks. And that little goat over there with horns."

"I think that's an ibex," said Toby.

"Is that some kind of goat?"

"It is," replied Toby. "I don't know if they're still around or extinct."

"They still have them in the Pyrenees," I offered. Could have kept it to myself.

"They're cute," said Dotty, addressing Toby. "The mammoths are extinct for sure, aren't they?"

"For sure," I observed dryly.

"What about that rhinoceros? I thought they only lived in Africa."

"Back then they lived in Europe too, until they died off," explained Toby patiently. "They had wooly coats and were different from the ones that live in Africa."

"Interesting," said Dotty.

Toby nodded. She fell silent for a moment. "It's mysterious, down here, isn't it? This is my favorite of everything I've seen so far on the trip."

With Dotty attached, we continued to amble around the chamber, heads craned up at the ceiling, until it was time for the return journey. On the ride in, Toby and I had occupied a bench in the last wagon on the train, and without giving it any thought, we headed to reclaim our seats. But Dotty beat me to it. Beaming girlishly, she squeezed in beside Toby in the next-to-last row. He shrugged, feigning helplessness, and so did I. She's hoping to make Marc jealous if our trains cross paths again, I thought.

The rows directly in front and in back of them were empty. I hadn't paid attention to where our other friends were sitting, but remembering my promise to keep Roz company, I looked for her beret. I couldn't locate her. By then the train was about to start, so I hopped onto the seat in front of Toby and Dotty. Later I tried to remember the person who had climbed onto the last bench in the car behind them just as our train pulled out. It was a man—at least I thought it was a man—wearing a cap with the brim pulled down, the lower part of his face wrapped in a scarf. He was dressed in that drab blue work outfit you see on farmers and store-keepers all over the country. I didn't recognize him, nor could I recall him being part of our group when the tour began.

As we returned through the darkened corridor, I could hear Dotty giggling about something with Toby in the row behind me. Meanwhile, the guide up front was recounting popular suppositions about the meanings of prehistoric art. None of it was new to me, so my mind began to wander. I was thinking how unlikely it was that any art at all survived from such a distant time.

The train's braking to a halt jolted me out of my reverie, as once again we approached the junction between branches. Our driver paused, waiting for Marc's train, which was now backing up out of the first gallery. I heard a sound I couldn't interpret in the row behind me, but I couldn't see anything in the dark. In another few moments, the beam from the other train lit up the junction. Then the two trains signaled one another by flashing their lights. Ours was given the right of way, and we continued onto the main stem leading back to the entrance. I turned to see if I could catch a glimpse of Marc as he backed through the junction, but all I could see was his train's brilliant light and the silhouettes of Dotty and Toby huddled shoulder to shoulder.

Now, that was too much! Just wait till I get you home, I thought. I fumed for the entire ride back and kept turning around. But a glare is wasted in the dark. In what little light there was, reflected from the headlight on the walls, Toby did look uncomfortable. He scrunched up, giving the hint to Dotty to back off, and when she leaned away from him, he moved as far as he could to his side of the bench. I gave him credit for that, but he shouldn't have been so accommodating in the first place. I told myself Toby had never made me jealous before, but then I remembered that blowsy nurse from Sonoma. Okay, that was before we were married, but, still, we were going out. And then there was that woman who came on to him at the art fair in Santa Rosa. And, of course, there was the time he forgot our anniversary and . . . Hold on, I thought, this is not the Nora I like. I made a conscious decision to cool off and to not look back again at the row behind me until the ride was over. For the most part I succeeded.

Afterward, I felt ashamed.

As we pulled up to the entrance at our starting point and the lights went on, I turned to make a wisecrack, but it died on my lips as soon as I saw the alarm on Toby's face. He was trying to rouse Dotty, whose head was lolling on her chest. She was slumped at her end of the bench. Her beret was in her lap, and a loop of thin wire, blood oozing out from around it, circled her neck. In the row in front of me, a child began to scream. The last row of the car was empty.

13

THERE WAS CHAOS at the entrance hall, compounded by the arrival of Marc's train, which disgorged its passengers as news of the murder spread. The cave swarmed with tourists protesting being detained or trying to use their cell phones to call home, while the head guide summoned the police. Some of the nervier tourists tried to leave, simply moving aside the metal chairs that the guides were setting up as a makeshift cordon. I saw several people being snatched back by one of the guides, and we all found ourselves trapped in the huge hall, exchanging accounts of what had happened. In the hubbub I spotted Marianne, who had just arrived, and I ran over to tell her the news. She immediately sought out Roz, to comfort her. I looked for Fernando but didn't see him. Marc was trying to calm a female passenger from his train who was distraught to the point of panic. The emotional temperature rose high enough to compensate for the cold of the cave entrance. Everyone was glad when the police arrived. Maybe they would restore order.

Soon Toby and I were riding in a police van, along with the French family from our train car, on our way to Périgueux for questioning. Jackie was the driver. The other members of our tour group were dispersed in additional vans filing behind us toward the gendarmerie.

Toby was beside himself. "I don't know what happened in there. I really don't!"

"You must have been aware something was wrong. Didn't you hear a struggle?"

"I'm not sure. I mean, going back over it, I should have realized what was happening, but in the dark and with the screeching of the tracks, I didn't."

"What *do* you remember?"

"Well, you saw how Dotty elbowed her way into the seat. I moved as far as I could away from her so that at least we weren't touching. She joked about hoping you weren't going to be jealous, and then the train started moving again and it was dark. I felt her squirming a little on the seat, adjusting her position. We picked up speed, and we were both holding on to the rail in front. Then, remember when we stopped at the junction to wait to see where the other train was? She shifted closer and I heard something, or maybe it was a movement—I don't know what. And then the train jolted, and I did what I could to get her to give me more space. You know, I hunched my shoulder, squeezed over to the side as far as I could—and she did lean away. After that, the train noise was so loud and it was so dark, that that's all I knew until we stopped and I saw her slumped over. I think she must have been strangled after we started up at the junction and she moved away from me. Whoever did it was sitting behind us. He must have jumped off while the train was still moving slowly, because when we got back to the entrance and I turned around, there was no one there."

"Did you get a look at whoever was behind you?"

"No, I never did. I remember the seat was empty when I got on, and then I heard someone get on behind us just as we were beginning to move, but I didn't turn around. I was preoccupied with Dotty. I can't even tell you if there was one person sitting behind us or two."

"One. I caught a glimpse of him but didn't pay much attention. Someone in a blue worker's smock and a cap, but I never saw his face. I was irked about Dotty and not thinking of who else was with us in the car."

"What about the others from our group?" asked Toby.

"They were sitting in the cars ahead of us. I know I looked for Roz, but I didn't see her. And another thing: I didn't notice anyone on the tour wearing a worker's smock when we started out. I think someone got on the train after we started out and then mingled with us in the gallery without getting noticed."

"Got on after we were moving?"

"Remember we stopped a couple of times on the way to the first gallery? Someone who knew the route could have waited in the dark and climbed aboard at one of the stops."

"Or here's another possibility. The killer could have been on board all along and changed into a disguise when we were in the second gallery."

"Someone would have seen him change, wouldn't they?"

"Not if he wandered out of the gallery a little way back up the track where it was pitch dark, changed, waited for the train to start pulling out, and then jumped back on at the last minute."

"But who would want to kill Dotty?"

"You don't get it, do you?" Toby locked eyes with me. He looked somber. "Someone was trying to kill *you*! Whoever it was mistook Dotty for you in the dark. He got on at the last minute as the train was leaving the second gallery, sat behind us—that is, sat behind me and Dotty thinking it was you and me—and attacked her just before we reached the junction."

I shuddered. I could see Toby was right. With both of us wearing the berets, somebody could have mistaken Dotty for me as she snuggled up against Toby. But that possibility raised the next question. Why me?

"Because the killer thought you were getting close to figuring out who murdered Malbert."

"But I don't know who killed Malbert."

"The killer thinks you do. Whoever killed Dotty is the same person who killed Malbert. The method is identical: strangulation using a loop of wire, the garrote. Silent but fatal. And you know what? I'm thinking it's Marc."

227

"Why Marc?"

"One, he's already the prime suspect for the murder in Lascaux; two, he shows up today in Rouffignac; and three, you may be getting close to uncovering information he doesn't want revealed."

"But look at the logistics. We just saw him driving the second train into the first gallery. Someone in his group would have noticed if their guide disappeared between driving in and driving them out, don't you think? And even if he could have gotten away from his group without being noticed, how could he have gone so quickly from the first gallery to the second gallery unless there's a passage between them?"

"Maybe there is. That's one thing that should be easy to find out."

"I suppose. But here's something else. Fernando was also in the cave today. At least, I saw him in the orientation hall, and at the time, I thought it was unusual to see him there. He always stays behind with the van when he takes us on excursions. Today he comes inside with us. Why?"

"I'll give you one reason. He could be working with Marc. Remember we saw them together the other day in Castelnaud? What if Marc uses Fernando to do his dirty work?" Toby paused, thinking for a moment and glancing out the window as trees blurred by. "Since we're talking about Fernando and what-ifs, what if he does his dirty work for the Cazelles?"

"You mean Guillaume?"

"Any of them. Last night at dinner you might have raised some hackles with your questions. Someone could have started worrying you were getting too close to the family secrets."

I remembered Guillaume's penetrating glance in my direction.

"If these two murders are connected," Toby was saying, "we can't forget about David, either. He was also listening to the conversation last night, and he was with us in Lascaux when Malbert was strangled. Two caves, two murders, present at both. By the way, did you notice where he was sitting when the train pulled out?"

I had no recollection of seeing David as we made ready to leave the second gallery. Toby and I rode on in silence for a few minutes, listening to the chattering of our fellow passengers in the van. Suddenly, a new thought entered my mind.

"Toby, what if we've been going at this the wrong way?"

He looked at me expectantly.

"What if the killer was after Dotty all along and knew it was Dotty and not me sitting with you?"

He raised his eyebrows, looking skeptical. "That's not very likely, if you ask me. There's no connection between Dotty and the Lascaux murder. And who would have a reason to kill Dotty?"

"About Lascaux, I agree. But I've been thinking about motive, and I don't like where it's leading."

"You don't mean Roz?"

"I don't want to mean Roz, but she does have a motive. Roz has been delaying the execution of her brother's will, arguing that a bequest he made orally should preempt the written will. She's determined to get that gift to the community center. With Dotty gone, the money will probably come through. Maybe all her brother's money, now that I think of it."

"And they had a quarrel at the dance last night, you told me. Was it about the will?"

"No, it was about Dotty throwing herself at men, namely Marc."

"Marc again. You don't suppose he had any reason to want Dotty dead?"

"No, that doesn't wash. But Roz has been having trouble containing her animosity against Dotty, and this might have been her opportunity to let it out."

"Nora, this wasn't a matter of letting out a little animosity. This was a calculated murder. And your friend Roz doesn't seem that cold-blooded. But, just for argument's sake, let's say she planned it. How would she have been able to carry it off? Besides, I thought you said it was a man who climbed aboard behind us."

"That's what I thought."

"But now you're saying it could have been a woman?"

"I'm just not sure."

"Think hard. Who else would have a motive for attacking Dotty?"

I thought about it. What if one of the men were sleeping with Dotty, and what if she wanted to let it be known? Would he have been desperate enough to kill her to keep the affair secret? Patrick? No, he was single and had nothing to lose if such an affair became public. Guillaume? He was a ladies' man, so why should he care if anyone learned of his conquest? David? Well, that was another matter. His young wife was pregnant and definitely concerned about some aspect of their relationship. If David had broken his marriage vows, he might well have wanted to preserve the secret. But would he have killed to do so?

"That brings us back to you," said Toby grimly. "It wasn't Dotty the killer was after."

At the Périgueux gendarmerie, we were ushered into a large room, where we waited our turns to be interrogated. Within minutes, the room was full, and new arrivals were shunted upstairs. Roz, Patrick, and David were among them. That left more than twenty of us in the downstairs waiting room—adults on the benches, teenagers standing, children on the floor. Toby was called first. Inspector Daglan himself led Toby down a narrow hallway. Shortly afterward, Jackie appeared at the hallway entrance.

"Follow me, please," Jackie piped in that strange fluty voice. He was pointing at the French couple who had been in our train car, and his gestures indicated that the whole family, two children included, should trail after him, down the same hallway that had swallowed Toby.

At intervals of roughly fifteen minutes, Jackie came in and out with his charges. I couldn't tell whether he was delivering them to another officer or interviewing them himself. He didn't return until they did, so either was possible. After two tedious hours, Jackie had thus dispatched everyone but me. And Toby had not returned.

"Madame Barnes, follow me if you please."

He led me down the corridor to an open door, which slammed behind me as I took a seat at the large wooden table that was the only furniture in the room.

Daglan looked exhausted. He nodded somberly. I acknowledged the nod.

"Strange, isn't it? Each time you and your husband visit one of our tourist attractions, we end up with a murder."

"But you can't think we had anything to do with this."

"I don't know what to think. So, from the beginning, please. Tell me what happened, as best you can." He sat back in his swivel chair, hands clasped behind his head, the very picture of patience tempered by a squint.

The inspector may have been up there in years, but his stamina was greater than mine. He held me for a good hour, going over and over the events at Rouffignac. When my answers became repetitious, he steered me in new directions by questioning me about the other suspects.

I welcomed the opportunity to unburden myself. I now knew more about Marc, Fernando, Guillaume, and Roz than I wanted to carry around with me. I told him about seeing Fernando and Marc together in Castelnaud, and I told him about Marc's relationship with the librarian who had provided his alibi for Lascaux. Daglan received it all with equanimity. He took notes only once, when I told him about the intended bequest by Roz's brother to his sister's charity and Dotty's reluctance to honor it. That made me feel so disloyal that I protested, arguing it was unfair to take that disclosure as an indictment of Roz.

"She hasn't been accused. No one has. I am merely trying to establish the facts."

"I've already told you everything I know."

"Yes? But what if there are certain facts you don't know?"

"What do you mean?"

"You keep talking about Madame Belnord. But I asked you once before how well you and your husband knew Madame Dexter. Let me ask that question in another way. Have you considered the possibility there might have been a relationship between your husband and Madame Dexter?"

Toby and Dotty? "That's nonsense. There wasn't any relationship! She was just another member of our group at the school."

"Would you have known of such a relationship, had there been one? Tell me, have there been times in the last few days when you were away from your husband and were unable to verify where he was?"

"Very few, Monsieur," I replied curtly. "We've been together the entire trip, except for a couple of early morning walks I took alone." That would hardly be the hour for a tryst with Dotty, especially with Madame Martin popping in and out of the rooms delivering breakfast and removing trays.

"Otherwise you were always together? That seems unlikely, even for an American couple."

I got the gibe. Frenchmen think American men are shackled to their wives. However, ignoring the quip, I had to admit, "Well, there were a few afternoons when I worked in the library and Toby went out antiquing."

That led Daglan to push for information as to Toby's whereabouts during those intervals. I countered that Toby's movements could be accounted for by Madame Martin, Patrick, Roz, and . . . I was going to say Dotty, but stopped.

"You see, Madame Barnes, your husband could have executed a murder, quietly, in the back of the train car, without any witnesses— except someone who only you claim was there, but who was seen by no one else."

"That's absurd. Toby had no reason to murder Dotty."

"As far as you know. But didn't you suggest to your husband that David Press might have murdered Madame Dexter to conceal from his wife that he and the murdered woman were lovers? Isn't it possible that if she had a lover, it was someone else?"

I was shocked at the suggested parallel and by the knowledge that Jackie must have overheard what I'd said to Toby in the van. So much for assuming the local police don't understand English. We'd been naive, but then, we had nothing to hide, no reason to suppress our natural urge to speculate about the murder. But we sure had one now, if Daglan suspected Toby. Of course, I didn't believe it for a minute.

"This line of questioning is a waste of time, Inspector. My husband was not having an affair with Dotty. And if he had been, he wouldn't have killed her to hide it." (Though I might have strangled her myself.)

"What if she had threatened your husband to expose their relationship?"

"He would take his chances." (And they'd be slim.)

The habitual squint gave way to raised eyebrows. "No man is that honest, in my experience. And no wife is that understanding."

I squirmed, recalling my petty jealousies on the train. But I wasn't about to let Daglan shake my faith in Toby, and he finally realized I wouldn't give ground.

"I see my questions have insulted you, Madame Barnes. You will appreciate that all possibilities must be explored, even those that are distasteful."

I did not reply.

"Or unlikely."

I sat there sullenly.

At last he said, "That will be all, for now. You and your husband may return to the château, but I must ask you to stay there until further notice."

"But we're supposed to leave for home on Wednesday morning."

To this Daglan made no reply except to steeple his hands and tilt back his head.

"You still have our passports," I said.

"And you will receive them when you are free to travel, Madame."

Now I felt that rush of anger that had overpowered David Press when his passport had been taken. I felt unjustly used. A week ago, I had thought David rash in reacting so hotly, but now I shared his outrage. There was nothing I could do.

The waiting room held Toby, along with the others from our party. They had been waiting for my interview to end, so we could all be driven back to the château. But where was Fernando? Detained, I was told, along with Marc. That meant they were active suspects, and Toby, after all, was not. Heading toward the police van, I brushed past Toby and said, "Watch out what you say in the van. Jackie understands English, and he reports what we say to Daglan."

"Really? Then it's lucky we don't have anything to hide."

"I know *I* don't." Sometimes my unconscious speaks for me.

"What?"

I jumped into the van and took the seat next to Roz. Toby, shaking his head in bewilderment, got in and sat in front of us alongside Patrick, while David climbed in back. As soon as I sat down, I was angry with myself for getting rattled so easily and for venting my stress on Toby. He didn't deserve it. No husband was ever more steadfast or more patient. With my Irish temper, I give the poor guy plenty of opportunities to snap back. But he's always calm and forgiving. I have a friend who had a bipolar period in college. She calls Toby my live-in lithium.

I put a hand on Toby's shoulder and leaned forward to whisper, "Sorry. I'll tell you about it later."

He turned around, still disconcerted, but he seemed reassured by my touch.

As the van pulled out, Roz started to cry. "I'm sorry I said those things about Dotty. She didn't deserve this," she sobbed. "She'd had such a hard life. And you'd never know it."

Was death gilding Roz's picture of her sister-in-law?

"That girl came from the most awful poverty. Never had an education," she went on. "We never accepted her. She was frozen out, from the first, and it wasn't until Tom got ill that I saw her true quality."

"Was she good to him?"

That sent Roz weeping again. When she'd calmed down and wiped away tears, she sighed and said, "She was the light of his life."

I could feel the case against Roz, slight as it was, collapsing in a heap on the van floor. Roz couldn't put on this kind of act; her grief was real. And it rang true, the way Roz judged Dotty by how she treated her brother, Tom. That's how I judge Eddie's wife. That's how most women view their sisters-in-law. Does she make my brother happy? If so, she's my friend.

I reached over to pat Roz's hand, but she took mine in hers and held it tight, for comfort.

Meanwhile, from the back, David entered the conversation. "It's just unimaginable." he said. "Toby, how could someone have murdered Dotty, when you were sitting right next to her?"

"That's what Inspector Daglan wanted to know. The only reason I'm in this van is because she was strangled from behind, so he finally had to concede I couldn't have done it. Otherwise, I'd still be at the police station. The garrote severed her vocal cords, so she couldn't cry out, and in the dark and with all that screeching, I had no idea what was happening."

It struck me that if Daglan had already arrived at this conclusion, he might have spared me those nasty suggestions of his. What did he have to gain by such insinuations? Did police the world over simply make up scenarios and throw mud at suspects until something stuck to the wall? I felt anger again welling up inside me.

Now that we were sharing our stories, David explained he and Patrick had been sitting together in the second car. "Where were you, Roz?" he asked. She drew back in her seat, releasing my hand, and stared at him with indignation.

"Hold on," Toby interjected, as a gentle rebuke, "the police don't think the murderer comes from our group. They've detained Marc and Fernando, not us. So let's make the same assumption."

"I wasn't implying anything different," said David. "But anyhow, which car were you sitting in?" he asked Roz.

"In the first car," she said sadly.

"Right," said David, somewhat abashed. To Toby he added, "I know they arrested Marc, but how can he be implicated? I thought he was driving the other train."

"He was," replied Toby, "and that would seem to put him out of the question, but it's awfully strange he was even there."

"Roz," I broke my silence, "do you know whether Dotty mentioned to Marc that we were coming to Rouffignac today?"

"I'm not sure. It would be just like Dotty to tell the whole world her business. She didn't have an ounce of reserve about her."

"So, she might have. But I don't know why I even ask. If Marc was driving the other train, he couldn't have been behind Dotty at the time of the murder."

In the silence that ensued, the others glanced our way from time to time. I imagined them thinking the obvious. The two people seated closest to Dotty were Toby and yours truly. That made for an awkward ride home.

Descending from the van at the steps of the château, I delivered Roz into the care of Marianne, who had pulled up behind us. She had been allowed to drive her own car to the station, and then she followed the police van that held us. I let the two of them head off toward Roz's room. Toby and David were standing a few steps away from the van, in which Jackie was seated, talking into a two-way radio. The two men exchanged a few words and then walked my way.

David said, "I have to speak with you both. There are things you need to know, and we can't talk here. Let me get Lily, and we can go out somewhere."

"Inspector Daglan told us to stay put," I protested.

"We can go out to dinner. We just can't pack up and leave town."

"Are you sure?"

"Nora, your life is in danger. You need to hear what I have to say."

I looked at Toby to sense his response. He looked wary. "Okay," he said. "But if you don't mind, we'll go in separate cars."

"Fine. I'll get Lily. Let's meet in half an hour at that little crêpe place in Beynac, the one on the left just after the patisserie. Do you know it?"

"Yes," said Toby.

"Good. It's time you found out what I'm doing here."

A pitcher of *cidre doux* sat on the table in front of us. Toby poured a round of the amber-colored cider, raised his mug, and took a swallow. "So, is it true or isn't it, what you've told us, that you're a lawyer and that you two are here on a sort of honeymoon?" With this last question, he included Lily in his glance. "If not, what's the story? Cheers, by the way."

David raised his mug but lowered it without drinking. "Yes, that part is true, but I'm afraid this hasn't been much of a honeymoon for Lily." He squeezed her hand, and she smiled gamely to acknowledge the implied apology. "I thought this trip could serve a double purpose, but now I realize that was my mistake."

"So neither of you is really here for the cooking school," I said, looking at Lily.

"You could tell, couldn't you? You're right, Nora. It's all about David's work, actually."

"Which is?" Toby inquired.

David replied, "Restitution of artwork that was stolen by the Nazis. It's the pro bono work I do for our firm. Have you ever heard of the Monuments Men?"

I had. "You mean the commission the Allies set up toward the end of the war, to locate looted cultural artifacts in Europe?"

"That's right. The MFAA, for Monuments, Fine Arts, and Archives. The soldiers who worked for the program were called Monuments Men. My father was one of them. He was studying architecture before the war and ended up being assigned to the commission. I've heard stories about their work all my life. I was brought up to believe that anything we can do to restore the family possessions of the victims of the Holocaust is a moral obligation, and that's what I still believe. Did you know nearly one-third of the art that was privately owned in France before the war ended up in the hands of the Nazis? That's right—a huge amount. A lot of it was returned after the war thanks to the efforts of my father's team, but thousands of works are still missing, not only major pieces taken from galleries and museums but paintings confiscated from private homes, family treasures that would have gone to the children and grandchildren of the victims but which are lost or have been resold or are still hidden or may be gathering dust in the basements of museums under false provenances. Well, I'm part of a volunteer group of lawyers in the United States who try to help families recover property confiscated during the war, especially paintings that might have some value."

"And you suspect the Cazelle family is still shielding art that was either looted or hidden during the war," said Toby, more as a statement than a question.

"That's what I'm here to find out. At the beginning of the war, Jewish families with connections—and even some Jewish-owned galleries— sent art down from the North to be hidden away from the Germans. A couple of well-known collections ended up in local castles. Some of those collections are still missing."

"Like the Bernheim-Jeune collection," I said.

"That's right. Recently my group came across an affidavit in connection with one of those cases that stated that the Château de Cazelle had been among the hiding places, along with others that were better known. It's not a certainty. There isn't any mention of Cazelle in my father's records, and there's no record of art that had been stored in the château being returned to original owners after the war. But there have been rumors of hidden art and family secrets, and that's what I'm here to investigate. Enrolling in the cooking school made a convenient cover. I've searched pretty much the entire château since we've been here, but so far I've come up empty-handed."

"David thinks the man who was murdered in Lascaux was trying to investigate the same rumors and that's why he was killed," said Lily.

"I do. Which is why you're in danger, Nora. Whoever killed Malbert is trying to kill you too, and for the same reason—to keep a secret. I don't understand why he thinks you've uncovered it, but I'm hoping you'll tell me. We need to pool our information to protect ourselves." David took a breath, held it a few seconds, and slowly exhaled. "So, please, you two, tell me what you've learned."

"All right," Toby began, "we've heard those rumors too about wartime art hidden in the château. We met an artist in Meyrals who thinks they're true. And we've been doing some snooping on our own. In fact, we were searching the attic the night you came up there and almost found us. We wondered if you had been following us."

"What? I had no idea anybody was up there. I heard a noise from downstairs and thought someone was on to me, so I left in a hurry. But I went back the next night and didn't find anything."

"Neither did we. If there are paintings hidden somewhere, they're not in the attic. But we have another lead. We've been told there's a cave somewhere on the castle grounds that could be a hiding place. In fact, Malbert was trying to gain access to that cave before he was killed."

David slammed his palm on the table. "I knew it! That's got to be it."

"Hold on a minute," I cautioned. "I'm not convinced you're on the right track."

David was taken aback. "Why do you say that?" He looked at Lily, then at me again.

I explained what I had learned about Jenny Marie Cazelle, including our discovery of the hidden notebook. If there had been paintings hidden in the château for safekeeping during the war, she would have mentioned them, I felt sure. She had risked her own safety and that of her brother to protect a Jewish child, so she certainly would have voiced misgivings about a scheme to appropriate victims' art. Besides, hadn't she collected works by some of her old friends from the academy for resale at provincial auctions? Perhaps that was how rumors about a cache of art gained currency. No, I said, the family may have secrets to protect, but they weren't necessarily about stolen paintings.

David looked crestfallen. Our food arrived, and we received it in silence. When the waitress left, I continued. The others listened as they ate.

"But something unusual did take place here during the war." I recounted Jenny Marie's references to the Nazi archaeologist who befriended her nephew and who made regular visits to the château to pursue his interests. "What he was studying I don't know, but he sent drawings back to Germany, and it seems they went directly to Himmler. My guess is they were sketches of prehistoric art, but I don't know any more than that."

David almost tipped over his mug in excitement. "Say that again? An archaeologist who was writing to Himmler?"

I repeated that I didn't know the subject of the sketches and reviewed everything I had gleaned about the mysterious German professor. I added that Jenny Marie had painted a portrait of him that now hung in the corridor near our room.

"That could be Anders Voellmer, one of Himmler's crackpot scholars in the Ahnenerbe."

"The what?" asked Toby.

"The Ahnenerbe. It was an organization Himmler created to trump up evidence to support the theory of a 'master race.' They had an institute, an offshoot of the SS, which drafted academics and packed them off to dig up traces of Germanic ancestors, whether real or mythical. Voellmer was a Paleolithic archaeologist in the excavations department. He headed an expedition to the Dordogne before the war to try to prove the Cro-Magnons were the forefathers of the Aryan race, based on some theory he had about spear points and racial superiority. I think he believed the Cro-Magnons evolved from the Neanderthals and that they populated Germany before they settled anywhere else. He also wrote a couple of articles about Cro-Magnon art and symbolism, which have been completely discredited, but Himmler loved the stuff."

"So, do you think he might have found something here that he thought helped prove his theory?" I asked.

"It's possible," said David. "Something that happened last night at dinner is just beginning to make sense. I noticed Guillaume glared at you when you mentioned the Cathars. I had no idea why, but now I think I do."

"Go on," said Toby.

"If Voellmer was the Nazi who was visiting the château, then there's another part of his story that might be significant. You see, Voellmer bought into the occult in a big way. So did Himmler. While Voellmer was here in the Dordogne, studying the Cro-Magnons, he also became obsessed with the Cathars. He thought they were the preservers of ancient truth and carriers of the spark of human genius through the Middle Ages. He even concocted a theory that the Cathars were keepers of the ancient symbols that had come down from the cave artists and which later fed into the legend of the Holy Grail the Germans gushed over. But according to Voellmer, the Church distorted the legend; it was the Cathars who preserved the ancient knowledge of the Aryan fore-fathers and who understood the true meaning of the symbols. Well, there you are. It was all hogwash, of course, but Himmler lapped it up. Voellmer died in the war, but he's still a cult figure in some circles."

Toby edged his chair closer to the table and leaned forward over his plate. "So whatever it is the family wants to protect may have something to do with the Cathars? Is that what you're saying?"

"I'm not sure, but I'd like to find out what's in that cave you mentioned."

"We think we know where the entrance is located," I said.

"Where?" David asked, with surprise in his voice.

I told him about the ceremony I had observed in the family chapel and how the men inside had disappeared, leading us to suspect a secret exit that must lead underground. Toby filled in the details of our search for the passageway, which, though unsuccessful, had yielded Jenny Marie's notebook.

"Let's try again," urged David. "That's where we'll find the answer."

"No!" Lily protested. "It's too dangerous! Two people are dead already. Don't you know when to stop?" I couldn't tell whether that last remark was meant for David or for Toby and me. In any case, David took it as a rebuke and began defending the righteousness of his project. Lily shook her head, looked away, and murmured, "There's a time to let go. You just can't see it."

She was right. David was not to be deterred. In the end, Toby agreed to go with him. And I wasn't about to stay behind.

14

THERE WERE A FEW LIGHTS ON upstairs in the château when we returned, but the downstairs was dark except for the entrance way and the central salon. Once we were upstairs, David escorted Lily to their room and then quietly knocked on our door. He was carrying a heavy-duty flashlight. Toby and I led him down the corridor to where the portrait of Anders Voellmer was hanging.

"So that's him, is it?" David whispered. "Looks nasty, and he *was* nasty." In the glare of David's flashlight, the portrait seemed even more sinister than it had before under the more subdued light of the *minuterie*. We tiptoed back into our room.

"Did he actually believe those myths about the Cathars, or do you think he was just sucking up to Himmler?" Toby asked.

"Who knows?" David said with a shrug. "You could ask that about all those academics who ended up working for the Third Reich. And which was worse, believing that crap or just pretending to in order to advance your career?"

"Good point," I acknowledged. "You said he was killed in the war. Do you know how it happened?"

"Voellmer was recalled to Berlin in the early part of '45 to finish his book on the precursors of the Aryans, but he never completed it. He was probably killed in the bombing of Berlin. We know he was in Berlin then, from Himmler's correspondence. I'm not aware of any sketches Voellmer sent from the Dordogne surviving in Himmler's papers, but when I get back to New York, I'll try to use my contacts to institute a search."

Right now it was more important to investigate the Cazelle cave. We agreed to remain in our rooms until midnight, turn out the lights, wait another half-hour, and then rendezvous at the old stables. At the appointed time, Toby and I crept silently down the stairs, out the front door, and across the whispering gravel to the meeting place, guided only by the dim moonlight. David was waiting for us.

"We'd better not use our flashlights in the yard," cautioned Toby, "but once we're on the cliff path, we'll go round a bend where the light won't be visible from the house."

I took the lead as we set out, since I'd done this walk several times. I kept David on my left to make sure he didn't veer too far toward the cliff's edge. Once we were around the bend, I took the big flashlight from him and used it to light the dangerous edge of the path. In the dark, the topiary figures loomed frighteningly, sometimes blocking, sometimes revealing what would otherwise have been a fairy-tale view of the opposite cliffs, which were lit up dramatically for the summer tourists. It was a starry night, but the view overhead blinked on and off as we walked under oak trees and then out in the open again. I was so nervous that I nearly forgot to breathe. I kept worrying about being followed.

When we reached the chapel, I kept the lead. I wasn't going to let a little fear keep me from completing my quest with dignity. The door was closed, but it opened with normal pressure on the latch. That would seem to say the family had no fear of prying eyes. Well, we were going to pry now. David already knew we had examined the walls and floor. We had agreed that the place to look was behind the small altar, the one space we had not explored.

I lifted the altar cloth and aimed the flashlight at the altar's base. The surface looked like marble, but a knock on its face said wood. I asked Toby and David to examine the right and left sides of the altar, to see if there might be a crawl space behind. There wasn't. But I thought I'd try the simplest solution.

"Guys, take the Virgin and the candles off the altar, would you?" When they did, I put David's flashlight down and gave a big push upward on the overhang of the altar. It budged.

"Now help me lift the altar up and then away from the wall." With a "one-two-three" heft, we had her up in the air and then back a few inches into the room. Another few tries, and there was a space big enough to walk into, and behind it was a hole in the wall as high as the altar. I went back to pick up the big flashlight, came round to where Toby and David were standing, and shone the beam into the opening. I saw a narrow corridor with walls of unpolished stone.

"I'm going in," I said. "What about you?"

They were coming too. We agreed Toby would follow me, and David would follow him. David would use Toby's little flashlight. We would keep close together.

The way in was difficult. We had to crouch to get through the opening, and once we were in the corridor we had to walk with bent knees. Sometimes the walls were so close together that it was hard to move. But we managed to travel this way for what seemed a long while, descending gradually, and then rounding a corner, only to find ourselves at a wall with a very low opening. To get through that opening, we had to drop to our hands and knees. David was so big that he had to get on his stomach and crawl through like an overgrown child.

What I saw on the other side made our toils worthwhile. As David's shoulders came through, I beamed the flashlight toward the ceiling, which glowed a moonlike white, as the light caught hundreds of stalactites hanging high above us. I rose to my feet, my mouth agape with wonder.

"Shine the light around the room," Toby whispered. I moved the beam downward, and then swept it around. We were in a spacious chamber, surrounded by delicate formations of every size and shape. The earthen floor was damp with moisture. The larger stalagmites twisted upward, a few of them joining stalactites hanging from the ceiling. Clusters of thin columns near the opposite wall formed a pattern of eerie beauty. Closer at hand, on an outcrop of stone that formed a natural platform, stood a brass candelabra that held six long tapers.

"Does anyone have a match?" David asked.

"I do," said Toby, fumbling in his pockets. He came up with a matchbook, struck a match, and lit the candles. A soft glow embraced the chamber as the tiny flames danced back and forth, casting intricate shadows. Carefully, we looked around. Aside from the candelabra, the chamber appeared empty. There were no traces of prehistoric drawings on the walls, no storage bins packed with paintings from the Nazi era, nothing out of the ordinary except for the natural rock formations.

"Is this it, do you think, or are there other sections?" David asked, disappointment showing in his voice.

"We'll soon find out," answered Toby. "You circle that way. We'll go this way." With a twirl of his finger, he motioned David to the left, while he slowly began circling the perimeter in the opposite direction. I followed behind Toby, carefully lighting the surfaces of the walls.

It wasn't long before David cried out: "Look here!"

We hurried over to find him bending around a thin curtain of stone that joined another wall behind it at a peak a few feet above our heads, forming a natural triangle that resembled a tent opening. It was possible to enter if you turned sideways. I was the smallest, so I went first. After a few steps, the passage turned to the right and widened so I could move forward. "There's room to walk," I called back. Toby and David followed quickly. Ahead of me, the flashlight bounced along the gleaming walls until we came to another abrupt turn, also to the right. This turn led us into another chamber, even larger and more magical than the one we'd left.

Candles stood in niches evenly placed around the walls. As Toby began lighting them, I stood in awe, staring up. From the ceiling, high above our heads, hundreds of stalactites hung like organ pipes, some as large as chimneys, others merely finger-length, while up from the ground rose thick stalagmites, a few as sturdy as cathedral columns (the analogy to church architecture seemed inescapable). And in the middle of the rotunda, where a massive stalagmite had been transformed into a pedestal, stood a figure of startling beauty.

We approached the natural altar, which gleamed a ghostly, translucent white. Rising from the pedestal was a magnificent sculpture of a bird in flight, its outstretched wings resembling a cross. Nature had provided the formation, but human hands had shaped it, giving it life. The long neck was carved lovingly from the calcite, the noble head stretched forward as the bird glided. The filigreed work of the wings and tail rippled with a suggestion of feathers. Power and grace bespoke the work of a gifted sculptor.

"The Cathar Dove," I murmured, with admiration.

"*Oui, la colombe*," said an unfriendly voice behind me.

Guillaume had followed us down.

He stepped into the chamber. "There is only one other sculpture like it in the whole of France: the little dove of Montségur that was found after our people were massacred. But this one is more beautiful and more profound. It is the most important Cathar shrine in the world, and no one outside the faith has ever seen it. You have no right to be here!"

I gazed down at his hand, half-expecting to find a gun in it, but Guillaume held only a candle. Its small blue flame shook as he spoke, trying to control his fury. "I mean what I say! This sacred stone was carved by one of the faithful in the Middle Ages, and we have guarded it ever since. It has been our duty to protect this site and to keep its secret, and now you have broken in like vandals. How dare you! You know nothing about our history or traditions. Even you, Madame, who are supposed to be an expert on art. You have violated my family's trust and hospitality."

For a few moments we were all too shocked to say a word. Guillaume stood stiffly, quaking with anger. I was the first to speak. "We owe you an apology, Monsieur. We should not have entered without permission."

"The harm you have done cannot be undone," Guillaume said fiercely, advancing toward me. "What did you expect to find?"

David now stepped forward. "I'm responsible. My work involves recovering property stolen during the Holocaust. I was searching for paintings I thought might have been hidden here during the war and which ought to be returned to their rightful owners."

"Paintings? Do you see any paintings here?" Guillaume demanded. "Who told you there were paintings here?"

"Obviously, my information was incorrect," David conceded in a mollifying tone.

"What arrogance!" exclaimed Guillaume. "We have never had anything to do with such things. See for yourself." He made an exaggerated sweep around the room with his candle, revealing nothing but the marvel at its center.

I had been holding the flashlight at my side with its beam striking the ground, but now I turned it on the shimmering sculpture. It was mesmerizing, a work of superb craftsmanship. "What does it signify?" I asked in a quiet voice.

"You mean, you don't know?"

"I'm not sure I do, other than that the dove was a symbol of the Holy Spirit in the Cathar faith," I ventured hesitantly. The shame of having been caught out was beginning to weigh on me.

As a stern professor might rebuke a backward student, Guillaume waved his free hand in a dismissive motion. "It is still a symbol of the Holy Spirit. But it has an even more particular meaning. It is the image we associate with Esclarmonde the Great." Our faces, I'm sure, looked uncomprehending. "Esclarmonde of Foix. She was the sister of Raymond Roger, the Count of Foix, and the most celebrated woman of our tradition. She became a perfect, *une parfaite*, in 1204."

As he spoke, Guillaume walked slowly around the statue. "She founded convents, schools, and hospitals. She brought many women to the faith. She helped establish the fortress of Montségur. And after she died, she became a legend. There are even some who believe she turned into a dove and flew away to escape the persecutors who came to burn her at the stake. And have you never heard the story of the Holy Grail? They say that while the walls of Montségur were still standing, the pure ones were entrusted with the Grail to guard it from their enemies. When the evil ones came to claim it, a white dove flew down from the sky and split the mountain in two. Esclarmonde saved the Grail by throwing it deep into the broken mountain, and then she, too, changed into a white dove and flew away.

"Now, those may be tales, but Esclarmonde was real. She lived an exemplary life, she inspires all of us who are not yet perfect. We honor her memory, and we venerate her symbol, which is the dove. And this"—he pointed to the statue—"is its most important representation." He now spoke directly to me. "That should answer your question, Madame, but the answer will not help you, because you are motivated solely by curiosity. Those who are merely curious will never recognize the truth. One needs a higher motivation if one wants wisdom, and that is what my people had—a higher motivation."

"But why keep the statue secret?" David wanted to know. "Why not share this beautiful object with the world?"

At this, Guillaume, who until now had been speaking with emotion but rationally, exploded: "You want to turn this shrine into a tourist attraction, do you? Charge admission? Print postcards? Organize tours down here and sell miniature doves on key chains? Why not ruin everything, as they have done with all the other caves of Périgord—violate their sanctity, pollute their atmosphere, destroy their art, and then make copies so thousands of tourists can come and gape at pictures. Is that what you want, another Lascaux II? Is that what you'd like, Monsieur? A 'Montségur II' for tourists? Never, Monsieur! Never!"

I listened, fascinated, as another avian image slowly worked its way into my consciousness, prompted by the mention of Lascaux. As I stared at the opalescent sculpture, listening to Guillaume's diatribe, I thought of the death we had witnessed in Lascaux and the baffling symbol that had been left alongside the body. Had Guillaume killed Malbert to protect the secrecy of his shrine and in so doing left a tribute to a Cathar saint?

Toby must have been thinking the same thought, for he stepped quickly between Guillaume and me and said in a challenging voice, "And is that why you were willing to kill two people? To keep this place a secret?" As he spoke, he advanced toward Guillaume aggressively.

At the same time, I turned the flashlight full on Guillaume's face, momentarily blinding him. Guillaume staggered back, confused, waving a hand in front of his eyes. "What are you talking about? I haven't killed anyone!"

"No? It wasn't you who killed Michel Malbert and left a dead dove next to him? It wasn't you who tried to attack my wife in Rouffignac but killed Dotty Dexter by mistake? You maniac, of course it was you!" Toby seized him roughly by the collar and shoved him against the wall.

But if Toby was hoping for a confession, he wasn't getting one. Guillaume pushed back with his free hand and shook him off, somehow retaining his grip on the candle with the other, though the flame snuffed out as it waved through the air. "Damn you, Monsieur! Take your hands off me. You commit a trespass, violate a shrine, and then you accuse me of horrible crimes. It is insupportable! I have never harmed anyone. My religion forbids violence. But I tell you, if you don't leave here immediately—all of you—I may not be responsible for what will happen next." His voice was trembling. "I tell you that in all sincerity, you will regret your actions and your words. Now, go!"

We had no option but to obey. Guillaume pushed the air with one hand, commanding us to back off and return through the passageway by which we had entered. When Toby hesitated, I took his elbow. Grudgingly, we retraced our steps. Once we had regained the chapel, Guillaume propelled us out the door into the cool night air. He stayed behind to restore the altar we had disturbed and, I gathered, to brood on our despoliation of his shrine.

The three of us began making our way back to the château along the cliff walk.

"Do you think it really was Guillaume who committed the murders?"

David asked. "And I thought the Cathars all died out in the Middle Ages."

"Well, obviously they're back," said Toby. "And yes, I'd say Guillaume is our killer. But without a confession, I'm not sure what can be proved."

"Shouldn't we let Daglan know what we've found?" I asked. "Keeping his cave secret gives Guillaume a motive for the murders, after all."

"Right," said David. "I'll call him. Can it wait until morning?" It was now the middle of the night.

"Do you think we'll be safe until then?" I asked.

"From Guillaume?" asked Toby. "That's what puzzles me. If he's the murderer and wanted to silence us, he just had the perfect opportunity. He had us trapped and could have killed us all, but he didn't. In fact, he wasn't armed. If he's trying to cover up a murder, it's strange he'd confront us like that without trying to do something about us."

"Maybe not so strange," said David. "How would he explain the disappearance of three Americans on his property? What would he do, leave our bodies down there? Or try to haul them out by himself? Maybe he's smart enough to take his chances with our suspicions. I've seen plenty of cases fall apart that were based on nothing more than circumstantial evidence. He could be biding his time. That's what I'd do, in his place."

We walked along for a few minutes in silence. Then David added: "Make sure your door is locked tight, and bolt your shutters when you get in. I wouldn't take any chances."

We were getting ready for bed when I heard distressed voices rising from downstairs. Guillaume and Marianne. Toby was in the bathroom, so I let myself out of the room and crept down the corridor as quietly as I could to listen at the top of the staircase. Guillaume was shouting, anguished and distraught, while Marianne's voice was low and indistinct. She was trying to placate him, to no avail. "*Calme-toi,*" I heard her say several times. But Guillaume was not to be assuaged. "*Inutile!*" he howled.

"Useless! All that we've done to protect our treasure for so many generations—useless! Our shrine defiled, our family trust betrayed. What will Father say? What will the others say?"

Marianne was shushing him, but he continued. "Think of it! The publicity—newspapers, television, and the government intrusion. The secret is exposed after all these centuries, and we were the guardians, the ones entrusted to keep our faith alive. We are disgraced. The family is disgraced."

"Hush," whispered Marianne. "They'll hear you upstairs."

"Will they?" said Guillaume. "It's too late. The harm is already done. My life's work is over. I've failed. We've failed. The family has failed."

But Marianne was insistent, and he did lower his voice. I took a few steps down the stairs, careful to remain out of sight as I strained to overhear. There was nothing for a while, and then a series of moans and gasps, which it took me a while to recognize as the sound of Guillaume sobbing.

"It's not too late," I heard Marianne say. "We haven't failed. Go to bed, Guillaume. It's not too late. You'll see."

"How?" he whimpered.

"We'll find a way. Come. Go to bed. We'll talk in the morning. Come."

I heard her leading him away, and I returned to our room, locking the door behind me. Toby was just emerging from the bathroom. I recounted the conversation I'd overheard.

"He's right, you know," said Toby. "Once this hits the news, his cult will never be the same. They depend on secret ceremonies, secret places of worship, even a secret idol. Without the secrets, it probably won't hold together. No wonder he's upset."

"And now we're in for it. I don't know how I'm going to face Marianne in the morning." I remembered Madame Martin had invited me to help prepare the baked eggs for breakfast. I felt obliged to appear in the kitchen, but Marianne was sure to be there, and I was dreading an encounter with her.

"Well, there's nothing we can do about it tonight," said Toby, yawning. "So let's get some sleep. You did lock the door again, didn't you?"

I tossed and turned until daylight. It took will power to get out of bed and to shower, dress, and go downstairs while Toby still slept. The claws of fear pressed into my gut when I saw that Marianne was standing outside the kitchen door, as if in wait for me. Not that I was the only one with whom she had a quarrel, but I was the one she had entrusted with the family history. So I opened with sincere regret.

"I'm so sorry, Marianne. Guillaume must have told you about last night." I searched for the next sentence.

"I can't tell you how hurt I am," Marianne said, with sand in her voice. "You, of all people. You seemed to admire our family, but now I see it was all a pretense, to get information you could use to advance your career. Guillaume is right. You don't care about our family at all."

"That's not true, Marianne. I do respect your family. The reason I came here is because I so admire Jenny Marie's art."

"And how did that require you to break into our private cave? I told you there was nothing down there that concerned you."

No hidden paintings, true enough, but Marianne hadn't been completely honest with me, either. Of course she knew about the statue. But it was awkward enough having this conversation without accusing her of duplicity.

"I'm truly sorry. These murders have us terrified, and they've made us all suspicious. I agree we had no right to enter the cave, but you see . . ." I had nowhere comfortable to go with my explanation.

"What have those crimes got to do with us or with your behavior? Did your husband really accuse my brother of committing a murder?"

Two murders, actually, but I bit my tongue.

"I'm extremely disappointed in you, Nora. Such accusations are absurd and completely baseless."

"Of course," I stammered, unconvincingly.

We both heard Lily walking in from the hall.

"Good morning, Marianne. I know about the trouble last night. I don't know what to say."

"So stop. Nothing you can say would help. I've come to a decision. Breakfast will be served on the terrace as usual, but after that, I would like you all to leave. I'll look after Roz myself."

"She's had a terrible shock," said Lily cautiously. "Is there anything we can do for her? Wouldn't she like one of us to keep her company?"

"Madame Martin will take breakfast up to her, and after you all are served, I'll stay with her. The last thing she needs right now is the attention of strangers." That was meant to sting.

"All right, Marianne," I agreed. "We'll leave. And Lily and I will let the others know about breakfast. But may I go into the kitchen to apologize to Madame Martin for not helping her prepare the eggs? Yesterday she invited me to help her this morning."

"So she told me. I have already told Agnes not to expect you. You'll excuse me." And with that, she opened the door to the kitchen and closed it firmly behind her.

Lily and I looked at each other with chagrin. Without speaking, we headed back through the hall. At the foot of the staircase, I stopped. I wanted to somehow explain things to her. "We may have made a big mistake, Lily. I feel awful about what we did. But if Guillaume is the murderer, then all our intrusions were justified. I don't know what to think."

"David told me all about it," she replied quietly. "He's called the police. I'll go let him know about breakfast, and about getting out of here fast. Would you tell Toby and Patrick?"

I said I would. When I went back to our room, Toby was just getting ready to come out.

"Would you knock on Patrick's door and let him know we'll be having breakfast soon on the terrace?" I asked. It struck me as more seemly to have a man knock on a man's door at this early hour. Toby went out to convey the message. When he came back, I told him the situation.

Within minutes, our group, minus two members, was assembled at the French doors leading to the terrace. The tables had been set again for three. Patrick, having been brought up to speed about last night's adventure, looked askance at the rest of us, as if sizing us up a second time. He probably was asking himself if we were intrepid adventurers or complete fools. Lily touched my elbow and indicated that she wanted me to join David at their table. Toby and Patrick were left to form a table with an empty chair. Guillaume wasn't there, and I hoped he wouldn't appear.

While David sheepishly kept his head down, Lily turned to me with an expression of concern. "We're really sorry to have led you into this fiasco, Nora," she whispered. "Sometimes David just doesn't know when to stop." David focused his concentration on the bit of toast and jam he'd just taken. "For him, the moral stakes are so high they justify actions that would otherwise be unconscionable. This time he seems to have overreached himself."

His head tilted up. "We don't know that, Lily."

"What? You think playing detective in a foreign country in the middle of the night won't get you in trouble?"

"Yes, but . . ."

Marianne came through the doorway carrying a round covered baking dish. She carefully put the hot dish down on a table between ours and Toby and Patrick's. "Good morning," she said icily through clenched lips. "I don't want any more talk about last night. In spite of what's happened, Madame Martin has prepared her breakfast specialty for you—*oeufs sur le plat*. As you see here, that means eggs in a baking dish. It's a special way of baking eggs so the yolk remains liquid." I sat there amazed as she continued: "That is important, because it allows the cook to add fresh herbs or truffles or mushrooms to the yolk, and they cook there, blending their flavor into the yolk."

Marianne seemed determined to assert control by going through her final cooking lesson. Her face was grim. She turned to Patrick. "Would you lift the cover, please?" On the round platter were six perfect eggs. "Can you tell me, Patrick, whether the mushrooms are truffles, girolles, or *cèpes*?" She duly slipped each of us what looked like a perfectly poached egg, with finely diced, black specks sprinkled over the yolk.

"Well, they aren't girolles," Patrick speculated. "Those would be more golden. These are dark. It's between truffles and *cèpes*, I would say." He raised his fork in the air and was poised to plunge it into the golden yolk, when Madame Martin came running through the doorway, with a cupped hand held out in front of her.

"Stop! Marianne, you've made a mistake! Those mushrooms aren't edible, they're poison!"

"What? I chopped those mushrooms myself. They're girolles."

"No, they're not." She pushed her hand forward. "Here are some you didn't chop. See? They're trumpet-shaped. They look like girolles, but these are pitch-black. Mother used to call them 'trumpets of death'! They're absolutely deadly!"

"Agnes, you don't know what you're talking about. Go back to the kitchen."

"Marianne! What are you doing? You know your mushrooms as well as I do."

"That's enough, Agnes!"

"No, Madame! I just came down to the kitchen to get some honey for Madame Belnord's tea, and I saw these mushrooms on the cutting board. I tell you, they're poison!"

We all had dropped our forks by now. Toby pulled his chair back from the table. "Maybe we'd better wait until we can sort this out," he said in his most matter-of-fact way. "Is it possible someone's made a mistake?"

Just then, Guillaume came through the door. "What's going on?" he asked, addressing Marianne. "I heard shouting out here."

"We are disputing the safety of my mushrooms," Marianne replied tersely. "Our guests seem to fear we have poisoned them."

"No, it was I who raised the alarm," corrected Madame Martin. "I'm sorry, Monsieur Guillaume. But I'm sure there's been an error. Marianne has mistaken black trumpets for girolles."

Guillaume looked angrily at Madame Martin, as if resenting her impertinence. But then he looked closely at the mushrooms, and with a shocked expression, he turned to Marianne. "You wouldn't—"

"Guillaume, let me handle this." She looked straight at Toby. "Let me show you, Monsieur, that the eggs are perfectly fine." From next to his coffee cup, she snatched his spoon, then pivoted toward the serving platter and dunked the spoon into the center of the one egg remaining there. But Guillaume was swifter than she was. Before she could lift the spoon to her mouth, he had her arm twisted behind her.

"What are you doing?" cried Guillaume. "You could poison yourself!"

"Let me go, Guillaume!" she spat in exasperation. "Let me go! It's better this way. I'd rather die than spend the rest of my life in prison!"

"Prison? What are you talking about? Were you really trying to poison these people?"

She seemed to slump in his arms. "It's over, Guillaume. Finished. Everything is finished. But believe me, what I did, I did for you."

"Did what? I never asked you to do such a thing!"

"No, you couldn't ask me, could you? You were too weak, dear brother." There was sarcasm in her words. "I was always the stronger."

We looked on in disbelief, and then a familiar voice spoke from the other side of the French doors. "Keep your grip on her, please, Monsieur. My man will take her from you." In lumbered Inspector Daglan. Jackie followed, with handcuffs ready. "Those won't be necessary, will they?" asked Daglan.

Marianne shook her head, almost defiantly, as if keeping her pride even in defeat. Her hands dropped to her sides. Guillaume was still standing, and I don't know how he kept steady on his feet. His face bore grief, and his body collapsed in stages. First his chest went concave. Then his head fell to his knees, and his hands pulled at his cheeks. His words were muffled, incomprehensible.

The inspector picked up one of the mushrooms and held it up to the light, turning it slowly from side to side. "Marianne de Cazelle," he said, "I arrest you on suspicion of the murders of Michel Malbert and

Dorothy Dexter, and for the attempted murder of your guests." Turning to Guillaume, he added: "Monsieur, you will come with us for questioning as well." To the rest of us, who sat stunned, he said simply, "Remain here, if you please." And to his subordinate, almost as an afterthought: "Jackie, collect these mushrooms and bring them to the station, will you?"

Jackie nodded and began gathering the mushrooms in a basket. As he followed Guillaume and Marianne through the door, the inspector said over his shoulder, "Don't eat any."

15

Waiting for Inspector Daglan's return, we shifted aimlessly like kids whose mother has been whisked away to the hospital. No one was in charge. No one knew precisely what had happened. In the first hour, Lily and I sat in the dining room with Madame Martin. Her mind ricocheted between the horror of discovering the mushrooms were poison and the shock of suspecting Marianne knew what they were. First she would lecture Lily and me about the distinctive color and size of the poison trumpets of death. Then she would fall into confused denials of Marianne's culpability. "She couldn't have known! Why would she want to poison her first group of students? The cooking school was her refuge. After so much sadness, she was doing something for herself, something she was good at."

We listened and comforted her until, finally, Madame Martin declared she must now tend to Madame Belnord. She stood, used her hands to iron her apron to her body, and headed upstairs.

Jackie had declared the kitchen off limits, using just a chair to bar the door. There would be no lunch coming through that door today. We'd been told not to return to the terrace, either. So Lily and I kept our seats at the dining table and took advantage of the chance to talk.

"I feel awful," I confessed. Our escapade last night nearly led to us all getting killed. It pushed Marianne right over the edge."

"It looks that way. But how were you to know Marianne was capable of murder? None of us had any idea."

"That's not the point. We might have been better off if we had listened to you last night."

Lily gave me a look of chagrin. "And then a murderer would have been no closer to being uncovered."

"Maybe so. But we could have reported our suspicions to Inspector Daglan and let his team inspect the cave in the morning."

"You did what your instinct told you was right. Maybe I need to respect David's instincts more than I do. I was pretty hard on him about what you did last night."

"It works both ways. That's what marriage is about—living by your own lights, but learning to see by your partner's lights too. Toby and I have been at this long enough that we now have a common way of seeing most things. But it wasn't always so."

"Really?"

And with that, Lily drew me into relating a disagreement Toby and I once had about a consigner of old paintings who charmed Toby but set my teeth on edge. When it turned out the man had falsely attributed a painting (and supplied it with a fake signature), I managed to hold my tongue, and since then Toby has always checked with me on consignments. Of course, it has worked the other way too. Toby has taught me to have more patience with colleagues I might have soured on because of the petty disagreements that often occur in department meetings. Over the years, I've become more tolerant, and he's become more cautious, and that's worked out well for both of us. As she listened, Lily nodded her assent.

Soon Madame Martin was back in the dining room, looking grim but composed. She sent us up to visit Roz, whom we found dressed in black and sitting despondently in a chair by the window. She rose and gave us both a hug. "Tell me what's happened," she insisted. "I can't believe what Madame Martin has been saying."

It took several rounds of explanation. First I described the breakfast incident. Then Lily explained about David's mission to find looted art at the château. Finally, I told Roz about my research on Jenny Marie, my eavesdropping on the ritual in the chapel, and our attempt to locate and explore the cave. Each part of the story seemed to strike another blow.

"Do you have a perspective on all this?" I asked Roz.

She sighed, and her eyes watered. "I've been worried about Marianne, but I never dreamed it could get this bad. I should have spoken up long ago."

"Why do you say that? Did you suspect she had anything to do with the murders?"

"Oh, no. Nothing like that. But I sensed, soon after her husband died, that Marianne wasn't grieving well. Instead of talking about Ben or trying to adjust to her life as a widow, she kept going on about her home in the Dordogne, especially about her brother. She kept saying that only he could understand her loss, that only being back home with him could make her whole again. I thought it was strange at the time, and when she announced she was coming back to Cazelle, I thought of telling her she was leaning too much on the idea that her brother could mend her heart. But I didn't say anything. When Marianne wrote me that she had decided to start a cooking school in the castle, I thought I'd been wrong all along."

"Are you saying she was mentally unstable after her husband died?"

"That's harsher wording than I would have used, but maybe it's true. Even before Ben's death, I thought she had an unhealthy focus on her brother. She was always saying how much she missed him and how they were soul mates. But after Ben died, it became an obsession, and I wasn't surprised when she returned to live with him here."

"This morning, when Guillaume asked her what she had done, she said she had done it all for him."

"Committed murder?" asked Roz.

I hated to admit how it all fit together, but it was time to say it. "It appears Marianne knew all about Guillaume's religious cult and his insistence that the shrine should remain secret, known only to devotees. When Malbert kept pushing in his attempts to inspect the cave, both of them must have been upset about it, but it was Marianne who decided to act. Guillaume probably never thought Marianne could go so far as to kill for him."

Roz frowned. "But what about Dotty? Are you saying Marianne killed her too? Why?"

"By mistake. From the start, Toby thought whoever killed Dotty really meant to kill me. Marianne must have worried I'd find out Guillaume's secret from all the questions I was asking. So she tried to end my poking around, and poor Dotty got in the way. On the train and in the dark we must have looked alike from behind. We were both wearing those berets Dotty bought us. And Dotty was sitting next to Toby, where I should have been."

Lily broke into the conversation. "Marianne didn't go with you to Rouffignac because she said she had shopping to do. But she must have found a way to get into the cave and join your group without being seen."

Roz put her hand to her brow as if fending off a headache. "If only I had stayed with Dotty at the cave. I was trying to avoid her. Maybe if I hadn't been so childish, she'd still be alive."

Yes, and maybe I'd be dead.

I went back to our room, hoping to get in a nap before the inspector returned, and noticed that my international cell phone was still charging in the outlet next to the chair; I had forgotten about it. I unplugged it, turned it on, and checked for messages. There was one, left overnight, from Angie. When it came to calculating time differences, she took after Mom. I fit the phone against my ear.

"Hi, Nora!" Angie had never sounded cheerier. "Just to say, don't worry about me. I decided not to go for that motorbike thing. In fact, Hank and I are over, which you'll be happy to hear. Gramps wanted that money used for education, so I've got this great idea. I'm going to

London for a month of training in hair-styling, and my salon is cool with that. They'll keep my job waiting for me. I'll tell you all about it when you get back. Bye."

I broke out laughing: maybe it was the result of pent-up nerves. Angie always lands on her feet, with a little help. I should have known that. And I had my brother, Eddie, to thank when I got home.

I stretched out on the bed not expecting to fall asleep, but when Toby nudged me awake, it was an hour later.

Around one o'clock Madame Martin reported that Inspector Daglan had called to say he was returning to distribute our passports. We were all assembled when he entered the grand salon, looking smug.

"I know your holiday has been disrupted, but the investigation is now over. If any of you have been inconvenienced, I apologize." Eager to retrieve our passports, we kept silent. Daglan searched our faces. "*Bon.*" He wore a satisfied expression as Jackie went around the room handing back the passports. "I can tell you we already have a signed confession to the murders and that you all are free to return to the United States when you wish."

"That's good news," said Toby. "But would you mind answering some questions for us?"

"Not at all."

David was the first to get an oar in. "What about Guillaume's part in all of this? Has he been charged?"

"No, Monsieur. His sister has made a full confession. As for Monsieur de Cazelle, he insists he knew nothing of her crimes, which she confirms. He seems profoundly affected by his sister's actions, and unless there is additional evidence to implicate him, he will not be charged. Of course, we will question him further before releasing him."

David looked dubious and pursed his lips.

"Inspector, did Marianne explain why she acted as she did?"

"*Oui, Madame Barnes.* She spoke quite freely once she began her confession. She seemed eager, in fact, to describe her actions."

"And she admitted she killed Malbert for her brother's sake?"

"For the sake of his delusions, I would say, this affair about a Cathar statue and her brother's dedication to the ancient ways—all nonsense in my opinion. But it appears Guillaume's entire life was devoted to the cult and to his shrine, which he insisted be kept secret. Well, it's a secret no longer. But yes, to protect him she killed Malbert. And she went about it very cleverly."

"How did she manage to get into Lascaux?" asked Toby.

"According to what she has told us, she acquired the key and the security code information from her brother without his knowledge. And how did Guillaume come into their possession? From Monsieur Gounot, the guardian of the cave."

That seemed to put Marc in the clear. I was glad to hear it.

"You see, every year at the time of the Félibrée, Guillaume presides over a Cathar ceremony for his band of followers at some location that has special meaning for them. This year it was held here. Last year, it was held in Lascaux, thanks to Monsieur Gounot, who is a member of the cult. But Gounot got sick at the last minute and gave the key and code to Guillaume so that the ceremony could take place. That, by the way, was a grave indiscretion, and Gounot will certainly lose his position over it. In any event, Guillaume held his ceremony in the Hall of Bulls, and then copied the key and wrote down the code, for future use. And Marianne knew where he kept them."

"But how did she know Monsieur Malbert would be in the cave on that particular day?" I asked.

"Malbert visited the château the day before he was murdered, to press for access to the Cazelle cave. At that time, Marianne learned he was planning an inspection visit to Lascaux on the following afternoon. So the next morning she lets herself into Lascaux and hides in the pit, which the tour never visits. Now she stalks her victim, using the darkness of the cave for cover. She observes that Malbert is always the last in line, trips the lights, strikes, and gets away back to her hiding place in the ensuing confusion."

David asked, "How did she escape from the cave without being seen? Didn't the police search it carefully?"

"Her plan was simple. She waited until you all ran out. While everyone was back at the guide's station, out of sight of the entrance to the cave, waiting for us to arrive, she quietly walked out and went home. *Voilà!*"

We sat transfixed, following Daglan's description. Then Toby spoke up. "Inspector, what about the second murder? Am I right that she killed Dotty by mistake?"

"No, Monsieur, and that is what I find most astonishing about this case. Naturally, once Marianne had confessed to two murders, I concluded, as you have done, that her motives in both were identical: to protect her brother. But it appears I was wrong."

I could hardly believe my ears. What other motive could there be?

Daglan wagged his finger. "It was no mistake that Marianne killed Madame Dexter in Rouffignac; that was her intention."

"That can't possibly be true!" Roz protested. "Why would she do that to Dotty? Why would she do that to me?"

"Not *to* you, Madame Belnord. *For* you."

"What?"

"Marianne had already committed one murder to protect her brother. She knew she could not be punished more severely for a second murder to protect her friend; the penalty was the same. I understand, Madame, that there are some questions about your brother's will and that Madame Dexter was an obstacle to your interests. Marianne decided to remove that obstacle."

"Oh, no!"

"I'm afraid so. That she carried out her plan successfully in Lascaux gave her the confidence to try a second attack in Rouffignac. I wonder, Madame Belnord, if Marianne said anything to you that hinted she was planning to harm your sister-in-law."

"No! I can hardly believe it. We talked about Dotty, and I did mention the problems over my brother's will. But that couldn't have given Marianne the idea I wanted Dotty dead."

"Did she say anything at all to you about Madame Dexter?"

Roz's face clouded. "Well, yes. She was angry that Dotty was ignoring my brother's wishes, and she did say something that took me aback. She said that Dotty lacked respect for our family, that she lacked respect for a sister's love. The awful thing was that when she said it, it rang true. I hated to think it, but that's how I felt. Yes, I said, Dotty did lack respect for my feelings, and she did lack respect for my brother's intentions. But I never meant any harm to come to her. I never imagined that Marianne would . . ." Roz began to cry. Lily comforted her, leading her to a sofa with an arm protectively around her shoulder.

That Marianne had committed both murders for the sake of people dear to her was beginning to make sense. I thought of that moment in *Macbeth* when Shakespeare's protagonist realizes that once he's stepped into a river of blood, he might just as well go forward as go back; in fact, there is no going back to the shore of innocence.

> I am in blood
> Stepp'd in so far that, should I wade no more,
> Returning were as tedious as go o'er.

The logic was pernicious.

"How did she get away with it?" asked Toby.

"Her plan in Rouffignac was ingenious, but it depended on exact timing. She simply bought a ticket for the last tour before lunch. She was familiar with the trains' stopping points. At the right moment, she got off in the dark without being noticed and found a comfortable hiding place in one of those bear's dens along the tracks. She chose her spot well. It was just a few meters away from the section of track where the train always stops on its return from the first chamber. While waiting for you, she changed into her disguise, the workman's smock and cap, which she had carried in her bag. When your group came through on the first train of the afternoon, she was able to climb aboard while your train was parked at the customary position, close to her hiding place. No one saw her get on, and no one noticed her when your group entered the second gallery. When the train was ready to begin its return journey, she got on in the seat behind you, in disguise. She knew exactly when to use the garrote—after your train made its next stop, as it always did, at the junction on its return trip.

"As the train pulled out again, she got off, removed her disguise, stuffed it in her bag, and waited at her hiding place until the next train came through and stopped at the same place. The final step was obvious. She mounted the second train and then got off, no longer in disguise, with the other passengers. You were expecting to meet her at the entrance after your tour, so there was no reason for you to be surprised at finding her there. In the confusion no one noticed she had dismounted from the second train instead of entering the hall from outside."

I thought hard about Daglan's summary. The pieces fit.

"But why did she try to poison the rest of us?" Patrick demanded.

"The mushrooms? Well, Monsieur, by then things were out of her control. After Rouffignac, as far as Marianne was concerned, both her friend's problem and her brother's had been solved. That is, until the three of you (he pointed at David, Toby, and me) discovered the shrine, and then she felt compelled to go one step further."

"But all of us? Did she think she could get away with it?" asked Patrick.

"Not all of you. Her friend Madame Belnord was in her room. Yes, it was reckless, but an accident in the cooking class would draw the least suspicion, she reasoned, and so she tried to feed you those mushrooms this morning. Afterward she could try to claim she had made an unfortunate mistake. The rest you know."

That Marianne could be so cold-blooded was appalling.

"Any other questions?" asked Daglan.

"There's still something that puzzles me about the first murder," said Toby. "That dead bird Marianne left next to the corpse, why?"

"Ah, the dead dove. I think she calculated that the bird would throw us off her trail and cast suspicion elsewhere. For a while, that's exactly what happened. We assumed the murderer was someone who had knowledge of the Lascaux symbolism, a prehistorian most likely. We wasted our time going over Malbert's old cases, looking for a colleague or a researcher who might bear him a grudge. That's how Marc Gounot became a suspect."

"And now you're sure he wasn't involved?" I asked.

"Yes, and he has been released. We have a confession. As far as I am concerned, the case is closed."

Was it? I thought of all the people whose lives had been altered by what Marianne had done. The case would never be closed for them. Roz would grieve for the sister-in-law whom she had just begun to understand and for her dearest friend, whom she had not understood at all. Guillaume's shrine would be the focus of a media circus, and his sister would spend the rest of her life in prison. Gounot would lose his position as the guardian at Lascaux. And who knows who would grieve for Malbert?

I felt very tired. The others seemed subdued as well, as we said goodbye to Inspector Daglan and his assistant. We lingered on in the salon, talking through the logistics of our departure. David offered to help Roz make phone calls back to the United States. We realized she would need to stay on for at least a few more days, to arrange for transport of Dotty's body to Baltimore. Patrick, who of all of us had been least touched by the whole affair, proved a good friend in this regard. Insisting he had no immediate need to return home, he offered to stay with Roz and help her through the arrangements. He would book hotel rooms for them in Sarlat. We were thinking of doing the same thing ourselves.

We were just settling the details when we heard a knock at the front door. We tensed, expecting the awkward return of Guillaume. But when the door swung open, it was Marc Gounot who walked in. "I was waiting for that policeman to leave. I've seen quite enough of him. I've come to say how sorry I am about Dotty," he said apologetically. "Roz, I especially want to offer you my sympathy." He walked across the room and took Roz's hand. Lily stood and left them talking quietly for a few minutes, Roz occasionally patting her cheeks to dry tears.

After a while he rose to go, but Toby was waiting for him near the door. "Would you mind if we talked to you before you leave?" Marc nodded and followed us out the front door. Across the driveway, under a linden tree, there were a few metal tables set out for the guests, and he and I sat down at one while Toby dragged over a third chair. By now Marc knew Marianne had been arrested, but he hadn't heard the details of her confession, and he was eager to know what Inspector Daglan had told us. When we finished our summary of events, he scratched his head in disbelief. Then it was our turn to ask him questions. First, about Rouffignac.

Yes, he knew in advance about our group's visit to Rouffignac, because Dotty had mentioned it to him at Domme. He told Dotty he was scheduled to work at Rouffignac that day and that it would be fun to keep it a surprise for the rest of us in case he ended up as the driver of our train. As it turned out, he enjoyed seeing our reaction when he waved to us.

Fernando? Yes, they did business from time to time. Fernando would bring his finds to the mineral shop for sale: rocks, artifacts if he was lucky, once in a while an arrowhead or spear point. He had good eyes for the ground and was something of a magpie. He also did odd jobs for the owner of the Château of Castelnaud. That day we saw them together, Fernando was finishing some masonry work at Castelnaud and had dropped in to try to sell Marc an old flintstone.

"So that's how Inspector Daglan came up with the idea Fernando and I were involved in a conspiracy, is it? It was because you told him you had seen us talking together."

I admitted that we had.

"Well, perhaps I shouldn't blame you. I know that Fernando has a police record and that he's not the most agreeable sort, but I seem to get on with him pretty well."

I was glad Marc wasn't resentful that I had shared my suspicions with the inspector. And I was glad that Fernando had played no role in the murders. In fact, I felt somewhat guilty about him. My grandfather had been a Portuguese laborer too. How might his life had been different had he not come to America? I regretted my hostility toward Fernando. I might have been more generous.

There was one other matter I wanted to clear up before we parted. I needed to ask Marc how much he knew about his father's relationship with the German archaeologist who had visited Cazelle during the war. I told him what I had learned about his father and Anders Voellmer from reading Jenny Marie's notebook.

"Anders Voellmer? Of course, I know about him. How could I not know? It was the work my father did with Voellmer that got him into trouble. It's true they worked together, on one research project, mind you, but my father wasn't a Nazi. In fact, he was completely naive about politics. His only interest was his research, and Voellmer was interested in the same subject. It's unfortunate Voellmer also was a member of the Nazi Party."

Marc's claim that his father had been an innocent when it came to politics struck me as evasive. According to Daglan, Henri Gounot had purged his Jewish colleagues from their positions to placate the Vichy authorities. For that he was personally responsible. I felt I couldn't remain silent on this point and confronted Marc about it.

"My father wasn't perfect. He made mistakes as many Frenchmen did during that period, and maybe he did some things I would rather not know about. But he was determined not to let the war interrupt his research, and that's where the authorities had influence over him. Anders Voellmer especially, too much influence, I admit."

There was a lot more to be said on this score, but I held back. Right now I wanted to coax additional information from Marc, not drive him away. "What was their research about? Do you know?"

"Ancient symbolism, the symbolism of prehistoric cave art, to be specific."

"Such as the tableau of the bird beside the falling man in Lascaux?"

"Precisely. My father spent a lot of time trying to analyze those images."

"And did he reach any conclusions?" Toby asked.

"Only that the drawings were made to illustrate a story, a myth, if you want to use that term—a myth that was as important to the

Cro-Magnons as the stories in the Bible are to us. The difficulty of knowing what the meaning was is that we have no other references to the story except for the drawings. My father had a theory, though. It's too bad he never lived to complete his work. Did I tell you I have kept all his notes and papers? Well, I have them, and one day I will complete his work and restore his reputation."

It would take more than a clever theory to do that. But I pressed on. "Are you willing to share his ideas with us?"

"There's no reason not to, now. His point was that images of birds appear very rarely in prehistoric art. But when they do appear, they are always painted in an abstract style, in the simplest of outlines without much detail, whereas all the other animals are drawn as realistically as possible. Why? He thought the answer must be that the bird was treated as a special creature, different from all the others, more sacred perhaps."

"But isn't that true as well for the human figures in cave art?" I remembered that the falling man in Lascaux was presented as a stick figure without any suggestion of volume or dimensions.

"That's so," replied Marc. "And that's what my father noticed, too. So in the mind of the cave artists there must have been a special connection between birds and human beings, but what was it? As an anthropologist, my father knew a lot about comparative religions. In one of his papers, he argued that in almost every culture around the world, birds are associated with gods or spirits. It's a natural association. Birds fly in the air, they inhabit the sky, and that's where the spirits live. So the bird becomes a symbol of the soul.

"That was one of his insights. Another was his recognition that for the Cro-Magnons, a human being wasn't just another animal but a special being with a soul. And that's why humans and birds are linked in cave art and why they are depicted differently from other animals. At least, that was his theory. But if I can ever prove him right, the world will have to recognize that my father was the first to show that the Cro-Magnons believed in the soul and that their art wasn't merely about hunting. It was essentially religious."

"So you think the bird in Lascaux symbolizes the soul of the dying man?" asked Toby.

"I do," replied Marc.

"It's an interesting theory," I said, "but how does Anders Voellmer fit into the picture?"

"The Cathar Dove," Marc answered flatly. "Another bird image meant to represent the soul, but this time the Holy Spirit in the Middle Ages. Voellmer convinced himself Périgord was somehow endowed with mystical properties that inspired both the Cro-Magnons and the Cathars to create similar images in their art and religion. But that wasn't enough for Voellmer. On top of that, he came to believe the dove was associated with the Holy Grail. For him, the Grail was a code word for a sacred work of art, never named, that was entrusted to the Cathars until such time as humanity could rediscover its ancient wisdom and realize its potential. Possessing the sacred work of art would confer almost supernatural powers on those who could claim it."

"Namely, the Nazis?" Toby asked with irony in his voice.

"Of course. That's why Himmler was interested. And just what was this mystical object according to Voellmer, and where did he think it was hidden?"

"I think I can guess the answer," responded Toby. "It was hidden in the cave of Cazelle."

"Yes. Lascaux and Cazelle, two caves that shared a common destiny. In Lascaux, Voellmer saw a bird next to a falling man, predicting, he thought, the end of the Cro-Magnons, who were supposed to be the first Aryans. In Cazelle he saw a bird perched atop a pedestal ready to soar, foretelling the glory of the renewed Aryan race! Well, that's what Voellmer made of it, anyway; that's not what my father thought. When Voellmer saw the statue of the dove, the fool actually thought he had found the Holy Grail. And he dragged my father down with him, discrediting a theory that otherwise might have made sense."

"A lot of things are beginning to make sense," said Toby. "So you do know about the statue underneath the Cazelle chapel. That's what

Voellmer was sketching, isn't it? He was sending pictures of it back to Himmler."

"I've never seen the dove in person, but yes. I know about the statue from my father's notes and from what my uncle has told me. Only members of Guillaume's cult are allowed inside the cave, and joining up would have been too high a price for me to pay. Besides, as I've told you, I don't buy the parallels between the cave artists and the Cathars. All that was Voellmer's idea. What I want to do is pursue my father's study of Cro-Magnon bird imagery. I think I can do that without bothering about the Holy Grail."

I had been mulling things over while listening to Marc's description of his father's theory and the crackpot views of Anders Voellmer. "Marc, how much do you think Marianne knew about the interest taken by the Nazis in the Cathar statue?"

"She must have been aware of it."

"What about Guillaume?"

"Of course, what she knew, he knew."

I now had the last piece of the puzzle, and it meant Daglan was wrong. "The inspector told us Marianne left the bird by the corpse to throw the police off her trail, to send them looking into Malbert's old cases rather than investigating the family. But the real reason was that she was leaving a message for Guillaume! Who else would understand the connection between the Lascaux bird and the Cathar Dove? She was telling him someone who knew the Cathar secrets had taken care of Malbert and stopped him from violating the shrine."

"And the garrote was another part of the message," added Toby. "Didn't you tell me it was a method of execution used against the Cathars?"

"That's right."

Toby frowned. "So that means Guillaume knew all along that someone from his cult or his family had killed Malbert."

"They all knew," I said, "including the old baron."

We said our goodbyes and returned to our room to pack. I took Jenny Marie's notebook out of my drawer and, after a moment's silent debate, brought it to the dining room to give to Madame Martin. Finding she wasn't there, I wrote a note saying that since the notebook had last been in her mother's hands, it seemed right to entrust it to her. I guessed she would give it to Guillaume, but in my mind's eye I pictured her returning it to the offering box in the chapel where her mother had placed it when Jenny Marie died. I left the note and the notebook in the center of the table where Marianne had served us our first meal together.

On our way out the gates of the grounds, I asked Toby to make a stop. I wanted to visit the ancient church on the opposite hill. Toby drove our little car up the winding dirt drive and then joined me in walking round to the back of the building, where the graveyard lay. Rows of headstones fell away, down the sloping hill behind the church. Any visitor to those rows had a magnificent view of the two châteaux, Cazelle and Beynac, and the Dordogne River sparkling beneath them. I suspected, though, that what I sought would lie in the other direction, at the top of the hill. That's where we found it, built right against a church buttress: a small mausoleum marked "Cazelle."

There was no door, no latch, to deter anyone who might wish to enter the marble enclosure. Inside, resting against the mossy walls were four stone caskets carved with flowers, the forms of which were now worn down. Near the entrance was a metal sign, of modern vintage, listing family members placed here since the beginning of the nineteenth century. One was Jenny Marie Cazelle, 1870–1944.

"Some day," I said, "Marianne and Guillaume will rest here, alongside their ancestors. Well, with most of them. Did you notice, there's no entry for Jenny Marie's brother, Antoine?"

"They didn't have a body to bury. It's too bad the one hero in the family won't be remembered."

"I'm going to try to see to it that he *is* remembered. Jenny Marie's story isn't complete without Antoine. She was devoted to her brother, and he gave his life trying to help her in a good cause. The essay I want to write won't be just about her art. It will be about her relationship to her brother and to this place."

Toby took my hand. "Good. That's a story worth telling. You know, it's odd, when you stop to think about it."

"What?"

"This brother and sister thing. They're awfully close in this family. Look at Guillaume and Marianne. Maybe Antoine sacrificed his life for his sister, but Marianne killed for her brother. That's way too close, if you ask me."

It was true. Each woman lost a lover, and like a homing pigeon, flew back to the family for comfort. Then as the years passed, each grew closer to her brother. In Jenny Marie's case, the relationship was noble, but in Marianne's case it led to murder.

Could I kill for my brother or sister? Would I sacrifice my life? I found it hard to think along those lines. Life in my family was fraught enough, but I was thankful it wasn't lived at that pitch.

A low late afternoon sun spread its orange rays across the hills. As we headed toward Sarlat to spend the night, I was struck, not for the first time, by the beauty of this gentle valley—its tranquil river, golden cliffs, the lush greenery of its fields—and by the violence of its inhabitants. Not only Marianne de Cazelle. I thought of the Cro-Magnons, who lived here thousands of years ago and created art but who spent their brutish existence battling predators. I thought of the Cathars, whose quest for perfection was crushed by a pitiless crusade that wiped them out. I thought of Jenny Marie's landscapes and of her lover lying dead on a battlefield of the Great War. I thought of villages burned to the ground in 1944 and of a Nazi scholar's obsession with a statue of unearthly grace. I pondered why blood and beauty are so often expressed in tandem.

We humans are a mysterious breed.

Then I recalled the road sign that had greeted us upon entering the Dordogne, and I thought how fitting its words were, after all. *Bienvenue au pays d'homme.*

"Welcome to the home of man."

Authors' Note

At this writing, Lascaux remains completely closed to the public for reasons of conservation, but some years ago, we had the privilege of visiting the authentic cave when five people a day were allowed in. Our guide was Jacques Marsal, who as a boy had helped discover Lascaux. He was a charming and urbane man, then in his sixties, and the tour he provided was memorable. He bears no resemblance to our fictional guide, who is purely imaginary, as are the other characters in this novel.

We wish to thank our editor at the University of Wisconsin Press, Raphael Kadushin, for his steadfast support and helpful suggestions during various stages of this manuscript. His guidance was essential, though any remaining shortcomings are our own. Thanks to Aaron Elkins, our favorite mystery writer, for his encouragement and generosity; to Owen Pell for information on missing art during the Holocaust; to Lynn Miller for revision suggestions; to Maria Duha, Shaina Robbins, and Barb Flaherty for background information; and to friends and relatives for good wishes and support.

For historical background, we gratefully acknowledge the usefulness of the following sources: Hector Feliciano, *The Lost Museum: The Nazi Conspiracy to Steal the World's Greatest Works of Art* (New York: Basic

Books, 1997); Julian Jackson, *France: The Dark Years, 1940–1944* (New York: Oxford University Press, 2005); Heather Pringle, *The Master Plan: Himmler's Scholars and the Holocaust* (New York: Hyperion, 2006); Lynn H. Nicholas, *The Rape of Europa: The Fate of Europe's Treasure in the Third Reich and the Second World War* (New York: Vintage, 1995); Stephen O'Shea, *The Perfect Heresy: The Revolutionary Life and Death of the Medieval Cathars* (New York: Walker Company, 2000); Otto Rahn, *Crusade against the Grail: The Struggle between the Cathars, the Templars, and the Church of Rome*, trans. Christopher Jones (1933; reprint, Rochester, VT: Inner Traditions, 2006); Gabriel Weisberg and Jane R. Becker, eds., *Overcoming All Obstacles: The Women of the Académie Julian* (New Brunswick, NJ: Rutgers University Press, 1999).

A final note: although Lascaux is closed to tourists, a number of other caves in the Dordogne containing Cro-Magnon art remain open. Among these are Bara-Bahau, Bernifal, Les Combarelles, Commarque, Font-de-Gaume, La Mouthe, and Rouffignac, which we describe in the novel. Lascaux II (the replica) is worth seeing, as well, but nothing compares with visiting one of the original caves. Our memories of such visits led to the writing of this book.